eclipse

STEPHENIE MEYER

Megan Tingley Books

LITTLE, BROWN AND COMPANY

New York   Boston

Little, Brown and Company

Hachette Book Group
237 Park Avenue, New York, NY 10017
Visit our Web site at www.lb-teens.com

Little, Brown and Company is a division of Hachette Book Group, Inc.
The Little, Brown name and logo are trademarks of Hachette Book Group, Inc.

First Hardcover Edition: August 2007
First Paperback Edition: August 2009

The characters and events portrayed in this book are fictitious. Any similarity
to real persons, living or dead, is coincidental and not intended by the author.

Meyer, Stephenie, 1973-
Eclipse / by Stephenie Meyer.—1st ed.
p. cm.
Summary: Bella must choose between her friendship with Jacob
and her relationship with Edward, but when Seattle is ravaged by
a mysterious string of killings, the three of them
need to decide whether their personal lives are more important
than the well-being of an entire city.
ISBN: 978-0-316-02765-6
[1. Vampire—Fiction. 2. Werewolves—Fiction. 3. Interpersonal
relations—Fiction. 4. High schools—Fiction. 5. Schools—Fiction.
6. Seattle (Wash.)—Fiction. 7. Washington (State)—Fiction.] I. Title.
PZ7.M57188Ec 2007
[Fic]—dc   2007012325

10 9 8 7 6 5 4 3 2 1

RRD-C

Printed in United States of America

To my husband, Pancho,
for your patience, love, friendship, humor,
and willingness to eat out.

And also to my children, Gabe, Seth, and Eli,
for letting me experience the kind of love
that people freely die for.

⤙ ⤚

CONTENTS

-+- -+-

Fire *and* Ice

-+- -+-

Some say the world will end in fire,
Some say in ice.
From what I've tasted of desire
I hold with those who favor fire.
But if it had to perish twice,
I think I know enough of hate
To say that for destruction ice
Is also great
And would suffice.

Robert Frost

PREFACE

ALL OUR ATTEMPTS AT SUBTERFUGE HAD BEEN IN VAIN.

With ice in my heart, I watched him prepare to defend me. His intense concentration betrayed no hint of doubt, though he was outnumbered. I knew that we could expect no help — at this moment, his family was fighting for their lives just as surely as he was for ours.

Would I ever learn the outcome of that other fight? Find out who the winners and the losers were? Would I live long enough for that?

The odds of that didn't look so great.

Black eyes, wild with their fierce craving for my death, watched for the moment when my protector's attention would be diverted. The moment when I would surely die.

Somewhere, far, far away in the cold forest, a wolf howled.

1. ULTIMATUM

Bella,

~~I don't know why you're making~~
~~charlie carry notes to Billy like~~
~~we're in second grade - if I wanted~~
~~to talk to you I would answer the~~

~~You made the choice here, okay?~~
~~You can't have it both ways when~~

~~What part of 'mortal enemies' is too~~
~~complicated for you to~~

~~Look, I know I'm being a jerk, but there's just no way around~~

~~We can't be friends when you're spending all your time with a bunch of~~

~~It just makes it worse when I think about you too much, so don't write anymore~~

Yeah, I miss you, too. A lot.
Doesn't change anything. Sorry.

Jacob

I ran my fingers across the page, feeling the dents where he had pressed the pen to the paper so hard that it had nearly broken through. I could picture him writing this — scrawling the angry letters in his rough handwriting, slashing through line after line when the words came out wrong, maybe even snapping the pen in his too-big hand; that would explain the ink splatters. I could imagine the frustration pulling his black eyebrows together and crumpling his forehead. If I'd been there, I might have laughed. *Don't give yourself a brain hemorrhage, Jacob,* I would have told him. *Just spit it out.*

Laughing was the last thing I felt like doing now as I reread the words I'd already memorized. His answer to my pleading note — passed from Charlie to Billy to him, just like second grade, as he'd pointed out — was no surprise.

I'd known the essence of what it would say before I'd opened it.

What was surprising was how much each crossed-out line wounded me — as if the points of the letters had cutting edges. More than that, behind each angry beginning lurked a vast pool of hurt; Jacob's pain cut me deeper than my own.

While I was pondering this, I caught the unmistakable scent of a smoking burner rising from the kitchen. In another house, the fact that someone besides myself was cooking might not be a cause for panicking.

I shoved the wrinkled paper into my back pocket and ran, making it downstairs in the nick of time.

The jar of spaghetti sauce Charlie'd stuck in the microwave was only on its first revolution when I yanked the door open and pulled it out.

"What did I do wrong?" Charlie demanded.

"You're supposed to take the lid off first, Dad. Metal's bad for microwaves." I swiftly removed the lid as I spoke, poured half the sauce into a bowl, and then put the bowl inside the microwave and the jar back in the fridge; I fixed the time and pressed start.

Charlie watched my adjustments with pursed lips. "Did I get the noodles right?"

I looked in the pan on the stove — the source of the smell that had alerted me. "Stirring helps," I said mildly. I found a spoon and tried to de-clump the mushy hunk that was scalded to the bottom.

Charlie sighed.

"So what's all this about?" I asked him.

He folded his arms across his chest and glared out the back windows into the sheeting rain. "Don't know what you're talking about," he grumbled.

I was mystified. Charlie cooking? And what was with the surly attitude? Edward wasn't here yet; usually my dad reserved this kind of behavior for my boyfriend's benefit, doing his best to illustrate the theme of "unwelcome" with every word and posture. Charlie's efforts were unnecessary — Edward knew exactly what my dad was thinking without the show.

The word *boyfriend* had me chewing on the inside of my cheek with a familiar tension while I stirred. It wasn't the right word, not at all. I needed something more expressive of eternal commitment. . . . But words like *destiny* and *fate* sounded hokey when you used them in casual conversation.

Edward had another word in mind, and that word was the source of the tension I felt. It put my teeth on edge just to think it to myself.

Fiancée. Ugh. I shuddered away from the thought.

"Did I miss something? Since when do you make dinner?" I asked Charlie. The pasta lump bobbed in the boiling water as I poked it. "Or *try* to make dinner, I should say."

Charlie shrugged. "There's no law that says I can't cook in my own house."

"You would know," I replied, grinning as I eyed the badge pinned to his leather jacket.

"Ha. Good one." He shrugged out of the jacket as if my glance had reminded him he still had it on, and hung it on the peg reserved for his gear. His gun belt was already slung in place — he hadn't felt the need to wear that to the station for a few weeks. There had been no more disturbing disappearances to trouble the small town of Forks, Washington, no more sightings of the giant, mysterious wolves in the ever-rainy woods. . . .

I prodded the noodles in silence, guessing that Charlie would get around to talking about whatever was bothering him in his own time. My dad was not a man of many words, and the effort he had put into trying to orchestrate a sit-down dinner with me made it clear there were an uncharacteristic number of words on his mind.

I glanced at the clock routinely — something I did every few minutes around this time. Less than a half hour to go now.

Afternoons were the hardest part of my day. Ever since my former best friend (and werewolf), Jacob Black, had informed on me about the motorcycle I'd been riding on the sly — a betrayal he had devised in order to get me grounded so that I couldn't spend time with my boyfriend (and vampire), Edward Cullen — Edward had been allowed to see me only from seven till nine-thirty p.m., always inside the confines of my home and under the supervision of my dad's unfailingly crabby glare.

This was an escalation from the previous, slightly less stringent grounding that I'd earned for an unexplained three-day disappearance and one episode of cliff diving.

Of course, I still saw Edward at school, because there wasn't anything Charlie could do about that. And then, Edward spent almost every night in my room, too, but

Charlie wasn't precisely aware of that. Edward's ability to climb easily and silently through my second-story window was almost as useful as his ability to read Charlie's mind.

Though the afternoon was the only time I spent away from Edward, it was enough to make me restless, and the hours always dragged. Still, I endured my punishment without complaining because — for one thing — I knew I'd earned it, and — for another — because I couldn't bear to hurt my dad by moving out now, when a much more permanent separation hovered, invisible to Charlie, so close on my horizon.

My dad sat down at the table with a grunt and unfolded the damp newspaper there; within seconds he was clucking his tongue in disapproval.

"I don't know why you read the news, Dad. It only ticks you off."

He ignored me, grumbling at the paper in his hands. "This is why everyone wants to live in a small town! Ridiculous."

"What have big cities done wrong now?"

"Seattle's making a run for murder capital of the country. Five unsolved homicides in the last two weeks. Can you imagine living like that?"

"I think Phoenix is actually higher up the homicide list, Dad. I *have* lived like that." And I'd never come close to being a murder victim until after I moved to his safe little town. In fact, I was still on several hit lists. . . . The spoon shook in my hands, making the water tremble.

"Well, you couldn't pay me enough," Charlie said.

I gave up on saving dinner and settled for serving it; I had to use a steak knife to cut a portion of spaghetti for Charlie and then myself, while he watched with a sheepish expression. Charlie coated his helping with sauce and dug in. I disguised my own clump as well as I could and followed his example without much enthusiasm. We ate in silence for a moment. Charlie was still scanning the news, so I picked up my much-abused copy of *Wuthering Heights* from where I'd left it this morning at breakfast, and tried to lose myself in turn-of-the-century England while I waited for him to start talking.

I was just to the part where Heathcliff returns when Charlie cleared his throat and threw the paper to the floor.

"You're right," Charlie said. "I did have a reason for doing this." He waved his fork at the gluey spread. "I wanted to talk to you."

I laid the book aside; the binding was so destroyed that it slumped flat to the table. "You could have just asked."

He nodded, his eyebrows pulling together. "Yeah. I'll remember that next time. I thought taking dinner off your hands would soften you up."

I laughed. "It worked — your cooking skills have me soft as a marshmallow. What do you need, Dad?"

"Well, it's about Jacob."

I felt my face harden. "What about him?" I asked through stiff lips.

"Easy, Bells. I know you're still upset that he told on you, but it was the right thing. He was being responsible."

"Responsible," I repeated scathingly, rolling my eyes. "Right. So, what about Jacob?"

The careless question repeated inside my head, anything but trivial. *What about Jacob?* What *was* I going to do about him? My former best friend who was now . . . what? My enemy? I cringed.

Charlie's face was suddenly wary. "Don't get mad at me, okay?"

"Mad?"

"Well, it's about Edward, too."

My eyes narrowed.

Charlie's voice got gruffer. "I let him in the house, don't I?"

"You do," I admitted. "For brief periods of time. Of course, you might let me *out* of the house for brief periods now and then, too," I continued — only jokingly; I knew I was on lockdown for the duration of the school year. "I've been pretty good lately."

"Well, that's kind of where I was heading with this. . . ." And then Charlie's face stretched into an unexpected eye-crinkling grin; for a second he looked twenty years younger.

I saw a dim glimmer of possibility in that smile, but I proceeded slowly. "I'm confused, Dad. Are we talking about Jacob, or Edward, or me being grounded?"

The grin flashed again. "Sort of all three."

"And how do they relate?" I asked, cautious.

"Okay." He sighed, raising his hands as if in surrender. "So I'm thinking maybe you deserve a parole for good behavior. For a teenager, you're amazingly non-whiney."

My voice and eyebrows shot up. "Seriously? I'm free?"

Where was this coming from? I'd been positive I would be under house arrest until I actually moved out, and Edward hadn't picked up any wavering in Charlie's thoughts. . . .

Charlie held up one finger. "Conditionally."

The enthusiasm vanished. "Fantastic," I groaned.

"Bella, this is more of a request than a demand, okay? You're free. But I'm hoping you'll use that freedom . . . judiciously."

"What does that mean?"

He sighed again. "I know you're satisfied to spend all of your time with Edward —"

"I spend time with Alice, too," I interjected. Edward's sister had no hours of visitation; she came and went as she pleased. Charlie was putty in her capable hands.

"That's true," he said. "But you have other friends besides the Cullens, Bella. Or you *used* to."

We stared at each other for a long moment.

"When was the last time you spoke to Angela Weber?" he threw at me.

"Friday at lunch," I answered immediately.

Before Edward's return, my school friends had polarized into two groups. I liked to think of those groups as *good* vs. *evil*. *Us* and *them* worked, too. The good guys were Angela, her steady boyfriend Ben Cheney, and Mike Newton; these three had all very generously forgiven me for going crazy when Edward left. Lauren Mallory was the evil core of the *them* side, and almost everyone else, including my first friend in Forks, Jessica Stanley, seemed content to go along with her anti-Bella agenda.

With Edward back at school, the dividing line had become even more distinct.

Edward's return had taken its toll on Mike's friendship, but Angela was unswervingly loyal, and Ben followed her lead. Despite the natural aversion most humans felt toward the Cullens, Angela sat dutifully beside Alice every day at lunch. After a few weeks, Angela even looked comfortable there. It was difficult not to be charmed by the Cullens — once one gave them the chance to be charming.

"Outside of school?" Charlie asked, calling my attention back.

"I haven't seen *anyone* outside of school, Dad. Grounded, remember? And Angela has a boyfriend, too. She's always with Ben. *If* I'm really free," I added, heavy on the skepticism, "maybe we could double."

"Okay. But then . . ." He hesitated. "You and Jake used to be joined at the hip, and now —"

I cut him off. "Can you get to the point, Dad? What's your condition — exactly?"

"I don't think you should dump all your other friends for your boyfriend, Bella," he said in a stern voice. "It's not nice, and I think your life would be better balanced if you kept some other people in it. What happened last September . . ."

I flinched.

"Well," he said defensively. "If you'd had more of a life outside of Edward Cullen, it might not have been like that."

"It would have been exactly like that," I muttered.

"Maybe, maybe not."

"The point?" I reminded him.

"Use your new freedom to see your other friends, too. Keep it balanced."

I nodded slowly. "Balance is good. Do I have specific time quotas to fill, though?"

He made a face, but shook his head. "I don't want to make this complicated. Just don't forget your friends . . ."

It was a dilemma I was already struggling with. My friends. People who, for their own safety, I would never be able to see again after graduation.

So what was the better course of action? Spend time with them while I could? Or start the separation now to make it more gradual? I quailed at the idea of the second option.

". . . particularly Jacob," Charlie added before I could think things through more than that.

A greater dilemma than the first. It took me a moment to find the right words. "Jacob might be . . . difficult."

"The Blacks are practically family, Bella," he said, stern and fatherly again. "And Jacob has been a very, *very* good friend to you."

"I know that."

"Don't you miss him at all?" Charlie asked, frustrated.

My throat suddenly felt swollen; I had to clear it twice before I answered. "Yes, I do miss him," I admitted, still looking down. "I miss him a lot."

"Then why is it difficult?"

It wasn't something I was at liberty to explain. It was against the rules for normal people — *human* people like me and Charlie — to know about the clandestine world full of myths and monsters that existed secretly around us.

I knew all about that world — and I was in no small amount of trouble as a result. I wasn't about to get Charlie in the same trouble.

"With Jacob there is a . . . conflict," I said slowly. "A conflict about the friendship thing, I mean. Friendship doesn't always seem to be enough for Jake." I wound my excuse out of details that were true but insignificant, hardly crucial compared to the fact that Jacob's werewolf pack bitterly hated Edward's vampire family — and therefore me, too, as I fully intended to join that family. It just wasn't something I could work out with him in a note, and he wouldn't answer my calls. But my plan to deal with the werewolf in person had definitely not gone over well with the vampires.

"Isn't Edward up for a little healthy competition?" Charlie's voice was sarcastic now.

I leveled a dark look at him. "There's no competition."

"You're hurting Jake's feelings, avoiding him like this. He'd rather be just friends than nothing."

Oh, now *I* was avoiding *him?*

"I'm pretty sure Jake doesn't want to be friends at all." The words burned in my mouth. "Where'd you get that idea, anyway?"

Charlie looked embarrassed now. "The subject might have come up today with Billy. . . ."

"You and Billy gossip like old women," I complained, stabbing my fork viciously into the congealed spaghetti on my plate.

"Billy's worried about Jacob," Charlie said. "Jake's having a hard time right now. . . . He's depressed."

I winced, but kept my eyes on the blob.

"And then you were always so happy after spending the day with Jake." Charlie sighed.

"I'm happy *now*," I growled fiercely through my teeth.

The contrast between my words and tone broke through the tension. Charlie burst into laughter, and I had to join in.

"Okay, okay," I agreed. "Balance."

"And Jacob," he insisted.

"I'll try."

"Good. Find that balance, Bella. And, oh, yeah, you've got some mail," Charlie said, closing the subject with no attempt at subtlety. "It's by the stove."

I didn't move, my thoughts twisting into snarls around Jacob's name. It was most likely junk mail; I'd just gotten a package from my mom yesterday and I wasn't expecting anything else.

Charlie shoved his chair away from the table and stretched as he got to his feet. He took his plate to the sink, but before he turned the water on to rinse it, he paused to toss a thick envelope at me. The letter skidded across the table and *thunk*ed into my elbow.

"Er, thanks," I muttered, puzzled by his pushiness. Then I saw the return address — the letter was from the University of Alaska Southeast. "That was quick. I guess I missed the deadline on that one, too."

Charlie chuckled.

I flipped the envelope over and then glared up at him. "It's open."

"I was curious."

"I'm shocked, Sheriff. That's a federal crime."

"Oh, just read it."

I pulled out the letter, and a folded schedule of courses.

"Congratulations," he said before I could read anything. "Your first acceptance."

"Thanks, Dad."

"We should talk about tuition. I've got some money saved up —"

"Hey, hey, none of that. I'm not touching your retirement, Dad. I've got my college fund." What was left of it — and there hadn't been much to begin with.

Charlie frowned. "Some of these places are pretty pricey, Bells. I want to help. You don't have to go all the way to Alaska just because it's cheaper."

It wasn't cheaper, not at all. But it *was* far away, and Juneau had an average of three hundred twenty-one overcast days per year. The first was my prerequisite, the second was Edward's.

"I've got it covered. Besides, there's lots of financial aid out there. It's easy to get loans." I hoped my bluff wasn't too obvious. I hadn't actually done a lot of research on the subject.

"So . . . ," Charlie began, and then he pursed his lips and looked away.

"So what?"

"Nothing. I was just . . ." He frowned. "Just wondering what . . . Edward's plans are for next year?"

"Oh."

"Well?"

Three quick raps on the door saved me. Charlie rolled his eyes and I jumped up.

"Coming!" I called while Charlie mumbled something that sounded like, "Go away." I ignored him and went to let Edward in.

I wrenched the door out of my way — ridiculously eager — and there he was, my personal miracle.

Time had not made me immune to the perfection of his face, and I was sure that I would never take any aspect of him for granted. My eyes traced over his pale white features: the hard square of his jaw, the softer curve of his full lips — twisted up into a smile now, the straight line of his nose, the sharp angle of his cheekbones, the smooth marble span of his forehead — partially obscured by a tangle of rain-darkened bronze hair. . . .

I saved his eyes for last, knowing that when I looked into them I was likely to lose my train of thought. They were wide, warm with liquid gold, and framed by a thick fringe of black lashes. Staring into his eyes always made me feel extraordinary — sort of like my bones were turning spongy. I was also a little lightheaded, but that could have been because I'd forgotten to keep breathing. Again.

It was a face any male model in the world would trade his soul for. Of course, that might be exactly the asking price: one soul.

No. I didn't believe that. I felt guilty for even thinking it, and was glad — as I was often glad — that I was the one person whose thoughts were a mystery to Edward.

I reached for his hand, and sighed when his cold fingers found mine. His touch brought with it the strangest sense of relief — as if I'd been in pain and that pain had suddenly ceased.

"Hey." I smiled a little at my anticlimactic greeting.

He raised our interlaced fingers to brush my cheek with the back of his hand. "How was your afternoon?"

"Slow."

"For me, as well."

He pulled my wrist up to his face, our hands still twisted together. His eyes closed as his nose skimmed along the skin there, and he smiled gently without opening them. Enjoying the bouquet while resisting the wine, as he'd once put it.

I knew that the scent of my blood — so much sweeter to him than any other person's blood, truly like wine beside water to an alcoholic — caused him actual pain from the burning thirst it engendered. But he didn't seem to shy away from it as much as he once had. I could only dimly imagine the Herculean effort behind this simple gesture.

It made me sad that he had to try so hard. I comforted myself with the knowledge that I wouldn't be causing him pain much longer.

I heard Charlie approaching then, stamping his feet on the way to express his customary displeasure with our guest. Edward's eyes snapped open and he let our hands fall, keeping them twined.

"Good evening, Charlie." Edward was always flawlessly polite, though Charlie didn't deserve it.

Charlie grunted at him, and then stood there with his arms crossed over his chest. He was taking the idea of parental supervision to extremes lately.

"I brought another set of applications," Edward told me

then, holding up a stuffed manila envelope. He was wearing a roll of stamps like a ring around his littlest finger.

I groaned. How were there any colleges left that he hadn't forced me to apply to already? And how did he keep finding these loophole openings? It was so late in the year.

He smiled as if he *could* read my thoughts; they must have been very obvious on my face. "There are still a few open deadlines. And a few places willing to make exceptions."

I could just imagine the motivations behind such exceptions. And the dollar amounts involved.

Edward laughed at my expression.

"Shall we?" he asked, towing me toward the kitchen table.

Charlie huffed and followed behind, though he could hardly complain about the activity on tonight's agenda. He'd been pestering me to make a decision about college on a daily basis.

I cleared the table quickly while Edward organized an intimidating stack of forms. When I moved *Wuthering Heights* to the counter, Edward raised one eyebrow. I knew what he was thinking, but Charlie interrupted before Edward could comment.

"Speaking of college applications, Edward," Charlie said, his tone even more sullen — he tried to avoid addressing Edward directly, and when he had to, it exacerbated his bad mood. "Bella and I were just talking about next year. Have you decided where you're going to school?"

Edward smiled up at Charlie and his voice was friendly. "Not yet. I've received a few acceptance letters, but I'm still weighing my options."

"Where have you been accepted?" Charlie pressed.

"Syracuse . . . Harvard . . . Dartmouth . . . and I just got accepted to the University of Alaska Southeast today." Edward turned his face slightly to the side so that he could wink at me. I stifled a giggle.

"Harvard? Dartmouth?" Charlie mumbled, unable to conceal his awe. "Well that's pretty . . . that's something. Yeah, but the University of Alaska . . . you wouldn't really consider that when you could go Ivy League. I mean, your father would want you to . . . ."

"Carlisle's always fine with whatever I choose to do," Edward told him serenely.

"Hmph."

"Guess what, Edward?" I asked in a bright voice, playing along.

"What, Bella?"

I pointed to the thick envelope on the counter. "I just got *my* acceptance to the University of Alaska!"

"Congratulations!" He grinned. "What a coincidence."

Charlie's eyes narrowed and he glared back and forth between the two of us. "Fine," he muttered after a minute. "I'm going to go watch the game, Bella. Nine-thirty."

That was his usual parting command.

"Er, Dad? Remember the very recent discussion about my freedom . . . ?"

He sighed. "Right. Okay, *ten*-thirty. You still have a curfew on school nights."

"Bella's no longer grounded?" Edward asked. Though I knew he wasn't really surprised, I couldn't detect any false note to the sudden excitement in his voice.

"Conditionally," Charlie corrected through his teeth. "What's it to you?"

I frowned at my dad, but he didn't see.

"It's just good to know," Edward said. "Alice has been itching for a shopping partner, and I'm sure Bella would love to see some city lights." He smiled at me.

But Charlie growled, "No!" and his face flushed purple.

"Dad! What's the problem?"

He made an effort to unclench his teeth. "I don't want you going to Seattle right now."

"Huh?"

"I told you about that story in the paper — there's some kind of gang on a killing spree in Seattle and I want you to steer clear, okay?"

I rolled my eyes. "Dad, there's a better chance that I'll get struck by lightning than that the one day I'm in Seattle —"

"No, that's fine, Charlie," Edward said, interrupting me. "I didn't mean Seattle. I was thinking Portland, actually. I wouldn't have Bella in Seattle, either. Of course not."

I looked at him in disbelief, but he had Charlie's newspaper in his hands and he was reading the front page intently.

He must have been trying to appease my father. The idea of being in danger from even the most deadly of humans while I was with Alice or Edward was downright hilarious.

It worked. Charlie stared at Edward for one second more, and then shrugged. "Fine." He stalked off toward the living room, in a bit of a hurry now — maybe he didn't want to miss tip-off.

I waited till the TV was on, so that Charlie wouldn't be able to hear me.

"What —," I started to ask.

"Hold on," Edward said without looking up from the paper. His eyes stayed focused on the page as he pushed the first application toward me across the table. "I think you can recycle your essays for this one. Same questions."

Charlie must still be listening. I sighed and started to fill out the repetitive information: name, address, social. . . . After a few minutes I glanced up, but Edward was now staring pensively out the window. As I bent my head back to my work, I noticed for the first time the name of the school.

I snorted and shoved the papers aside.

"Bella?"

"Be serious, Edward. *Dartmouth?*"

Edward lifted the discarded application and laid it gently in front of me again. "I think you'd like New Hampshire," he said. "There's a full complement of night courses for me, and the forests are very conveniently located for the avid hiker. Plentiful wildlife." He pulled out the crooked smile he knew I couldn't resist.

I took a deep breath through my nose.

"I'll let you pay me back, if that makes you happy," he promised. "If you want, I can charge you interest."

"Like I could even get in without some enormous bribe. Or was that part of the loan? The new Cullen wing of the library? Ugh. Why are we having this discussion again?"

"Will you just fill out the application, please, Bella? It won't hurt you to apply."

My jaw flexed. "You know what? I don't think I will."

I reached for the papers, planning to crumple them into a suitable shape for lobbing at the trashcan, but they were already gone. I stared at the empty table for a moment, and then at Edward. He didn't appear to have moved, but the application was probably already tucked away in his jacket.

"What are you doing?" I demanded.

"I sign your name better than you do yourself. You've already written the essays."

"You're going way overboard with this, you know." I whispered on the off chance that Charlie wasn't completely lost in his game. "I really don't need to apply anywhere else. I've been accepted in Alaska. I can almost afford the first semester's tuition. It's as good an alibi as any. There's no need to throw away a bunch of money, no matter whose it is."

A pained looked tightened his face. "Bella —"

"Don't start. I agree that I need to go through the motions for Charlie's sake, but we both know I'm not going to be in any condition to go to school next fall. To be anywhere near people."

My knowledge of those first few years as a new vampire was sketchy. Edward had never gone into details — it wasn't his favorite subject — but I knew it wasn't pretty. Self-control was apparently an acquired skill. Anything more than correspondence school was out of the question.

"I thought the timing was still undecided," Edward

reminded me softly. "You might enjoy a semester or two of college. There are a lot of human experiences you've never had."

"I'll get to those afterward."

"They won't be *human* experiences afterward. You don't get a second chance at humanity, Bella."

I sighed. "You've got to be reasonable about the timing, Edward. It's just too dangerous to mess around with."

"There's no danger yet," he insisted.

I glared at him. No danger? Sure. I only had a sadistic vampire trying to avenge her mate's death with my own, preferably through some slow and torturous method. Who was worried about Victoria? And, oh yeah, the Volturi — the vampire royal family with their small army of vampire warriors — who insisted that my heart stop beating one way or another in the near future, because humans weren't allowed to know they existed. Right. No reason at all to panic.

Even with Alice keeping watch — Edward was relying on her uncannily accurate visions of the future to give us advance warning — it was insane to take chances.

Besides, I'd already won this argument. The date for my transformation was tentatively set for shortly after my graduation from high school, only a handful of weeks away.

A sharp jolt of unease pierced my stomach as I realized how short the time really was. Of course this change was necessary — and the key to what I wanted more than everything else in the world put together — but I was deeply conscious of Charlie sitting in the other room enjoying his game, just like every other night. And my mother, Renée, far away in sunny Florida, still pleading with me to spend the summer on the beach with her and her new husband. And Jacob, who, unlike my parents, would know exactly what was going on when I disappeared to some distant school. Even if my parents didn't grow suspicious for a long time, even if I could put off visits with excuses about travel expenses or study loads or illnesses, Jacob would know the truth.

For a moment, the idea of Jacob's certain revulsion overshadowed every other pain.

"Bella," Edward murmured, his face twisting when he read the distress in mine. "There's no hurry. I won't let anyone hurt you. You can take all the time you need."

"I want to hurry," I whispered, smiling weakly, trying to make a joke of it. "I want to be a monster, too."

His teeth clenched; he spoke through them. "You have no idea what you're saying." Abruptly, he flung the damp newspaper onto the table in between us. His finger stabbed the headline on the front page:

DEATH TOLL ON THE RISE, POLICE FEAR GANG ACTIVITY

"What does that have to do with anything?"

"Monsters are not a joke, Bella."

I stared at the headline again, and then up to his hard expression. "A . . . a *vampire* is doing this?" I whispered.

He smiled without humor. His voice was low and cold. "You'd be surprised, Bella, at how often my kind are the source behind the horrors in your human news. It's easy to recognize, when you know what to look for. The information here indicates a newborn vampire is loose in Seattle. Bloodthirsty, wild, out of control. The way we all were."

I let my gaze drop to the paper again, avoiding his eyes.

"We've been monitoring the situation for a few weeks. All the signs are there — the unlikely disappearances, always in the night, the poorly disposed-of corpses, the lack of other evidence. . . . Yes, someone brand-new. And no one seems to be taking responsibility for the neophyte. . . ." He took a deep breath. "Well, it's not our problem. We wouldn't even pay attention to the situation if it wasn't going on so close to home. Like I said, this happens all the time. The existence of monsters results in monstrous consequences."

I tried not to see the names on the page, but they jumped out from the rest of the print like they were in bold. The five people whose lives were over, whose families were mourning now. It was different from considering murder in the abstract, reading those names. Maureen Gardiner, Geoffrey Campbell, Grace Razi, Michelle O'Connell, Ronald Albrook. People who'd had parents and children and friends and pets and jobs and hopes and plans and memories and futures. . . .

"It won't be the same for me," I whispered, half to myself. "You won't let me be like that. We'll live in Antarctica."

Edward snorted, breaking the tension. "Penguins. Lovely."

I laughed a shaky laugh and knocked the paper off the table so I wouldn't have to see those names; it hit the linoleum with a thud. Of course Edward would consider

the hunting possibilities. He and his "vegetarian" family —
all committed to protecting human life — preferred the
flavor of large predators for satisfying their dietary needs.
"Alaska, then, as planned. Only somewhere much more
remote than Juneau — somewhere with grizzlies galore."

"Better," he allowed. "There are polar bears, too. Very
fierce. And the wolves get quite large."

My mouth fell open and my breath blew out in a sharp
gust.

"What's wrong?" he asked. Before I could recover, the
confusion vanished and his whole body seemed to harden.
"Oh. Never mind the wolves, then, if the idea is offensive
to you." His voice was stiff, formal, his shoulders rigid.

"He was my best friend, Edward," I muttered. It stung
to use the past tense. "Of course the idea offends me."

"Please forgive my thoughtlessness," he said, still very
formal. "I shouldn't have suggested that."

"Don't worry about it." I stared at my hands, clenched
into a double fist on the table.

We were both silent for a moment, and then his cool
finger was under my chin, coaxing my face up. His expression was much softer now.

"Sorry. Really."

"I know. I know it's not the same thing. I shouldn't
have reacted that way. It's just that . . . well, I was already
thinking about Jacob before you came over." I hesitated.
His tawny eyes seemed to get a little bit darker whenever
I said Jacob's name. My voice turned pleading in response.
"Charlie says Jake is having a hard time. He's hurting
right now, and . . . it's my fault."

"You've done nothing wrong, Bella."

I took a deep breath. "I need to make it better, Edward. I owe him that. And it's one of Charlie's conditions, anyway —"

His face changed while I spoke, turning hard again, statue-like.

"You know it's out of the question for you to be around a werewolf unprotected, Bella. And it would break the treaty if any of us cross over onto their land. Do you want us to start a war?"

"Of course not!"

"Then there's really no point in discussing the matter further." He dropped his hand and looked away, searching for a subject change. His eyes paused on something behind me, and he smiled, though his eyes stayed wary.

"I'm glad Charlie has decided to let you out — you're sadly in need of a visit to the bookstore. I can't believe you're reading *Wuthering Heights* again. Don't you know it by heart yet?"

"Not all of us have photographic memories," I said curtly.

"Photographic memory or not, I don't understand why you like it. The characters are ghastly people who ruin each others' lives. I don't know how Heathcliff and Cathy ended up being ranked with couples like Romeo and Juliet or Elizabeth Bennet and Mr. Darcy. It isn't a love story, it's a hate story."

"You have some serious issues with the classics," I snapped.

"Perhaps it's because I'm not impressed by antiquity." He smiled, evidently satisfied that he'd distracted me.

"Honestly, though, why *do* you read it over and over?" His eyes were vivid with real interest now, trying — again — to unravel the convoluted workings of my mind. He reached across the table to cradle my face in his hand. "What is it that appeals to you?"

His sincere curiosity disarmed me. "I'm not sure," I said, scrambling for coherency while his gaze unintentionally scattered my thoughts. "I think it's something about the inevitability. How nothing can keep them apart — not her selfishness, or his evil, or even death, in the end. . . ."

His face was thoughtful as he considered my words. After a moment he smiled a teasing smile. "I still think it would be a better story if either of them had one redeeming quality."

"I think that may be the point," I disagreed. "Their love *is* their only redeeming quality."

"I hope you have better sense than that — to fall in love with someone so . . . malignant."

"It's a bit late for me to worry about who I fall in love with," I pointed out. "But even without the warning, I seem to have managed fairly well."

He laughed quietly. "I'm glad *you* think so."

"Well, I hope you're smart enough to stay away from someone so selfish. Catherine is really the source of all the trouble, not Heathcliff."

"I'll be on my guard," he promised.

I sighed. He was so good at distractions.

I put my hand over his to hold it to my face. "I need to see Jacob."

His eyes closed. "No."

"It's truly not dangerous at all," I said, pleading again. "I used to spend all day in La Push with the whole lot of them, and nothing ever happened."

But I made a slip; my voice faltered at the end because I realized as I was saying the words that they were a lie. It was not true that *nothing* had ever happened. A brief flash of memory — an enormous gray wolf crouched to spring, baring his dagger-like teeth at me — had my palms sweating with an echo of remembered panic.

Edward heard my heart accelerate and nodded as if I'd acknowledged the lie aloud. "Werewolves are unstable. Sometimes, the people near them get hurt. Sometimes, they get killed."

I wanted to deny it, but another image slowed my rebuttal. I saw in my head the once beautiful face of Emily Young, now marred by a trio of dark scars that dragged down the corner of her right eye and left her mouth warped forever into a lopsided scowl.

He waited, grimly triumphant, for me to find my voice.

"You don't know them," I whispered.

"I know them better than you think, Bella. I was here the last time."

"The last time?"

"We started crossing paths with the wolves about seventy years ago. . . . We had just settled near Hoquiam. That was before Alice and Jasper were with us. We outnumbered them, but that wouldn't have stopped it from turning into a fight if not for Carlisle. He managed to convince Ephraim Black that coexisting was possible, and eventually we made the truce."

Jacob's great-grandfather's name startled me.

"We thought the line had died out with Ephraim," Edward muttered; it sounded like he was talking to himself now. "That the genetic quirk which allowed the transmutation had been lost. . . ." He broke off and stared at me accusingly. "Your bad luck seems to get more potent every day. Do you realize that your insatiable pull for all things deadly was strong enough to recover a pack of mutant canines from extinction? If we could bottle your luck, we'd have a weapon of mass destruction on our hands."

I ignored the ribbing, my attention caught by his assumption — was he serious? "But I didn't bring them back. Don't you know?"

"Know what?"

"My bad luck had nothing to do with it. The werewolves came back because the vampires did."

Edward stared at me, his body motionless with surprise.

"Jacob told me that your family being here set things in motion. I thought you would already know. . . ."

His eyes narrowed. "Is that what they think?"

"Edward, look at the facts. Seventy years ago, you came here, and the werewolves showed up. You come back now, and the werewolves show up again. Do you think that's a coincidence?"

He blinked and his glare relaxed. "Carlisle will be interested in that theory."

"Theory," I scoffed.

He was silent for a moment, staring out the window into the rain; I imagined he was contemplating the fact that his family's presence was turning the locals into giant dogs.

"Interesting, but not exactly relevant," he murmured after a moment. "The situation remains the same."

I could translate that easily enough: no werewolf friends.

I knew I must be patient with Edward. It wasn't that he was unreasonable, it was just that he didn't *understand*. He had no idea how very much I owed Jacob Black — my life many times over, and possibly my sanity, too.

I didn't like to talk about that barren time with anyone, and especially not Edward. He had only been trying to save me when he'd left, trying to save my soul. I didn't hold him responsible for all the stupid things I'd done in his absence, or the pain I had suffered.

He did.

So I would have to word my explanation very carefully.

I got up and walked around the table. He opened his arms for me and I sat on his lap, nestling into his cool stone embrace. I looked at his hands while I spoke.

"Please just listen for a minute. This is so much more important than some whim to drop in on an old friend. Jacob is in *pain*." My voice distorted around the word. "I can't *not* try to help him — I can't give up on him now, when he needs me. Just because he's not human all the time. . . . Well, he was there for me when I was . . . not so human myself. You don't know what it was like. . . ." I hesitated. Edward's arms were rigid around me; his hands were in fists now, the tendons standing out. "If Jacob hadn't helped me . . . I'm not sure what you would have come home to. I owe him better than this, Edward."

I looked up at his face warily. His eyes were closed, and his jaw was strained.

"I'll never forgive myself for leaving you," he whispered. "Not if I live a hundred thousand years."

I put my hand against his cold face and waited until he sighed and opened his eyes.

"You were just trying to do the right thing. And I'm sure it would have worked with anyone less mental than me. Besides, you're here now. That's the part that matters."

"If I'd never left, you wouldn't feel the need to go risk your life to comfort a *dog*."

I flinched. I was used to Jacob and all his derogatory slurs — *bloodsucker, leech, parasite*. . . . Somehow it sounded harsher in Edward's velvet voice.

"I don't know how to phrase this properly," Edward said, and his tone was bleak. "It's going to sound cruel, I suppose. But I've come too close to losing you in the past. I know what it feels like to think I have. I am *not* going to tolerate anything dangerous."

"You have to trust me on this. I'll be fine."

His face was pained again. "Please, Bella," he whispered.

I stared into his suddenly burning golden eyes. "Please what?"

"Please, for me. Please make a conscious effort to keep yourself safe. I'll do everything I can, but I would appreciate a little help."

"I'll work on it," I murmured.

"Do you really have any idea how important you are to me? Any concept at all of how much I love you?" He pulled me tighter against his hard chest, tucking my head under his chin.

I pressed my lips against his snow-cold neck. "I know how much *I* love *you*," I answered.

"You compare one small tree to the entire forest."

I rolled my eyes, but he couldn't see. "Impossible."

He kissed the top of my head and sighed.

"No werewolves."

"I'm not going along with that. I have to see Jacob."

"Then I'll have to stop you."

He sounded utterly confident that this wouldn't be a problem.

I was sure he was right.

"We'll see about that," I bluffed anyway. "He's still my friend."

I could feel Jacob's note in my pocket, like it suddenly weighed ten pounds. I could hear the words in his voice, and he seemed to be agreeing with Edward — something that would never happen in reality.

Doesn't change anything. Sorry.

2. EVASION

I FELT ODDLY BUOYANT AS I WALKED FROM SPANISH toward the cafeteria, and it wasn't just because I was holding hands with the most perfect person on the planet, though that was certainly part of it.

Maybe it was the knowledge that my sentence was served and I was a free woman again.

Or maybe it wasn't anything to do with me specifically. Maybe it was the atmosphere of freedom that hung over the entire campus. School was winding down, and, for the senior class especially, there was a perceptible thrill in the air.

Freedom was so close it was touchable, taste-able. Signs of it were everywhere. Posters crowded together on the cafeteria walls, and the trashcans wore a colorful skirt of spilled-over fliers: reminders to buy yearbooks, class rings, and announcements; deadlines to order graduation gowns, hats, and tassels; neon-bright sales pitches — the juniors campaigning for class office; ominous, rose-wreathed advertisements for this year's prom. The big dance was this coming weekend, but I had an ironclad promise from Edward that I would not be subjected to that again. After all, I'd already had *that* human experience.

No, it must be my personal freedom that lightened me today. The ending of the school year did not give me the pleasure it seemed to give the other students. Actually, I felt nervous to the point of nausea whenever I thought of it. I tried to *not* think of it.

But it was hard to escape such an omnipresent topic as graduation.

"Have you sent your announcements, yet?" Angela asked when Edward and I sat down at our table. She had her light brown hair pulled back into a sloppy ponytail instead of her usual smooth hairdo, and there was a slightly frantic look about her eyes.

Alice and Ben were already there, too, on either side of Angela. Ben was intent over a comic book, his glasses sliding down his narrow nose. Alice was scrutinizing my boring jeans-and-a-t-shirt outfit in a way that made me self-conscious. Probably plotting another makeover. I sighed. My indifferent attitude to fashion was a constant thorn in her side. If I'd allow it, she'd love to dress me every day — perhaps several times a day — like some oversized three-dimensional paper doll.

"No," I answered Angela. "There's no point, really. Renée knows when I'm graduating. Who else is there?"

"How about you, Alice?"

Alice smiled. "All done."

"Lucky you." Angela sighed. "My mother has a thousand cousins and she expects me to hand-address one to everybody. I'm going to get carpal tunnel. I can't put it off any longer and I'm just dreading it."

"I'll help you," I volunteered. "If you don't mind my awful handwriting."

Charlie would like that. From the corner of my eye, I saw Edward smile. He must like that, too — me fulfilling Charlie's conditions without involving werewolves.

Angela looked relieved. "That's so nice of you. I'll come over any time you want."

"Actually, I'd rather go to your house if that's okay — I'm sick of mine. Charlie un-grounded me last night." I grinned as I announced my good news.

"Really?" Angela asked, mild excitement lighting her always-gentle brown eyes. "I thought you said you were in for life."

"I'm more surprised than you are. I was sure I would at least have finished high school before he set me free."

"Well, this is great, Bella! We'll have to go out to celebrate."

"You have no idea how good that sounds."

"What should we do?" Alice mused, her face lighting up at the possibilities. Alice's ideas were usually a little grandiose for me, and I could see it in her eyes now — the tendency to take things too far kicking into action.

"Whatever you're thinking, Alice, I doubt I'm *that* free."

"Free is free, right?" she insisted.

"I'm sure I still have boundaries — like the continental U.S., for example."

Angela and Ben laughed, but Alice grimaced in real disappointment.

"So what are we doing tonight?" she persisted.

"Nothing. Look, let's give it a couple of days to make sure he wasn't joking. It's a school night, anyway."

"We'll celebrate this weekend, then." Alice's enthusiasm was impossible to repress.

"Sure," I said, hoping to placate her. I knew I wasn't going to do anything too outlandish; it would be safer to take it slow with Charlie. Give him a chance to appreciate how trustworthy and mature I was before I asked for any favors.

Angela and Alice started talking about options; Ben joined the conversation, setting his comics aside. My attention drifted. I was surprised to find that the subject of my freedom was suddenly not as gratifying as it had been just a moment ago. While they discussed things to do in Port Angeles or maybe Hoquiam, I began to feel disgruntled.

It didn't take long to determine where my restlessness stemmed from.

Ever since I'd said goodbye to Jacob Black in the forest outside my home, I'd been plagued by a persistent, uncomfortable intrusion of a specific mental picture. It popped into my thoughts at regular intervals like some annoying alarm clock set to sound every half hour, filling my head with the image of Jacob's face crumpled in pain. This was the last memory I had of him.

As the disturbing vision struck again, I knew exactly why I was dissatisfied with my liberty. Because it was incomplete.

Sure, I was free to go to anywhere I wanted — except La Push; free to do anything I wanted — except see Jacob. I frowned at the table. There *had* to be some kind of middle ground.

"Alice? Alice!"

Angela's voice yanked me from my reverie. She was waving her hand back and forth in front of Alice's blank, staring face. Alice's expression was something I recognized — an expression that sent an automatic shock of panic through my body. The vacant look in her eyes told me that she was seeing something very different from the mundane lunchroom scene that surrounded us, but something that was every bit as real in its own way. Something that was coming, something that would happen soon. I felt the blood slither from my face.

Then Edward laughed, a very natural, relaxed sound. Angela and Ben looked toward him, but my eyes were locked on Alice. She jumped suddenly, as if someone had kicked her under the table.

"Is it naptime already, Alice?" Edward teased.

Alice was herself again. "Sorry, I was daydreaming, I guess."

"Daydreaming's better than facing two more hours of school," Ben said.

Alice threw herself back into the conversation with more animation than before — just a little bit too much. Once I saw her eyes lock with Edward's, only for a moment, and then she looked back to Angela before anyone else noticed. Edward was quiet, playing absentmindedly with a strand of my hair.

I waited anxiously for a chance to ask Edward what Alice had seen in her vision, but the afternoon passed without one minute of alone time.

It felt odd to me, almost deliberate. After lunch, Edward slowed his pace to match Ben's, talking about some assignment I knew he'd already finished. Then there was always someone else there between classes, though we usually had a few minutes to ourselves. When the final bell rang, Edward struck up a conversation with Mike Newton of all people, falling into step beside him as Mike headed for the parking lot. I trailed behind, letting Edward tow me along.

I listened, confused, while Mike answered Edward's unusually friendly queries. It seemed Mike was having car troubles.

". . . but I just replaced the battery," Mike was saying. His eyes darted ahead and then back to Edward warily. Mystified, just like I was.

"Perhaps it's the cables?" Edward offered.

"Maybe. I really don't know anything about cars," Mike admitted. "I need to have someone look at it, but I can't afford to take it to Dowling's."

I opened my mouth to suggest my mechanic, and then

snapped it shut again. My mechanic was busy these days — busy running around as a giant wolf.

"I know a few things — I could take a look, if you like," Edward offered. "Just let me drop Alice and Bella at home."

Mike and I both stared at Edward with our mouths hanging open.

"Er . . . thanks," Mike mumbled when he recovered. "But I have to get to work. Maybe some other time."

"Absolutely."

"See ya." Mike climbed into his car, shaking his head in disbelief.

Edward's Volvo, with Alice already inside, was just two cars away.

"What was *that* about?" I muttered as Edward held the passenger door for me.

"Just being helpful," Edward answered.

And then Alice, waiting in the backseat, was babbling at top speed.

"You're really not *that* good a mechanic, Edward. Maybe you should have Rosalie take a look at it tonight, just so you look good if Mike decides to let you help, you know. Not that it wouldn't be fun to watch his face if *Rosalie* showed up to help. But since Rosalie is supposed to be across the country attending college, I guess that's not the best idea. Too bad. Though I suppose, for Mike's car, you'll do. It's only within the finer tunings of a good Italian sports car that you're out of your depth. And speaking of Italy and sports cars that I stole there, you still owe me a yellow Porsche. I don't know that I want to wait for Christmas. . . ."

I stopped listening after a minute, letting her quick voice become just a hum in the background as I settled into my patient mode.

It looked to me like Edward was trying to avoid my questions. Fine. He would have to be alone with me soon enough. It was only a matter of time.

Edward seemed to realize that, too. He dropped Alice at the mouth of the Cullens' drive as usual, though by this point I half expected him to drive her to the door and walk her in.

As she got out, Alice threw a sharp look at his face. Edward seemed completely at ease.

"See you later," he said. And then, ever so slightly, he nodded.

Alice turned to disappear into the trees.

He was quiet as he turned the car around and headed back to Forks. I waited, wondering if he would bring it up himself. He didn't, and this made me tense. What *had* Alice seen today at lunch? Something he didn't want to tell me, and I tried to think of a reason why he would keep secrets. Maybe it would be better to prepare myself before I asked. I didn't want to freak out and have him think I couldn't handle it, whatever it was.

So we were both silent until we got back to Charlie's house.

"Light homework load tonight," he commented.

"Mmm," I assented.

"Do you suppose I'm allowed inside again?"

"Charlie didn't throw a fit when you picked me up for school."

But I was sure Charlie was going to turn sulky fast when he got home and found Edward here. Maybe I should make something extra-special for dinner.

Inside, I headed up the stairs, and Edward followed. He lounged on my bed and gazed out the window, seeming oblivious to my edginess.

I stowed my bag and turned the computer on. There was an unanswered e-mail from my mom to attend to, and she got panicky when I took too long. I drummed my fingers as I waited for my decrepit computer to wheeze awake; they snapped against the desk, staccato and anxious.

And then his fingers were on mine, holding them still.

"Are we a little impatient today?" he murmured.

I looked up, intending to make a sarcastic remark, but his face was closer than I'd expected. His golden eyes were smoldering, just inches away, and his breath was cool against my open lips. I could taste his scent on my tongue.

I couldn't remember the witty response I'd been about to make. I couldn't remember my name.

He didn't give me a chance to recover.

If I had my way, I would spend the majority of my time kissing Edward. There wasn't anything I'd experienced in my life that compared to the feeling of his cool lips, marble hard but always so gentle, moving with mine.

I didn't often get my way.

So it surprised me a little when his fingers braided themselves into my hair, securing my face to his. My arms locked behind his neck, and I wished I was stronger — strong enough to keep him prisoner here. One hand slid down my back, pressing me tighter against his stone chest. Even through his sweater, his skin was cold enough to make me shiver — it was a shiver of pleasure, of happiness, but his hands began to loosen in response.

I knew I had about three seconds before he would sigh and slide me deftly away, saying something about how we'd risked my life enough for one afternoon. Making the most of my last seconds, I crushed myself closer, molding myself to the shape of him. The tip of my tongue traced the curve of his lower lip; it was as flawlessly smooth as if it had been polished, and the *taste* —

He pulled my face away from his, breaking my hold with ease — he probably didn't even realize that I was using all my strength.

He chuckled once, a low, throaty sound. His eyes were bright with the excitement he so rigidly disciplined.

"Ah, Bella." He sighed.

"I'd say I'm sorry, but I'm not."

"And I should feel sorry that you're not sorry, but I don't. Maybe I should go sit on the bed."

I exhaled a little dizzily. "If you think that's necessary. . . ."

He smiled crookedly and disentangled himself.

I shook my head a few times, trying to clear it, and turned back to my computer. It was all warmed up and humming now. Well, not as much humming as groaning.

"Tell Renée I said hello."

"Sure thing."

I scanned through Renée's e-mail, shaking my head now and then at some of the dippier things she'd done. I was just as entertained and horrified as the first time I'd read this. It was so like my mother to forget exactly how paralyzed she was by heights until she was already strapped to a parachute and a dive instructor. I felt a little frustrated with Phil, her husband of almost two years, for allowing that one. I would have taken better care of her. I knew her so much better.

You have to let them go their own way eventually, I reminded myself. You have to let them have their own life. . . .

I'd spent most of my life taking care of Renée, patiently guiding her away from her craziest plans, good-naturedly enduring the ones I couldn't talk her out of. I'd always been indulgent with my mom, amused by her, even a little condescending to her. I saw her cornucopia of mistakes and laughed privately to myself. Scatterbrained Renée.

I was a very different person from my mother. Someone thoughtful and cautious. The responsible one, the grown-up. That's how I saw myself. That was the person I knew.

With the blood still pounding in my head from Edward's kiss, I couldn't help but think of my mother's most life-altering mistake. Silly and romantic, getting married fresh out of high school to a man she barely knew, then producing me a year later. She'd always promised me that she had no regrets, that I was the best gift her life had ever given her. And yet she'd drilled it into me over and over — smart people took marriage seriously. Mature people went to college and started careers before they got deeply involved in a relationship. She knew I would never be as thoughtless and goofy and *small-town* as she'd been. . . .

I gritted my teeth and tried to concentrate as I answered her letter.

Then I hit her parting line and remembered why I'd neglected to write sooner.

You haven't said anything about Jacob in a long time, she'd written. *What's he up to these days?*

Charlie was prompting her, I was sure.

I sighed and typed quickly, tucking the answer to her question between two less sensitive paragraphs.

```
Jacob is fine, I guess. I don't see him
much; he spends most of his time with a
pack of his friends down at La Push these
days.
```

Smiling wryly to myself, I added Edward's greeting and hit "send."

I didn't realize that Edward was standing silently behind me again until after I'd turned off the computer and shoved away from the desk. I was about to scold him for reading over my shoulder when I realized that he wasn't paying any attention to me. He was examining a flat black box with wires curling crookedly away from the main square in a way that didn't look healthy for whatever it was. After a second, I recognized the car stereo Emmett, Rosalie, and Jasper had given me for my last birthday. I'd forgotten about the birthday presents hiding under a growing pile of dust on the floor of my closet.

"What did you *do* to this?" he asked in a horrorstruck voice.

"It didn't want to come out of the dashboard."

"So you felt the need to torture it?"

"You know how I am with tools. No pain was inflicted intentionally."

He shook his head, his face a mask of faux tragedy. "You killed it."

I shrugged. "Oh, well."

"It would hurt their feelings if they saw this," he said. "I guess it's a good thing that you've been on house arrest. I'll have to get another one in place before they notice."

"Thanks, but I don't need a fancy stereo."

"It's not for your sake that I'm going to replace it."

I sighed.

"You didn't get much good out of your birthday presents last year," he said in a disgruntled voice. Suddenly, he was fanning himself with a stiff rectangle of paper.

I didn't answer, for fear my voice would shake. My disastrous eighteenth birthday — with all its far-reaching consequences — wasn't something I cared to remember, and I was surprised that he would bring it up. He was even more sensitive about it than I was.

"Do you realize these are about to expire?" he asked, holding the paper out to me. It was another present — the voucher for airplane tickets that Esme and Carlisle had given me so that I could visit Renée in Florida.

I took a deep breath and answered in a flat voice. "No. I'd forgotten all about them, actually."

His expression was carefully bright and positive; there was no trace of any deep emotion as he continued. "Well, we still have a little time. You've been liberated . . . and we have no plans this weekend, as you refuse to go to the prom with me." He grinned. "Why not celebrate your freedom this way?"

I gasped. "By going to Florida?"

"You did say something about the continental U.S. being allowable."

I glared at him, suspicious, trying to understand where this had come from.

"Well?" he demanded. "Are we going to see Renée or not?"

"Charlie will never allow it."

"Charlie can't keep you from visiting your mother. She still has primary custody."

"Nobody has custody of me. I'm an adult."

He flashed a brilliant smile. "Exactly."

I thought it over for a short minute before deciding that it wasn't worth the fight. Charlie would be furious — not that I was going to see Renée, but that Edward was going with me. Charlie wouldn't speak to me for months, and I'd probably end up grounded again. It was definitely smarter not to even bring it up. Maybe in a few weeks, as a graduation favor or something.

But the idea of seeing my mother *now*, not weeks from now, was hard to resist. It had been so long since I'd seen Renée. And even longer since I'd seen her under pleasant circumstances. The last time I'd been with her in Phoenix, I'd spent the whole time in a hospital bed. The last time she'd come here, I'd been more or less catatonic. Not exactly the best memories to leave her with.

And maybe, if she saw how happy I was with Edward, she would tell Charlie to ease up.

Edward scrutinized my face while I deliberated.

I sighed. "Not this weekend."

"Why not?"

"I don't want to fight with Charlie. Not so soon after he's forgiven me."

His eyebrows pulled together. "I think this weekend is perfect," he muttered.

I shook my head. "Another time."

"You aren't the only one who's been trapped in this house, you know." He frowned at me.

Suspicion returned. This kind of behavior was unlike him. He was always so impossibly selfless; I knew it was making me spoiled.

"You can go anywhere you want," I pointed out.

"The outside world holds no interest for me without you."

I rolled my eyes at the hyperbole.

"I'm serious," he said.

"Let's take the outside world slowly, all right? For example, we could start with a movie in Port Angeles. . . ."

He groaned. "Never mind. We'll talk about it later."

"There's nothing left to talk about."

He shrugged.

"Okay, then, new subject," I said. I'd almost forgotten

my worries about this afternoon — had that been his intention? "What did Alice see today at lunch?"

My eyes were fixed on his face as I spoke, measuring his reaction.

His expression was composed; there was only the slightest hardening of his topaz eyes. "She's been seeing Jasper in a strange place, somewhere in the southwest, she thinks, near his former . . . family. But he has no conscious intentions to go back." He sighed. "It's got her worried."

"Oh." That was nothing close to what I'd been expecting. But of course it made sense that Alice would be watching out for Jasper's future. He was her soul mate, her true other half, though they weren't as flamboyant about their relationship as Rosalie and Emmett were. "Why didn't you tell me before?"

"I didn't realize you'd noticed," he said. "It's probably nothing important, in any case."

My imagination was sadly out of control. I'd taken a perfectly normal afternoon and twisted it until it looked like Edward was going out of his way to keep things from me. I needed therapy.

We went downstairs to work on our homework, just in case Charlie showed up early. Edward finished in minutes; I slogged laboriously through my calculus until I decided it was time to fix Charlie's dinner. Edward helped, making faces every so often at the raw ingredients — human food was mildly repulsive to him. I made stroganoff from Grandma Swan's recipe, because I was sucking up. It wasn't one of my favorites, but it would please Charlie.

Charlie seemed to already be in a good mood when he got home. He didn't even go out of his way to be rude to Edward. Edward excused himself from eating with us, as usual. The sound of the nightly news drifted from the front room, but I doubted Edward was really watching.

After forcing down three helpings, Charlie kicked his feet up on the spare chair and folded his hands contentedly across his distended stomach.

"That was great, Bells."

"I'm glad you liked it. How was work?" He'd been eating with too much concentration for me to make conversation before.

"Sort of slow. Well, dead slow really. Mark and I played cards for a good part of the afternoon," he admitted with a grin. "I won, nineteen hands to seven. And then I was on the phone with Billy for a while."

I tried to keep my expression the same. "How is he?"

"Good, good. His joints are bothering him a little."

"Oh. That's too bad."

"Yeah. He invited us down to visit this weekend. He was thinking of having the Clearwaters and the Uleys over too. Sort of a playoff party. . . ."

"Huh," was my genius response. But what could I say? I knew I wouldn't be allowed to hit a werewolf party, even with parental supervision. I wondered if Edward would have a problem with Charlie hanging out in La Push. Or would he suppose that, since Charlie was mostly spending time with Billy, who was only human, my father wouldn't be in danger?

I got up and piled the dishes together without looking at Charlie. I dumped them into the sink and started the water. Edward appeared silently and grabbed a dishtowel.

Charlie sighed and gave up for the moment, though I imagined he would revisit the subject when we were alone again. He heaved himself to his feet and headed for the TV, just like every other night.

"Charlie," Edward said in a conversational tone.

Charlie stopped in the middle of his little kitchen. "Yeah?"

"Did Bella ever tell you that my parents gave her airplane tickets on her last birthday, so that she could visit Renée?"

I dropped the plate I was scrubbing. It glanced off the counter and clattered noisily to the floor. It didn't break, but it spattered the room, and all three of us, with soapy water. Charlie didn't even seem to notice.

"Bella?" he asked in a stunned voice.

I kept my eyes on the plate as I retrieved it. "Yeah, they did."

Charlie swallowed loudly, and then his eyes narrowed as he turned back to Edward. "No, she never mentioned it."

"Hmm," Edward murmured.

"Was there a reason you brought it up?" Charlie asked in a hard voice.

Edward shrugged. "They're about to expire. I think it might hurt Esme's feelings if Bella doesn't use her gift. Not that she'd say anything."

I stared at Edward in disbelief.

Charlie thought for a minute. "It's probably a good

idea for you to visit your mom, Bella. She'd love that. I'm surprised you didn't say anything about this, though."

"I forgot," I admitted.

He frowned. "You forgot that someone gave you plane tickets?"

"Mmm," I murmured vaguely, and turned back to the sink.

"I noticed that you said *they're* about to expire, Edward," Charlie went on. "How many tickets did your parents give her?"

"Just one for her . . . and one for me."

The plate I dropped this time landed in the sink, so it didn't make as much noise. I could easily hear the sharp huff as my father exhaled. The blood rushed into my face, fueled by irritation and chagrin. Why was Edward doing this? I glared at the bubbles in the sink, panicking.

"That's out of the question!" Charlie was abruptly in a rage, shouting the words.

"Why?" Edward asked, his voice saturated with innocent surprise. "You just said it was a good idea for her to see her mother."

Charlie ignored him. "You're not going anywhere with him, young lady!" he yelled. I spun around and he was jabbing a finger at me.

Anger pulsed through me automatically, an instinctive reaction to his tone.

"I'm not a child, Dad. And I'm not grounded anymore, remember?"

"Oh yes, you are. Starting now."

"For what?!"

"Because I said so."

"Do I need to remind you that I'm a legal adult, Charlie?"

"This is my house — you follow my rules!"

My glare turned icy. "If that's how you want it. Do you want me to move out tonight? Or can I have a few days to pack?"

Charlie's face went bright red. I instantly felt horrible for playing the move-out card.

I took a deep breath and tried to make my tone more reasonable. "I'll do my time without complaining when I've done something wrong, Dad, but I'm not going to put up with your prejudices."

He sputtered, but managed nothing coherent.

"Now, I know that *you* know that I have every right to see Mom for the weekend. You can't honestly tell me you'd object to the plan if I was going with Alice or Angela."

"Girls," he grunted, with a nod.

"Would it bother you if I took Jacob?"

I'd only picked the name because I knew of my father's preference for Jacob, but I quickly wished I hadn't; Edward's teeth clenched together with an audible snap.

My father struggled to compose himself before he answered. "Yes," he said in an unconvincing voice. "That would bother me."

"You're a rotten liar, Dad."

"Bella —"

"It's not like I'm headed off to Vegas to be a showgirl or anything. I'm going to see *Mom*," I reminded him. "She's just as much my parental authority as you are."

He threw me a withering look.

"Are you implying something about Mom's ability to look after me?"

Charlie flinched at the threat implicit in my question.

"You'd better hope I don't mention this to her," I said.

"You'd better not," he warned. "I'm not happy about this, Bella."

"There's no reason for you to be upset."

He rolled his eyes, but I could tell the storm was over.

I turned to pull the plug out of the sink. "So my homework is done, your dinner is done, the dishes are done, and I'm not grounded. I'm going out. I'll be back before ten-thirty."

"Where are you going?" His face, almost back to normal, flushed light red again.

"I'm not sure," I admitted. "I'll keep it within a ten-mile radius, though. Okay?"

He grunted something that did not sound like approval, and stalked out of the room. Naturally, as soon as I'd won the fight, I began to feel guilty.

"We're going out?" Edward asked, his voice low but enthusiastic.

I turned to glower at him. "Yes. I think I'd like to speak to you *alone*."

He didn't look as apprehensive as I thought he should.

I waited to begin until we were safely in his car.

"What was *that*?" I demanded.

"I know you want to see your mother, Bella — you've been talking about her in your sleep. Worrying actually."

"I have?"

He nodded. "But, clearly, you were too much of a coward to deal with Charlie, so I interceded on your behalf."

"Interceded? You threw me to the sharks!"

He rolled his eyes. "I don't think you were in any danger."

"I told you I didn't want to fight with Charlie."

"Nobody said that you had to."

I glowered at him. "I can't help myself when he gets all bossy like that — my natural teenage instincts overpower me."

He chuckled. "Well, that's not my fault."

I stared at him, speculating. He didn't seem to notice. His face was serene as he gazed out the windshield. Something was off, but I couldn't put my finger on it. Or maybe it was just my imagination again, running wild like it had this afternoon.

"Does this sudden urge to see Florida have anything to do with the party at Billy's place?"

His jaw flexed. "Nothing at all. It wouldn't matter if you were here or on the other side of the world, you still wouldn't be going."

It was just like with Charlie before — just like being treated as a misbehaving child. I gritted my teeth together so I wouldn't start shouting. I didn't want to fight with Edward, too.

Edward sighed, and when he spoke his voice was warm and velvet again. "So what do you want to do tonight?" he asked.

"Can we go to your house? I haven't seen Esme in so long."

He smiled. "She'll like that. Especially when she hears what we're doing this weekend."

I groaned in defeat.

We didn't stay out late, as I'd promised. I was not surprised to see the lights still on when we pulled up in front of the house — I knew Charlie would be waiting to yell at me some more.

"You'd better not come inside," I said. "It will only make things worse."

"His thoughts are relatively calm," Edward teased. His expression made me wonder if there was some additional joke I was missing. The corners of his mouth twitched, fighting a smile.

"I'll see you later," I muttered glumly.

He laughed and kissed the top of my head. "I'll be back when Charlie's snoring."

The TV was loud when I got inside. I briefly considered trying to sneak past him.

"Could you come in here, Bella?" Charlie called, sinking that plan.

My feet dragged as I took the five necessary steps.

"What's up, Dad?"

"Did you have a nice time tonight?" he asked. He seemed ill at ease. I looked for hidden meanings in his words before I answered.

"Yes," I said hesitantly.

"What did you do?"

I shrugged. "Hung out with Alice and Jasper. Edward beat Alice at chess, and then I played Jasper. He buried me."

I smiled. Edward and Alice playing chess was one of the funniest things I'd ever seen. They'd sat there nearly motionless, staring at the board, while Alice foresaw the moves he would make and he picked the moves she would make in return out of her head. They played most of the game in their minds; I think they'd each moved two pawns when Alice suddenly flicked her king over and surrendered. It took all of three minutes.

Charlie hit the mute button — an unusual action.

"Look, there's something I need to say." He frowned, looking very uncomfortable.

I sat still, waiting. He met my gaze for a second before shifting his eyes to the floor. He didn't say anything more.

"What is it, Dad?"

He sighed. "I'm not good at this kind of thing. I don't know how to start. . . ."

I waited again.

"Okay, Bella. Here's the thing." He got up from the couch and started pacing back and forth across the room, looking at his feet all the time. "You and Edward seem pretty serious, and there are some things that you need to be careful about. I know you're an adult now, but you're still young, Bella, and there are a lot of important things you need to know when you . . . well, when you're physically involved with —"

"Oh, please, *please* no!" I begged, jumping to my feet. "Please tell me you are not trying to have a sex talk with me, Charlie."

He glared at the floor. "I am your father. I have responsibilities. Remember, I'm just as embarrassed as you are."

"I don't think that's humanly possible. Anyway, Mom beat you to the punch about ten years ago. You're off the hook."

"Ten years ago you didn't have a boyfriend," he muttered unwillingly. I could tell he was battling with his desire to drop the subject. We were both standing up, looking at the floor, and facing away from each other.

"I don't think the essentials have changed that much," I mumbled, and my face had to be as red as his. This was beyond the seventh circle of Hades; even worse was realizing that Edward had known this was coming. No wonder he'd seemed so smug in the car.

"Just tell me that you two are being responsible," Charlie pled, obviously wishing a pit would open in the floor so that he could fall in.

"Don't worry about it, Dad, it's not like that."

"Not that I don't trust you, Bella, but I know you don't want to tell me anything about this, and you know I don't really want to hear it. I will try to be open-minded, though. I know the times have changed."

I laughed awkwardly. "Maybe the times have, but Edward is very old-fashioned. You have nothing to worry about."

Charlie sighed. "Sure he is," he muttered.

"Ugh!" I groaned. "I really wish you were not forcing me to say this out loud, Dad. *Really.* But . . . I am a . . . virgin, and I have no immediate plans to change that status."

We both cringed, but then Charlie's face smoothed out. He seemed to believe me.

"Can I go to bed, now? *Please.*"

"In a minute," he said.

"Aw, please, Dad? I'm begging you."

"The embarrassing part's over, I promise," he assured me.

I shot a glance at him, and was grateful to see that he looked more relaxed, that his face was back to its regular color. He sank down onto the sofa, sighing with relief that he was past the sex speech.

"What now?"

"I just wanted to know how the balance thing is coming along."

"Oh. Good, I guess. I made plans with Angela today. I'm going to help her with her graduation announcements. Just us girls."

"That's nice. And what about Jake?"

I sighed. "I haven't figured that one out yet, Dad."

"Keep trying, Bella. I know you'll do the right thing. You're a good person."

Nice. So if I didn't figure out some way to make things right with Jacob, then I was a *bad* person? That was below the belt.

"Sure, sure," I agreed. The automatic response almost made me smile — it was something I'd picked up from Jacob. I even said it in the same patronizing tone he used with his own father.

Charlie grinned and turned the sound back on. He slumped lower into the cushions, pleased with his night's work. I could tell he would be up with the game for a while.

"'Night, Bells."

"See you in the morning!" I sprinted for the stairs.

Edward was long gone and he wouldn't be back until Charlie was asleep — he was probably out hunting or something to pass the time — so I was in no hurry to undress for bed. I wasn't in the mood to be alone, but I certainly wasn't going to go back downstairs to hang out with my Dad, just in case he thought of some topic of sex education that he hadn't touched on before; I shuddered.

So, thanks to Charlie, I was wound up and anxious. My homework was done and I didn't feel mellow enough for reading or just listening to music. I considered calling Renée with the news of my visit, but then I realized that it was three hours later in Florida, and she would be asleep.

I could call Angela, I supposed.

But suddenly I knew that it wasn't Angela that I wanted to talk to. That I needed to talk to.

I stared at the blank black window, biting my lip. I don't know how long I stood there weighing the pros against the cons — doing the right thing by Jacob, seeing my closest friend again, being a good person, versus making Edward furious with me. Ten minutes maybe. Long enough to decide that the pros were valid while the cons were not. Edward was only concerned about my safety, and I knew that there was really no problem on that count.

The phone wasn't any help; Jacob had refused to answer my phone calls since Edward's return. Besides, I needed to *see* him — see him smiling again the way he used to. I needed to replace that awful last memory of his face warped and twisted by pain if I was ever going to have any peace of mind.

I had an hour probably. I could make a quick run down

to La Push and be back before Edward realized I had gone. It was past my curfew, but would Charlie really care about that when Edward wasn't involved? One way to find out.

I grabbed my jacket and shoved my arms through the sleeves as I ran down the stairs.

Charlie looked up from the game, instantly suspicious.

"You care if I go see Jake tonight?" I asked breathlessly. "I won't stay long."

As soon as I said Jake's name, Charlie's expression relaxed into a smug smile. He didn't seem surprised at all that his lecture had taken effect so quickly. "Sure, kid. No problem. Stay as long as you like."

"Thanks, Dad," I said as I darted out the door.

Like any fugitive, I couldn't help looking over my shoulder a few times while I jogged to my truck, but the night was so black that there really was no point. I had to feel my way along the side of the truck to the handle.

My eyes were just beginning to adjust as I shoved my keys in the ignition. I twisted them hard to the left, but instead of roaring deafeningly to life, the engine just clicked. I tried it again with the same results.

And then a small motion in my peripheral vision made me jump.

"Gah!" I gasped in shock when I saw that I was not alone in the cab.

Edward sat very still, a faint bright spot in the darkness, only his hands moving as he turned a mysterious black object around and around. He stared at the object as he spoke.

"Alice called," he murmured.

Alice! Damn. I'd forgotten to account for her in my plans. He must have her watching me.

"She got nervous when your future rather abruptly disappeared five minutes ago."

My eyes, already wide with surprise, popped wider.

"Because she can't see the wolves, you know," he explained in the same low murmur. "Had you forgotten that? When you decide to mingle your fate with theirs, you disappear, too. You couldn't know that part, I realize that. But can you understand why that might make me a little . . . anxious? Alice saw you disappear, and she couldn't even tell if you'd come home or not. Your future got lost, just like theirs.

"We're not sure why this is. Some natural defense they're born with?" He spoke as if he were talking to himself now, still looking at the piece of my truck's engine as he twirled it in his hands. "That doesn't seem entirely likely, since I haven't had any trouble reading their thoughts. The Blacks' at least. Carlisle theorizes that it's because their lives are so ruled by their transformations. It's more an involuntary reaction than a decision. Utterly unpredictable, and it changes everything about them. In that instant when they shift from one form to the other, they don't really even exist. The future can't hold them. . . ."

I listened to his musing in stony silence.

"I'll put your car back together in time for school, in case you'd like to drive yourself," he assured me after a minute.

With my lips mashed together, I retrieved my keys and stiffly climbed out of the truck.

"Shut your window if you want me to stay away tonight. I'll understand," he whispered just before I slammed the door.

I stomped into the house, slamming that door, too.

"What's wrong?" Charlie demanded from the couch.

"Truck won't start," I growled.

"Want me to look at it?"

"No. I'll try it in the morning."

"Want to use my car?"

I wasn't supposed to drive his police cruiser. Charlie must be really desperate to get me to La Push. Nearly as desperate as I was.

"No. I'm tired," I grumbled. "'Night."

I stamped my way up the stairs, and went straight to my window. I shoved the metal frame roughly — it crashed shut and the glass trembled.

I stared at the shivering black glass for a long moment, until it was still. Then I sighed, and opened the window as wide as it would go.

3. MOTIVES

THE SUN WAS SO DEEPLY BURIED BEHIND THE CLOUDS that there was no way to tell if it had set or not. After the long flight — chasing the sun westward so that it seemed unmoving in the sky — it was especially disorienting; time seemed oddly variable. It took me by surprise when the forest gave way to the first buildings, signaling that we were nearly home.

"You've been very quiet," Edward observed. "Did the plane make you sick?"

"No, I'm okay."

"Are you sad to leave?"

"More relieved than sad, I think."

He raised one eyebrow at me. I knew it was useless

and — much as I hated to admit it — unnecessary to ask him to keep his eyes on the road.

"Renée is so much more . . . *perceptive* than Charlie in some ways. It was making me jumpy."

Edward laughed. "Your mother has a very interesting mind. Almost childlike, but very insightful. She sees things differently than other people."

Insightful. It was a good description of my mother — when she was paying attention. Most of the time Renée was so bewildered by her own life that she didn't notice much else. But this weekend she'd been paying plenty of attention to me.

Phil was busy — the high school baseball team he coached was in the playoffs — and being alone with Edward and me had only sharpened Renée's focus. As soon as the hugs and squeals of delight were out of the way, Renée began to watch. And as she'd watched, her wide blue eyes had become first confused and then concerned.

This morning we'd gone for a walk along the beach. She wanted to show off all the beauties of her new home, still hoping, I think, that the sun might lure me away from Forks. She'd also wanted to talk with me alone, and that was easily arranged. Edward had fabricated a term paper to give himself an excuse to stay indoors during the day.

In my head, I went through the conversation again. . . .

Renée and I ambled along the sidewalk, trying to stay in the range of the infrequent palm tree shadows. Though it was early, the heat was smothering. The air was so heavy with moisture that just breathing in and out was giving my lungs a workout.

"Bella?" my mother asked, looking out past the sand to the lightly crashing waves as she spoke.

"What is it, Mom?"

She sighed, not meeting my gaze. "I'm worried. . . ."

"What's wrong?" I asked, anxious at once. "What can I do?"

"It's not me." She shook her head. "I'm worried about you . . . and Edward."

Renée finally looked at me when she said his name, her face apologetic.

"Oh," I mumbled, fixing my eyes on a pair of joggers as they passed us, drenched with sweat.

"You two are more serious than I'd been thinking," she went on.

I frowned, quickly reviewing the last two days in my head. Edward and I had barely touched — in front of her, at least. I wondered if Renée was about to give me a lecture on responsibility, too. I didn't mind that the way I had with Charlie. It wasn't embarrassing with my mom. After all, I'd been the one giving her that lecture time and time again in the last ten years.

"There's something . . . strange about the way you two are together," she murmured, her forehead creasing over her troubled eyes. "The way he watches you — it's so . . . protective. Like he's about to throw himself in front of a bullet to save you or something."

I laughed, though I was still not able to meet her gaze. "That's a bad thing?"

"No." She frowned as she struggled for the words. "It's just *different*. He's very intense about you . . . and very careful. I feel like I don't really understand your relationship. Like there's some secret I'm missing. . . ."

"I think you're imagining things, Mom," I said quickly, struggling to keep my voice light. There was a flutter in my stomach. I'd forgotten how much my mother *saw*. Something about her simple view of the world cut through all the distractions and pierced right to the truth of things. This had never been a problem before. Until now, there had never been a secret I couldn't tell her.

"It's not just him." She set her lips defensively. "I wish you could see how you move around him."

"What do you mean?"

"The way you move — you orient yourself around him without even thinking about it. When he moves, even a little bit, you adjust your position at the same time. Like magnets . . . or gravity. You're like a . . . satellite, or something. I've never seen anything like it."

She pursed her lips and stared down.

"Don't tell me," I teased, forcing a smile. "You're reading mysteries again, aren't you? Or is it sci-fi this time?"

Renée flushed a delicate pink. "That's beside the point."

"Found anything good?"

"Well, there was one — but that doesn't matter. We're talking about you right now."

"You should stick to romance, Mom. You know how you freak yourself out."

Her lips turned up at the corners. "I'm being silly, aren't I?"

For half a second I couldn't answer. Renée was so easily

swayed. Sometimes it was a good thing, because not all of her ideas were practical. But it pained me to see how quickly she caved in to my trivializing, especially since she was dead right this time.

She looked up, and I controlled my expression.

"Not silly — just being a mom."

She laughed and then gestured grandly toward the white sands stretching to the blue water.

"And all this isn't enough to get you to move back in with your silly mom?"

I wiped my hand dramatically across my forehead, and then pretended to wring my hair out.

"You get used to the humidity," she promised.

"You can get used to rain, too," I countered.

She elbowed me playfully and then took my hand as we walked back to her car.

Other than her worries about me, she seemed happy enough. Content. She still looked at Phil with goo-goo eyes, and that was comforting. Surely her life was full and satisfying. Surely she didn't miss me that much, even now. . . .

Edward's icy fingers brushed my cheek. I looked up, blinking, coming back to the present. He leaned down and kissed my forehead.

"We're home, Sleeping Beauty. Time to awake."

We were stopped in front of Charlie's house. The porch light was on and the cruiser was parked in the driveway. As I examined the house, I saw the curtain twitch in the living room window, flashing a line of yellow light across the dark lawn.

I sighed. Of course Charlie was waiting to pounce.

Edward must have been thinking the same thing, because his expression was stiff and his eyes remote as he came to get my door for me.

"How bad?" I asked.

"Charlie's not going to be difficult," Edward promised, his voice level with no hint of humor. "He missed you."

My eyes narrowed in doubt. If that was the case, then why was Edward tensed as if for a battle?

My bag was small, but he insisted on carrying it into the house. Charlie held the door open for us.

"Welcome home, kid!" Charlie shouted like he really meant it. "How was Jacksonville?"

"Moist. And buggy."

"So Renée didn't sell you on the University of Florida?"

"She tried. But I'd rather drink water than inhale it."

Charlie's eyes flickered unwillingly to Edward. "Did you have a nice time?"

"Yes," Edward answered in a serene voice. "Renée was very hospitable."

"That's . . . um, good. Glad you had fun." Charlie turned away from Edward and pulled me in for an unexpected hug.

"Impressive," I whispered in his ear.

He rumbled a laugh. "I really missed you, Bells. The food around here sucks when you're gone."

"I'll get on it," I said as he let me go.

"Would you call Jacob first? He's been bugging me every five minutes since six o'clock this morning. I promised I'd have you call him before you even unpacked."

I didn't have to look at Edward to feel that he was too still, too cold beside me. So this was the cause of his tension.

"Jacob wants to talk to me?"

"Pretty bad, I'd say. He wouldn't tell me what it was about — just said it was important."

The phone rang then, shrill and demanding.

"That's him again, I'd bet my next paycheck," Charlie muttered.

"I got it." I hurried to the kitchen.

Edward followed after me while Charlie disappeared into the living room.

I grabbed the phone mid-ring, and twisted around so that I was facing the wall. "Hello?"

"You're back," Jacob said.

His familiar husky voice sent a wave of wistfulness through me. A thousand memories spun in my head, tangling together — a rocky beach strewn with driftwood trees, a garage made of plastic sheds, warm sodas in a paper bag, a tiny room with one too-small shabby loveseat. The laughter in his deep-set black eyes, the feverish heat of his big hand around mine, the flash of his white teeth against his dark skin, his face stretching into the wide smile that had always been like a key to a secret door where only kindred spirits could enter.

It felt sort of like homesickness, this longing for the place and person who had sheltered me through my darkest night.

I cleared the lump from my throat. "Yes," I answered.

"Why didn't you call me?" Jacob demanded.

His angry tone instantly got my back up. "Because I've been in the house for exactly four seconds and your call interrupted Charlie telling me that you'd called."

"Oh. Sorry."

"Sure. Now, why are you harassing Charlie?"

"I need to talk to you."

"Yeah, I figured out that part all by myself. Go ahead."

There was a short pause.

"You going to school tomorrow?"

I frowned to myself, unable to make sense of this question. "Of course I am. Why wouldn't I?"

"I dunno. Just curious."

Another pause.

"So what did you want to talk about, Jake?"

He hesitated. "Nothing really, I guess. I . . . wanted to hear your voice."

"Yeah, I know. I'm *so* glad you called me, Jake. I . . ." But I didn't know what more to say. I wanted to tell him I was on my way to La Push right now. And I couldn't tell him that.

"I have to go," he said abruptly.

"What?"

"I'll talk to you soon, okay?"

"But Jake —"

He was already gone. I listened to the dial tone with disbelief.

"That was short," I muttered.

"Is everything all right?" Edward asked. His voice was low and careful.

I turned slowly to face him. His expression was perfectly smooth — impossible to read.

"I don't know. I wonder what that was about." It didn't make sense that Jacob had been hounding Charlie all day just to ask me if I was going to school. And if he'd wanted to hear my voice, then why did he hang up so quickly?

"Your guess is probably better than mine," Edward said, the hint of a smile tugging at the corner of his mouth.

"Mmm," I murmured. That was true. I knew Jake inside and out. It shouldn't be that complicated to figure out his motivations.

With my thoughts miles away — about fifteen miles away, up the road to La Push — I started combing through the fridge, assembling ingredients for Charlie's dinner. Edward leaned against the counter, and I was distantly aware that his eyes were on my face, but too preoccupied to worry about what he saw there.

The school thing seemed like the key to me. That was the only real question Jake had asked. And he had to be after an answer to something, or he wouldn't have been bugging Charlie so persistently.

Why would my attendance record matter to him, though?

I tried to think about it in a logical way. So, if I *hadn't* been going to school tomorrow, what would be the problem with that, from Jacob's perspective? Charlie had given me a little grief about missing a day of school so close to finals, but I'd convinced him that one Friday wasn't going to derail my studies. Jake would hardly care about that.

My brain refused to come up with any brilliant insights. Maybe I was missing some vital piece of information.

What could have changed in the past three days that was so important that Jacob would break his long streak of refusing to answer my phone calls and contact me? What difference could three days make?

I froze in the middle of the kitchen. The package of icy hamburger in my hands slipped through my numb fingers. It took me a slow second to miss the thud it should have made against the floor.

Edward had caught it and thrown it onto the counter. His arms were already around me, his lips at my ear.

"What's wrong?"

I shook my head, dazed.

Three days could change everything.

Hadn't I just been thinking about how impossible college was? How I couldn't be anywhere near people after I'd gone through the painful three-day conversion that would set me free from mortality, so that I could spend eternity with Edward? The conversion that would make me forever a prisoner to my own thirst. . . .

Had Charlie told Billy that I'd vanished for three days? Had Billy jumped to conclusions? Had Jacob really been asking me if I was still human? Making sure that the werewolves' treaty was unbroken — that none of the Cullens had dared to bite a human . . . bite, not kill . . . ?

But did he honestly think I would come home to Charlie if that was the case?

Edward shook me. "Bella?" he asked, truly anxious now.

"I think . . . I think he was checking," I mumbled. "Checking to make sure. That I'm human, I mean."

Edward stiffened, and a low hiss sounded in my ear.

"We'll have to leave," I whispered. "Before. So that it doesn't break the treaty. We won't ever be able to come back."

His arms tightened around me. "I know."

"Ahem." Charlie cleared his voice loudly behind us.

I jumped, and then pulled free of Edward's arms, my face getting hot. Edward leaned back against the counter. His eyes were tight. I could see worry in them, and anger.

"If you don't want to make dinner, I can call for a pizza," Charlie hinted.

"No, that's okay, I'm already started."

"Okay," Charlie said. He propped himself against the doorframe, folding his arms.

I sighed and got to work, trying to ignore my audience.

"If I asked you to do something, would you trust me?" Edward asked, an edge to his soft voice.

We were almost to school. Edward had been relaxed and joking just a moment ago, and now suddenly his hands were clenched tight on the steering wheel, his knuckles straining in an effort not to snap it into pieces.

I stared at his anxious expression — his eyes were far away, like he was listening to distant voices.

My pulse sped in response to his stress, but I answered carefully. "That depends."

We pulled into the school lot.

"I was afraid you would say that."

"What do you want me to do, Edward?"

"I want you to stay in the car." He pulled into his usual spot and turned the engine off as he spoke. "I want you to wait here until I come back for you."

"But . . . *why?*"

That was when I saw him. He would have been hard to miss, towering over the students the way he did, even if he hadn't been leaning against his black motorcycle, parked illegally on the sidewalk.

"Oh."

Jacob's face was a calm mask that I recognized well. It was the face he used when he was determined to keep his emotions in check, to keep himself under control. It made him look like Sam, the oldest of the wolves, the leader of the Quileute pack. But Jacob could never quite manage the perfect serenity Sam always exuded.

I'd forgotten how much this face bothered me. Though I'd gotten to know Sam pretty well before the Cullens had come back — to like him, even — I'd never been able to completely shake the resentment I felt when Jacob mimicked Sam's expression. It was a stranger's face. He wasn't my Jacob when he wore it.

"You jumped to the wrong conclusion last night," Edward murmured. "He asked about school because he knew that I would be where you were. He was looking for a safe place to talk to me. A place with witnesses."

So I'd misinterpreted Jacob's motives last night. Missing information, that was the problem. Information like why in the world Jacob would want to talk to Edward.

"I'm not staying in the car," I said.

Edward groaned quietly. "Of course not. Well, let's get this over with."

Jacob's face hardened as we walked toward him, hand in hand.

I noticed other faces, too — the faces of my classmates. I noticed how their eyes widened as they took in all six foot seven inches of Jacob's long body, muscled up the way no normal sixteen-and-a-half-year-old ever had been. I saw those eyes rake over his tight black t-shirt — short-sleeved, though the day was unseasonably cool — his ragged, grease-smeared jeans, and the glossy black bike he leaned against. Their eyes didn't linger on his face — something about his expression had them glancing quickly away. And I noticed the wide berth everyone gave him, the bubble of space that no one dared to encroach on.

With a sense of astonishment, I realized that Jacob looked *dangerous* to them. How odd.

Edward stopped a few yards away from Jacob, and I could tell that he was uncomfortable having me so close to a werewolf. He drew his hand back slightly, pulling me halfway behind his body.

"You could have called us," Edward said in a steel-hard voice.

"Sorry," Jacob answered, his face twisting into a sneer. "I don't have any leeches on my speed dial."

"You could have reached me at Bella's house, of course."

Jacob's jaw flexed, and his brows pulled together. He didn't answer.

"This is hardly the place, Jacob. Could we discuss this later?"

"Sure, sure. I'll stop by your crypt after school." Jacob snorted. "What's wrong with now?"

Edward looked around pointedly, his eyes resting on the witnesses who were just barely out of hearing range. A few people were hesitating on the sidewalk, their eyes bright with expectation. Like they were hoping a fight might break out to alleviate the tedium of another Monday morning. I saw Tyler Crowley nudge Austin Marks, and they both paused on their way to class.

"I already know what you came to say," Edward reminded Jacob in a voice so low that I could barely make it out. "Message delivered. Consider us warned."

Edward glanced down at me for a fleeting second with worried eyes.

"Warned?" I asked blankly. "What are you talking about?"

"You didn't tell her?" Jacob asked, his eyes widening with disbelief. "What, were you afraid she'd take our side?"

"Please drop it, Jacob," Edward said in an even voice.

"Why?" Jacob challenged.

I frowned in confusion. "What don't I know? Edward?"

Edward just glared at Jacob as if he hadn't heard me.

"Jake?"

Jacob raised his eyebrow at me. "He didn't tell you that his big . . . *brother* crossed the line Saturday night?" he asked, his tone thickly layered with sarcasm. Then his eyes flickered back to Edward. "Paul was totally justified in —"

"It was no-man's land!" Edward hissed.

"Was not!"

Jacob was fuming visibly. His hands trembled. He shook his head and sucked in two deep lungfuls of air.

"Emmett and Paul?" I whispered. Paul was Jacob's most volatile pack brother. He was the one who'd lost control that day in the woods — the memory of the snarling gray wolf was suddenly vivid in my head. "What happened? Were they fighting?" My voice strained higher in panic. "Why? Did Paul get hurt?"

"No one fought," Edward said quietly, only to me. "No one got hurt. Don't be anxious."

Jacob was staring at us with incredulous eyes. "You didn't tell her anything at all, did you? Is that why you took her away? So she wouldn't know that —?"

"Leave now." Edward cut him off mid-sentence, and his face was abruptly frightening — truly frightening. For a second, he looked like . . . like a *vampire*. He glared at Jacob with vicious, unveiled loathing.

Jacob raised his eyebrows, but made no other move. "Why haven't you told her?"

They faced each other in silence for a long moment. More students gathered behind Tyler and Austin. I saw Mike next to Ben — Mike had one hand on Ben's shoulder, like he was holding him in place.

In the dead silence, all the details suddenly fell into place for me with a burst of intuition.

Something Edward didn't want me to know.

Something that Jacob wouldn't have kept from me.

Something that had the Cullens and the wolves both in the woods, moving in hazardous proximity to each other.

Something that would cause Edward to insist that I fly across the country.

Something that Alice had seen in a vision last week — a vision Edward had lied to me about.

Something I'd been waiting for anyway. Something I knew would happen again, as much as I might wish it never would. It was never going to end, was it?

I heard the quick *gasp, gasp, gasp, gasp* of the air dragging through my lips, but I couldn't stop it. It looked like the school was shaking, like there was an earthquake, but I knew it was my own trembling that caused the illusion.

"She came back for me," I choked out.

Victoria was never going to give up till I was dead. She would keep repeating the same pattern — feint and run, feint and run — until she found a hole through my defenders.

Maybe I'd get lucky. Maybe the Volturi would come for me first — they'd kill me quicker, at least.

Edward held me tight to his side, angling his body so that he was still between me and Jacob, and stroked my face with anxious hands. "It's fine," he whispered to me. "It's fine. I'll never let her get close to you, it's fine."

Then he glared at Jacob. "Does that answer your question, mongrel?"

"You don't think Bella has a right to know?" Jacob challenged. "It's her life."

Edward kept his voice muted; even Tyler, edging forward by inches, would be unable to hear. "Why should she be frightened when she was never in danger?"

"Better frightened than lied to."

I tried to pull myself together, but my eyes were swimming in moisture. I could see it behind my lids — I could see Victoria's face, her lips pulled back over her teeth, her crimson eyes glowing with the obsession of her vendetta; she held Edward responsible for the demise of her love, James. She wouldn't stop until his love was taken from him, too.

Edward wiped the tears from my cheek with his fingertips.

"Do you really think hurting her is better than protecting her?" he murmured.

"She's tougher than you think," Jacob said. "And she's been through worse."

Abruptly, Jacob's expression shifted, and he was staring at Edward with an odd, speculative expression. His eyes narrowed like he was trying to do a difficult math problem in his head.

I felt Edward cringe. I glanced up at him, and his face was contorted in what could only be pain. For one ghastly moment, I was reminded of our afternoon in Italy, in the macabre tower room of the Volturi, where Jane had tortured Edward with her malignant gift, burning him with her thoughts alone. . . .

The memory snapped me out of my near hysteria and put everything in perspective. Because I'd rather Victoria killed me a hundred times over than watch Edward suffer that way again.

"That's funny," Jacob said, laughing as he watched Edward's face.

Edward winced, but smoothed his expression with a little effort. He couldn't quite hide the agony in his eyes.

I glanced, wide-eyed, from Edward's grimace to Jacob's sneer.

"What are you doing to him?" I demanded.

"It's nothing, Bella," Edward told me quietly. "Jacob just has a good memory, that's all."

Jacob grinned, and Edward winced again.

"Stop it! Whatever you're doing."

"Sure, if you want." Jacob shrugged. "It's his own fault if he doesn't like the things I remember, though."

I glared at him, and he smiled back impishly — like a kid caught doing something he knows he shouldn't by someone who he knows won't punish him.

"The principal's on his way to discourage loitering on school property," Edward murmured to me. "Let's get to English, Bella, so you're not involved."

"Overprotective, isn't he?" Jacob said, talking just to me. "A little trouble makes life fun. Let me guess, you're not allowed to have fun, are you?"

Edward glowered, and his lips pulled back from his teeth ever so slightly.

"Shut up, Jake," I said.

Jacob laughed. "That sounds like a *no*. Hey, if you ever feel like having a life again, you could come see me. I've still got your motorcycle in my garage."

This news distracted me. "You were supposed to sell that. You promised Charlie you would." If I hadn't begged on Jake's behalf — after all, he'd put weeks of labor into both motorcycles, and he deserved some kind of payback —

Charlie would have thrown my bike in a Dumpster. And possibly set that Dumpster on fire.

"Yeah, right. Like I would do that. It belongs to you, not me. Anyway, I'll hold on to it until you want it back."

A tiny hint of the smile I remembered was suddenly playing around the edges of his lips.

"Jake . . ."

He leaned forward, his face earnest now, the bitter sarcasm fading. "I think I might have been wrong before, you know, about not being able to be friends. Maybe we could manage it, on my side of the line. Come see me."

I was vividly conscious of Edward, his arms still wrapped protectively around me, motionless as a stone. I shot a look at his face — it was calm, patient.

"I, er, don't know about that, Jake."

Jacob dropped the antagonistic façade completely. It was like he'd forgotten Edward was there, or at least he was determined to act that way. "I miss you every day, Bella. It's not the same without you."

"I know and I'm sorry, Jake, I just . . ."

He shook his head, and sighed. "I know. Doesn't matter, right? I guess I'll survive or something. Who needs friends?" He grimaced, trying to cover the pain with a thin attempt at bravado.

Jacob's suffering had always triggered my protective side. It was not entirely rational — Jacob was hardly in need of any physical protection I could offer. But my arms, pinned beneath Edward's, yearned to reach out to him. To wrap around his big, warm waist in a silent promise of acceptance and comfort.

Edward's shielding arms had become restraints.

"Okay, get to class," a stern voice sounded behind us. "Move along, Mr. Crowley."

"Get to school, Jake," I whispered, anxious as soon as I recognized the principal's voice. Jacob went to the Quileute school, but he might still get in trouble for trespassing or the equivalent.

Edward released me, taking just my hand and pulling me behind his body again.

Mr. Greene pushed through the circle of spectators, his brows pressing down like ominous storm clouds over his small eyes.

"I mean it," he was threatening. "Detention for anyone who's still standing here when I turn around again."

The audience melted away before he was finished with his sentence.

"Ah, Mr. Cullen. Do we have a problem here?"

"Not at all, Mr. Greene. We were just on our way to class."

"Excellent. I don't seem to recognize your friend." Mr. Greene turned his glower on Jacob. "Are you a new student here?"

Mr. Greene's eyes scrutinized Jacob, and I could see that he'd come to the same conclusion everyone else had: dangerous. A troublemaker.

"Nope," Jacob answered, half a smirk on his broad lips.

"Then I suggest you remove yourself from school property at once, young man, before I call the police."

Jacob's little smirk became a full-blown grin, and I

knew he was picturing Charlie showing up to arrest him. This grin was too bitter, too full of mocking to satisfy me. This wasn't the smile I'd been waiting to see.

Jacob said, "Yes, sir," and snapped a military salute before he climbed on his bike and kicked it to a start right there on the sidewalk. The engine snarled and then the tires squealed as he spun it sharply around. In a matter of seconds, Jacob raced out of sight.

Mr. Greene gnashed his teeth together while he watched the performance.

"Mr. Cullen, I expect you to ask your friend to refrain from trespassing again."

"He's no friend of mine, Mr. Greene, but I'll pass along the warning."

Mr. Greene pursed his lips. Edward's perfect grades and spotless record were clearly a factor in Mr. Greene's assessment of the incident. "I see. If you're worried about any trouble, I'd be happy to —"

"There's nothing to worry about, Mr. Greene. There won't be any trouble."

"I hope that's correct. Well, then. On to class. You, too, Miss Swan."

Edward nodded, and pulled me quickly along toward the English building.

"Do you feel well enough to go to class?" he whispered when we were past the principal.

"Yes," I whispered back, not quite sure if this was a lie.

Whether I felt well or not was hardly the most important consideration. I needed to talk to Edward right away, and English class wasn't the ideal place for the conversation I had in mind.

But with Mr. Greene right behind us, there weren't a lot of other options.

We got to class a little late and took our seats quickly. Mr. Berty was reciting a Frost poem. He ignored our entrance, refusing to let us break his rhythm.

I yanked a blank page out of my notebook and started writing, my handwriting more illegible than normal thanks to my agitation.

What happened? Tell me everything. And screw the protecting me crap, please.

I shoved the note at Edward. He sighed, and then began writing. It took him less time than me, though he wrote an entire paragraph in his own personal calligraphy before he slipped the paper back.

Alice saw that Victoria was coming back. I took you out of town merely as a precaution — there was never a chance that she would have gotten anywhere close to you. Emmett and Jasper very nearly had her, but Victoria seems to have some instinct for evasion. She escaped right down the Quileute boundary line as if she were reading it from a map. It didn't help that Alice's abilities were nullified by the Quileutes' involvement. To be fair, the Quileutes might have had her, too, if we hadn't gotten in the way. The big gray one thought

Emmett was over the line, and he got defensive. Of course Rosalie reacted to that, and everyone left the chase to protect their companions. Carlisle and Jasper got things calmed down before it got out of hand. But by then, Victoria had slipped away. That's everything.

I frowned at the letters on the page. All of them had been in on it — Emmett, Jasper, Alice, Rosalie, and Carlisle. Maybe even Esme, though he hadn't mentioned her. And then Paul and the rest of the Quileute pack. It might so easily have turned into a fight, pitting my future family and my old friends against each other. Any one of them could have been hurt. I imagined the wolves would be in the most danger, but picturing tiny Alice next to one of the huge werewolves, *fighting* . . .

I shuddered.

Carefully, I scrubbed out the entire paragraph with my eraser and then I wrote over the top:

What about Charlie? She could have been after him.

Edward was shaking his head before I finished, obviously going to downplay any danger on Charlie's behalf. He held a hand out, but I ignored that and started again.

You can't know that she wasn't thinking that, because you weren't here. Florida was a bad idea.

He took the paper from underneath my hand.

I wasn't about to send you off alone. With your luck, not even the black box would survive.

That wasn't what I'd meant at all; I hadn't thought of going without him. I'd meant that we should have stayed here together. But I was sidetracked by his response, and a little miffed. Like I couldn't fly cross country without bringing the plane down. Very funny.

So let's say my bad luck did crash the plane. What exactly were you going to do about it?

Why is the plane crashing?

He was trying to hide a smile now.

The pilots are passed out drunk.

Easy. I'd fly the plane.

Of course. I pursed my lips and tried again.

Both engines have exploded and we're falling in a death spiral toward the earth.

I'd wait till we were close enough to the ground, get a good grip on you, kick out the wall, and jump. Then

I'd run you back to the scene of the accident, and we'd stumble around like the two luckiest survivors in history.

I stared at him wordlessly.

"What?" he whispered.

I shook my head in awe. "Nothing," I mouthed.

I scrubbed out the disconcerting conversation and wrote one more line.

You will tell me next time.

I knew there would be a next time. The pattern would continue until someone lost.

Edward stared into my eyes for a long moment. I wondered what my face looked like — it felt cold, so the blood hadn't returned to my cheeks. My eyelashes were still wet.

He sighed and then nodded once.

Thanks.

The paper disappeared from under my hand. I looked up, blinking in surprise, just as Mr. Berty came down the aisle.

"Is that something you'd like to share there, Mr. Cullen?"

Edward looked up innocently and held out the sheet of paper on top of his folder. "My notes?" he asked, sounding confused.

Mr. Berty scanned the notes — no doubt a perfect transcription of his lecture — and then walked away frowning.

*   *   *

It was later, in Calculus — my one class without Edward — that I heard the gossip.

"My money's on the big Indian," someone was saying.

I peeked up to see that Tyler, Mike, Austin, and Ben had their heads bent together, deep in conversation.

"Yeah," Mike whispered. "Did you see the *size* of that Jacob kid? I think he could take Cullen down." Mike sounded pleased by the idea.

"I don't think so," Ben disagreed. "There's something about Edward. He's always so . . . confident. I have a feeling he can take care of himself."

"I'm with Ben," Tyler agreed. "Besides, if that other kid messed Edward up, you know those big brothers of his would get involved."

"Have you been down to La Push lately?" Mike asked. "Lauren and I went to the beach a couple of weeks ago, and believe me, Jacob's friends are all just as big as he is."

"Huh," Tyler said. "Too bad it didn't turn into anything. Guess we'll never know how it would have turned out."

"It didn't look over to me," Austin said. "Maybe we'll get to see."

Mike grinned. "Anyone in the mood for a bet?"

"Ten on Jacob," Austin said at once.

"Ten on Cullen," Tyler chimed in.

"Ten on Edward," Ben agreed.

"Jacob," Mike said.

"Hey, do you guys know what it was about?" Austin wondered. "That might affect the odds."

"I can guess," Mike said, and then he shot a glance at me at the same time that Ben and Tyler did.

From their expressions, none of them had realized I was in easy hearing distance. They all looked away quickly, shuffling the papers on their desks.

"I still say Jacob," Mike muttered under his breath.

4. NATURE

I WAS HAVING A BAD WEEK.

I knew that essentially nothing had changed. Okay, so Victoria had not given up, but had I ever dreamed for one moment that she had? Her reappearance had only confirmed what I'd already known. No reason for fresh panic.

In theory. Not panicking was easier said than done.

Graduation was only a few weeks away, but I wondered if it wasn't a little foolish to sit around, weak and tasty, waiting for the next disaster. It seemed too dangerous to be human — just begging for trouble. Someone like me shouldn't *be* human. Someone with my luck ought to be a little less helpless.

But no one would listen to me.

Carlisle had said, "There are seven of us, Bella. And with Alice on our side, I don't think Victoria's going to catch us off guard. I think it's important, for Charlie's sake, that we stick with the original plan."

Esme had said, "We'd never allow anything to happen to you, sweetheart. You know that. Please don't be anxious." And then she'd kissed my forehead.

Emmett had said, "I'm really glad Edward didn't kill you. Everything's so much more fun with you around."

Rosalie had glared at him.

Alice had rolled her eyes and said, "I'm offended. You're not honestly *worried* about this, are you?"

"If it's no big deal, then why did Edward drag me to Florida?" I'd demanded.

"Haven't you noticed yet, Bella, that Edward is just the teeniest bit prone to overreaction?"

Jasper had silently erased all the panic and tension in my body with his curious talent of controlling emotional atmospheres. I'd felt reassured, and let them talk me out of my desperate pleading.

Of course, that calm had worn off as soon as Edward and I had walked out of the room.

So the consensus was that I was just supposed to forget that a deranged vampire was stalking me, intent on my death. Go about my business.

I did try. And surprisingly, there *were* other things almost as stressful to dwell on besides my status on the endangered species list. . . .

Because Edward's response had been the most frustrating of them all.

"That's between you and Carlisle," he'd said. "Of course, you know that I'm willing to make it between you and me at any time that you wish. You know my condition." And he had smiled angelically.

Ugh. I did know his condition. Edward had promised that he would change me himself whenever I wanted . . . just as long as I was *married* to him first.

Sometimes I wondered if he was only pretending that he couldn't read my mind. How else had he struck upon the one condition that I would have trouble accepting? The one condition that would slow me down.

All in all, a very bad week. And today was the worst day in it.

It was always a bad day when Edward was away. Alice had foreseen nothing out of the ordinary this weekend, and so I'd insisted that he take the opportunity to go hunting with his brothers. I knew how it bored him to hunt the easy, nearby prey.

"Go have fun," I'd told him. "Bag a few mountain lions for me."

I would never admit to him how hard it was for me when he was gone — how it brought back the abandonment nightmares. If he knew that, it would make him feel horrible and he would be afraid to ever leave me, even for the most necessary reasons. It had been like that in the beginning, when he'd first returned from Italy. His golden eyes had turned black and he'd suffered from his thirst more than it was already necessary that he suffer. So I put on a brave face and all but kicked him out the door whenever Emmett and Jasper wanted to go.

I think he saw through me, though. A little. This morning there had been a note left on my pillow:

I'll be back so soon you won't have time to miss me. Look after my heart — I've left it with you.

So now I had a big empty Saturday with nothing but my morning shift at Newton's Olympic Outfitters to distract me. And, of course, the oh-so-comforting promise from Alice.

"I'm staying close to home to hunt. I'll only be fifteen minutes away if you need me. I'll keep an eye out for trouble."

Translation: don't try anything funny just because Edward is gone.

Alice was certainly just as capable of crippling my truck as Edward was.

I tried to look on the bright side. After work, I had plans to help Angela with her announcements, so that would be a distraction. And Charlie was in an excellent mood due to Edward's absence, so I might as well enjoy that while it lasted. Alice would spend the night with me if I was pathetic enough to ask her to. And then tomorrow, Edward would be home. I would survive.

Not wanting to be ridiculously early for work, I ate my breakfast slowly, one Cheerio at a time. Then, when I'd washed the dishes, I arranged the magnets on the fridge into a perfect line. Maybe I was developing obsessive-compulsive disorder.

The last two magnets — round black utilitarian pieces

that were my favorites because they could hold ten sheets of paper to the fridge without breaking a sweat — did not want to cooperate with my fixation. Their polarities were reversed; every time I tried to line the last one up, the other jumped out of place.

For some reason — impending mania, perhaps — this really irritated me. Why couldn't they just play nice? Stupid with stubbornness, I kept shoving them together as if I was expecting them to suddenly give up. I could have flipped one over, but that felt like losing. Finally, exasperated at myself more than the magnets, I pulled them from the fridge and held them together with two hands. It took a little effort — they were strong enough to put up a fight — but I forced them to coexist side-by-side.

"See," I said out loud — talking to inanimate objects, never a good sign — "That's not so horrible, is it?"

I stood there like an idiot for a second, not quite able to admit that I wasn't having any lasting effect against scientific principles. Then, with a sigh, I put the magnets back on the fridge, a foot apart.

"There's no need to be so inflexible," I muttered.

It was still too early, but I decided I'd better get out of the house before the inanimate objects started talking back.

When I got to Newton's, Mike was methodically dry mopping the aisles while his mom arranged a new counter display. I caught them in the middle of an argument, unaware that I had arrived.

"But it's the only time that Tyler can go," Mike complained. "You said after graduation —"

"You're just going to have to wait," Mrs. Newton snapped. "You and Tyler can think of something else to do. You are not going to Seattle until the police stop whatever it is that is going on there. I know Beth Crowley has told Tyler the same thing, so don't act like I'm the bad guy — oh, good morning, Bella," she said when she caught sight of me, brightening her tone quickly. "You're early."

Karen Newton was the last person I'd think to ask for help in an outdoor sports equipment store. Her perfectly highlighted blond hair was always smoothed into an elegant twist on the back of her neck, her fingernails were polished by professionals, as were her toenails — visible through the strappy high heels that didn't resemble anything Newton's offered on the long row of hiking boots.

"Light traffic," I joked as I grabbed my hideous fluorescent orange vest out from under the counter. I was surprised that Mrs. Newton was as worked up about this Seattle thing as Charlie. I'd thought he was going to extremes.

"Well, er . . ." Mrs. Newton hesitated for a moment, playing uncomfortably with a stack of flyers she was arranging by the register.

I stopped with one arm in my vest. I knew that look.

When I'd let the Newtons know that I wouldn't be working here this summer — abandoning them in their busiest season, in effect — they'd started training Katie Marshall to take my place. They couldn't really afford both of us on the payroll at the same time, so when it looked like a slow day . . .

"I was going to call," Mrs. Newton continued. "I don't

think we're expecting a ton of business today. Mike and I can probably handle things. I'm sorry you got up and drove out. . . ."

On a normal day, I would be ecstatic with this turn of events. Today . . . not so much.

"Okay," I sighed. My shoulders slumped. What was I going to do now?

"That's not fair, Mom," Mike said. "If Bella wants to work —"

"No, it's okay, Mrs. Newton. Really, Mike. I've got finals to study for and stuff. . . ." I didn't want to be a source of familial discord when they were already arguing.

"Thanks, Bella. Mike, you missed aisle four. Um, Bella, do you mind throwing these flyers in a Dumpster on the way out? I told the girl who left them here that I'd put them on the counter, but I really don't have the room."

"Sure, no problem." I put my vest away, and then tucked the flyers under my arm and headed out into the misty rain.

The Dumpster was around the side of Newton's, next to where we employees were supposed to park. I shuffled along, kicking pebbles petulantly on my way. I was about to fling the stack of bright yellow papers into the trash when the heading printed in bold across the top caught my eye. One word in particular seized my attention.

I clutched the papers in both hands as I stared at the picture beneath the caption. A lump rose in my throat.

SAVE THE OLYMPIC WOLF

Under the words, there was a detailed drawing of a wolf in front of a fir tree, its head thrown back in the act of baying at the moon. It was a disconcerting picture; something about the wolf's plaintive posture made him look forlorn. Like he was howling in grief.

And then I was running to my truck, the flyers still locked in my grip.

Fifteen minutes — that's all I had. But it should be long enough. It was only fifteen minutes to La Push, and surely I would cross the boundary line a few minutes before I hit the town.

My truck roared to life without any difficulty.

Alice couldn't have seen me doing this, because I hadn't been planning it. A snap decision, that was the key! And as long as I moved fast enough, I should be able to capitalize on it.

I'd thrown the damp flyers in my haste and they were scattered in a bright mess across the passenger seat — a hundred bolded captions, a hundred dark howling wolves outlined against the yellow background.

I barreled down the wet highway, turning the windshield wipers on high and ignoring the groan of the ancient engine. Fifty-five was the most I could coax out of my truck, and I prayed it would be enough.

I had no clue where the boundary line was, but I began to feel safer as I passed the first houses outside La Push. This must be beyond where Alice was allowed to follow.

I'd call her when I got to Angela's this afternoon, I reasoned, so that she'd know I was fine. There was no reason for her to get worked up. She didn't need to be mad at me — Edward would be angry enough for two when he got back.

My truck was positively wheezing by the time it grated to a stop in front of the familiar faded red house. The lump came back to my throat as I stared at the little place that had once been my refuge. It had been so long since I'd been here.

Before I could cut the engine, Jacob was standing in the door, his face blank with shock.

In the sudden silence when the truck-roar died, I heard him gasp.

"Bella?"

"Hey, Jake!"

"Bella!" he yelled back, and the smile I'd been waiting for stretched across his face like the sun breaking free of the clouds. His teeth gleamed bright against his russet skin. "I can't believe it!"

He ran to the truck and half-yanked me through the open door, and then we were both jumping up and down like kids.

"How did you get here?"

"I snuck out!"

"*Awe*some!"

"Hey, Bella!" Billy had rolled himself into the doorway to see what all the commotion was about.

"Hey, Bil —!"

Just then my air choked off — Jacob grabbed me up in a bear hug too tight to breathe and swung me around in a circle.

"Wow, it's good to see you here!"

"Can't . . . breathe," I gasped.

He laughed and put me down.

"Welcome back, Bella," he said, grinning. And the way he said the words made it sound like *welcome home*.

We started walking, too keyed up to sit still in the house. Jacob was practically bouncing as he moved, and I had to remind him a few times that my legs weren't ten feet long.

As we walked, I felt myself settling into another version of myself, the self I had been with Jacob. A little younger, a little less responsible. Someone who might, on occasion, do something really stupid for no good reason.

Our exuberance lasted through the first few topics of conversation: how we were doing, what we were up to, how long I had, and what had brought me here. When I hesitantly told him about the wolf flyer, his bellowing laugh echoed back from the trees.

But then, as we ambled past the back of the store and shoved through the thick scrub that ringed the far edge of First Beach, we got to the hard parts. All too soon we had to talk about the reasons behind our long separation, and I watched as the face of my friend hardened into the bitter mask that was already too familiar.

"So what's the story, anyway?" Jacob asked me, kicking a piece of driftwood out of his way with too much force. It sailed over the sand and then clattered against the rocks. "I mean, since the last time we . . . well, before, you know . . ." He struggled for the words. He took a deep breath and tried again. "What I'm asking is . . . everything is just back to the way it was before *he* left? You forgave him for all of that?"

I took a deep breath. "There was nothing to forgive."

I wanted to skip past this part, the betrayals, the accusations, but I knew that we had to talk it through before we'd be able to move on to anything else.

Jacob's face puckered up like he'd just licked a lemon. "I wish Sam had taken a picture when he found you that night last September. It would be exhibit A."

"Nobody's on trial."

"Maybe somebody should be."

"Not even you would blame him for leaving, if you knew the reason why."

He glared at me for a few seconds. "Okay," he challenged acidly. "Amaze me."

His hostility was wearing on me — chafing against the raw; it hurt to have him angry with me. It reminded me of the bleak afternoon, long ago, when — under orders from Sam — he'd told me we couldn't be friends. I took a second to compose myself.

"Edward left me last fall because he didn't think I should be hanging out with vampires. He thought it would be healthier for me if he left."

Jacob did a double take. He had to scramble for a minute. Whatever he'd been planning to say, it clearly no longer applied. I was glad he didn't know the catalyst behind Edward's decision. I could only imagine what he'd think if he knew Jasper had tried to kill me.

"He came back, though, didn't he?" Jacob muttered. "Too bad he can't stick to a decision."

"If you remember, *I* went and got *him*."

Jacob stared at me for a moment, and then he backed off. His face relaxed, and his voice was calmer when he spoke.

"That's true. So I never did get the story. What happened?"

I hesitated, biting my lip.

"Is it a secret?" His voice took on a taunting edge. "Are you not allowed to tell me?"

"No," I snapped. "It's just a really long story."

Jacob smiled, arrogant, and turned to walk up the beach, expecting me to follow.

It was no fun being with Jacob if he was going to act like this. I trailed behind him automatically, not sure if I shouldn't turn around and leave. I was going to have to face Alice, though, when I got home. . . . I supposed I wasn't in any rush.

Jacob walked to a huge, familiar piece of driftwood — an entire tree, roots and all, bleached white and beached deep in the sand; it was *our* tree, in a way.

Jacob sat down on the natural bench, and patted the space next to him.

"I don't mind long stories. Is there any action?"

I rolled my eyes as I sat next to him. "There's some action," I allowed.

"It wouldn't be real horror without action."

"Horror!" I scoffed. "Can you listen, or will you be interrupting me with rude comments about my friends?"

He pretended to lock his lips and then threw the invisible key over his shoulder. I tried not to smile, and failed.

"I'll have to start with the stuff you were already there for," I decided, working to organize the stories in my head before I began.

Jacob raised his hand.

"Go ahead."

"That's good," he said. "I didn't understand much that was going on at the time."

"Yeah, well, it gets complicated, so pay attention. You know how Alice *sees* things?"

I took his scowl — the wolves weren't thrilled that the legends of vampires possessing supernatural gifts were true — for a yes, and proceeded with the account of my race through Italy to rescue Edward.

I kept it as succinct as possible — leaving out anything that wasn't essential. I tried to read Jacob's reactions, but his face was enigmatic as I explained how Alice had seen Edward plan to kill himself when he'd heard that I was dead. Sometimes Jacob seemed so deep in thought, I wasn't sure if he was listening. He only interrupted one time.

"The fortune-telling bloodsucker can't see us?" he echoed, his face both fierce and gleeful. "Seriously? That's *excellent*!"

I clenched my teeth together, and we sat in silence, his face expectant as he waited for me to continue. I glared at him until he realized his mistake.

"Oops!" he said. "Sorry." He locked his lips again.

His response was easier to read when I got to the part about the Volturi. His teeth clenched together, goose bumps rose on his arms, and his nostrils flared. I didn't go into specifics, I just told him that Edward had talked us out of trouble, without revealing the promise we'd had to make, or the visit we were anticipating. Jacob didn't need to have my nightmares.

"Now you know the whole story," I concluded. "So it's your turn to talk. What happened while I was with my mom this weekend?" I knew Jacob would give me more details than Edward had. He wasn't afraid of scaring me.

Jacob leaned forward, instantly animated. "So Embry and Quil and I were running patrol on Saturday night, just routine stuff, when out of nowhere — bam!" He threw his arms out, impersonating an explosion. "There it is — a fresh trail, not fifteen minutes old. Sam wanted us to wait for him, but I didn't know you were gone, and I didn't know if your bloodsuckers were keeping an eye on you or not. So we took off after her at full speed, but she'd crossed the treaty line before we caught up. We spread out along the line, hoping she'd cross back over. It was frustrating, let me tell you." He wagged his head and his hair — growing out from the short crop he'd adopted when he'd joined the pack — flopped into his eyes. "We ended up too far south. The Cullens chased her back to our side just a few miles north of us. Would have been the perfect ambush if we'd known where to wait."

He shook his head, grimacing now. "That's when it got dicey. Sam and the others caught up to her before we did, but she was dancing right along the line, and the whole coven was right there on the other side. The big one, what's-his-name —"

"Emmett."

"Yeah, him. He made a lunge for her, but that redhead is fast! He flew right behind her and almost rammed into Paul. So, Paul . . . well, you know Paul."

"Yeah."

"Lost his focus. Can't say that I blame him — the big bloodsucker was right on top of him. He sprang — hey, don't give me that look. The vampire was on our land."

I tried to compose my face so that he would go on. My nails were digging into my palms with the stress of the story, even though I knew it had turned out fine.

"Anyway, Paul missed, and the big one got back on his side. But by then the, er, well the, uh, blonde . . ." Jacob's expression was a comical mix of disgust and unwilling admiration as he tried to come up with a word to describe Edward's sister.

"Rosalie."

"Whatever. She got real territorial, so Sam and I fell back to get Paul's flanks. Then their leader and the other blond male —"

"Carlisle and Jasper."

He gave me an exasperated look. "You know I don't really care. Anyway, so *Carlisle* spoke to Sam, trying to calm things down. Then it was weird, because everyone got really calm really fast. It was that other one you told me about, messing with our heads. But even though we knew what he was doing, we couldn't *not* be calm."

"Yeah, I know how it feels."

"Really annoying, that's how it feels. Only you can't be annoyed until afterwards." He shook his head angrily. "So Sam and the head vamp agreed that Victoria was the priority, and we started after her again. Carlisle gave us the line, so that we could follow the scent properly, but then she hit the cliffs just north of Makah country, right where the line hugs the coast for a few miles. She took off into the water again. The big one and the calm one wanted permission to cross the line to go after her, but of course we said no."

"Good. I mean, you were being stupid, but I'm glad. Emmett's never cautious enough. He could have gotten hurt."

Jacob snorted. "So did your vampire tell you we attacked for no reason and his totally innocent coven —"

"No," I interrupted. "Edward told me the same story, just without quite as many details."

"Huh," Jacob said under his breath, and he bent over to pick up a rock from among the millions of pebbles at our feet. With a casual flick, he sent it flying a good hundred meters out into the bay. "Well, she'll be back, I guess. We'll get another shot at her."

I shuddered; of course she would be back. Would Edward really tell me next time? I wasn't sure. I'd have to keep an eye on Alice, to look for the signs that the pattern was about to repeat. . . .

Jacob didn't seem to notice my reaction. He was staring across the waves with a thoughtful expression on his face, his broad lips pursed.

"What are you thinking about?" I asked after a long, quiet time.

"I'm thinking about what you told me. About when the fortune-teller saw you cliff jumping and thought you'd committed suicide, and how it all got out of control. . . . Do you realize that if you had just waited for me like you were supposed to, then the bl — *Alice* wouldn't have been able to see you jump? Nothing would have changed. We'd probably be in my garage right now, like any other Saturday. There wouldn't be any vampires in Forks, and you and me . . ." He trailed off, deep in thought.

It was disconcerting the way he said this, like it would be a good thing to have no vampires in Forks. My heart thumped unevenly at the emptiness of the picture he painted.

"Edward would have come back anyway."

"Are you sure about that?" he asked, belligerent again as soon as I spoke Edward's name.

"Being apart . . . It didn't work out so well for either of us."

He started to say something, something angry from his expression, but he stopped himself, took a breath, and began again.

"Did you know Sam is mad at you?"

"Me?" It took me a second. "Oh. I see. He thinks they would have stayed away if I wasn't here."

"No. That's not it."

"What's his problem then?"

Jacob leaned down to scoop up another rock. He turned it over and over in his fingers; his eyes were riveted on the black stone while he spoke in a low voice.

"When Sam saw . . . how you were in the beginning, when Billy told them how Charlie worried when you didn't get better, and then when you started jumping off cliffs . . ."

I made a face. No one was ever going to let me forget that.

Jacob's eyes flashed up to mine. "He thought you were the one person in the world with as much reason to hate the Cullens as he does. Sam feels sort of . . . betrayed that you would just let them back into your life like they never hurt you."

I didn't believe for a second that Sam was the only one who felt that way. And the acid in my voice now was for both of them.

"You can tell Sam to go right to —"

"Look at that," Jacob interrupted me, pointing to an eagle in the act of plummeting down toward the ocean from an incredible height. It checked itself at the last minute, only its talons breaking the surface of the waves, just for an instant. Then it flapped away, its wings straining against the load of the huge fish it had snagged.

"You see it everywhere," Jacob said, his voice suddenly distant. "Nature taking its course — hunter and prey, the endless cycle of life and death."

I didn't understand the point of the nature lecture; I guessed that he was just trying to change the subject. But then he looked down at me with dark humor in his eyes.

"And yet, you don't see the fish trying to plant a kiss on the eagle. You never see *that*." He grinned a mocking grin.

I grinned back tightly, though the acid taste was still in my mouth. "Maybe the fish was trying," I suggested.

"It's hard to tell what a fish is thinking. Eagles are good-looking birds, you know."

"Is that what it comes down to?" His voice was abruptly sharper. "Good looks?"

"Don't be stupid, Jacob."

"Is it the money, then?" he persisted.

"That's nice," I muttered, getting up from the tree. "I'm flattered that you think so much of me." I turned my back on him and paced away.

"Aw, don't get mad." He was right behind me; he caught my wrist and spun me around. "I'm serious! I'm trying to understand here, and I'm coming up blank."

His eyebrows pushed together angrily, and his eyes were black in their deep shadow.

"I love *him*. Not because he's beautiful or because he's *rich*!" I spat the word at Jacob. "I'd much rather he weren't either one. It would even out the gap between us just a little bit — because he'd still be the most loving and unselfish and brilliant and *decent* person I've ever met. Of course I love him. How hard is that to understand?"

"It's impossible to understand."

"Please enlighten me, then, Jacob." I let the sarcasm flow thick. "What *is* a valid reason for someone to love someone else? Since apparently I'm doing it wrong."

"I think the best place to start would be to look within your own species. That usually works."

"Well, that just sucks!" I snapped. "I guess I'm stuck with Mike Newton after all."

Jacob flinched back and bit his lip. I could see that my words had hurt him, but I was too mad to feel bad about that yet. He dropped my wrist and folded his arms across his chest, turning from me to glare toward the ocean.

"I'm human," he muttered, his voice almost inaudible.

"You're not as human as Mike," I continued ruthlessly. "Do you still think that's the most important consideration?"

"It's not the same thing." Jacob didn't look away from the gray waves. "I didn't choose this."

I laughed once in disbelief. "Do you think Edward did? He didn't know what was happening to him any more than you did. He didn't exactly sign up for this."

Jacob was shaking his head back and forth with a small, quick movement.

"You know, Jacob, you're awfully self-righteous — considering that you're a werewolf and all."

"It's not the same," Jacob repeated, glowering at me.

"I don't see why not. You could be a *bit* more understanding about the Cullens. You have no idea how truly good they are — to the core, Jacob."

He frowned more deeply. "They shouldn't exist. Their existence goes against nature."

I stared at him for a long moment with one eyebrow raised incredulously. It was a while before he noticed.

"What?"

"Speaking of unnatural . . . ," I hinted.

"Bella," he said, his voice slow and different. Aged. I realized that he sounded suddenly older than me — like a parent or a teacher. "What I am was born in me. It's a part of who I am, who my family is, who we all are as a tribe — it's the reason why we're still here.

"Besides that" — he looked down at me, his black eyes unreadable — "I *am* still human."

He picked up my hand and pressed it to his fever-warm chest. Through his t-shirt, I could feel the steady beating of his heart under my palm.

"Normal humans can't throw motorcycles around the way you can."

He smiled a faint, half-smile. "Normal humans run away from monsters, Bella. And I never claimed to be normal. Just human."

Staying angry with Jacob was too much work. I started to smile as I pulled my hand away from his chest.

"You look plenty human to me," I allowed. "At the moment."

"I feel human." He stared past me, his face far away. His lower lip trembled, and he bit down on it hard.

"Oh, Jake," I whispered, reaching for his hand.

This was why I was here. This was why I would take whatever reception waited for me when I got back. Because, underneath all the anger and the sarcasm, Jacob was in pain. Right now, it was very clear in his eyes. I didn't know how to help him, but I knew I had to try. It was more than that I owed him. It was because his pain hurt me, too. Jacob had become a part of me, and there was no changing that now.

5. IMPRINT

"ARE YOU OKAY, JAKE? CHARLIE SAID YOU WERE HAVING a hard time. . . . Isn't it getting any better?"

His warm hand curled around mine. "'S not so bad," he said, but he wouldn't meet my eyes.

He walked slowly back to the driftwood bench, staring at the rainbow-colored pebbles, and pulling me along at his side. I sat back down on our tree, but he sat on the wet, rocky ground rather than next to me. I wondered if it was so that he could hide his face more easily. He kept my hand.

I started babbling to fill the silence. "It's been so long since I was here. I've probably missed a ton of things. How are Sam and Emily? And Embry? Did Quil —?"

I broke off mid-sentence, remembering that Jacob's friend Quil had been a sensitive subject.

"Ah, Quil," Jacob sighed.

So then it must have happened — Quil must have joined the pack.

"I'm sorry," I mumbled.

To my surprise, Jacob snorted. "Don't say that to *him*."

"What do you mean?"

"Quil's not looking for pity. Just the opposite — he's jazzed. Totally thrilled."

This made no sense to me. All the other wolves had been so depressed at the idea of their friend sharing their fate. "Huh?"

Jacob tilted his head back to look at me. He smiled and rolled his eyes.

"Quil thinks it's the coolest thing that's ever happened to him. Part of it is finally knowing what's going on. And he's excited to have his friends back — to be part of the 'in crowd.'" Jacob snorted again. "Shouldn't be surprised, I guess. It's so *Quil*."

"He *likes* it?"

"Honestly . . . most of them do," Jacob admitted slowly. "There are definitely good sides to this — the speed, the freedom, the strength . . . the sense of — of *family*. . . . Sam and I are the only ones who ever felt really bitter. And Sam got past that a long time ago. So I'm the crybaby now." Jacob laughed at himself.

There were so many things I wanted to know. "Why are you and Sam different? What happened to Sam anyway? What's his problem?" The questions tumbled out without room to answer them, and Jacob laughed again.

"That's a long story."

"I told you a long story. Besides, I'm not in any hurry to get back," I said, and then I grimaced as I thought of the trouble I would be in.

He looked up at me swiftly, hearing the double edge in my words. "Will he be mad at you?"

"Yes," I admitted. "He really hates it when I do things he considers . . . risky."

"Like hanging out with werewolves."

"Yeah."

Jacob shrugged. "So don't go back. I'll sleep on the couch."

"That's a great idea," I grumbled. "Because then he would come looking for me."

Jacob stiffened, and then smiled bleakly. "Would he?"

"If he was afraid I was hurt or something — probably."

"My idea's sounding better all the time."

"Please, Jake. That really bugs me."

"What does?"

"That you two are so ready to kill each other!" I complained. "It makes me crazy. Why can't you both just be civilized?"

"Is he ready to kill me?" Jacob asked with a grim smile, unconcerned by my anger.

"Not like you seem to be!" I realized I was yelling. "At least *he* can be a grown-up about this. He knows that hurting you would hurt me — and so he never would. You don't seem to care about that at all!"

"Yeah, right," Jacob muttered. "I'm sure he's quite the pacifist."

"Ugh!" I ripped my hand out of his and shoved his head away. Then I pulled my knees up to my chest and wrapped my arms tightly around them.

I glared out toward the horizon, fuming.

Jacob was quiet for a few minutes. Finally, he got up off the ground and sat beside me, putting his arm around my shoulders. I shook it off.

"Sorry," he said quietly. "I'll try to behave myself."

I didn't answer.

"Do you still want to hear about Sam?" he offered.

I shrugged.

"Like I said, it's a long story. And very . . . strange. There're so many strange things about this new life. I haven't had time to tell you the half of it. And this thing with Sam — well, I don't know if I'll even be able to explain it right."

His words pricked my curiosity in spite of my irritation.

"I'm listening," I said stiffly.

Out of the corner of my eye, I saw the side of his face pull up in a smile.

"Sam had it so much harder than the rest of us. Because he was the first, and he was alone, and he didn't have anyone to tell him what was happening. Sam's grandfather died before he was born, and his father has never been around. There was no one there to recognize the signs. The first time it happened — the first time he phased — he thought he'd gone insane. It took him two weeks to calm down enough to change back.

"This was before you came to Forks, so you wouldn't remember. Sam's mother and Leah Clearwater had the forest rangers searching for him, the police. People thought there had been an accident or something. . . ."

"Leah?" I asked, surprised. Leah was Harry's daughter. Hearing her name sent an automatic surge of pity through me. Harry Clearwater, Charlie's life-long friend, had died of a heart attack this past spring.

His voice changed, became heavier. "Yeah. Leah and Sam were high school sweethearts. They started dating when she was just a freshman. She was frantic when he disappeared."

"But he and Emily —"

"I'll get to that — it's part of the story," he said. He inhaled slowly, and then exhaled in a gust.

I supposed it was silly for me to imagine that Sam had never loved anyone before Emily. Most people fall in and out of love many times in their lives. It was just that I'd seen Sam with Emily, and I couldn't imagine him with someone else. The way he looked at her . . . well, it reminded me of a look I'd seen sometimes in Edward's eyes — when he was looking at me.

"Sam came back," Jacob said, "but he wouldn't talk to anyone about where he'd been. Rumors flew — that he was up to no good, mostly. And then Sam happened to run in to Quil's grandfather one afternoon when Old Quil Ateara came to visit Mrs. Uley. Sam shook his hand. Old Quil just about had a stroke." Jacob paused to laugh.

"Why?"

Jacob put his hand on my cheek and pulled my face around to look at him — he was leaning toward me, his face was just a few inches away. His palm burned my skin, like he had a fever.

"Oh, right," I said. It was uncomfortable, having my face so close to his with his hand hot against my skin. "Sam was running a temperature."

Jacob laughed again. "Sam's hand felt like he'd left it sitting on a hot stovetop."

He was so close, I could feel his warm breath. I reached up casually, to take his hand away and free my face, but wound my fingers through his so that I wouldn't hurt his feelings. He smiled and leaned back, undeceived by my attempt at nonchalance.

"So Mr. Ateara went straight to the other elders," Jacob went on. "They were the only ones left who still knew, who remembered. Mr. Ateara, Billy, and Harry had actually seen their grandfathers make the change. When Old Quil told them, they met with Sam secretly and explained.

"It was easier when he understood — when he wasn't alone anymore. They knew he wouldn't be the only one affected by the Cullens' return" — he pronounced the name with unconscious bitterness — "but no one else was old enough. So Sam waited for the rest of us to join him. . . ."

"The Cullens had no idea," I said in a whisper. "They didn't think that werewolves still existed here. They didn't know that coming here would change you."

"It doesn't change the fact that it did."

"Remind me not to get on your bad side."

"You think I should be as forgiving as you are? We can't all be saints and martyrs."

"Grow up, Jacob."

"I wish I could," he murmured quietly.

I stared at him, trying to make sense of his response. "What?"

Jacob chuckled. "One of those many strange things I mentioned."

"You . . . can't . . . grow up?" I said blankly. "You're what? Not . . . *aging*? Is that a joke?"

"Nope." He popped his lips on the *P*.

I felt blood flood my face. Tears — tears of rage — filled my eyes. My teeth mashed together with an audible grinding sound.

"Bella? What did I say?"

I was on my feet again, my hands balled up into fists, my whole frame shaking.

"You. Are. Not. Aging," I growled through my teeth.

Jacob tugged my arm gently, trying to make me sit. "None of us are. What's wrong with you?"

"Am I the only one who has to get *old*? I get older every stinking day!" I nearly shrieked, throwing my hands in the air. Some little part of me recognized that I was throwing a Charlie-esque fit, but that rational part was greatly overshadowed by the irrational part. "*Damn* it! What kind of world is this? Where's the *justice*?"

"Take it easy, Bella."

"Shut up, Jacob. Just shut up! This is *so* unfair!"

"Did you seriously just stamp your foot? I thought girls only did that on TV."

I growled unimpressively.

"It's not as bad as you seem to think it is. Sit down and I'll explain."

"I'll stand."

He rolled his eyes. "Okay. Whatever you want. But listen, I *will* get older . . . someday."

"Explain."

He patted the tree. I glowered for a second, but then sat; my temper had burned out as suddenly as it had flared and I'd calmed down enough to realize that I was making a fool of myself.

"When we get enough control to quit . . . ," Jacob said. "When we stop phasing for a solid length of time, we age again. It's not easy." He shook his head, abruptly doubtful. "It's gonna take a really long time to learn that kind of restraint, I think. Even Sam's not there yet. 'Course it doesn't help that there's a huge coven of vampires right down the road. We can't even think about quitting when the tribe needs protectors. But you shouldn't get all bent out of shape about it, anyway, because I'm already older than you, physically at least."

"What are you talking about?"

"Look at me, Bells. Do I look sixteen?"

I glanced up and down his mammoth frame, trying to be unbiased. "Not exactly, I guess."

"Not at all. Because we reach full growth inside of a few months when the werewolf gene gets triggered. It's one hell of a growth spurt." He made a face. "Physically, I'm probably twenty-five or something. So there's no need for you to freak out about being too old for me for at least another seven years."

Twenty-five or something. The idea messed with my head. But I remembered that growth spurt — I remembered watching him shoot up and fill out right before my eyes. I remembered how he would look different from one day to the next. . . . I shook my head, feeling dizzy.

"So, did you want to hear about Sam, or did you want to scream at me some more for things that are out of my control?"

I took a deep breath. "Sorry. Age is a touchy subject for me. That hit a nerve."

Jacob's eyes tightened, and he looked as if he were trying to decide how to word something.

Since I didn't want to talk about the truly touchy stuff — my plans for the future, or treaties that might be broken by said plans, I prompted him. "So once Sam understood what was going on, once he had Billy and Harry and Mr. Ateara, you said it wasn't so hard anymore. And, like you also said, there are the cool parts. . . ." I hesitated briefly. "Why does Sam hate them so much? Why does he wish I would hate them?"

Jacob sighed. "This is the really weird part."

"I'm a pro at weird."

"Yeah, I know." He grinned before he continued. "So, you're right. Sam knew what was going on, and everything was almost okay. In most ways, his life was back to, well, not normal. But better." Then Jacob's expression tightened, like something painful was coming. "Sam couldn't tell Leah. We aren't supposed to tell anyone who doesn't have to know. And it wasn't really safe for him to be around her — but he cheated, just like I did with you. Leah was furious that he wouldn't tell her what was going on — where he'd been, where he went at night, why he was always so exhausted — but they were working it out. They were trying. They really loved each other."

"Did she find out? Is that what happened?"

He shook his head. "No, that wasn't the problem. Her cousin, Emily Young, came down from the Makah reservation to visit her one weekend."

I gasped. "Emily is Leah's cousin?"

"Second cousins. They're close, though. They were like sisters when they were kids."

"That's . . . horrible. How could Sam . . . ?" I trailed off, shaking my head.

"Don't judge him just yet. Did anyone ever tell you . . . Have you ever heard of *imprinting*?"

"Imprinting?" I repeated the unfamiliar word. "No. What's that mean?"

"It's one of those bizarre things we have to deal with. It doesn't happen to everyone. In fact, it's the rare exception, not the rule. Sam had heard all the stories by then, the stories we all used to think were legends. He'd heard of imprinting, but he never dreamed . . ."

"What is it?" I prodded.

Jacob's eyes strayed to the ocean. "Sam did love Leah. But when he saw Emily, that didn't matter anymore. Sometimes . . . we don't exactly know why . . . we find our mates that way." His eyes flashed back to me, his face reddening. "I mean . . . our soul mates."

"What way? Love at first sight?" I snickered.

Jacob wasn't smiling. His dark eyes were critical of my reaction. "It's a little bit more powerful than that. More absolute."

"Sorry," I muttered. "You're serious, aren't you?"

"Yeah, I am."

"Love at first sight? But more powerful?" My voice still sounded dubious, and he could hear that.

"It's not easy to explain. It doesn't matter, anyway." He shrugged indifferently. "You wanted to know what happened to Sam to make him hate the vampires for changing him, to make him hate himself. And that's what happened. He broke Leah's heart. He went back on every promise he'd ever made her. Every day he has to see the accusation in her eyes, and know that she's right."

He stopped talking abruptly, as if he'd said something he hadn't meant to.

"How did Emily deal with this? If she was so close to Leah . . . ?" Sam and Emily were utterly *right* together, two puzzle pieces, shaped for each other exactly. Still . . . how had Emily gotten past the fact that he'd belonged to someone else? Her sister, almost.

"She was real angry, in the beginning. But it's hard to resist that level of commitment and adoration." Jacob sighed. "And then, Sam could tell her everything. There are no rules that can bind you when you find your other half. You know how she got hurt?"

"Yeah." The story in Forks was that she was mauled by a bear, but I was in on the secret.

Werewolves are unstable, Edward had said. *The people near them get hurt.*

"Well, weirdly enough, that was sort of how they resolved things. Sam was so horrified, so sickened by himself, so full of hate for what he'd done. . . . He would have thrown himself under a bus if it would have made her feel better. He might have anyway, just to escape what he'd done. He was shattered. . . . Then, somehow, *she* was the one comforting *him*, and after that. . . ."

Jacob didn't finish his thought, and I sensed the story had gotten too personal to share.

"Poor Emily," I whispered. "Poor Sam. Poor Leah. . . ."

"Yeah, Leah got the worst end of the stick," he agreed. "She puts on a brave face. She's going to be a bridesmaid."

I gazed away, toward the jagged rocks that rose from the ocean like stubby broken-off fingers on the south rim of the harbor, while I tried to make sense of it all. I could feel his eyes on my face, waiting for me to say something.

"Did it happen to you?" I finally asked, still looking away. "This love-at-first-sight thing?"

"No," he answered briskly. "Sam and Jared are the only ones."

"Hmm," I said, trying to sound only politely interested. I was relieved, and I tried to explain my reaction to myself. I decided I was just glad he didn't claim there was some mystical, wolfy connection between the two of us. Our relationship was confusing enough as it was. I didn't need any more of the supernatural than I already had to deal with.

He was quiet, too, and the silence felt a little awkward. My intuition told me that I didn't want to hear what he was thinking.

"How did that work out for Jared?" I asked to break the silence.

"No drama there. It was just a girl he'd sat next to in school every day for a year and never looked at twice. And then, after he changed, he saw her again and never looked away. Kim was thrilled. She'd had a huge crush on him. She'd had his last name tacked on to the end of hers all over in her diary." He laughed mockingly.

I frowned. "Did Jared tell you that? He shouldn't have."

Jacob bit his lip. "I guess I shouldn't laugh. It was funny, though."

"Some soul mate."

He sighed. "Jared didn't tell us anything on purpose. I already told you this part, remember?"

"Oh, yeah. You can hear each other's thoughts, but only when you're wolves, right?"

"Right. Just like your bloodsucker." He glowered.

"Edward," I corrected.

"Sure, sure. That's how come I know so much about how Sam felt. It's not like he would have told us all that if he'd had a choice. Actually, that's something we all hate." The bitterness was abruptly harsh in his voice. "It's awful. No privacy, no secrets. Everything you're ashamed of, laid out for everyone to see." He shuddered.

"It sounds horrible," I whispered.

"It *is* sometimes helpful when we need to coordinate,"

he said grudgingly. "Once in a blue moon, when some bloodsucker crosses into our territory. Laurent was fun. And if the Cullens hadn't gotten in our way last Saturday . . . ugh!" he groaned. "We could have had her!" His fists clenched into angry balls.

I flinched. As much as I worried about Jasper or Emmett getting hurt, it was nothing like the panic I felt at the idea of Jacob going up against Victoria. Emmett and Jasper were the closest thing to indestructible I could imagine. Jacob was still warm, still comparatively human. Mortal. I thought of Jacob facing Victoria, her brilliant hair blowing around her oddly feline face . . . and shuddered.

Jacob looked up at me with a curious expression. "But isn't it like that for you all the time? Having *him* in your head?"

"Oh, no. Edward's never in my head. He only wishes." Jacob's expression became confused.

"He can't hear me," I explained, my voice a tiny bit smug from old habit. "I'm the only one like that, for him. We don't know *why* he can't."

"Weird," Jacob said.

"Yeah." The smugness faded. "It probably means there's something wrong with my brain," I admitted.

"I already knew there was something wrong with your brain," Jacob muttered.

"Thanks."

The sun broke through the clouds suddenly, a surprise I hadn't been expecting, and I had to narrow my eyes against the glare off the water. Everything changed color — the waves turned from gray to blue, the trees from dull olive to brilliant jade, and the rainbow-hued pebbles glittered like jewels.

We squinted for a moment, letting our eyes adjust. There were no sounds besides the hollow roar of the waves that echoed from every side of the sheltered harbor, the soft grinding of the stones against each other under the water's movement, and the cry of gulls high overhead. It was very peaceful.

Jacob settled closer to me, so that he was leaning against my arm. He was so warm. After a minute of this, I shrugged out of my rain jacket. He made a little sound of contentment in the back of his throat, and rested his cheek on the top of my head. I could feel the sun heat my skin — though it was not quite as warm as Jacob — and I wondered idly how long it would take me to burn.

Absentmindedly, I twisted my right hand to the side, and watched the sunlight glitter subtly off the scar James had left there.

"What are you thinking about?" he murmured.

"The sun."

"Mmm. It's nice."

"What are you thinking about?" I asked.

He chuckled to himself. "I was remembering that moronic movie you took me to. And Mike Newton puking all over everything."

I laughed, too, surprised by how time had changed the memory. It used to be one of stress, of confusion. So much had changed that night. . . . And now I could laugh. It was the last night Jacob and I had had before he'd learned the truth about his heritage. The last human memory. An oddly pleasant memory now.

"I miss that," Jacob said. "The way it used to be so easy . . . uncomplicated. I'm glad I've got a good memory." He sighed.

He felt the sudden tension in my body as his words triggered a memory of my own.

"What is it?" he asked.

"About that good memory of yours . . ." I pulled away from him so that I could read his face. At the moment, it was confused. "Do you mind telling me what you were doing Monday morning? You were thinking something that bothered Edward." *Bothered* wasn't quite the word for it, but I wanted an answer, so I thought it was best not to start out too severely.

Jacob's face brightened with understanding, and he laughed. "I was just thinking about you. Didn't like that much, did he?"

"*Me?* What about me?"

Jacob laughed, with a harder edge this time. "I was remembering the way you looked that night Sam found you — I've seen it in his head, and it's like I was there; that memory has always haunted Sam, you know. And then I remembered how you looked the first time you came to my place. I bet you don't even realize what a mess you were then, Bella. It was weeks before you started to look human again. And I remembered how you always used to have your arms wrapped around yourself, trying to hold yourself together. . . ." Jacob winced, and then shook his head. "It's hard for me to remember how sad you were, and it wasn't *my* fault. So I figured it would be harder for him. And I thought he ought to get a look at what he'd done."

I smacked his shoulder. It hurt my hand. "Jacob Black, don't you ever do that again! Promise me you won't."

"No way. I haven't had that much fun in months."

"So help me, Jake —"

"Oh, get a grip, Bella. When am I ever going to see him again? Don't worry about it."

I got to my feet, and he caught my hand as I started to walk away. I tried to tug free.

"I'm leaving, Jacob."

"No, don't go yet," he protested, his hand tightening around mine. "I'm sorry. And . . . okay, I won't do it again. Promise."

I sighed. "Thanks, Jake."

"Come on, we'll go back to my house," he said eagerly.

"Actually, I think I really do need to go. Angela Weber is expecting me, and I know Alice is worried. I don't want to upset her too much."

"But you just got here!"

"It feels that way," I agreed. I glared up at the sun, somehow already directly overhead. How had the time passed so quickly?

His eyebrows pulled down over his eyes. "I don't know when I'll see you again," he said in a hurt voice.

"I'll come back the next time he's away," I promised impulsively.

"*Away?*" Jacob rolled his eyes. "That's a nice way to describe what he's doing. Disgusting parasites."

"If you can't be nice, I won't come back at all!" I threatened, trying to pull my hand free. He refused to let go.

"Aw, don't be mad," he said, grinning. "Knee-jerk reaction."

"If I'm going to try to come back again, you're going to have to get something straight, okay?"

He waited.

"See," I explained. "I don't care who's a vampire and who's a werewolf. That's irrelevant. You are Jacob, and he is Edward, and I am Bella. And nothing else matters."

His eyes narrowed slightly. "But I *am* a werewolf," he said unwillingly. "And he *is* a vampire," he added with obvious revulsion.

"And I'm a Virgo!" I shouted, exasperated.

He raised his eyebrows, measuring my expression with curious eyes. Finally, he shrugged.

"If you can really see it that way . . ."

"I can. I do."

"Okay. Just Bella and Jacob. None of those freaky Virgos here." He smiled at me, the warm, familiar smile that I had missed so much. I felt the answering smile spread across my face.

"I've really missed you, Jake," I admitted impulsively.

"Me, too," his smile widened. His eyes were happy and clear, free for once of the angry bitterness. "More than you know. Will you come back soon?"

"As soon as I can," I promised.

6. SWITZERLAND

As I drove home, I wasn't paying much attention to the road that shimmered wetly in the sun. I was thinking about the flood of information Jacob had shared with me, trying to sort it out, to force it all to make sense. Despite the overload, I felt lighter. Seeing Jacob smile, having all the secrets thrashed out . . . it didn't make things perfect, but it made them better. I was right to have gone. Jacob needed me. And obviously, I thought as I squinted into the glare, there was no danger.

It came out of nowhere. One minute there was nothing but bright highway in my rearview mirror. The next minute, the sun was glinting off a silver Volvo right on my tail.

"Aw, crap," I whimpered.

I considered pulling over. But I was too much of a coward to face him right away. I'd been counting on some prep time . . . and having Charlie nearby as a buffer. At least that would force him to keep his voice down.

The Volvo followed inches behind me. I kept my eyes on the road ahead.

Chicken through and through, I drove straight to Angela's without once meeting the gaze I could feel burning a hole in my mirror.

He followed me until I pulled to the curb in front of the Webers' house. He didn't stop, and I didn't look up as he passed. I didn't want to see the expression on his face. I ran up the short concrete walk to Angela's door as soon as he was out of sight.

Ben answered the door before I could finish knocking, like he'd been standing right behind it.

"Hey, Bella!" he said, surprised.

"Hi, Ben. Er, is Angela here?" I wondered if Angela had forgotten our plans, and cringed at the thought of going home early.

"Sure," Ben said just as Angela called, "Bella!" and appeared at the top of the stairs.

Ben peered around me as we both heard the sound of a car on the road; the sound didn't scare me — this engine stuttered to a stop, followed by the loud pop of a backfire. Nothing like the purr of the Volvo. This must be the visitor Ben had been waiting for.

"Austin's here," Ben said as Angela reached his side.

A horn honked on the street.

"I'll see you later," Ben promised. "Miss you already."

He threw his arm around Angela's neck and pulled her face down to his height so that he could kiss her enthusiastically. After a second of this, Austin honked again.

"'Bye, Ang! Love you!" Ben shouted as he dashed past me.

Angela swayed, her face slightly pink, then recovered herself and waved until Ben and Austin were out of sight. Then she turned to me and grinned ruefully.

"Thank you for doing this, Bella," she said. "From the bottom of my heart. Not only are you saving my hands from permanent injury, you also just spared me two long hours of a plot-less, badly dubbed martial arts film." She sighed in relief.

"Happy to be of service." I was feeling a bit less panicked, able to breathe a little more evenly. It felt so ordinary here. Angela's easy human dramas were oddly reassuring. It was nice to know that life was normal *somewhere*.

I followed Angela up the stairs to her room. She kicked toys out of the way as she went. The house was unusually quiet.

"Where's your family?"

"My parents took the twins to a birthday party in Port Angeles. I can't believe you're really going to help me with this. Ben's pretending he has tendonitis." She made a face.

"I don't mind at all," I said, and then I walked into Angela's room and saw the stacks of waiting envelopes.

"Oh!" I gasped. Angela turned to look at me, apologies

in her eyes. I could see why she'd been putting this off, and why Ben had weaseled out.

"I thought you were exaggerating," I admitted.

"I wish. Are you sure you want to do this?"

"Put me to work. I've got all day."

Angela divided a pile in half and put her mother's address book between us on her desk. For a while we concentrated, and there was just the sound of our pens scratching quietly across the paper.

"What's Edward doing tonight?" she asked after a few minutes.

My pen dug into the envelope I was working on. "Emmet's home for the weekend. They're *supposed* to be hiking."

"You say that like you're not sure."

I shrugged.

"You're lucky Edward has his brothers for all the hiking and camping. I don't know what I'd do if Ben didn't have Austin for the guy stuff."

"Yeah, the outdoors thing is not really for me. And there's no way I'd ever be able to keep up."

Angela laughed. "I prefer the indoors myself."

She focused on her pile for a minute. I wrote out four more addresses. There was never any pressure to fill a pause with meaningless chatter around Angela. Like Charlie, she was comfortable with silence.

But, like Charlie, she was also too observant sometimes.

"Is something wrong?" she asked in a low voice now. "You seem . . . anxious."

I smiled sheepishly. "Is it that obvious?"

"Not really."

She was probably lying to make me feel better.

"You don't have to talk about it unless you want to," she assured me. "I'll listen if you think it will help."

I was about to say *thanks, but no thanks*. After all, there were just too many secrets I was bound to keep. I really couldn't discuss my problems with someone human. That was against the rules.

And yet, with a strange, sudden intensity, that's exactly what I wanted. I wanted to talk to a normal human girlfriend. I wanted to moan a little bit, like any other teenage girl. I wanted my problems to be that simple. It would also be nice to have someone outside the whole vampire-werewolf mess to put things in perspective. Someone unbiased.

"I'll mind my own business," Angela promised, smiling down at the address she was working on.

"No," I said. "You're right. I am anxious. It's . . . it's Edward."

"What's wrong?"

It was so easy to talk to Angela. When she asked a question like that, I could tell that she wasn't just morbidly curious or looking for gossip, like Jessica would have been. She cared that I was upset.

"Oh, he's mad at me."

"That's hard to imagine," she said. "What's he mad about?"

I sighed. "Do you remember Jacob Black?"

"Ah," she said.

"Yeah."

"He's jealous."

"No, not *jealous* . . ." I should have kept my mouth shut. There was no way to explain this right. But I wanted to keep talking anyway. I hadn't realized I was so starved for human conversation. "Edward thinks Jacob is . . . a bad influence, I guess. Sort of . . . dangerous. You know how much trouble I got in a few months back. . . . It's all ridiculous, though."

I was surprised to see Angela shaking her head.

"What?" I asked.

"Bella, I've seen how Jacob Black looks at you. I'd bet the real problem is jealousy."

"It's not like that with Jacob."

"For you, maybe. But for Jacob . . ."

I frowned. "Jacob knows how I feel. I've told him everything."

"Edward's only human, Bella. He's going to react like any other boy."

I grimaced. I didn't have a response to that.

She patted my hand. "He'll get over it."

"I hope so. Jake's going through kind of a tough time. He needs me."

"You and Jacob are pretty close, aren't you?"

"Like family," I agreed.

"And Edward doesn't like him. . . . That must be hard. I wonder how Ben would handle that?" she mused.

I half-smiled. "Probably just like any other boy."

She grinned. "Probably."

Then she changed the subject. Angela wasn't one to pry, and she seemed to sense I wouldn't — couldn't — say any more.

"I got my dorm assignment yesterday. The farthest building from campus, naturally."

"Does Ben know where he's staying yet?"

"The closest dorm to campus. He's got all the luck. How about you? Did you decide where you're going?"

I stared down, concentrating on the clumsy scrawl of my handwriting. For a second I was distracted by the thought of Angela and Ben at the University of Washington. They would be off to Seattle in just a few months. Would it be safe then? Would the wild young vampire menace have moved elsewhere? Would there be a new place by then, some other city flinching from horror-movie headlines?

Would those new headlines be *my* fault?

I tried to shake it off and answered her question a beat late. "Alaska, I think. The university there in Juneau."

I could hear the surprise in her voice. "Alaska? Oh. Really? I mean, that's great. I just figured you'd go somewhere . . . warmer."

I laughed a little, still staring at the envelope. "Yeah. Forks has really changed my perspective on life."

"And Edward?"

Though his name set butterflies fluttering in my stomach, I looked up and grinned at her. "Alaska's not too cold for Edward, either."

She grinned back. "Of course not." And then she sighed. "It's so far. You won't be able to come home very often. I'll miss you. Will you e-mail me?"

A swell of quiet sadness crashed over me; maybe it was a mistake to get closer to Angela now. But wouldn't it be sadder still to miss out on these last chances? I shook off the unhappy thoughts, so that I could answer her teasingly.

"If I can type again after this." I nodded toward the stack of envelopes I'd done.

We laughed, and it was easy then to chat cheerfully about classes and majors while we finished the rest — all I had to do was not think about it. Anyway, there were more urgent things to worry about today.

I helped her put the stamps on, too. I was afraid to leave.

"How's your hand?" she asked.

I flexed my fingers. "I think I'll recover the full use of it . . . someday."

The door banged downstairs, and we both looked up.

"Ang?" Ben called.

I tried to smile, but my lips trembled. "I guess that's my cue to leave."

"You don't have to go. Though he's probably going to describe the movie for me . . . in detail."

"Charlie will be wondering where I am anyway."

"Thanks for helping me."

"I had a good time, actually. We should do something like this again. It was nice to have some girl time."

"Definitely."

There was a light knock on the bedroom door.

"Come in, Ben," Angela said.

I got up and stretched.

"Hey, Bella! You survived," Ben greeted me quickly before going to take my place by Angela. He eyed our work. "Nice job. Too bad there's nothing left to do, I would have . . ." He let the thought trail off, and then restarted excitedly. "Ang, I can't believe you missed this one! It was awesome. There was this final fight sequence — the choreography was unbelievable! This one guy — well, you're going to have to see it to know what I'm talking about —"

Angela rolled her eyes at me.

"See you at school," I said with a nervous laugh.

She sighed. "See you."

I was jumpy on the way out to my truck, but the street was empty. I spent the whole drive glancing anxiously in all my mirrors, but there was never any sign of the silver car.

His car was not in front of the house, either, though that meant little.

"Bella?" Charlie called when I opened the front door.

"Hey, Dad."

I found him in the living room, in front of the TV.

"So, how was your day?"

"Good," I said. Might as well tell him everything — he'd hear it from Billy soon enough. Besides, it would make him happy. "They didn't need me at work, so I went down to La Push."

There wasn't enough surprise in his face. Billy had already talked to him.

"How's Jacob?" Charlie asked, attempting to sound indifferent.

"Good," I said, just as casual.

"You get over to the Webers'?"

"Yep. We got all her announcements addressed."

"That's nice." Charlie smiled a wide smile. He was strangely focused, considering that there was a game on. "I'm glad you spent some time with your friends today."

"Me, too."

I ambled toward the kitchen, looking for busy work. Unfortunately, Charlie had already cleaned up his lunch. I stood there for a few minutes, staring at the bright patch of light the sun made on the floor. But I knew I couldn't delay this forever.

"I'm going to go study," I announced glumly as I headed up the stairs.

"See you later," Charlie called after me.

If I survive, I thought to myself.

I shut my bedroom door carefully before I turned to face my room.

Of course he was there. He stood against the wall across from me, in the shadow beside the open window. His face was hard and his posture tense. He glared at me wordlessly.

I cringed, waiting for the torrent, but it didn't come. He just continued to glare, possibly too angry to speak.

"Hi," I finally said.

His face could have been carved from stone. I counted to a hundred in my head, but there was no change.

"Er . . . so, I'm still alive," I began.

A growl rumbled low in his chest, but his expression didn't change.

"No harm done," I insisted with a shrug.

He moved. His eyes closed, and he pinched the bridge of his nose between the fingers of his right hand.

"Bella," he whispered. "Do you have *any* idea how close I came to crossing the line today? To breaking the treaty and coming after you? Do you know what that would have meant?"

I gasped and his eyes opened. They were as cold and hard as night.

"You can't!" I said too loudly. I worked to modulate the volume of my voice so Charlie wouldn't hear, but I wanted to shout the words. "Edward, they'd use any excuse for a fight. They'd love that. You can't ever break the rules!"

"Maybe they aren't the only ones who would enjoy a fight."

"Don't you start," I snapped. "You made the treaty — you stick to it."

"If he'd hurt you —"

"Enough!" I cut him off. "There's nothing to worry about. Jacob isn't dangerous."

"Bella." He rolled his eyes. "You aren't exactly the best judge of what is or isn't dangerous."

"I know I don't have to worry about Jake. And neither do you."

He ground his teeth together. His hands were balled up in fists at his sides. He was still standing against the wall, and I hated the space between us.

I took a deep breath, and crossed the room. He didn't move when I wrapped my arms around him. Next to the warmth of the last of the afternoon sun streaming through the window, his skin felt especially icy. He seemed like ice, too, frozen the way he was.

"I'm sorry I made you anxious," I muttered.

He sighed, and relaxed a little. His arms wound around my waist.

"*Anxious* is a bit of an understatement," he murmured. "It was a very long day."

"You weren't supposed to know about it," I reminded him. "I thought you'd be hunting longer."

I looked up at his face, at his defensive eyes; I hadn't noticed in the stress of the moment, but they were too dark. The rings under them were deep purple. I frowned in disapproval.

"When Alice saw you disappear, I came back," he explained.

"You shouldn't have done that. Now you'll have to go away again." My frown intensified.

"I can wait."

"That's ridiculous. I mean, I know she couldn't see me with Jacob, but you should have known —"

"But I didn't," he broke in. "And you can't expect me to let you —"

"Oh, yes, I can," I interrupted him. "That's exactly what I expect —"

"This won't happen again."

"That's right! Because you're not going to overreact next time."

"Because there isn't going to be a next time."

"I understand when you have to leave, even if I don't like it —"

"That's not the same. I'm not risking my life."

"Neither am I."

"Werewolves constitute a risk."

"I disagree."

"I'm not negotiating this, Bella."

"Neither am I."

His hands were in fists again. I could feel them against my back.

The words popped out thoughtlessly. "Is this really just about my safety?"

"What do you mean?" he demanded.

"You aren't . . ." Angela's theory seemed sillier now than before. It was hard to finish the thought. "I mean, you know better than to be jealous, right?"

He raised one eyebrow. "Do I?"

"Be serious."

"Easily — there's nothing remotely humorous about this."

I frowned suspiciously. "Or . . . is this something else altogether? Some vampires-and-werewolves-are-always-enemies nonsense? Is this just a testosterone-fueled —"

His eyes blazed. "This is *only* about you. All I care is that you're safe."

The black fire in his eyes was impossible to doubt.

"Okay," I sighed. "I believe that. But I want you to know something — when it comes to all this *enemies* nonsense, I'm out. I am a neutral country. I am Switzerland. I refuse to be affected by territorial disputes between mythical creatures. Jacob is family. You are . . . well, not exactly the love of my life, because I expect to love you for much longer than that. The love of my existence. I don't care who's a werewolf and who's a vampire. If Angela turns out to be a witch, she can join the party, too."

He stared at me silently through narrowed eyes.

"Switzerland," I repeated again for emphasis.

He frowned at me, and then sighed. "Bella . . . ," he began, but he paused, and his nose wrinkled in disgust.

"What now?"

"Well . . . don't be offended, but you smell like a dog," he told me.

And then he smiled crookedly, so I knew the fight was over. For now.

Edward had to make up for the missed hunting trip, and so he was leaving Friday night with Jasper, Emmett, and Carlisle to hit some reserve in Northern California with a mountain lion problem.

We'd come to no agreement on the werewolf issue, but I didn't feel guilty calling Jake — during my brief window of opportunity when Edward took the Volvo home before climbing back in through my window — to let him know I'd be coming over on Saturday again. It wasn't sneaking around. Edward knew how I felt. And if he broke my truck again, then I'd have Jacob pick me up. Forks was neutral, just like Switzerland — just like me.

So when I got off work Thursday and it was Alice rather than Edward waiting for me in the Volvo, I was not suspicious at first. The passenger door was open, and music I didn't recognize was shaking the frame when the bass played.

"Hey, Alice," I shouted over the wailing as I climbed in. "Where's your brother?"

She was singing along to the song, her voice an octave higher than the melody, weaving through it with a complicated harmony. She nodded at me, ignoring my question as she concentrated on the music.

I shut my door and put my hands over my ears. She grinned, and turned the volume down until it was just background. Then she hit the locks and the gas in the same second.

"What's going on?" I asked, starting to feel uneasy. "Where is Edward?"

She shrugged. "They left early."

"Oh." I tried to control the absurd disappointment. If he left early, that meant he'd be back sooner, I reminded myself.

"All the boys went, and we're having a slumber party!" she announced in a trilling, singsong voice.

"A slumber party?" I repeated, the suspicion finally settling in.

"Aren't you excited?" she crowed.

I met her animated gaze for a long second.

"You're kidnapping me, aren't you?"

She laughed and nodded. "Till Saturday. Esme cleared it with Charlie; you're staying with me two nights, and I will drive you to and from school tomorrow."

I turned my face to the window, my teeth grinding together.

"Sorry," Alice said, not sounding in the least bit penitent. "He paid me off."

"How?" I hissed through my teeth.

"The Porsche. It's exactly like the one I stole in Italy." She sighed happily. "I'm not supposed to drive it around Forks, but if you want, we could see how long it takes to get from here to L.A. — I bet I could have you back by midnight."

I took a deep breath. "I think I'll pass," I sighed, repressing a shudder.

We wound, always too fast, down the long drive. Alice pulled around to the garage, and I quickly looked over the cars. Emmett's big jeep was there, with a shiny canary yellow Porsche between it and Rosalie's red convertible.

Alice hopped out gracefully and went to stroke her hand along the length of her bribe. "Pretty, isn't it?"

"Pretty over-the-top," I grumbled, incredulous. "He gave you *that* just for two days of holding me hostage?"

Alice made a face.

A second later, comprehension came and I gasped in horror. "It's for every time he's gone, isn't it?"

She nodded.

I slammed my door and stomped toward the house. She danced along next to me, still unrepentant.

"Alice, don't you think this is just a little bit controlling? Just a tiny bit psychotic, maybe?"

"Not really." She sniffed. "You don't seem to grasp how dangerous a young werewolf can be. Especially when I can't see them. Edward has no way to know if you're safe. You shouldn't be so reckless."

My voice turned acidic. "Yes, because a vampire slumber party is the pinnacle of safety conscious behavior."

Alice laughed. "I'll give you a pedicure and everything," she promised.

It wasn't so bad, except for the fact that I was being

held against my will. Esme brought Italian food — the good stuff, all the way from Port Angeles — and Alice was prepared with my favorite movies. Even Rosalie was there, quietly in the background. Alice did insist on the pedicure, and I wondered if she was working from a list — maybe something she'd compiled from watching bad sitcoms.

"How late do you want to stay up?" she asked when my toenails were glistening a bloody red. Her enthusiasm remained untouched by my mood.

"I don't want to stay up. We have school in the morning."

She pouted.

"Where am I supposed to sleep, anyway?" I measured the couch with my eyes. It was a little short. "Can't you just keep me under surveillance at my house?"

"What kind of a slumber party would that be?" Alice shook her head in exasperation. "You're sleeping in Edward's room."

I sighed. His black leather sofa *was* longer than this one. Actually, the gold carpet in his room was probably thick enough that the floor wouldn't be half bad either.

"Can I go back to my place to get my things, at least?"

She grinned. "Already taken care of."

"Am I allowed to use your phone?"

"Charlie knows where you are."

"I wasn't going to call Charlie." I frowned. "Apparently, I have some plans to cancel."

"Oh." She deliberated. "I'm not sure about that."

"Alice!" I whined loudly. "C'mon!"

"Okay, okay," she said, flitting from the room. She was

back in half a second, cell phone in hand. "He didn't *specifically* prohibit this . . . ," she murmured to herself as she handed it to me.

I dialed Jacob's number, hoping he wasn't out running with his friends tonight. Luck was with me — Jacob was the one to answer.

"Hello?"

"Hey, Jake, it's me." Alice watched me with expressionless eyes for a second, before she turned and went to sit between Rosalie and Esme on the sofa.

"Hi, Bella," Jacob said, suddenly cautious. "What's up?"

"Nothing good. I can't come over Saturday after all."

It was silent for a minute. "Stupid bloodsucker," he finally muttered. "I thought he was leaving. Can't you have a life when he's gone? Or does he lock you in a coffin?"

I laughed.

"I don't think that's funny."

"I'm only laughing because you're close," I told him. "But he's going to be here Saturday, so it doesn't matter."

"Will he be feeding there in Forks, then?" Jacob asked cuttingly.

"No." I didn't let myself get irritated with him. I wasn't that far from being as angry as he was. "He left early."

"Oh. Well, hey, come over now, then," he said with sudden enthusiasm. "It's not that late. Or I'll come up to Charlie's."

"I wish. I'm not at Charlie's," I said sourly. "I'm kind of being held prisoner."

He was silent as that sunk in, and then he growled.

"We'll come and get you," he promised in a flat voice, slipping automatically into a plural.

A chill slid down my spine, but I answered in a light and teasing voice. "Tempting. I *have* been tortured — Alice painted my toenails."

"I'm serious."

"Don't be. They're just trying to keep me safe."

He growled again.

"I know it's silly, but their hearts are in the right place."

"Their *hearts*!" he scoffed.

"Sorry about Saturday," I apologized. "I've got to hit the sack" — the couch, I corrected mentally — "but I'll call you again soon."

"Are you sure they'll let you?" he asked in a scathing tone.

"Not completely." I sighed. "'Night, Jake."

"See you around."

Alice was abruptly at my side, her hand held out for the phone, but I was already dialing. She saw the number.

"I don't think he'll have his phone on him," she said.

"I'll leave a message."

The phone rang four times, followed by a beep. There was no greeting.

"You are in trouble," I said slowly, emphasizing each word. "Enormous trouble. Angry grizzly bears are going to look tame next to what is waiting for you at home."

I snapped the phone shut and placed it in her waiting hand. "I'm done."

She grinned. "This hostage stuff is fun."

"I'm going to sleep now," I announced, heading for the stairs. Alice tagged along.

"Alice," I sighed. "I'm not going to sneak out. You would know if I was planning to, and you'd catch me if I tried."

"I'm just going to show you where your things are," she said innocently.

Edward's room was at the farthest end of the third floor hallway, hard to mistake even when the huge house had been less familiar. But when I switched the light on, I paused in confusion. Had I picked the wrong door?

Alice giggled.

It was the same room, I realized quickly; the furniture had just been rearranged. The couch was pushed to the north wall and the stereo shoved up against the vast shelves of CDs — to make room for the colossal bed that now dominated the central space.

The southern wall of glass reflected the scene back like a mirror, making it look twice as bad.

It matched. The coverlet was a dull gold, just lighter than the walls; the frame was black, made of intricately patterned wrought iron. Sculpted metal roses wound in vines up the tall posts and formed a bowery lattice overhead. My pajamas were folded neatly on the foot of the bed, my bag of toiletries to one side.

"What the hell is all this?" I spluttered.

"You didn't really think he would make you sleep on the couch, did you?"

I mumbled unintelligibly as I stalked forward to snatch my things off the bed.

"I'll give you some privacy," Alice laughed. "See you in the morning."

After my teeth were brushed and I was dressed, I grabbed a puffy feather pillow off the huge bed and dragged the gold cover to the couch. I knew I was being silly, but I didn't care. Porsches as bribes and king-sized beds in houses where nobody slept — it was beyond irritating. I flipped off the lights and curled up on the sofa, wondering if I was too annoyed to sleep.

In the dark, the glass wall was no longer a black mirror, doubling the room. The light of the moon brightened the clouds outside the window. As my eyes adjusted, I could see the diffused glow highlighting the tops of the trees, and glinting off a small slice of the river. I watched the silver light, waiting for my eyes to get heavy.

There was a light knock on the door.

"What, Alice?" I hissed. I was on the defensive, imagining her amusement when she saw my makeshift bed.

"It's me," Rosalie said softly, opening the door enough that I could see the silver glow touch her perfect face. "Can I come in?"

7. UNHAPPY ENDING

ROSALIE HESITATED IN THE DOORWAY, HER BREATHTAK-
ing face unsure.

"Of course," I replied, my voice an octave high with
surprise. "Come on in."

I sat up, sliding to the end of the sofa to make room.
My stomach twisted nervously as the one Cullen who did
not like me moved silently to sit down in the open space.
I tried to come up with a reason why she would want to
see me, but my mind was a blank on that point.

"Do you mind talking to me for a few minutes?" she
asked. "I didn't wake you or anything, did I?" Her eyes
shifted to the stripped bed and back to my couch.

"No, I was awake. Sure, we can talk." I wondered if she could hear the alarm in my voice as clearly as I could.

She laughed lightly, and it sounded like a chorus of bells. "He so rarely leaves you alone," she said. "I figured I'd better make the best of this opportunity."

What did she want to say that couldn't be said in front of Edward? My hands twisted and untwisted around the edge of the comforter.

"Please don't think I'm horribly interfering," Rosalie said, her voice gentle and almost pleading. She folded her hands in her lap and looked down at them as she spoke. "I'm sure I've hurt your feelings enough in the past, and I don't want to do that again."

"Don't worry about it, Rosalie. My feelings are great. What is it?"

She laughed again, sounding oddly embarrassed. "I'm going to try to tell you why I think you should stay human — why I would stay human if I were you."

"Oh."

She smiled at the shocked tone of my voice, and then she sighed.

"Did Edward ever tell you what led to this?" she asked, gesturing to her glorious immortal body.

I nodded slowly, suddenly somber. "He said it was close to what happened to me that time in Port Angeles, only no one was there to save *you*." I shuddered at the memory.

"Is that really all he told you?" she asked.

"Yes," I said, my voice blank with confusion. "Was there more?"

She looked up at me and smiled; it was a harsh, bitter — but still stunning — expression.

"Yes," she said. "There was more."

I waited while she stared out the window. She seemed to be trying to calm herself.

"Would you like to hear my story, Bella? It doesn't have a happy ending — but which of ours does? If we had happy endings, we'd all be under gravestones now."

I nodded, though I was frightened by the edge in her voice.

"I lived in a different world than you do, Bella. My human world was a much simpler place. It was nineteen thirty-three. I was eighteen, and I was beautiful. My life was perfect."

She stared out the window at the silver clouds, her expression far away.

"My parents were thoroughly middle class. My father had a stable job in a bank, something I realize now that he was smug about — he saw his prosperity as a reward for talent and hard work, rather than acknowledging the luck involved. I took it all for granted then; in my home, it was as if the Great Depression was only a troublesome rumor. Of course I saw the poor people, the ones who weren't as lucky. My father left me with the impression that they'd brought their troubles on themselves.

"It was my mother's job to keep our house — and myself and my two younger brothers — in spotless order. It was clear that I was both her first priority and her favorite. I didn't fully understand at the time, but I was always vaguely aware that my parents weren't satisfied with what they had, even if it was so much more than most. They wanted more. They had social aspirations — social climbers, I suppose you could call them. My beauty was like a gift to them. They saw so much more potential in it than I did.

"They weren't satisfied, but *I* was. I was thrilled to be me, to be Rosalie Hale. Pleased that men's eyes watched me everywhere I went, from the year I turned twelve. Delighted that my girlfriends sighed with envy when they touched my hair. Happy that my mother was proud of me and that my father liked to buy me pretty dresses.

"I knew what I wanted out of life, and there didn't seem to be any way that I wouldn't get exactly what I wanted. I wanted to be loved, to be adored. I wanted to have a huge, flowery wedding, where everyone in town would watch me walk down the aisle on my father's arm and think I was the most beautiful thing they'd ever seen. Admiration was like air to me, Bella. I was silly and shallow, but I was content." She smiled, amused at her own evaluation.

"My parents' influence had been such that I also wanted the material things of life. I wanted a big house with elegant furnishings that someone else would clean and a modern kitchen that someone else would cook in. As I said, shallow. Young and very shallow. And I didn't see any reason why I wouldn't get these things.

"There were a few things I wanted that were more meaningful. One thing in particular. My very closest friend was a girl named Vera. She married young, just seventeen. She married a man my parents would never have considered for me — a carpenter. A year later she had a son, a beautiful little boy with dimples and curly black hair. It was the first time I'd ever felt truly jealous of anyone else in my entire life."

She looked at me with unfathomable eyes. "It was a different time. I was the same age as you, but I was ready for it all. I yearned for my own little baby. I wanted my own house and a husband who would kiss me when he got home from work — just like Vera. Only I had a very different kind of house in mind. . . ."

It was hard for me to imagine the world that Rosalie had known. Her story sounded more like a fairy tale than history to me. With a slight shock, I realized that this was very close to the world that Edward would have experienced when he was human, the world he had grown up in. I wondered — while Rosalie sat silent for a moment — if my world seemed as baffling to him as Rosalie's did to me?

Rosalie sighed, and when she spoke again her voice was different, the wistfulness gone.

"In Rochester, there was one royal family — the Kings, ironically enough. Royce King owned the bank my father worked at, and nearly every other really profitable business in town. That's how his son, Royce King the Second" — her mouth twisted around the name, it came out through her teeth — "saw me the first time. He was going to take over at the bank, and so he began overseeing the different positions. Two days later, my mother conveniently forgot to send my father's lunch to work with him. I remember being confused when she insisted that I wear my white organza and roll my hair up just to run over to the bank." Rosalie laughed without humor.

"I didn't notice Royce watching me particularly. Everyone watched me. But that night the first of the roses came. Every night of our courtship, he sent a bouquet of roses to me. My room was always overflowing with them. It got to the point that I would smell like roses when I left the house.

"Royce was handsome, too. He had lighter hair than I did, and pale blue eyes. He said my eyes were like violets, and then those started showing up alongside the roses.

"My parents approved — that's putting it mildly. This was everything they'd dreamed of. And Royce seemed to be everything *I'd* dreamed of. The fairy tale prince, come to make me a princess. Everything I wanted, yet it was still no more than I expected. We were engaged before I'd known him for two months.

"We didn't spend a great deal of time alone with each other. Royce told me he had many responsibilities at work, and, when we were together, he liked people to look at us, to see me on his arm. I liked that, too. There were lots of parties, dancing, and pretty dresses. When you were a King, every door was open for you, every red carpet rolled out to greet you.

"It wasn't a long engagement. Plans went ahead for the most lavish wedding. It was going to be everything I'd ever wanted. I was completely happy. When I called at Vera's, I no longer felt jealous. I pictured my fair-haired children playing on the huge lawns of the Kings' estate, and I pitied her."

Rosalie broke off suddenly, clenching her teeth together. It pulled me out of her story, and I realized that the horror was not far off. There would be no happy ending, as she'd promised. I wondered if this was why she had so much more bitterness in her than the rest of them — because she'd been within reach of everything she'd wanted when her human life was cut short.

"I was at Vera's that night," Rosalie whispered. Her face was smooth as marble, and as hard. "Her little Henry really was adorable, all smiles and dimples — he was just sitting up on his own. Vera walked me to the door as I was leaving, her baby in her arms and her husband at her side, his arm around her waist. He kissed her on the cheek when he thought I wasn't looking. That bothered me. When Royce kissed me, it wasn't quite the same — not so sweet somehow. . . . I shoved that thought aside. Royce was my prince. Someday, I would be queen."

It was hard to tell in the moonlight, but it looked like her bone white face got paler.

"It was dark in the streets, the lamps already on. I hadn't realized how late it was." She continued to whisper almost inaudibly. "It was cold, too. Very cold for late April. The wedding was only a week away, and I was worrying about the weather as I hurried home — I can remember that clearly. I remember every detail about that night. I clung to it so hard . . . in the beginning. I thought of nothing else. And so I remember this, when so many pleasant memories have faded away completely. . . ."

She sighed, and began whispering again. "Yes, I was

worrying about the weather. . . . I didn't want to have to move the wedding indoors. . . .

"I was a few streets from my house when I heard them. A cluster of men under a broken streetlamp, laughing too loud. Drunk. I wished I'd called my father to escort me home, but the way was so short, it seemed silly. And then he called my name.

"'Rose!' he yelled, and the others laughed stupidly.

"I hadn't realized the drunks were so well dressed. It was Royce and some of his friends, sons of other rich men.

"'Here's my Rose!' Royce shouted, laughing with them, sounding just as stupid. 'You're late. We're cold, you've kept us waiting so long.'"

"I'd never seen him drink before. A toast, now and then, at a party. He'd told me he didn't like champagne. I hadn't realized that he preferred something much stronger.

"He had a new friend — the friend of a friend, come up from Atlanta.

"'What did I tell you, John,' Royce crowed, grabbing my arm and pulling me closer. 'Isn't she lovelier than all your Georgia peaches?'

"The man named John was dark-haired and suntanned. He looked me over like I was a horse he was buying.

"'It's hard to tell,' he drawled slowly. 'She's all covered up.'

"They laughed, Royce like the rest.

"Suddenly, Royce ripped my jacket from my shoulders — it was a gift from him — popping the brass buttons off. They scattered all over the street.

"'Show him what you look like, Rose!' He laughed again and then he tore my hat out of my hair. The pins wrenched my hair from the roots, and I cried out in pain. They seemed to enjoy that — the sound of my pain. . . ."

Rosalie looked at me suddenly, as if she'd forgotten I was there. I was sure my face was as white as hers. Unless it was green.

"I won't make you listen to the rest," she said quietly. "They left me in the street, still laughing as they stumbled away. They thought I was dead. They were teasing Royce that he would have to find a new bride. He laughed and said he'd have to learn some patience first.

"I waited in the road to die. It was cold, though there was so much pain that I was surprised it bothered me. It started to snow, and I wondered why I wasn't dying. I was impatient for death to come, to end the pain. It was taking so long. . . .

"Carlisle found me then. He'd smelled the blood, and come to investigate. I remember being vaguely irritated as he worked over me, trying to save my life. I'd never liked Dr. Cullen or his wife and her brother — as Edward pretended to be then. It had upset me that they were all more beautiful than I was, especially that the men were. But they didn't mingle in society, so I'd only seen them once or twice.

"I thought I'd died when he pulled me from the ground and ran with me — because of the speed — it felt like I was flying. I remembered being horrified that the pain didn't stop. . . .

"Then I was in a bright room, and it was warm. I was

slipping away, and I was grateful as the pain began to dull. But suddenly something sharp was cutting me, my throat, my wrists, my ankles. I screamed in shock, thinking he'd brought me there to hurt me more. Then fire started burning through me, and I didn't care about anything else. I begged him to kill me. When Esme and Edward returned home, I begged them to kill me, too. Carlisle sat with me. He held my hand and said that he was so sorry, promising that it would end. He told me everything, and sometimes I listened. He told me what he was, what I was becoming. I didn't believe him. He apologized each time I screamed.

"Edward wasn't happy. I remember hearing them discuss me. I stopped screaming sometimes. It did no good to scream.

"'What were you thinking, Carlisle?' Edward said. 'Rosalie Hale?'" Rosalie imitated Edward's irritated tone to perfection. "I didn't like the way he said my name, like there was something wrong with me.

"'I couldn't just let her die,' Carlisle said quietly. 'It was too much — too horrible, too much waste.'

"'I know,' Edward said, and I thought he sounded dismissive. It angered me. I didn't know then that he really could see exactly what Carlisle had seen.

"'It was too much waste. I couldn't leave her,' Carlisle repeated in a whisper.

"'Of course you couldn't,' Esme agreed.

"'People die all the time,' Edward reminded him in a hard voice. 'Don't you think she's just a little recognizable, though? The Kings will have to put up a huge search — not that anyone suspects the fiend,' he growled.

"It pleased me that they seemed to know that Royce was guilty.

"I didn't realize that it was almost over — that I was getting stronger and that was why I was able to concentrate on what they were saying. The pain was beginning to fade from my fingertips.

"'What are we going to do with her?' Edward said disgustedly — or that's how it sounded to me, at least.

"Carlisle sighed. 'That's up to her, of course. She may want to go her own way.'

"I'd believed enough of what he'd told me that his words terrified me. I knew that my life was ended, and there was no going back for me. I couldn't stand the thought of being alone. . . .

"The pain finally ended and they explained to me again what I was. This time I believed. I felt the thirst, my hard skin; I saw my brilliant red eyes.

"Shallow as I was, I felt better when I saw my reflection in the mirror the first time. Despite the eyes, I was the most beautiful thing I'd ever seen." She laughed at herself for a moment. "It took some time before I began to blame the beauty for what had happened to me — for me to see the curse of it. To wish that I had been . . . well, not ugly, but normal. Like Vera. So I could have been allowed to marry someone who loved *me,* and have pretty babies. That's what I'd really wanted, all along. It still doesn't seem like too much to have asked for."

She was thoughtful for a moment, and I wondered if she'd forgotten my presence again. But then she smiled at me, her expression suddenly triumphant.

"You know, my record is almost as clean as Carlisle's," she told me. "Better than Esme. A thousand times better than Edward. I've never tasted human blood," she announced proudly.

She understood my puzzled expression as I wondered why her record was only *almost* as clean.

"I did murder five humans," she told me in a complacent tone. "If you can really call them *human*. But I was very careful not to spill their blood — I knew I wouldn't be able to resist that, and I didn't want any part of them *in* me, you see.

"I saved Royce for last. I hoped that he would hear of his friends' deaths and understand, know what was coming for him. I hoped the fear would make the end worse for him. I think it worked. He was hiding inside a windowless room behind a door as thick as a bank vault's, guarded outside by armed men, when I caught up with him. Oops — seven murders," she corrected herself. "I forgot about his guards. They only took a second."

"I was overly theatrical. It was kind of childish, really. I wore a wedding dress I'd stolen for the occasion. He screamed when he saw me. He screamed a lot that night. Saving him for last was a good idea — it made it easier for me to control myself, to make it slower —"

She broke off suddenly, and she glanced down at me. "I'm sorry," she said in a chagrined voice. "I'm frightening you, aren't I?"

"I'm fine," I lied.

"I got carried away."

"Don't worry about it."

"I'm surprised Edward didn't tell you more about it."

"He doesn't like to tell other people's stories — he feels like he's betraying confidences, because he hears so much more than just the parts they mean for him to hear."

She smiled and shook her head. "I probably ought to give him more credit. He's really quite decent, isn't he?"

"*I* think so."

"I can tell." Then she sighed. "I haven't been fair to you, either, Bella. Did he tell you why? Or was that too confidential?"

"He said it was because I was human. He said it was harder for you to have someone on the outside who knew."

Rosalie's musical laughter interrupted me. "Now I really feel guilty. He's been much, much kinder to me than I deserve." She seemed warmer as she laughed, like she'd let down some guard that had never been absent in my presence before. "What a liar that boy is." She laughed again.

"He was lying?" I asked, suddenly wary.

"Well, that's probably putting it too strongly. He just didn't tell you the whole story. What he told you was true, even truer now than it was before. However, at the time . . ." She broke off, chuckling nervously. "It's embarrassing. You see, at first, I was mostly jealous because he wanted *you* and not me."

Her words sent a thrill of fear through me. Sitting there in the silver light, she was more beautiful than anything else I could imagine. I could not compete with Rosalie.

"But you love Emmett . . . ," I mumbled.

She shook her head back and forth, amused. "I don't

want Edward that way, Bella. I never did — I love him as a brother, but he's irritated me from the first moment I heard him speak. You have to understand, though . . . I was so used to people wanting *me*. And Edward wasn't the least bit interested. It frustrated me, even offended me in the beginning. But he never wanted anyone, so it didn't bother me long. Even when we first met Tanya's clan in Denali — all those females! — Edward never showed the slightest preference. And then he met you." She looked at me with confused eyes. I was only half paying attention. I was thinking about Edward and Tanya and *all those females,* and my lips pressed together in a hard line.

"Not that you aren't pretty, Bella," she said, misreading my expression. "But it just meant that he found you more attractive than me. I'm vain enough that I minded."

"But you said 'at first.' That doesn't still . . . bother you, does it? I mean, we both know you're the most beautiful person on the planet."

I laughed at having to say the words — it was so obvious. How odd that Rosalie should need such reassurances.

Rosalie laughed, too. "Thanks, Bella. And no, it doesn't really bother me anymore. Edward has always been a little strange." She laughed again.

"But you still don't like me," I whispered.

Her smile faded. "I'm sorry about that."

We sat in silence for a moment, and she didn't seem inclined to go on.

"Would you tell me why? Did I do something . . . ?" Was she angry that I'd put her family — her Emmett —

in danger? Time and time again. James, and now Victoria . . .

"No, you haven't done anything," she murmured. "Not yet."

I stared at her, perplexed.

"Don't you see, Bella?" Her voice was suddenly more passionate than before, even while she'd told her unhappy story. "You already have *everything*. You have a whole life ahead of you — everything I want. And you're going to just *throw it away*. Can't you see that I'd trade everything I have to be you? You have the choice that I didn't have, and you're choosing *wrong*!"

I flinched back from her fierce expression. I realized my mouth had fallen open and I snapped it shut.

She stared at me for a long moment and, slowly, the fervor in her eyes dimmed. Abruptly, she was abashed.

"And I was so sure that I could do this calmly." She shook her head, seeming a little dazed by the flood of emotion. "It's just that it's harder now than it was then, when it was no more than vanity."

She stared at the moon in silence. It was a few moments before I was brave enough to break into her reverie.

"Would you like me better if I chose to stay human?"

She turned back to me, her lips twitching into a hint of a smile. "Maybe."

"You did get some of your happy ending, though," I reminded her. "You got Emmett."

"I got half." She grinned. "You know that I saved Emmett from a bear that was mauling him, and carried him home to Carlisle. But can you guess why I stopped the bear from eating him?"

I shook my head.

"With the dark curls . . . the dimples that showed even while he was grimacing in pain . . . the strange innocence that seemed so out of place on a grown man's face . . . he reminded me of Vera's little Henry. I didn't want him to die — so much that, even though I hated this life, I was selfish enough to ask Carlisle to change him for me.

"I got luckier than I deserved. Emmett is everything I would have asked for if I'd known myself well enough to know what to ask for. He's exactly the kind of person someone like me needs. And, oddly enough, he needs me, too. That part worked out better than I could have hoped. But there will never be more than the two of us. And I'll never sit on a porch somewhere, with him gray-haired by my side, surrounded by our grandchildren."

Her smile was kind now. "That sounds quite bizarre to you, doesn't it? In some ways, you are much more mature than I was at eighteen. But in other ways . . . there are many things you've probably never thought about seriously. You're too young to know what you'll want in ten years, fifteen years — and too young to give it all up without thinking it through. You don't want to be rash about permanent things, Bella." She patted my head, but the gesture didn't feel condescending.

I sighed.

"Just think about it a little. Once it's done, it can't be undone. Esme's made do with us as substitutes . . . and

Alice doesn't remember anything human so she can't miss it. . . . You will remember, though. It's a lot to give up."

But more to get in return, I didn't say aloud. "Thanks, Rosalie. It's nice to understand . . . to know you better."

"I apologize for being such a monster." She grinned. "I'll try to behave myself from now on."

I grinned back at her.

We weren't friends yet, but I was pretty sure she wouldn't always hate me so much.

"I'll let you sleep now." Rosalie's eyes flickered to the bed, and her lips twitched. "I know you're frustrated that he's keeping you locked up like this, but don't give him too bad a time when he gets back. He loves you more than you know. It terrifies him to be away from you." She got up silently and ghosted to the door. "Goodnight, Bella," she whispered as she shut it behind herself.

"Goodnight, Rosalie," I murmured a second too late.

It took me a long time to fall asleep after that.

When I did sleep, I had a nightmare. I was crawling across the dark, cold stones of an unfamiliar street, under lightly falling snow, leaving a trail of blood smeared behind me. A shadowy angel in a long white dress watched my progress with resentful eyes.

The next morning, Alice drove me to school while I stared grumpily out the windshield. I was feeling sleep-deprived, and it made the irritation of my imprisonment that much stronger.

"Tonight we'll go out to Olympia or something," she promised. "That would be fun, right?"

"Why don't you just lock me in the basement," I suggested, "and forget the sugar coating?"

Alice frowned. "He's going to take the Porsche back. I'm not doing a very good job. You're supposed to be having fun."

"It's not your fault," I muttered. I couldn't believe I actually felt guilty. "I'll see you at lunch."

I trudged off to English. Without Edward, the day was guaranteed to be unbearable. I sulked through my first class, well aware that my attitude wasn't helping anything.

When the bell rang, I got up without much enthusiasm. Mike was there at the door, holding it open for me.

"Edward hiking this weekend?" he asked sociably as we walked out into the light rain.

"Yeah."

"You want to do something tonight?"

How could he still sound hopeful?

"Can't. I've got a slumber party," I grumbled. He gave me a strange look as he processed my mood.

"Who are you —"

Mike's question was cut short as a loud, growling roar erupted from behind us in the parking lot. Everyone on the sidewalk turned to look, staring in disbelief as the noisy black motorcycle screeched to a stop on the edge of the concrete, the engine still snarling.

Jacob waved to me urgently.

"Run, Bella!" he yelled over the engine's roar.

I was frozen for a second before I understood.

I looked at Mike quickly. I knew I only had seconds. How far would Alice go to restrain me in public?

"I got really sick and went home, okay?" I said to Mike, my voice filled with sudden excitement.

"Fine," he muttered.

I pecked Mike swiftly on the cheek. "Thanks, Mike. I owe you one!" I called as I sprinted away.

Jacob revved his engine, grinning. I jumped on the back of his seat, wrapping my arms tightly around his waist.

I caught sight of Alice, frozen at the edge of the cafeteria, her eyes sparking with fury, her lip curled back over her teeth.

I shot her one pleading glance.

Then we were racing across the blacktop so fast that my stomach got lost somewhere behind me.

"Hold on," Jacob shouted.

I hid my face in his back as he sped down the highway. I knew he would slow down when we hit the Quileute border. I just had to hold on till then. I prayed silently and fervently that Alice wouldn't follow, and that Charlie wouldn't happen to see me. . . .

It was obvious when we had reached the safe zone. The bike slowed, and Jacob straightened up and howled with laughter. I opened my eyes.

"We made it," he shouted. "Not bad for a prison break, eh?"

"Good thinking, Jake."

"I remembered what you said about the psychic leech not being about to predict what *I'm* going to do. I'm glad *you* didn't think of this — she wouldn't have let you go to school."

"That's why I didn't consider it."

He laughed triumphantly. "What do you want to do today?"

"Anything!" I laughed back. It felt great to be free.

8. TEMPER

W<small>E ENDED UP ON THE BEACH AGAIN, WANDERING AIM</small>-lessly. Jacob was still full of himself for engineering my escape.

"Do you think they'll come looking for you?" he asked, sounding hopeful.

"No." I was certain about that. "They're going to be furious with me tonight, though."

He picked up a rock and chucked it into the waves. "Don't go back, then," he suggested again.

"Charlie would love that," I said sarcastically.

"I bet he wouldn't mind."

I didn't answer. Jacob was probably right, and that

made me grind my teeth together. Charlie's blatant preference for my Quileute friends was so unfair. I wondered if he would feel the same if he knew the choice was really between vampires and werewolves.

"So what's the latest pack scandal?" I asked lightly.

Jacob skidded to a halt, and he stared down at me with shocked eyes.

"What? That was a joke."

"Oh." He looked away.

I waited for him to start walking again, but he seemed lost in thought.

"*Is* there a scandal?" I wondered.

Jacob chuckled once. "I forget what it's like, not having everyone know everything all the time. Having a quiet, private place inside my head."

We walked along the stony beach quietly for a few minutes.

"So what is it?" I finally asked. "That everyone in your head already knows?"

He hesitated for a moment, as if he weren't sure how much he was going to tell me. Then he sighed and said, "Quil imprinted. That's three now. The rest of us are starting to get worried. Maybe it's more common than the stories say. . . ." He frowned, and then turned to stare at me. He gazed into my eyes without speaking, his eyebrows furrowed in concentration.

"What are you staring at?" I asked, feeling self-conscious.

He sighed. "Nothing."

Jacob started walking again. Without seeming to think

about it, he reached out and took my hand. We paced silently across the rocks.

I thought of how we must look walking hand and hand down the beach — like a couple, certainly — and wondered if I should object. But this was the way it had always been with Jacob. . . . No reason to get worked up about it now.

"Why is Quil's imprinting such a scandal?" I asked when it didn't look like he was going to go on. "Is it because he's the newest one?"

"That doesn't have anything to do with it."

"Then what's the problem?"

"It's another one of those legend things. I wonder when we're going to stop being surprised that they're *all* true?" he muttered to himself.

"Are you going to tell me? Or do I have to guess?"

"You'd never get it right. See, Quil hasn't been hanging out with us, you know, until just recently. So he hadn't been around Emily's place much."

"Quil imprinted on Emily, too?" I gasped.

"No! I told you not to guess. Emily had her two nieces down for a visit . . . and Quil met Claire."

He didn't continue. I thought about that for a moment.

"Emily doesn't want her niece with a werewolf? That's a little hypocritical," I said.

But I could understand why she of all people might feel that way. I thought again of the long scars that marred her face and extended all the way down her right arm. Sam had lost control just once when he was standing too close to her. Once was all it took. . . . I'd seen the pain in Sam's eyes when he looked at what he'd done to Emily. I could understand why Emily might want to protect her niece from that.

"Would you please stop guessing? You're way off. Emily doesn't mind that part, it's just, well, a little early."

"What do you mean *early*?"

Jacob appraised me with narrowed eyes. "Try not to be judgmental, okay?"

I nodded cautiously.

"Claire is two," Jacob told me.

Rain started to fall. I blinked furiously as the drops pelted my face.

Jacob waited in silence. He wore no jacket, as usual; the rain left a spatter of dark spots on his black T-shirt, and dripped through his shaggy hair. His face was expressionless as he watched mine.

"Quil . . . imprinted . . . with a *two-year-old*?" I was finally able to ask.

"It happens." Jacob shrugged. He bent to grab another rock and sent it flying out into the bay. "Or so the stories say."

"But she's a baby," I protested.

He looked at me with dark amusement. "Quil's not getting any older," he reminded me, a bit of acid in his tone. "He'll just have to be patient for a few decades."

"I . . . don't know what to say."

I was trying my hardest not to be critical, but, in truth, I was horrified. Until now, nothing about the werewolves had bothered me since the day I'd found out they weren't committing the murders I'd suspected them of.

"You're making judgments," he accused. "I can see it on your face."

"Sorry," I muttered. "But it sounds really creepy."

"It's not like that; you've got it all wrong," Jacob defended his friend, suddenly vehement. "I've seen what it's like, through his eyes. There's nothing *romantic* about it at all, not for Quil, not now." He took a deep breath, frustrated. "It's so hard to describe. It's not like love at first sight, really. It's more like . . . gravity moves. When you see *her,* suddenly it's not the earth holding you here anymore. She does. And nothing matters more than her. And you would do anything for her, be anything for her. . . . You become whatever she needs you to be, whether that's a protector, or a lover, or a friend, or a brother.

"Quil will be the best, kindest big brother any kid ever had. There isn't a toddler on the planet that will be more carefully looked after than that little girl will be. And then, when she's older and needs a friend, he'll be more understanding, trustworthy, and reliable than anyone else she knows. And then, when she's grown up, they'll be as happy as Emily and Sam." A strange, bitter edge sharpened his tone at the very end, when he spoke of Sam.

"Doesn't Claire get a choice here?"

"Of course. But why wouldn't she choose him, in the end? He'll be her perfect match. Like he was designed for her alone."

We walked in silence for a moment, till I paused to toss

a rock toward the ocean. It fell to the beach several meters short. Jacob laughed at me.

"We can't all be freakishly strong," I muttered.

He sighed.

"When do you think it will happen for you?" I asked quietly.

His answer was flat and immediate. "Never."

"It's not something you can control, is it?"

He was silent for a few minutes. Unconsciously, we both walked slower, barely moving at all.

"It's not supposed to be," he admitted. "But you have to *see* her — the one that's supposedly meant for you."

"And you think that if you haven't seen her yet, then she's not out there?" I asked skeptically. "Jacob, you haven't really seen much of the world — less than me, even."

"No, I haven't," he said in a low voice. He looked at my face with suddenly piercing eyes. "But I'll never see anyone else, Bella. I only see you. Even when I close my eyes and try to see something else. Ask Quil or Embry. It drives them all crazy."

I dropped my eyes to the rocks.

We weren't walking anymore. The only sound was of the waves beating against the shore. I couldn't hear the rain over their roar.

"Maybe I'd better go home," I whispered.

"No!" he protested, surprised by this conclusion.

I looked up at him again, and his eyes were anxious now.

"You have the whole day off, right? The bloodsucker won't be home yet."

I glared at him.

"No offense intended," he said quickly.

"Yes, I have the whole day. But, Jake . . ."

He held up his hands. "Sorry," he apologized. "I won't be like that anymore. I'll just be Jacob."

I sighed. "But if that's what you're *thinking* . . ."

"Don't worry about me," he insisted, smiling with deliberate cheer, too brightly. "I know what I'm doing. Just tell me if I'm upsetting you."

"I don't know. . . ."

"C'mon, Bella. Let's go back to the house and get our bikes. You've got to ride a motorcycle regularly to keep it in tune."

"I really don't think I'm allowed."

"By who? Charlie or the blood — or *him?*"

"Both."

Jacob grinned *my* grin, and he was suddenly the Jacob I missed the most, sunny and warm.

I couldn't help grinning back.

The rain softened, turned to mist.

"I won't tell anyone," he promised.

"Except every one of your friends."

He shook his head soberly and raised his right hand. "I promise not to think about it."

I laughed. "If I get hurt, it was because I tripped."

"Whatever you say."

We rode our motorcycles on the back roads around La Push until the rain made them too muddy and Jacob insisted that he was going to pass out if he didn't eat soon. Billy greeted me easily when we got to the house, as if my sudden reappearance meant nothing more complicated than that I'd wanted to spend the day with my friend. After we ate the sandwiches Jacob made, we went out to the garage and I helped him clean up the bikes. I hadn't been here in months — since Edward had returned — but there was no sense of import to it. It was just another afternoon in the garage.

"This is nice," I commented when he pulled the warm sodas from the grocery bag. "I've missed this place."

He smiled, looking around at the plastic sheds bolted together over our heads. "Yeah, I can understand that. All the splendor of the Taj Mahal, without the inconvenience and expense of traveling to India."

"To Washington's little Taj Mahal," I toasted, holding up my can.

He touched his can to mine.

"Do you remember last Valentine's Day? I think that was the last time you were here — the last time when things were still . . . normal, I mean."

I laughed. "Of course I remember. I traded a lifetime of servitude for a box of conversation hearts. That's not something I'm likely to forget."

He laughed with me. "That's right. Hmm, servitude. I'll have to think of something good." Then he sighed. "It feels like it was years ago. Another era. A happier one."

I couldn't agree with him. This was my happy era now. But I was surprised to realize how many things I missed from my own personal dark ages. I stared through the opening at the murky forest. The rain had picked up again, but it was warm in the little garage, sitting next to Jacob. He was as good as a furnace.

His fingers brushed my hand. "Things have really changed."

"Yeah," I said, and then I reached out and patted the back tire of my bike. "Charlie *used* to like me. I hope Billy doesn't say anything about today. . . ." I bit my lip.

"He won't. He doesn't get worked up about things the way Charlie does. Hey, I never did apologize officially for that stupid move with the bike. I'm real sorry about ratting you out to Charlie. I wish I hadn't."

I rolled my eyes. "Me, too."

"I'm really, really sorry."

He looked at me hopefully, his wet, tangled black hair sticking up in every direction around his pleading face.

"Oh, fine! You're forgiven."

"Thanks, Bells!"

We grinned at each other for a second, and then his face clouded over.

"You know that day, when I brought the bike over . . . I've been wanting to ask you something," he said slowly. "But also . . . not wanting to."

I held very still — a reaction to stress. It was a habit I'd picked up from Edward.

"Were you just being stubborn because you were mad at me, or were you really serious?" he whispered.

"About what?" I whispered back, though I was sure I knew what he meant.

He glared at me. "You know. When you said it was

none of my business . . . if — if he bit you." He cringed visibly at the end.

"Jake . . ." My throat felt swollen. I couldn't finish.

He closed his eyes and took a deep breath. "Were you serious?"

He was trembling just slightly. His eyes stayed closed.

"Yes," I whispered.

Jacob inhaled, slow and deep. "I guess I knew that."

I stared at his face, waiting for his eyes to open.

"You know what this will mean?" He demanded suddenly. "You do understand that, don't you? What will happen if they break the treaty?"

"We'll leave first," I said in a small voice.

His eyes flashed open, their black depths full of anger and pain. "There wasn't a geographic limit to the treaty, Bella. Our great-grandfathers only agreed to keep the peace because the Cullens swore that they were different, that humans weren't in danger from them. They promised they would never kill or change anyone ever again. If they go back on their word, the treaty is meaningless, and they are no different than any other vampires. Once that's established, when we find them again —"

"But, Jake, didn't you break the treaty already?" I asked, grasping at straws. "Wasn't part of it that you not tell people about the vampires? And you told me. So isn't the treaty sort of moot, anyhow?"

Jacob didn't like the reminder; the pain in his eyes hardened into animosity. "Yeah, I broke the treaty — back before I believed any of it. And I'm sure they were informed of that." He glared sourly at my forehead, not meeting my shamed gaze. "But it's not like that gives them a freebie or anything. There's no fault for a fault. They have only one option if they object to what I did. The same option we'll have when they break the treaty: to attack. To start the war."

He made it sound so inevitable. I shuddered.

"Jake, it doesn't have to be that way."

His teeth ground together. "It *is* that way."

The silence after his declaration felt very loud.

"Will you never forgive me, Jacob?" I whispered. As soon as I said the words, I wished I hadn't. I didn't want to hear his answer.

"You won't be Bella anymore," he told me. "My friend won't exist. There'll be no one to forgive."

"That sounds like a *no,*" I whispered.

We faced each other for an endless moment.

"Is this goodbye then, Jake?"

He blinked rapidly, his fierce expression melting in surprise. "Why? We still have a few years. Can't we be friends until we're out of time?"

"Years? No, Jake, not years." I shook my head, and laughed once without humor. "*Weeks* is more accurate."

I was not expecting his reaction.

He was suddenly on his feet, and there was a loud *pop* as the soda can exploded in his hand. Soda flew everywhere, soaking me, like it was spraying from a hose.

"Jake!" I started to complain, but I fell silent when I realized that his whole body was quivering with anger. He glared at me wildly, a growling sound building in his chest.

I froze in place, too shocked to remember how to move.

The shaking rolled through him, getting faster, until it looked like he was vibrating. His shape blurred. . . .

And then Jacob gritted his teeth together, and the growling stopped. He squeezed his eyes tight in concentration; the quivering slowed until only his hands were shaking.

"Weeks," Jacob said in a flat monotone.

I couldn't respond; I was still frozen.

He opened his eyes. They were beyond fury now.

"He's going to change you into a filthy bloodsucker in just a few *weeks*!" Jacob hissed through his teeth.

Too stunned to take offense at his words, I just nodded mutely.

His face turned green under the russet skin.

"Of course, Jake," I whispered after a long minute of silence. "He's *seventeen,* Jacob. And I get closer to nineteen every day. Besides, what's the point in waiting? He's all I want. What else can I do?"

I'd meant that as a rhetorical question.

His words cracked like snaps of a whip. "Anything. Anything else. You'd be better off dead. I'd rather you were."

I recoiled like he'd slapped me. It hurt worse than if he had.

And then, as the pain shot through me, my own temper burst into flame.

"Maybe you'll get lucky," I said bleakly, lurching to my feet. "Maybe I'll get hit by a truck on my way back."

I grabbed my motorcycle and pushed it out into the rain. He didn't move as I passed him. As soon as I was on the small, muddy path, I climbed on and kicked the bike to life. The rear tire spit a fountain of mud toward the garage, and I hoped that it hit him.

I got absolutely soaked as I sped across the slick highway toward the Cullens' house. The wind felt like it was freezing the rain against my skin, and my teeth were chattering before I was halfway there.

Motorcycles were too impractical for Washington. I would sell the stupid thing first chance I got.

I walked the bike into the Cullens' cavernous garage and was unsurprised to find Alice waiting for me, perched lightly on the hood of her Porsche. Alice stroked the glossy yellow paint.

"I haven't even had a chance to drive it." She sighed.

"Sorry," I spit through my rattling teeth.

"You look like you could use a hot shower," she said, offhand, as she sprang lightly to her feet.

"Yep."

She pursed her lips, taking in my expression carefully. "Do you want to talk about it?"

"Nope."

She nodded in assent, but her eyes were raging with curiosity.

"Do you want to go to Olympia tonight?"

"Not really. Can't I go home?"

She grimaced.

"Never mind, Alice," I said. "I'll stay if it makes things easier for you."

"Thanks," she sighed in relief.

I went to bed early that night, curling up on his sofa again.

It was still dark when I woke. I was groggy, but I knew it wasn't near morning yet. My eyes closed, and I stretched, rolling over. It took me a second before I realized that the movement should have dumped me onto the floor. And that I was much too comfortable.

I rolled back over, trying to see. It was darker than last night — the clouds were too thick for the moon to shine through.

"Sorry," he murmured so softly that his voice was part of the darkness. "I didn't mean to wake you."

I tensed, waiting for the fury — both his and mine — but it was only quiet and calm in the darkness of his room. I could almost taste the sweetness of reunion in the air, a separate fragrance from the perfume of his breath; the emptiness when we were apart left its own bitter after-taste, something I didn't consciously notice until it was removed.

There was no friction in the space between us. The stillness was peaceful — not like the calm before the tempest, but like a clear night untouched by even the dream of a storm.

And I didn't care that I was supposed to be angry with him. I didn't care that I was supposed to be angry with everyone. I reached out for him, found his hands in the darkness, and pulled myself closer to him. His arms encircled me, cradling me to his chest. My lips searched, hunting along his throat, to his chin, till I finally found his lips.

Edward kissed me softly for a moment, and then he chuckled.

"I was all braced for the wrath that was going to put grizzlies to shame, and this is what I get? I should infuriate you more often."

"Give me a minute to work up to it," I teased, kissing him again.

"I'll wait as long as you want," he whispered against my lips. His fingers knotted in my hair.

My breath was becoming uneven. "Maybe in the morning."

"Whatever you prefer."

"Welcome home," I said while his cold lips pressed under my jaw. "I'm glad you came back."

"That's a very good thing."

"Mmm," I agreed, tightening my arms around his neck.

His hand curved around my elbow, moving slowly down my arm, across my ribs and over my waist, tracing along my hip and down my leg, around my knee. He paused there, his hand curling around my calf. He pulled my leg up suddenly, hitching it around his hip.

I stopped breathing. This wasn't the kind of thing he usually allowed. Despite his cold hands, I felt suddenly warm. His lips moved in the hollow at the base of my throat.

"Not to bring on the ire prematurely," he whispered, "but do you mind telling me what it is about this bed that you object to?"

Before I could answer, before I could even concentrate

enough to make sense of his words, he rolled to the side, pulling me on top of him. He held my face in his hands, angling it up so that his mouth could reach my throat. My breathing was too loud — it was almost embarrassing, but I couldn't care quite enough to be ashamed.

"The bed?" he asked again. "*I* think it's nice."

"It's unnecessary," I managed to gasp.

He pulled my face back to his, and my lips shaped themselves around his. Slowly this time, he rolled till he hovered over me. He held himself carefully so that I felt none of his weight, but I could feel the cool marble of his body press against mine. My heart was hammering so loudly that it was hard to hear his quiet laughter.

"That's debatable," he disagreed. "This would be difficult on a couch."

Cold as ice, his tongue lightly traced the shape of my lips.

My head was spinning — the air was coming too fast and shallow.

"Did you change your mind?" I asked breathlessly. Maybe he'd rethought all his careful rules. Maybe there was more significance to this bed than I'd originally guessed. My heart pounded almost painfully as I waited for his answer.

Edward sighed, rolling back so that we were on our sides again.

"Don't be ridiculous, Bella," he said, disapproval strong in his voice — clearly, he understood what I meant. "I was just trying to illustrate the benefits of the bed you don't seem to like. Don't get carried away."

"Too late," I muttered. "And I like the bed," I added.

"Good." I could hear the smile in his voice as he kissed my forehead. "I do, too."

"But I still think it's unnecessary," I continued. "If we're not going to get carried away, what's the point?"

He sighed again. "For the hundredth time, Bella — it's too dangerous."

"I like danger," I insisted.

"I know." There was a sour edge to his voice, and I realized that he would have seen the motorcycle in the garage.

"I'll tell you what's dangerous," I said quickly, before he could move to a new topic of discussion. "I'm going to spontaneously combust one of these days — and you'll have no one but yourself to blame."

He started to push me away.

"What are you doing?" I objected, clinging to him.

"Protecting you from combustion. If this is too much for you. . . ."

"I can handle it," I insisted.

He let me worm myself back into the circle of his arms.

"I'm sorry I gave you the wrong impression," he said. "I didn't mean to make you unhappy. That wasn't nice."

"Actually, it was very, very nice."

He took a deep breath. "Aren't you tired? I should let you sleep."

"No, I'm not. I don't mind if you want to give me the wrong impression again."

"That's probably a bad idea. You're not the only one who gets carried away."

"Yes, I am," I grumbled.

He chuckled. "You have no idea, Bella. It doesn't help that you are so eager to undermine my self-control, either."

"I'm not going to apologize for that."

"Can *I* apologize?"

"For what?"

"You were angry with me, remember?"

"Oh, that."

"I'm sorry. I was wrong. It's much easier to have the proper perspective when I have you safely *here*." His arms tightened around me. "I go a little berserk when I try to leave you. I don't think I'll go so far again. It's not worth it."

I smiled. "Didn't you find any mountain lions?"

"Yes, I did, actually. Still not worth the anxiety. I'm sorry I had Alice hold you hostage, though. That was a bad idea."

"Yes," I agreed.

"I won't do it again."

"Okay," I said easily. He was already forgiven. "But slumber parties do have their advantages. . . ." I curled myself closer to him, pressing my lips into the indentation over his collarbone. "*You* can hold me hostage any time you want."

"Mmm," he sighed. "I may take you up on that."

"So is it my turn now?"

"Your turn?" his voice was confused.

"To apologize."

"What do you have to apologize for?"

"Aren't you mad at me?" I asked blankly.

"No."

It sounded like he really meant it.

I felt my eyebrows pull together. "Didn't you see Alice when you got home?"

"Yes — why?"

"Are you going to take her Porsche back?"

"Of course not. It was a gift."

I wished I could see his expression. His voice sounded as if I'd insulted him.

"Don't you want to know what I did?" I asked, starting to be puzzled by his apparent lack of concern.

I felt him shrug. "I'm always interested in everything you do — but you don't have to tell me unless you want to."

"But I went to La Push."

"I know."

"And I ditched school."

"So did I."

I stared toward the sound of his voice, tracing his features with my fingers, trying to understand his mood. "Where did all this tolerance come from?" I demanded.

He sighed.

"I decided that you were right. My problem before was more about my . . . prejudice against werewolves than anything else. I'm going to try to be more reasonable and trust your judgment. If you say it's safe, then I'll be-lieve you."

"Wow."

"And . . . most importantly . . . I'm not willing to let this drive a wedge between us."

I rested my head against his chest and closed my eyes, totally content.

"So," he murmured in a casual tone. "Did you make plans to go back to La Push again soon?"

I didn't answer. His question brought back the memory of Jacob's words, and my throat was suddenly tight.

He misread my silence and the tension in my body.

"Just so that I can make my own plans," he explained quickly. "I don't want you to feel like you have to hurry back because I'm sitting around waiting for you."

"No," I said in a voice that sounded strange to me. "I don't have plans to go back."

"Oh. You don't have to do that for me."

"I don't think I'm welcome anymore," I whispered.

"Did you run over someone's cat?" he asked lightly. I knew he didn't want to force the story out of me, but I could hear the curiosity burning behind his words.

"No." I took a deep breath, and then mumbled quickly through the explanation. "I thought Jacob would have realized . . . I didn't think it would surprise him."

Edward waited while I hesitated.

"He wasn't expecting . . . that it was so soon."

"Ah," Edward said quietly.

"He said he'd rather see me dead." My voice broke on the last word.

Edward was too still for a moment, controlling whatever reaction he didn't want me to see.

Then he crushed me gently to his chest. "I'm so sorry."

"I thought you'd be glad," I whispered.

"Glad over something that's hurt you?" he murmured into my hair. "I don't think so, Bella."

I sighed and relaxed, fitting myself to the stone shape of him. But he was motionless again, tense.

"What's wrong?" I asked.

"It's nothing."

"You can tell me."

He paused for a minute. "It might make you angry."

"I still want to know."

He sighed. "I could quite literally kill him for saying that to you. I *want* to."

I laughed halfheartedly. "I guess it's a good thing you've got so much self-control."

"I could slip." His tone was thoughtful.

"If you're going to have a lapse in control, I can think of a better place for it." I reached for his face, trying to pull myself up to kiss him. His arms held me tighter, restraining.

He sighed. "Must I always be the responsible one?"

I grinned in the darkness. "No. Let me be in charge of responsibility for a few minutes . . . or hours."

"Goodnight, Bella."

"Wait — there was something else I wanted to ask you about."

"What's that?"

"I was talking to Rosalie last night. . . ."

His body tensed again. "Yes. She was thinking about that when I got in. She gave you quite a lot to consider, didn't she?"

His voice was anxious, and I realized that he thought I wanted to talk about the reasons Rosalie'd given me for staying human. But I was interested in something much more pressing.

"She told me a little bit . . . about the time your family lived in Denali."

There was a short pause; this beginning took him by surprise. "Yes?"

"She mentioned something about a bunch of female vampires . . . and you."

He didn't answer, though I waited for a long moment.

"Don't worry," I said, after the silence had grown uncomfortable. "She told me you didn't . . . show any preference. But I was just wondering, you know, if any of *them* had. Shown a preference for you, I mean."

Again he said nothing.

"Which one?" I asked, trying to keep my voice casual, and not quite managing. "Or was there more than one?"

No answer. I wished I could see his face, so I could try to guess what this silence meant.

"Alice will tell me," I said. "I'll go ask her right now."

His arms tightened; I was unable to squirm even an inch away.

"It's late," he said. His voice had a little edge to it that was something new. Sort of nervous, maybe a little embarrassed. "Besides, I think Alice stepped out. . . ."

"It's bad," I guessed. "It's really bad, isn't it?" I started to panic, my heart accelerating as I imagined the gorgeous immortal rival I'd never realized I had.

"Calm down, Bella," he said, kissing the tip of my nose. "You're being absurd."

"Am I? Then why won't you tell me?"

"Because there's nothing to tell. You're blowing this wildly out of proportion."

"Which one?" I insisted.

He sighed. "Tanya expressed a little interest. I let her know, in a very courteous, gentlemanly fashion, that I did not return that interest. End of story."

I kept my voice as even as possible. "Tell me something — what does Tanya look like?"

"Just like the rest of us — white skin, gold eyes," he answered too quickly.

"And, of course, extraordinarily beautiful."

I felt him shrug.

"I suppose, to human eyes," he said, indifferent. "You know what, though?"

"What?" My voice was petulant.

He put his lips right to my ear; his cold breath tickled. "I prefer brunettes."

"She's a blonde. That figures."

"Strawberry blonde — not at all my type."

I thought about that for a while, trying to concentrate as his lips moved slowly along my cheek, down my throat, and back up again. He made the circuit three times before I spoke.

"I *guess* that's okay, then," I decided.

"Hmm," he whispered against my skin. "You're quite adorable when you're jealous. It's surprisingly enjoyable."

I scowled into the darkness.

"It's late," he said again, murmuring, almost crooning now, his voice smoother than silk. "Sleep, my Bella. Dream happy dreams. You are the only one who has ever touched my heart. It will always be yours. Sleep, my only love."

He started to hum my lullaby, and I knew it was only a matter of time till I succumbed, so I closed my eyes and snuggled closer into his chest.

9. TARGET

ALICE DROPPED ME OFF IN THE MORNING, IN KEEPING with the slumber party charade. It wouldn't be long until Edward showed up, officially returning from his "hiking" trip. All of the pretenses were starting to wear on me. I wouldn't miss this part of being human.

Charlie peeked through the front window when he heard me slam the car door. He waved to Alice, and then went to get the door for me.

"Did you have fun?" Charlie asked.

"Sure, it was great. Very . . . girlie."

I carried my stuff in, dumped it all at the foot of the stairs, and wandered into the kitchen to look for a snack.

"You've got a message," Charlie called after me.

On the kitchen counter, the phone message pad was propped up conspicuously against a saucepan.

Jacob called, Charlie had written.

He said he didn't mean it, and that he's sorry. He wants you to call him. Be nice and give him a break. He sounded upset.

I grimaced. Charlie didn't usually editorialize on my messages.

Jacob could just go ahead and be upset. I didn't want to talk to him. Last I'd heard, they weren't big on allowing phone calls from the other side. If Jacob preferred me dead, then maybe he should get used to the silence.

My appetite evaporated. I turned an about face and went to put my things away.

"Aren't you going to call Jacob?" Charlie asked. He was leaning around the living room wall, watching me pick up.

"No."

I started up the stairs.

"That's not very attractive behavior, Bella," he said. "Forgiveness is divine."

"Mind your own business," I muttered under my breath, much too low for him to hear.

I knew the laundry was building up, so after I put my toothpaste away and threw my dirty clothes in the hamper, I went to strip Charlie's bed. I left his sheets in a pile at the top of the stairs and went to get mine.

I paused beside the bed, cocking my head to the side.

Where was my pillow? I turned in a circle, scanning the room. No pillow. I noticed that my room looked oddly tidy. Hadn't my gray sweatshirt been draped over the low bedpost on the footboard? And I would swear there had been a pair of dirty socks behind the rocking chair, along with the red blouse I'd tried on two mornings ago, but decided was too dressy for school, hanging over the arm. . . . I spun around again. My hamper wasn't empty, but it wasn't overflowing, the way I thought it had been.

Was Charlie doing laundry? That was out of character.

"Dad, did you start the wash?" I shouted out my door.

"Um, no," he shouted back, sounding guilty. "Did you want me to?"

"No, I got it. Were you looking for something in my room?"

"No. Why?"

"I can't find . . . a shirt. . . ."

"I haven't been in there."

And then I remembered that Alice had been here to get my pajamas. I hadn't noticed that she'd borrowed my pillow, too — probably since I'd avoided the bed. It looked like she had cleaned while she was passing through. I blushed for my slovenly ways.

But that red shirt really wasn't dirty, so I went to save it from the hamper.

I expected to find it near the top, but it wasn't there. I dug through the whole pile and still couldn't find it. I knew I was probably getting paranoid, but it seemed like something else was missing, or maybe more than one something. I didn't even have half a load here.

I ripped my sheets off and headed for the laundry closet, grabbing Charlie's on the way. The washing machine was empty. I checked the dryer, too, half-expecting to find a washed load waiting for me, courtesy of Alice. Nothing. I frowned, mystified.

"Did you find what you were looking for?" Charlie yelled.

"Not yet."

I went back upstairs to search under my bed. Nothing but dust bunnies. I started to dig through my dresser. Maybe I'd put the red shirt away and forgotten.

I gave up when the doorbell rang. That would be Edward.

"Door," Charlie informed me from the couch as I skipped past him.

"Don't strain yourself, Dad."

I pulled the door open with a big smile on my face.

Edward's golden eyes were wide, his nostrils flared, his lips pulled back over his teeth.

"Edward?" My voice was sharp with shock as I read his expression. "What —?"

He put his finger to my lips. "Give me two seconds," he whispered. "Don't move."

I stood frozen on the doorstep and he . . . disappeared. He moved so quickly that Charlie wouldn't even have seen him pass.

Before I could compose myself enough to count to two,

he was back. He put his arm around my waist and pulled me swiftly toward the kitchen. His eyes darted around the room, and he held me against his body as if he were shielding me from something. I threw a glance toward Charlie on the couch, but he was studiously ignoring us.

"Someone's been here," he murmured in my ear after he pulled me to the back of the kitchen. His voice was strained; it was difficult to hear him over the thumping of the washing machine.

"I swear that no werewolves —" I started to say.

"Not one of them," he interrupted me quickly, shaking his head. "One of us."

His tone made it clear that he didn't mean a member of his family.

I felt the blood empty from my face.

"Victoria?" I choked.

"It's not a scent I recognize."

"One of the Volturi," I guessed.

"Probably."

"When?"

"That's why I think it must have been them — it wasn't long ago, early this morning while Charlie was sleeping. And whoever it was didn't touch him, so there must have been another purpose."

"Looking for me."

He didn't answer. His body was frozen, a statue.

"What are you two hissing about in here?" Charlie asked suspiciously, rounding the corner with an empty popcorn bowl in his hands.

I felt green. A vampire had been in the house looking

for me while Charlie slept. Panic overwhelmed me, closed my throat. I couldn't answer, I just stared at him in horror.

Charlie's expression changed. Abruptly, he was grinning. "If you two are having a fight . . . well, don't let me interrupt."

Still grinning, he put his bowl in the sink and sauntered out of the room.

"Let's go," Edward said in a low hard voice.

"But Charlie!" The fear was squeezing my chest, making it hard to breathe.

He deliberated for a short second, and then his phone was in his hand.

"Emmett," he muttered into the receiver. He began talking so fast that I couldn't understand the words. It was over in half a minute. He started pulling me toward the door.

"Emmett and Jasper are on their way," he whispered when he felt my resistance. "They'll sweep the woods. Charlie is fine."

I let him drag me along then, too panicked to think clearly. Charlie met my frightened eyes with a smug grin, which suddenly turned to confusion. Edward had me out the door before Charlie could say anything.

"Where are we going?" I couldn't stop whispering, even after we were in the car.

"We're going to talk to Alice," he told me, his volume normal but his voice bleak.

"You think maybe she saw something?"

He stared at the road through narrowed eyes. "Maybe."

They were waiting for us, on alert after Edward's call.

It was like walking into a museum, everyone still as statues in various poses of stress.

"What happened?" Edward demanded as soon as we were through the door. I was shocked to see that he was glowering at Alice, his hands fisted in anger.

Alice stood with her arms folded tight across her chest. Only her lips moved. "I have no idea. I didn't see anything."

"How is that *possible?*" he hissed.

"Edward," I said, a quiet reproof. I didn't like him talking to Alice this way.

Carlisle interrupted in a calming voice. "It's not an exact science, Edward."

"He was in her *room,* Alice. He could have still been there — waiting for her."

"I would have seen that."

Edward threw his hands up in exasperation. "Really? You're sure?"

Alice's voice was cold when she answered. "You've already got me watching the Volturis' decisions, watching for Victoria's return, watching Bella's every step. You want to add another? Do I just have to watch Charlie, or Bella's room, or the house, or the whole street, too? Edward, if I try to do too much, things are going to start slipping through the cracks."

"It looks like they already are," Edward snapped.

"She was never in any danger. There was nothing to see."

"If you're watching Italy, why didn't you see them send —"

"I don't think it's them," Alice insisted. "I would have seen that."

"Who else would leave Charlie alive?"

I shuddered.

"I don't know," Alice said.

"Helpful."

"Stop it, Edward," I whispered.

He turned on me, his face still livid, his teeth clenched together. He glared at me for half a second, and then, suddenly, he exhaled. His eyes widened and his jaw relaxed.

"You're right, Bella. I'm sorry." He looked at Alice. "Forgive me, Alice. I shouldn't be taking this out on you. That was inexcusable."

"I understand," Alice assured him. "I'm not happy about it, either."

Edward took a deep breath. "Okay, let's look at this logically. What are the possibilities?"

Everyone seemed to thaw out at once. Alice relaxed and leaned against the back of the couch. Carlisle walked slowly toward her, his eyes far away. Esme sat on the sofa in front of Alice, curling her legs up on the seat. Only Rosalie remained unmoving, her back to us, staring out the glass wall.

Edward pulled me to the sofa and I sat next to Esme, who shifted to put her arm around me. He held one of my hands tightly in both of his.

"Victoria?" Carlisle asked.

Edward shook his head. "No. I didn't know the scent. He might have been from the Volturi, someone I've never met. . . ."

Alice shook her head. "Aro hasn't asked anyone to look for her yet. I *will* see that. I'm waiting for it."

Edward's head snapped up. "You're watching for an official command."

"You think someone's acting on their own? Why?"

"Caius's idea," Edward suggested, his face tightening again.

"Or Jane's . . . ," Alice said. "They both have the resources to send an unfamiliar face. . . ."

Edward scowled. "And the motivation."

"It doesn't make sense, though," Esme said. "If whoever it was meant to wait for Bella, Alice would have seen that. He — or she — had no intention of hurting Bella. Or Charlie, for that matter."

I cringed at my father's name.

"It's going to be fine, Bella," Esme murmured, smoothing my hair.

"But what was the point then?" Carlisle mused.

"Checking to see if I'm still human?" I guessed.

"Possible," Carlisle said.

Rosalie breathed out a sigh, loud enough for me to hear. She'd unfrozen, and her face was turned expectantly toward the kitchen. Edward, on the other hand, looked discouraged.

Emmett burst through the kitchen door, Jasper right behind him.

"Long gone, hours ago," Emmett announced, disappointed. "The trail went East, then South, and disappeared on a side road. Had a car waiting."

"That's bad luck," Edward muttered. "If he'd gone west . . . well, it would be nice for those dogs to make themselves useful."

I winced, and Esme rubbed my shoulder.

Jasper looked at Carlisle. "Neither of us recognized him. But here." He held out something green and crumpled. Carlisle took it from him and held it to his face. I saw, as it exchanged hands, that it was a broken fern frond. "Maybe you know the scent."

"No," Carlisle said. "Not familiar. No one I've ever met."

"Perhaps we're looking at this the wrong way. Maybe it's a coincidence . . . ," Esme began, but stopped when she saw everyone else's incredulous expressions. "I don't mean a coincidence that a stranger happened to pick Bella's house to visit at random. I meant that maybe someone was just curious. Our scent is all around her. Was he wondering what draws us there?"

"Why wouldn't he just come here then? If he was curious?" Emmett demanded.

"You would," Esme said with a sudden, fond smile. "The rest of us aren't always so direct. Our family is very large — he or she might be frightened. But Charlie wasn't harmed. This doesn't have to be an enemy."

Just curious. Like James and Victoria had been curious, in the beginning? The thought of Victoria made me tremble, though the one thing they seemed certain of was that it had not been her. Not this time. She would stick to her obsessed pattern. This was just someone else, a stranger.

I was slowly realizing that vampires were much bigger participants in this world than I'd once thought. How many times did the average human cross paths with them, completely unaware? How many deaths, obliviously reported as crimes and accidents, were really due to their thirst? How crowded would this new world be when I finally joined it?

The shrouded future sent a shiver down my spine.

The Cullens pondered Esme's words with varying expressions. I could see that Edward did not accept her theory, and that Carlisle very much wanted to.

Alice pursed her lips. "I don't think so. The timing of it was too perfect. . . . This visitor was so careful to make no contact. Almost like he or she knew that I would see. . . ."

"He could have other reasons for not making contact," Esme reminded her.

"Does it really matter who it was?" I asked. "Just the chance that someone *was* looking for me . . . isn't that reason enough? We shouldn't wait for graduation."

"No, Bella," Edward said quickly. "It's not that bad. If you're really in danger, we'll know."

"Think of Charlie," Carlisle reminded me. "Think of how it would hurt him if you disappeared."

"I *am* thinking of Charlie! He's the one I'm worried about! What if my little guest had happened to be thirsty last night? As long as I'm around Charlie, he's a target, too. If anything happened to him, it would be all my fault!"

"Hardly, Bella," Esme said, patting my hair again. "And nothing will happen to Charlie. We're just going to have to be more careful."

"*More* careful?" I repeated in disbelief.

"It's all going to be fine, Bella," Alice promised; Edward squeezed my hand.

And I could see, looking at all of their beautiful faces one by one, that nothing I could say was going to change their minds.

It was a quiet ride home. I was frustrated. Against my better judgment, I was still human.

"You won't be alone for a second," Edward promised as he drove me to Charlie's. "Someone will always be there. Emmett, Alice, Jasper . . ."

I sighed. "This is ridiculous. They'll get so bored, they'll have to kill me themselves, just for something to do."

Edward gave me a sour look. "Hilarious, Bella."

Charlie was in a good mood when we got back. He could see the tension between me and Edward, and he was misinterpreting it. He watched me throw together his dinner with a smug smile on his face. Edward had excused himself for a moment, to do some surveillance, I assumed, but Charlie waited till he was back to pass on my messages.

"Jacob called again," Charlie said as soon as Edward was in the room. I kept my face empty as I set the plate in front of him.

"Is that a fact?"

Charlie frowned. "Don't be petty, Bella. He sounded really low."

"Is Jacob paying you for all the P.R., or are you a volunteer?"

Charlie grumbled incoherently at me until the food cut off his garbled complaint.

Though he didn't realize it, he'd found his mark.

My life was feeling a lot like a game of dice right now — would the next roll come up snake eyes? What if something *did* happen to me? It seemed worse than petty to leave Jacob feeling guilty about what he'd said.

But I didn't want to talk to him with Charlie around, to have to watch my every word so I didn't let the wrong thing slip. Thinking about this made me jealous of Jacob and Billy's relationship. How easy it must be when you had no secrets from the person you lived with.

So I would wait for the morning. I most likely wasn't going to die tonight, after all, and it wouldn't hurt him to feel guilty for twelve more hours. It might even be good for him.

When Edward officially left for the evening, I wondered who was out in the downpour, keeping an eye on Charlie and me. I felt awful for Alice or whoever else it might be, but still comforted. I had to admit it was nice, knowing I wasn't alone. And Edward was back in record time.

He sang me to sleep again and — aware even in unconsciousness that he was there — I slept free of nightmares.

In the morning, Charlie left to go fishing with Deputy Mark before I was up. I decided to use this lack of supervision to be divine.

"I'm going to let Jacob off the hook," I warned Edward after I'd eaten breakfast.

"I knew you'd forgive him," he said with an easy smile. "Holding grudges is not one of your many talents."

I rolled my eyes, but I was pleased. It seemed like Edward really was over the whole anti-werewolf thing.

I didn't look at the clock until after I'd dialed. It was a little early for calls, and I worried that I would wake Billy and Jake, but someone picked up before the second ring, so he couldn't have been too far from the phone.

"Hello?" a dull voice said.

"Jacob?"

"Bella!" he exclaimed. "Oh, Bella, I'm so sorry!" he tripped over the words as he hurried to get them out. "I swear I didn't mean it. I was just being stupid. I was angry — but that's no excuse. It was the stupidest thing I've ever said in my life and I'm sorry. Don't be mad at me, please? Please. Lifetime of servitude up for grabs — all you have to do is forgive me."

"I'm not mad. You're forgiven."

"Thank you," he breathed fervently. "I can't believe I was such a jerk."

"Don't worry about that — I'm used to it."

He laughed, exuberant with relief. "Come down to see me," he begged. "I want to make it up to you."

I frowned. "How?"

"Anything you want. Cliff diving," he suggested, laughing again.

"Oh, *there's* a brilliant idea."

"I'll keep you safe," he promised. "No matter what you want to do."

I glanced at Edward. His face was very calm, but I was sure this was not the time.

"Not right now."

"*He's* not thrilled with me, is he?" Jacob's voice was ashamed, rather than bitter, for once.

"That's not the problem. There's . . . well, there's this other problem that's slightly more worrisome than a bratty teenage werewolf. . . ." I tried to keep my tone joking, but I didn't fool him.

"What's wrong?" he demanded.

"Um." I wasn't sure what I should tell him.

Edward held his hand out for the phone. I looked at his face carefully. He *seemed* calm enough.

"Bella?" Jacob asked.

Edward sighed, holding his hand closer.

"Do you mind speaking to Edward?" I asked apprehensively. "He wants to talk to you."

There was a long pause.

"Okay," Jacob finally agreed. "This should be interesting."

I handed the phone to Edward; I hoped he could read the warning in my eyes.

"Hello, Jacob," Edward said, perfectly polite.

There was a silence. I bit my lip, trying to guess how Jacob would answer.

"Someone was here — not a scent I know," Edward explained. "Has your pack come across anything new?"

Another pause, while Edward nodded to himself, unsurprised.

"Here's the crux, Jacob. I won't be letting Bella out of my sight till I get this taken care of. It's nothing personal —"

Jacob interrupted him then, and I could hear the buzz of his voice from the receiver. Whatever he was saying, he was more intense than before. I tried unsuccessfully to make out the words.

"You might be right —," Edward began, but Jacob was arguing again. Neither of them sounded angry, at least.

"That's an interesting suggestion. We're quite willing to renegotiate. If Sam is amenable."

Jacob's voice was quieter now. I started chewing on my thumbnail as I tried to read Edward's expression.

"Thank you," Edward replied.

Then Jacob said something that caused a surprised expression to flicker across Edward's face.

"I'd planned to go alone, actually," Edward said, answering the unexpected question. "And leave her with the others."

Jacob's voice rose in pitch, and it sounded to me like he was trying to be persuasive.

"I'll try to consider it objectively," Edward promised. "As objectively as I'm capable of."

The pause was shorter this time.

"That's not a half-bad idea. When? . . . No, that's fine. I'd like a chance to follow the trail personally, anyway. Ten minutes . . . Certainly," Edward said. He held the phone out to me. "Bella?"

I took it slowly, feeling confused.

"What was that all about?" I asked Jacob, my voice peeved. I knew it was juvenile, but I felt excluded.

"A truce, I think. Hey, do me a favor," Jacob suggested. "Try to convince your bloodsucker that the safest place for you to be — especially when he leaves — is on the reservation. We're well able to handle anything."

"Is that what you were trying to sell him?"

"Yes. It makes sense. Charlie's probably better off here, too. As much as possible."

"Get Billy on it," I agreed. I hated that I was putting Charlie within the range of the crosshairs that always seemed to be centered on me. "What else?"

"Just rearranging some boundaries, so we can catch anyone who gets too near Forks. I'm not sure if Sam will go for it, but until he comes around, I'll keep an eye on things."

"What do you mean by 'keep an eye on things'?"

"I mean that if you see a wolf running around your house, don't shoot at it."

"Of course not. You really shouldn't do anything . . . risky, though."

He snorted. "Don't be stupid. I can take care of myself."

I sighed.

"I also tried to convince him to let you visit. He's prejudiced, so don't let him give you any crap about safety. He knows as well as I do that you'd be safe here."

"I'll keep that in mind."

"See you in a few," Jacob said.

"You're coming up?"

"Yeah. I'm going to get the scent of your visitor so we can track him if he comes back."

"Jake, I really don't like the idea of you tracking —"

"Oh *please,* Bella," he interrupted. Jacob laughed, and then hung up.

10. SCENT

IT WAS ALL VERY CHILDISH. WHY ON EARTH SHOULD ED-ward have to leave for Jacob to come over? Weren't we past this kind of immaturity?

"It's not that I feel any personal antagonism toward him, Bella, it's just easier for both of us," Edward told me at the door. "I won't be far away. You'll be safe."

"I'm not worried about *that*."

He smiled, and then a sly look came into his eye. He pulled me close, burying his face in my hair. I could feel his cool breath saturate the strands as he exhaled; it raised goose bumps on my neck.

"I'll be right back," he said, and then he laughed aloud as if I'd just told a good joke.

"What's so funny?"

But Edward just grinned and loped off toward the trees without answering.

Grumbling to myself, I went to clean up the kitchen. Before I even had the sink full of water, the doorbell rang. It was hard to get used to how much faster Jacob was *without* his car. How everyone seemed to be so much faster than me. . . .

"Come in, Jake!" I shouted.

I was concentrating on piling the dishes into the bubbly water, and I'd forgotten that Jacob moved like a ghost these days. So it made me jump when his voice was suddenly there behind me.

"Should you really leave your door unlocked like that? Oh, sorry."

I'd slopped myself with the dishwater when he'd startled me.

"I'm not worried about anyone who would be deterred by a locked door," I said while I wiped the front of my shirt with a dishtowel.

"Good point," he agreed.

I turned to look at him, eyeing him critically. "Is it really so impossible to wear clothes, Jacob?" I asked. Once again, Jacob was bare-chested, wearing nothing but a pair of old cut-off jeans. Secretly, I wondered if he was just so proud of his new muscles that he couldn't stand to cover them up. I had to admit, they were impressive — but I'd never thought of him as vain. "I mean, I know you don't get cold anymore, but still."

He ran a hand through his wet hair; it was falling in his eyes.

"It's just easier," he explained.

"What's easier?"

He smiled condescendingly. "It's enough of a pain to carry the shorts around with me, let alone a complete outfit. What do I look like, a pack mule?"

I frowned. "What are you talking about, Jacob?"

His expression was superior, like I was missing something obvious. "My clothes don't just pop in and out of existence when I change — I have to carry them with me while I run. Pardon me for keeping my burden light."

I changed color. "I guess I didn't think about that," I muttered.

He laughed and pointed to a black leather cord, thin as a strand of yarn, that was wound three times below his left calf like an anklet. I hadn't noticed before that his feet were bare, too. "That's more than just a fashion statement — it sucks to carry jeans in your mouth."

I didn't know what to say to that.

He grinned. "Does my being half-naked bother you?"

"No."

Jacob laughed again, and I turned my back on him to focus on the dishes. I hoped he realized my blush was left over from embarrassment at my own stupidity, and had nothing to do with his question.

"Well, I suppose I should get to work." He sighed. "I wouldn't want to give him an excuse to say I'm slacking on my side."

"Jacob, it's not your job —"

He raised a hand to cut me off. "I'm working on a volunteer basis here. Now, where is the intruder's scent the worst?"

"My bedroom, I think."

His eyes narrowed. He didn't like that any more than Edward had.

"I'll just be a minute."

I methodically scrubbed the plate I was holding. The only sound was the brush's plastic bristles scraping round and round on the ceramic. I listened for something from above, a creak of the floorboard, the click of a door. There was nothing. I realized I'd been cleaning the same plate far longer than necessary, and I tried to pay attention to what I was doing.

"Whew!" Jacob said, inches behind me, scaring me again.

"Yeesh, Jake, cut that out!"

"Sorry. Here —" Jacob took the towel and mopped up my new spill. "I'll make it up to you. You wash, I'll rinse and dry."

"Fine." I gave him the plate.

"Well, the scent was easy enough to catch. By the way, your room reeks."

"I'll buy some air freshener."

He laughed.

I washed and he dried in companionable silence for a few minutes.

"Can I ask you something?"

I handed him another plate. "That depends on what you want to know."

"I'm not trying to be a jerk or anything — I'm honestly curious," Jacob assured me.

"Fine. Go ahead."

He paused for half a second. "What's it like — having a vampire for a boyfriend?"

I rolled my eyes. "It's the best."

"I'm serious. The idea doesn't bother you — it never creeps you out?"

"Never."

He was silent as he reached for the bowl in my hands. I peeked up at his face — he was frowning, his lower lip jutting out.

"Anything else?" I asked.

He wrinkled his nose again. "Well . . . I was wondering . . . do you . . . y'know, *kiss* him?"

I laughed. "Yes."

He shuddered. "Ugh."

"To each her own," I murmured.

"You don't worry about the fangs?"

I smacked his arm, splashing him with dishwater. "Shut up, Jacob! You know he doesn't have fangs!"

"Close enough," he muttered.

I gritted my teeth and scrubbed a boning knife with more force than necessary.

"Can I ask another one?" he asked softly when I passed the knife to him. "Just curious, again."

"Fine," I snapped.

He turned the knife over and over in his hands under the stream of water. When he spoke, it was only a whisper. "You said a few weeks. . . . When, exactly . . . ?" He couldn't finish.

"Graduation," I whispered back, watching his face warily. Would this set him off again?

"So soon," he breathed, his eyes closing. It didn't sound like a question. It sounded like a lament. The muscles in his arms tightened and his shoulders were stiff.

"OW!" he shouted; it had gotten so still in the room that I jumped a foot in the air at his outburst.

His right hand had curled into a tense fist around the blade of the knife — he unclenched his hand and the knife clattered onto the counter. Across his palm was a long, deep gash. The blood streamed down his fingers and dripped on the floor.

"Damn it! Ouch!" he complained.

My head spun and my stomach rolled. I clung to the countertop with one hand, took a deep breath through my mouth, and forced myself to get a grip so that I could take care of him.

"Oh, no, Jacob! Oh, crap! Here, wrap this around it!" I shoved the dish towel at him, reaching for his hand. He shrugged away from me.

"It's nothing, Bella, don't worry about it."

The room started to shimmer a little around the edges.

I took another deep breath. "Don't worry?! You sliced your hand open!"

He ignored the dish towel I pushed at him. He put his hand under the faucet and let the water wash over the wound. The water ran red. My head whirled.

"Bella," he said.

I looked away from the wound, up to his face. He was frowning, but his expression was calm.

"What?"

"You look like you're going to pass out, and you're biting your lip off. Stop it. Relax. Breathe. I'm fine."

I inhaled through my mouth and removed my teeth from my lower lip. "Don't be brave."

He rolled his eyes.

"Let's go. I'll drive you to the ER." I was pretty sure I would be okay to drive. The walls were holding steady now, at least.

"Not necessary." Jake turned off the water and took the towel from my hand. He twisted it loosely around his palm.

"Wait," I protested. "Let me look at it." I clutched the counter more firmly, to hold myself upright if the wound made me woozy again.

"Do you have a medical degree that you never told me about?"

"Just give me the chance to decide whether or not I'm going to throw a fit over taking you to the hospital."

He made a face of mock horror. "Please, not a fit!"

"If you don't let me see your hand, a fit is guaranteed."

He inhaled deeply, and then let out a gusty sigh. "Fine."

He unwound the towel and, when I reached out to take the cloth, he laid his hand in mine.

It took me a few seconds. I even flipped his hand over, though I was sure he'd cut his palm. I turned his hand back up, finally realizing that the angry pink, puckered line was all that was left of his wound.

"But . . . you were bleeding . . . so much."

He pulled his hand back, his eyes steady and somber on mine.

"I heal fast."

"I'll say," I mouthed.

I'd seen the long gash clearly, seen the blood that flowed into the sink. The rust-and-salt smell of it had almost pulled me under. It should have needed stitches. It should have taken days to scab over and then weeks to fade into the shiny pink scar that marked his skin now.

He screwed his mouth up into half a smile and thumped his fist once against his chest. "Werewolf, remember?"

His eyes held mine for an immeasurable moment.

"Right," I finally said.

He laughed at my expression. "I told you this. You saw Paul's scar."

I shook my head to clear it. "It's a little different, seeing the action sequence firsthand."

I kneeled down and dug the bleach out of the cabinet under the sink. Then I poured some on a dusting rag and started scrubbing the floor. The burning scent of the bleach cleared the last of the dizziness from my head.

"Let me clean up," Jacob said.

"I got this. Throw that towel in the wash, will you?"

When I was sure the floor smelled of nothing but

bleach, I got up and rinsed the right side of the sink with bleach, too. Then I went to the laundry closet beside the pantry, and poured a cupful into the washing machine before starting it. Jacob watched me with a disapproving look on his face.

"Do you have obsessive-compulsive disorder?" he asked when I was done.

Huh. Maybe. But at least I had a good excuse this time. "We're a bit sensitive to blood around here. I'm sure you can understand that."

"Oh." He wrinkled his nose again.

"Why not make it as easy as possible for him? What he's doing is hard enough."

"Sure, sure. Why not?"

I pulled the plug, and let the dirty water drain from the sink.

"Can I ask you something, Bella?"

I sighed.

"What's it like — having a werewolf for a best friend?"

The question caught me off guard. I laughed out loud.

"Does it creep you out?" he pressed before I could answer.

"No. When the werewolf is being nice," I qualified, "it's the best."

He grinned widely, his teeth bright against his russet skin. "Thanks, Bella," he said, and then he grabbed my hand and wrenched me into one of his bone-crushing hugs.

Before I had time to react, he dropped his arms and stepped away.

"Ugh," he said, his nose wrinkling. "Your hair stinks worse than your room."

"Sorry," I muttered. I suddenly understood what Edward had been laughing about earlier, after breathing on me.

"One of the many hazards of socializing with vampires," Jacob said, shrugging. "It makes you smell bad. A minor hazard, comparatively."

I glared at him. "I only smell bad to you, Jake."

He grinned. "See you around, Bells."

"Are you leaving?"

"He's waiting for me to go. I can hear him outside."

"Oh."

"I'll go out the back," he said, and then he paused. "Hold up a sec — hey, do you think you can come to La Push tonight? We're having a bonfire party. Emily will be there, and you could meet Kim . . . And I know Quil wants to see you, too. He's pretty peeved that you found out before he did."

I grinned at that. I could just imagine how that would have irked Quil — Jacob's little human gal pal down with the werewolves while he was still clueless. And then I sighed. "Yeah, Jake, I don't know about that. See, it's a little tense right now. . . ."

"C'mon, you think somebody's going to get past all — all six of us?"

There was a strange pause as he stuttered over the end of his question. I wondered if he had trouble saying the word *werewolf* aloud, the way I often had difficulty with *vampire*.

His big dark eyes were full of unashamed pleading.

"I'll ask," I said doubtfully.

He made a noise in the back of his throat. "Is he your warden, now, too? You know, I saw this story on the news last week about controlling, abusive teenage relationships and —"

"Okay!" I cut him off, and then shoved his arm. "Time for the werewolf to get out!"

He grinned. "Bye, Bells. Be sure you ask *permission*."

He ducked out the back door before I could find something to throw at him. I growled incoherently at the empty room.

Seconds after he was gone, Edward walked slowly into the kitchen, raindrops glistening like diamonds set into the bronze of his hair. His eyes were wary.

"Did you two get into a fight?" he asked.

"Edward!" I sang, throwing myself at him.

"Hi, there." He laughed and wrapped his arms around me. "Are you trying to distract me? It's working."

"No, I didn't fight with Jacob. Much. Why?"

"I was just wondering why you stabbed him. Not that I object." With his chin, he gestured to the knife on the counter.

"Dang! I thought I got everything."

I pulled away from him and ran to put the knife in the sink before I doused it with bleach.

"I didn't stab him," I explained as I worked. "He forgot he had a knife in his hand."

Edward chuckled. "That's not nearly as fun as the way I imagined it."

"Be nice."

He took a big envelope from his jacket pocket and tossed it on the counter. "I got your mail."

"Anything good?"

"*I* think so."

My eyes narrowed suspiciously at his tone. I went to investigate.

He'd folded the legal-sized envelope in half. I smoothed it open, surprised at the weight of the expensive paper, and read the return address.

"Dartmouth? Is this a joke?"

"I'm sure it's an acceptance. It looks exactly like mine."

"Good grief, Edward — what did you *do*?"

"I sent in your application, that's all."

"I may not be Dartmouth material, but I'm not stupid enough to believe *that*."

"Dartmouth seems to think that you're Dartmouth material."

I took a deep breath and counted slowly to ten. "That's very generous of them," I finally said. "However, accepted or not, there is still the minor matter of tuition. I can't afford it, and I'm not letting you throw away enough money to buy yourself another sports car just so that I can pretend to go to Dartmouth next year."

"I don't need another sports car. And you don't have to pretend anything," he murmured. "One year of college wouldn't kill you. Maybe you'd even like it. Just think about it, Bella. Imagine how excited Charlie and Renée would be. . . ."

His velvet voice painted the picture in my head before I could block it. Of course Charlie would explode with pride — no one in the town of Forks would be able to escape the fallout from his excitement. And Renée would be hysterical with joy at my triumph — though she'd swear she wasn't at all surprised. . . .

I tried to shake the image out of my head. "Edward. I'm worried about living through graduation, let alone this summer or next fall."

His arms wrapped around me again. "No one is going to hurt you. You have all the time in the world."

I sighed. "I'm mailing the contents of my bank account to Alaska tomorrow. It's all the alibi I need. It's far enough away that Charlie won't expect a visit until Christmas at the earliest. And I'm sure I'll think of some excuse by then. You know," I teased halfheartedly, "this whole secrecy and deception thing is kind of a pain."

Edward's expression hardened. "It gets easier. After a few decades, everyone you know is dead. Problem solved."

I flinched.

"Sorry, that was harsh."

I stared down at the big white envelope, not seeing it. "But still true."

"If I get this resolved, whatever it is we're dealing with, will you please *consider* waiting?"

"Nope."

"Always so stubborn."

"Yep."

The washing machine thumped and stuttered to a halt.

"Stupid piece of junk," I muttered as I pulled away

from him. I moved the one small towel that had unbalanced the otherwise empty machine, and started it again.

"This reminds me," I said. "Could you ask Alice what she did with my stuff when she cleaned my room? I can't find it anywhere."

He looked at me with confused eyes. "Alice cleaned your room?"

"Yeah, I guess that's what she was doing. When she came to get my pajamas and pillow and stuff to hold me hostage." I glowered at him briefly. "She picked up everything that was lying around, my shirts, my socks, and I don't know where she put them."

Edward continued to look confused for one short moment, and then, abruptly, he was rigid.

"When did you notice your things were missing?"

"When I got back from the fake slumber party. Why?"

"I don't think Alice took anything. Not your clothes, or your pillow. The things that were taken, these were things you'd worn . . . and touched . . . and slept on?"

"Yes. What is it, Edward?"

His expression was strained. "Things with your scent."

"Oh!"

We stared into each other's eyes for a long moment.

"My visitor," I muttered.

"He was gathering traces . . . evidence. To prove that he'd found you?"

"Why?" I whispered.

"I don't know. But, Bella, I swear I *will* find out. I will."

"I know you will," I said, laying my head against his chest. Leaning there, I felt his phone vibrate in his pocket.

He pulled out his phone and glanced at the number. "Just the person I need to talk to," he murmured, and then he flipped it open. "Carlisle, I —" He broke off and listened, his face taut with concentration for a few minutes. "I'll check it out. Listen . . ."

He explained about my missing things, but from the side I was hearing, it sounded like Carlisle had no insights for us.

"Maybe I'll go . . . ," Edward said, trailing off as his eyes drifted toward me. "Maybe not. Don't let Emmett go alone, you know how he gets. At least ask Alice to keep an eye on things. We'll figure this out later."

He snapped the phone shut. "Where's the paper?" he asked me.

"Um, I'm not sure. Why?"

"I need to see something. Did Charlie already throw it out?"

"Maybe. . . ."

Edward disappeared.

He was back in half a second, new diamonds in his hair, a wet newspaper in his hands. He spread it out on the table, his eyes scanning quickly across the headlines. He leaned in, intent on something he was reading, one finger tracing passages that interested him most.

"Carlisle's right . . . yes . . . very sloppy. Young and crazed? Or a death wish?" he muttered to himself.

I went to peek over his shoulder.

The headline of the *Seattle Times* read: "Murder Epidemic Continues — Police Have No New Leads."

It was almost the same story Charlie had been complaining about a few weeks ago — the big-city violence that was pushing Seattle up the national murder hot-spot list. It wasn't exactly the same story, though. The numbers were a lot higher.

"It's getting worse," I murmured.

He frowned. "Altogether out of control. This can't be the work of just *one* newborn vampire. What's going on? It's as if they've never heard of the Volturi. Which is possible, I guess. No one has explained the rules to them . . . so who is creating them, then?"

"The Volturi?" I repeated, shuddering.

"This is exactly the kind of thing they routinely wipe out — immortals who threaten to expose us. They just cleaned up a mess like this a few years ago in Atlanta, and it hadn't gotten nearly this bad. They will intervene soon, very soon, unless we can find some way to calm the situation. I'd really rather they didn't come to Seattle just now. As long as they're this close . . . they might decide to check on you."

I shuddered again. "What can we do?"

"We need to know more before we can decide that. Perhaps if we can talk to these young ones, explain the rules, it can be resolved peacefully." He frowned, like he didn't think the chances of that were good. "We'll wait until Alice has an idea of what's going on. . . . We don't want to step in until it's absolutely necessary. After all, it's not our responsibility. But it's good we have Jasper," he added, almost to himself. "If we are dealing with newborns, he'll be helpful."

"Jasper? Why?"

Edward smiled darkly. "Jasper is sort of an expert on young vampires."

"What do you mean, an expert?"

"You'll have to ask him — the story is involved."

"What a mess," I mumbled.

"It does feel that way, doesn't it? Like it's coming at us from all sides these days." He sighed. "Do you ever think that your life might be easier if you weren't in love with me?"

"Maybe. It wouldn't be much of a life, though."

"For me," he amended quietly. "And now, I suppose," he continued with a wry smile, "you have something you want to ask me?"

I stared at him blankly. "I do?"

"Or maybe not." He grinned. "I was rather under the impression that you'd promised to ask my permission to go to some kind of werewolf soirée tonight."

"Eavesdropping again?"

He grinned. "Just a bit, at the very end."

"Well, I wasn't going to ask you anyway. I figured you had enough to stress about."

He put his hand under my chin, and held my face so that he could read my eyes. "Would you like to go?"

"It's no big thing. Don't worry about it."

"You don't have to ask my permission, Bella. I'm not your father — thank heaven for *that*. Perhaps you should ask Charlie, though."

"But you know Charlie will say yes."

"I do have a bit more insight into his probable answer than most people would, it's true."

I just stared at him, trying to understand what he wanted, and trying to put out of my mind the yearning I felt to go to La Push so that I wouldn't be swayed by my own wishes. It was stupid to want to go hang out with a bunch of big idiot wolf-boys right now when there was so much that was frightening and unexplained going on. Of course, that was *exactly* why I wanted to go. I wanted to escape the death threats, for just a few hours . . . to be the less-mature, more-reckless Bella who could laugh it off with Jacob, if only briefly. But that didn't matter.

"Bella," Edward said. "I told you that I was going to be reasonable and trust your judgment. I meant that. If you trust the werewolves, then I'm not going to worry about them."

"Wow," I said, as I had last night.

"And Jacob's right — about one thing, anyway — a pack of werewolves ought to be enough to protect even you for one evening."

"Are you sure?"

"Of course. Only . . ."

I braced myself.

"I hope you won't mind taking a few precautions? Allowing me to drive you to the boundary line, for one. And then taking a cell phone, so that I'll know when to pick you up?"

"That sounds . . . very reasonable."

"Excellent."

He smiled at me, and I could see no trace of apprehension in his jewel-like eyes.

To no one's surprise, Charlie had no problem at all with me going to La Push for a bonfire. Jacob crowed with undisguised exultation when I called to give him the news, and he seemed eager enough to embrace Edward's safety measures. He promised to meet us at the line between territories at six.

I had decided, after a short internal debate, that I would not sell my motorcycle. I would take it back to La Push where it belonged and, when I no longer needed it anymore . . . well, then, I would insist that Jacob profit from his work somehow. He could sell it or give it to a friend. It didn't matter to me.

Tonight seemed like a good opportunity to return the bike to Jacob's garage. As gloomy as I was feeling about things lately, every day seemed like a possible last chance. I didn't have time to procrastinate any task, no matter how minor.

Edward only nodded when I explained what I wanted, but I thought I saw a flicker of consternation in his eyes, and I knew he was no happier about the idea of me on a motorcycle than Charlie was.

I followed him back to his house, to the garage where I'd left the bike. It wasn't until I pulled the truck in and got out that I realized the consternation might not be entirely about my safety this time.

Next to my little antique motorcycle, overshadowing it, was another vehicle. To call this other vehicle a motorcycle hardly seemed fair, since it didn't seem to belong to the same family as my suddenly shabby-looking bike.

It was big and sleek and silver and — even totally motionless — it looked fast.

"What is *that*?"

"Nothing," Edward murmured.

"It doesn't *look* like nothing."

Edward's expression was casual; he seemed determined to blow it off. "Well, I didn't know if you were going to forgive your friend, or he you, and I wondered if you would still want to ride your bike anyway. It sounded like it was something that you enjoyed. I thought I could go with you, if you wished." He shrugged.

I stared at the beautiful machine. Beside it, my bike looked like a broken tricycle. I felt a sudden wave of sadness when I realized that this was not a bad analogy for the way I probably looked next to Edward.

"I wouldn't be able to keep up with you," I whispered.

Edward put his hand under my chin and pulled my face around so that he could see it straight on. With one finger, he tried to push the corner of my mouth up.

"I'd keep pace with you, Bella."

"That wouldn't be much fun for you."

"Of course it would, if we were together."

I bit my lip and imagined it for a moment. "Edward, if you thought I was going too fast or losing control of the bike or something, what would you do?"

He hesitated, obviously trying to find the right answer. I knew the truth: he'd find some way to save me before I crashed.

Then he smiled. It looked effortless, except for the tiny defensive tightening of his eyes.

"This is something you do with Jacob. I see that now."

"It's just that, well, I don't slow him down so much, you know. I could try, I guess. . . ."

I eyed the silver motorcycle doubtfully.

"Don't worry about it," Edward said, and then he laughed lightly. "I saw Jasper admiring it. Perhaps it's time he discovered a new way to travel. After all, Alice has her Porsche now."

"Edward, I —"

He interrupted me with a quick kiss. "I said not to worry. But would you do something for me?"

"Whatever you need," I promised quickly.

He dropped my face and leaned over the far side of the big motorcycle, retrieving something he had stashed there.

He came back with one object that was black and shapeless, and another that was red and easily identifiable.

"Please?" he asked, flashing the crooked smile that always destroyed my resistance.

I took the red helmet, weighing it in my hands. "I'll look stupid."

"No, you'll look smart. Smart enough not to get yourself hurt." He threw the black thing, whatever it was, over his arm and then took my face in his hands. "There are things between my hands right now that I can't live without. You could take care of them."

"Okay, fine. What's that other thing?" I asked suspiciously.

He laughed and shook out some kind of padded jacket. "It's a riding jacket. I hear road rash is quite uncomfortable, not that I would know myself."

He held it out for me. With a deep sigh, I flipped my hair back and stuffed the helmet on my head. Then I shoved my arms through the sleeves of the jacket. He zipped me in, a smile playing around the corners of his lips, and took a step back.

I felt bulky.

"Be honest, how hideous do I look?"

He took another step back and pursed his lips.

"That bad, huh?" I muttered.

"No, no, Bella. Actually . . ." he seemed to be struggling for the right word. "You look . . . sexy."

I laughed out loud. "Right."

"Very sexy, really."

"You are just saying that so that I'll wear it," I said. "But that's okay. You're right, it's smarter."

He wrapped his arms around me and pulled me against his chest. "You're silly. I suppose that's part of your charm. Though, I'll admit it, this helmet does have its drawbacks."

And then he pulled the helmet off so that he could kiss me.

As Edward drove me toward La Push a little while later, I realized that this unprecedented situation felt oddly familiar. It took me a moment of thought to pinpoint the source of the déjà vu.

"You know what this reminds me of?" I asked. "It's just

like when I was a kid and Renée would pass me off to Charlie for the summer. I feel like a seven-year-old."

Edward laughed.

I didn't mention it out loud, but the biggest difference between the two circumstances was that Renée and Charlie had been on better terms.

About halfway to La Push, we rounded the corner and found Jacob leaning against the side of the red Volkswagen he'd built for himself out of scraps. Jacob's carefully neutral expression dissolved into a smile when I waved from the front seat.

Edward parked the Volvo thirty yards away.

"Call me whenever you're ready to come home," he said. "And I'll be here."

"I won't be out late," I promised.

Edward pulled the bike and my new gear out of the trunk of his car — I'd been quite impressed that it had all fit. But it wasn't so hard to manage when you were strong enough to juggle full-sized vans, let alone small motorcycles.

Jacob watched, making no move to approach, his smile gone and his dark eyes indecipherable.

I tucked the helmet under my arm and threw the jacket across the seat.

"Do you have it all?" Edward asked.

"No problem," I assured him.

He sighed and leaned toward me. I turned my face up for a goodbye peck, but Edward took me by surprise, fastening his arms tightly around me and kissing me with as much enthusiasm as he had in the garage — before long, I was gasping for air.

Edward laughed quietly at something, and then let me go.

"Goodbye," he said. "I really do like the jacket."

As I turned away from him, I thought I saw a flash of something in his eyes that I wasn't supposed to see. I couldn't tell for sure what it was exactly. Worry, maybe. For a second I thought it was panic. But I was probably just making something out of nothing, as usual.

I could feel his eyes on my back as I pushed my bike toward the invisible vampire-werewolf treaty line to meet Jacob.

"What's all that?" Jacob called to me, his voice wary, scrutinizing the motorcycle with an enigmatic expression.

"I thought I should put this back where it belongs," I told him.

He pondered that for one short second, and then his wide smile stretched across his face.

I knew the exact point that I was in werewolf territory because Jacob shoved away from his car and loped quickly over to me, closing the distance in three long strides. He took the bike from me, balanced it on the kickstand, and grabbed me up in another vice-tight hug.

I heard the Volvo's engine growl, and I struggled to get free.

"Cut it out, Jake!" I gasped breathlessly.

He laughed and set me down. I turned to wave goodbye, but the silver car was already disappearing around the curve in the road.

"Nice," I commented, allowing some acid to leak into my voice.

His eyes widened in false innocence. "What?"

"He's being pretty dang pleasant about this; you don't need to push your luck."

He laughed again, louder than before — he found what I'd said very funny indeed. I tried to see the joke as he walked around the Rabbit to hold my door open for me.

"Bella," he finally said — still chuckling — as he shut the door behind me, "you can't push what you don't have."

11. LEGENDS

"ARE YOU GONNA EAT THAT HOT DOG?" PAUL ASKED JA-cob, his eyes locked on the last remnant of the huge meal the werewolves had consumed.

Jacob leaned back against my knees and toyed with the hot dog he had spitted on a straightened wire hanger; the flames at the edge of the bonfire licked along its blistered skin. He heaved a sigh and patted his stomach. It was somehow still flat, though I'd lost count of how many hot dogs he'd eaten after his tenth. Not to mention the super-sized bag of chips or the two-liter bottle of root beer.

"I guess," Jake said slowly. "I'm so full I'm about to puke, but I *think* I can force it down. I won't enjoy it at all, though." He sighed again sadly.

Despite the fact that Paul had eaten at least as much as Jacob, he glowered and his hands balled up into fists.

"Sheesh." Jacob laughed. "Kidding, Paul. Here."

He flipped the homemade skewer across the circle. I expected it to land hot-dog-first in the sand, but Paul caught it neatly on the right end without difficulty.

Hanging out with no one but extremely dexterous people all the time was going to give me a complex.

"Thanks, man," Paul said, already over his brief fit of temper.

The fire crackled, settling lower toward the sand. Sparks blew up in a sudden puff of brilliant orange against the black sky. Funny, I hadn't noticed that the sun had set. For the first time, I wondered how late it had gotten. I'd lost track of time completely.

It was easier being with my Quileute friends than I'd expected.

While Jacob and I had dropped off my bike at the garage — and he had admitted ruefully that the helmet was a good idea that he should have thought of himself — I'd started to worry about showing up with him at the bonfire, wondering if the werewolves would consider me a traitor now. Would they be angry with Jacob for inviting me? Would I ruin the party?

But when Jacob had towed me out of the forest to the clifftop meeting place — where the fire already roared brighter than the cloud-obscured sun — it had all been very casual and light.

"Hey, vampire girl!" Embry had greeted me loudly.

Quil had jumped up to give me a high five and kiss me on the cheek. Emily had squeezed my hand when we'd sat on the cool stone ground beside her and Sam.

Other than a few teasing complaints — mostly by Paul — about keeping the bloodsucker stench downwind, I was treated like someone who belonged.

It wasn't just kids in attendance, either. Billy was here, his wheelchair stationed at what seemed the natural head of the circle. Beside him on a folding lawn chair, looking quite brittle, was Quil's ancient, white-haired grandfather, Old Quil. Sue Clearwater, widow of Charlie's friend Harry, had a chair on his other side; her two children, Leah and Seth, were also there, sitting on the ground like the rest of us. This surprised me, but all three were clearly in on the secret now. From the way Billy and Old Quil spoke to Sue, it sounded to me like she'd taken Harry's place on the council. Did that make her children automatic members of La Push's most secret society?

I wondered how horrible it was for Leah to sit across the circle from Sam and Emily. Her lovely face betrayed no emotion, but she never looked away from the flames. Looking at the perfection of Leah's features, I couldn't help but compare them to Emily's ruined face. What did Leah think of Emily's scars, now that she knew the truth behind them? Did it seem like justice in her eyes?

Little Seth Clearwater wasn't so little anymore. With his huge, happy grin and his long, gangly build, he reminded me very much of a younger Jacob. The resemblance made me smile, and then sigh. Was Seth doomed to have his life change as drastically as the rest of these boys? Was that future why he and his family were allowed to be here?

The whole pack was there: Sam with his Emily, Paul, Embry, Quil, and Jared with Kim, the girl he'd imprinted upon.

My first impression of Kim was that she was a nice girl, a little shy, and a little plain. She had a wide face, mostly cheekbones, with eyes too small to balance them out. Her nose and mouth were both too broad for traditional beauty. Her flat black hair was thin and wispy in the wind that never seemed to let up atop the cliff.

That was my first impression. But after a few hours of watching Jared watch Kim, I could no longer find anything plain about the girl.

The way he stared at her! It was like a blind man seeing the sun for the first time. Like a collector finding an undiscovered Da Vinci, like a mother looking into the face of her newborn child.

His wondering eyes made me see new things about her — how her skin looked like russet-colored silk in the firelight, how the shape of her lips was a perfect double curve, how white her teeth were against them, how long her eyelashes were, brushing her cheek when she looked down.

Kim's skin sometimes darkened when she met Jared's awed gaze, and her eyes would drop as if in embarrassment, but she had a hard time keeping her eyes away from his for any length of time.

Watching them, I felt like I better understood what

Jacob had told me about imprinting before — *it's hard to resist that level of commitment and adoration.*

Kim was nodding off now against Jared's chest, his arms around her. I imagined she would be very warm there.

"It's getting late," I murmured to Jacob.

"Don't start *that* yet," Jacob whispered back — though certainly half the group here had hearing sensitive enough to hear us anyway. "The best part is coming."

"What's the best part? You swallowing an entire cow whole?"

Jacob chuckled his low, throaty laugh. "No. That's the finale. We didn't meet just to eat through a week's worth of food. This is technically a council meeting. It's Quil's first time, and he hasn't heard the stories yet. Well, he's *heard* them, but this will be the first time he knows they're true. That tends to make a guy pay closer attention. Kim and Seth and Leah are all first-timers, too."

"Stories?"

Jacob scooted back beside me, where I rested against a low ridge of rock. He put his arm over my shoulder and spoke even lower into my ear.

"The histories we always thought were legends," he said. "The stories of how we came to be. The first is the story of the spirit warriors."

It was almost as if Jacob's soft whisper was the introduction. The atmosphere changed abruptly around the low-burning fire. Paul and Embry sat up straighter. Jared nudged Kim and then pulled her gently upright.

Emily produced a spiral-bound notebook and a pen, looking exactly like a student set for an important lecture.

Sam twisted just slightly beside her — so that he was facing the same direction as Old Quil, who was on his other side — and suddenly I realized that the elders of the council here were not three, but four in number.

Leah Clearwater, her face still a beautiful and emotionless mask, closed her eyes — not like she was tired, but as if to help her concentration. Her brother leaned in toward the elders eagerly.

The fire crackled, sending another explosion of sparks glittering up against the night.

Billy cleared his throat, and, with no more introduction than his son's whisper, began telling the story in his rich, deep voice. The words poured out with precision, as if he knew them by heart, but also with feeling and a subtle rhythm. Like poetry performed by its author.

"The Quileutes have been a small people from the beginning," Billy said. "And we are a small people still, but we have never disappeared. This is because there has always been magic in our blood. It wasn't always the magic of shape-shifting — that came later. First, we were spirit warriors."

Never before had I recognized the ring of majesty that was in Billy Black's voice, though I realized now that this authority had always been there.

Emily's pen sprinted across the sheets of paper as she tried to keep up with him.

"In the beginning, the tribe settled in this harbor and became skilled ship builders and fishermen. But the tribe was small, and the harbor was rich in fish. There were others who coveted our land, and we were too small to hold it. A larger tribe moved against us, and we took to our ships to escape them.

"Kaheleha was not the first spirit warrior, but we do not remember the stories that came before his. We do not remember who was the first to discover this power, or how it had been used before this crisis. Kaheleha *was* the first great Spirit Chief in our history. In this emergency, Kaheleha used the magic to defend our land.

"He and all his warriors left the ship — not their bodies, but their spirits. Their women watched over the bodies and the waves, and the men took their spirits back to our harbor.

"They could not physically touch the enemy tribe, but they had other ways. The stories tell us that they could blow fierce winds into their enemy's camps; they could make a great screaming in the wind that terrified their foes. The stories also tell us that the animals could see the spirit warriors and understand them; the animals would do their bidding.

"Kaheleha took his spirit army and wreaked havoc on the intruders. This invading tribe had packs of big, thick-furred dogs that they used to pull their sleds in the frozen north. The spirit warriors turned the dogs against their masters and then brought a mighty infestation of bats up from the cliff caverns. They used the screaming wind to aid the dogs in confusing the men. The dogs and bats won. The survivors scattered, calling our harbor a cursed place. The dogs ran wild when the spirit warriors released them. The Quileutes returned to their bodies and their wives, victorious.

"The other nearby tribes, the Hohs and the Makahs, made treaties with the Quileutes. They wanted nothing to do with our magic. We lived in peace with them. When an enemy came against us, the spirit warriors would drive them off.

"Generations passed. Then came the last great Spirit Chief, Taha Aki. He was known for his wisdom, and for being a man of peace. The people lived well and content in his care.

"But there was one man, Utlapa, who was not content."

A low hiss ran around the fire. I was too slow to see where it came from. Billy ignored it and went on with the legend.

"Utlapa was one of Chief Taha Aki's strongest spirit warriors — a powerful man, but a grasping man, too. He thought the people should use their magic to expand their lands, to enslave the Hohs and the Makahs and build an empire.

"Now, when the warriors were their spirit selves, they knew each other's thoughts. Taha Aki saw what Utlapa dreamed, and was angry with Utlapa. Utlapa was commanded to leave the people, and never use his spirit self again. Utlapa was a strong man, but the chief's warriors outnumbered him. He had no choice but to leave. The furious outcast hid in the forest nearby, waiting for a chance to get revenge against the chief.

"Even in times of peace, the Spirit Chief was vigilant in protecting his people. Often, he would go to a sacred, secret place in the mountains. He would leave his body behind and sweep down through the forests and along the coast, making sure no threat approached.

"One day when Taha Aki left to perform this duty, Utlapa followed. At first, Utlapa simply planned to kill the chief, but this plan had its drawbacks. Surely the spirit warriors would seek to destroy him, and they could follow faster than he could escape. As he hid in the rocks and watched the chief prepare to leave his body, another plan occurred to him.

"Taha Aki left his body in the secret place and flew with the winds to keep watch over his people. Utlapa waited until he was sure the chief had traveled some distance with his spirit self.

"Taha Aki knew it the instant that Utlapa had joined him in the spirit world, and he also knew Utlapa's murderous plan. He raced back to his secret place, but even the winds weren't fast enough to save him. When he returned, his body was already gone. Utlapa's body lay abandoned, but Utlapa had not left Taha Aki with an escape — he had cut his own body's throat with Taha Aki's hands.

"Taha Aki followed his body down the mountain. He screamed at Utlapa, but Utlapa ignored him as if he were mere wind.

"Taha Aki watched with despair as Utlapa took his place as chief of the Quileutes. For a few weeks, Utlapa did nothing but make sure that everyone believed he was Taha Aki. Then the changes began — Utlapa's first edict was to forbid any warrior to enter the spirit world. He claimed that he'd had a vision of danger, but really he was afraid.

He knew that Taha Aki would be waiting for the chance to tell his story. Utlapa was also afraid to enter the spirit world himself, knowing Taha Aki would quickly claim his body. So his dreams of conquest with a spirit warrior army were impossible, and he sought to content himself with ruling over the tribe. He became a burden — seeking privileges that Taha Aki had never requested, refusing to work alongside his warriors, taking a young second wife and then a third, though Taha Aki's wife lived on — something unheard of in the tribe. Taha Aki watched in helpless fury.

"Eventually, Taha Aki tried to kill his body to save the tribe from Utlapa's excesses. He brought a fierce wolf down from the mountains, but Utlapa hid behind his warriors. When the wolf killed a young man who was protecting the false chief, Taha Aki felt horrible grief. He ordered the wolf away.

"All the stories tell us that it was no easy thing to be a spirit warrior. It was more frightening than exhilarating to be freed from one's body. This is why they only used their magic in times of need. The chief's solitary journeys to keep watch were a burden and a sacrifice. Being bodiless was disorienting, uncomfortable, horrifying. Taha Aki had been away from his body for so long at this point that he was in agony. He felt he was doomed — never to cross over to the final land where his ancestors waited, stuck in this torturous nothingness forever.

"The great wolf followed Taha Aki's spirit as he twisted and writhed in agony through the woods. The wolf was very large for its kind, and beautiful. Taha Aki was suddenly jealous of the dumb animal. At least it had a body. At least it had a life. Even life as an animal would be better than this horrible empty consciousness.

"And then Taha Aki had the idea that changed us all. He asked the great wolf to make room for him, to share. The wolf complied. Taka Aki entered the wolf's body with relief and gratitude. It was not his human body, but it was better than the void of the spirit world.

"As one, the man and the wolf returned to the village on the harbor. The people ran in fear, shouting for the warriors to come. The warriors ran to meet the wolf with their spears. Utlapa, of course, stayed safely hidden.

"Taha Aki did not attack his warriors. He retreated slowly from them, speaking with his eyes and trying to yelp the songs of his people. The warriors began to realize that the wolf was no ordinary animal, that there was a spirit influencing it. One older warrior, a man name Yut, decided to disobey the false chief's order and try to communicate with the wolf.

"As soon as Yut crossed to the spirit world, Taha Aki left the wolf — the animal waited tamely for his return — to speak to him. Yut gathered the truth in an instant, and welcomed his true chief home.

"At this time, Utlapa came to see if the wolf had been defeated. When he saw Yut lying lifeless on the ground, surrounded by protective warriors, he realized what was happening. He drew his knife and raced forward to kill Yut before he could return to his body.

"'Traitor,' he screamed, and the warriors did not know what to do. The chief had forbidden spirit journeys, and it was the chief's decision how to punish those who disobeyed.

"Yut jumped back into his body, but Utlapa had his knife at his throat and a hand covering his mouth. Taha Aki's body was strong, and Yut was weak with age. Yut could not say even one word to warn the others before Utlapa silenced him forever.

"Taha Aki watched as Yut's spirit slipped away to the final lands that were barred to Taha Aki for all eternity. He felt a great rage, more powerful than anything he'd felt before. He entered the big wolf again, meaning to rip Utlapa's throat out. But, as he joined the wolf, the greatest magic happened.

"Taha Aki's anger was the anger of a man. The love he had for his people and the hatred he had for their oppressor were too vast for the wolf's body, too human. The wolf shuddered, and — before the eyes of the shocked warriors and Utlapa — transformed into a man.

"The new man did not look like Taha Aki's body. He was far more glorious. He was the flesh interpretation of Taha Aki's spirit. The warriors recognized him at once, though, for they had flown with Taha Aki's spirit.

"Utlapa tried to run, but Taha Aki had the strength of the wolf in his new body. He caught the thief and crushed the spirit from him before he could jump out of the stolen body.

"The people rejoiced when they understood what had happened. Taha Aki quickly set everything right, working again with his people and giving the young wives back to their families. The only change he kept in place was the end of the spirit travels. He knew that it was too danger-ous now that the idea of stealing a life was there. The spirit warriors were no more.

"From that point on, Taha Aki was more than either wolf or man. They called him Taha Aki the Great Wolf, or Taha Aki the Spirit Man. He led the tribe for many, many years, for he did not age. When danger threatened, he would resume his wolf-self to fight or frighten the enemy. The people dwelt in peace. Taha Aki fathered many sons, and some of these found that, after they had reached the age of manhood, they, too, could transform into wolves. The wolves were all different, because they were spirit wolves and reflected the man they were inside."

"So that's why Sam is all black," Quil muttered under his breath, grinning. "Black heart, black fur."

I was so involved in the story, it was a shock to come back to the present, to the circle around the dying fire. With another shock, I realized that the circle was made up of Taha Aki's great — to however many degrees — grandsons.

The fire threw a volley of sparks into the sky, and they shivered and danced, making shapes that were almost de-cipherable.

"And your chocolate fur reflects what?" Sam whispered back to Quil. "How *sweet* you are?"

Billy ignored their jibes. "Some of the sons became warriors with Taha Aki, and they no longer aged. Others, who did not like the transformation, refused to join the pack of wolf-men. These began to age again, and the tribe discovered that the wolf-men could grow old like anyone else if they gave up their spirit wolves. Taha Aki had lived the span of three old men's lives. He had married a third wife after the deaths of the first two, and found in her his true spirit wife. Though he had loved the others, this was something else. He decided to give up his spirit wolf so that he would die when she did.

"That is how the magic came to us, but it is not the end of the story. . . ."

He looked at Old Quil Ateara, who shifted in his chair, straightening his frail shoulders. Billy took a drink from a bottle of water and wiped his forehead. Emily's pen never hesitated as she scribbled furiously on the paper.

"That was the story of the spirit warriors," Old Quil began in a thin tenor voice. "This is the story of the third wife's sacrifice.

"Many years after Taha Aki gave up his spirit wolf, when he was an old man, trouble began in the north, with the Makahs. Several young women of their tribe had disappeared, and they blamed it on the neighboring wolves, who they feared and mistrusted. The wolf-men could still read each other's thoughts while in their wolf forms, just like their ancestors had while in their spirit forms. They knew that none of their number was to blame. Taha Aki tried to pacify the Makah chief, but there was too much fear. Taha Aki did not want to have a war on his hands. He was no longer a warrior to lead his people. He charged his oldest wolf-son, Taha Wi, with finding the true culprit before hostilities began.

"Taha Wi led the five other wolves in his pack on a

search through the mountains, looking for any evidence of the missing Makahs. They came across something they had never encountered before — a strange, sweet scent in the forest that burned their noses to the point of pain."

I shrank a little closer to Jacob's side. I saw the corner of his mouth twitch with humor, and his arm tightened around me.

"They did not know what creature would leave such a scent, but they followed it," Old Quil continued. His quavering voice did not have the majesty of Billy's, but it had a strange, fierce edge of urgency about it. My pulse jumped as his words came faster.

"They found faint traces of human scent, and human blood, along the trail. They were sure this was the enemy they were searching for.

"The journey took them so far north that Taha Wi sent half the pack, the younger ones, back to the harbor to report to Taha Aki.

"Taha Wi and his two brothers did not return.

"The younger brothers searched for their elders, but found only silence. Taha Aki mourned for his sons. He wished to avenge his sons' death, but he was old. He went to the Makah chief in his mourning clothes and told him everything that had happened. The Makah chief believed his grief, and tensions ended between the tribes.

"A year later, two Makah maidens disappeared from their homes on the same night. The Makahs called on the Quileute wolves at once, who found the same sweet stink all through the Makah village. The wolves went on the hunt again.

"Only one came back. He was Yaha Uta, the oldest son of Taha Aki's third wife, and the youngest in the pack. He brought something with him that had never been seen in all the days of the Quileutes — a strange, cold, stony corpse that he carried in pieces. All who were of Taha Aki's blood, even those who had never been wolves, could smell the piercing smell of the dead creature. This was the enemy of the Makahs.

"Yaha Uta described what had happened: he and his brothers had found the creature, who looked like a man but was hard as a granite rock, with the two Makah daughters. One girl was already dead, white and bloodless on the ground. The other was in the creature's arms, his mouth at her throat. She may have been alive when they came upon the hideous scene, but the creature quickly snapped her neck and tossed her lifeless body to the ground when they approached. His white lips were covered in her blood, and his eyes glowed red.

"Yaha Uta described the fierce strength and speed of the creature. One of his brothers quickly became a victim when he underestimated that strength. The creature ripped him apart like a doll. Yaha Uta and his other brother were more wary. They worked together, coming at the creature from the sides, outmaneuvering it. They had to reach the very limits of their wolf strength and speed, something that had never been tested before. The creature was hard as stone and cold as ice. They found that only their teeth could damage it. They began to rip small pieces of the creature apart while it fought them.

"But the creature learned quickly, and soon was matching their maneuvers. It got its hands on Yaha Uta's brother. Yaha Uta found an opening on the creature's throat, and he lunged. His teeth tore the head off the creature, but the hands continued to mangle his brother.

"Yaha Uta ripped the creature into unrecognizable chunks, tearing pieces apart in a desperate attempt to save his brother. He was too late, but, in the end, the creature was destroyed.

"Or so they thought. Yaha Uta laid the reeking remains out to be examined by the elders. One severed hand lay beside a piece of the creature's granite arm. The two pieces touched when the elders poked them with sticks, and the hand reached out towards the arm piece, trying to reassemble itself.

"Horrified, the elders set fire to the remains. A great cloud of choking, vile smoke polluted the air. When there was nothing but ashes, they separated the ashes into many small bags and spread them far and wide — some in the ocean, some in the forest, some in the cliff caverns. Taha Aki wore one bag around his neck, so he would be warned if the creature ever tried to put himself together again."

Old Quil paused and looked at Billy. Billy pulled out a leather thong from around his neck. Hanging from the end was a small bag, blackened with age. A few people gasped. I might have been one of them.

"They called it The Cold One, the Blood Drinker, and lived in fear that it was not alone. They only had one wolf protector left, young Yaha Uta.

"They did not have long to wait. The creature had a mate, another blood drinker, who came to the Quileutes seeking revenge.

"The stories say that the Cold Woman was the most beautiful thing human eyes had ever seen. She looked like the goddess of the dawn when she entered the village that morning; the sun was shining for once, and it glittered off her white skin and lit the golden hair that flowed down to her knees. Her face was magical in its beauty, her eyes black in her white face. Some fell to their knees to worship her.

"She asked something in a high, piercing voice, in a language no one had ever heard. The people were dumbfounded, not knowing how to answer her. There was none of Taha Aki's blood among the witnesses but one small boy. He clung to his mother and screamed that the smell was hurting his nose. One of the elders, on his way to council, heard the boy and realized what had come among them. He yelled for the people to run. She killed him first.

"There were twenty witnesses to the Cold Woman's approach. Two survived, only because she grew distracted by the blood, and paused to sate her thirst. They ran to Taha Aki, who sat in counsel with the other elders, his sons, and his third wife.

"Yaha Uta transformed into his spirit wolf as soon as he heard the news. He went to destroy the blood drinker alone. Taha Aki, his third wife, his sons, and his elders followed behind him.

"At first they could not find the creature, only the evidence of her attack. Bodies lay broken, a few drained of blood, strewn across the road where she'd appeared. Then they heard the screams and hurried to the harbor.

"A handful of the Quileutes had run to the ships for refuge. She swam after them like a shark, and broke the bow of their boat with her incredible strength. When the ship sank, she caught those trying to swim away and broke them, too.

"She saw the great wolf on the shore, and she forgot the fleeing swimmers. She swam so fast she was a blur and came, dripping and glorious, to stand before Yaha Uta. She pointed at him with one white finger and asked another incomprehensible question. Yaha Uta waited.

"It was a close fight. She was not the warrior her mate had been. But Yaha Uta was alone — there was no one to distract her fury from him.

"When Yaha Uta lost, Taha Aki screamed in defiance. He limped forward and shifted into an ancient, white-muzzled wolf. The wolf was old, but this was Taha Aki the Spirit Man, and his rage made him strong. The fight began again.

"Taha Aki's third wife had just seen her son die before her. Now her husband fought, and she had no hope that he could win. She'd heard every word the witnesses to the slaughter had told the council. She'd heard the story of Yaha Uta's first victory, and knew that his brother's diversion had saved him.

"The third wife grabbed a knife from the belt of one of the sons who stood beside her. They were all young sons, not yet men, and she knew they would die when their father failed.

"The third wife ran toward the Cold Woman with the dagger raised high. The Cold Woman smiled, barely distracted from her fight with the old wolf. She had no fear of the weak human woman or the knife that would not even scratch her skin, and she was about to deliver the death blow to Taha Aki.

"And then the third wife did something the Cold Woman did not expect. She fell to her knees at the blood drinker's feet and plunged the knife into her own heart.

"Blood spurted through the third wife's fingers and splashed against the Cold Woman. The blood drinker could not resist the lure of the fresh blood leaving the third wife's body. Instinctively, she turned to the dying woman, for one second entirely consumed by thirst.

"Taha Aki's teeth closed around her neck.

"That was not the end of the fight, but Taha Aki was not alone now. Watching their mother die, two young sons felt such rage that they sprang forth as their spirit wolves, though they were not yet men. With their father, they finished the creature.

"Taha Aki never rejoined the tribe. He never changed back to a man again. He lay for one day beside the body of the third wife, growling whenever anyone tried to touch her, and then he went into the forest and never returned.

"Trouble with the cold ones was rare from that time on. Taha Aki's sons guarded the tribe until their sons were old enough to take their places. There were never more than three wolves at a time. It was enough. Occasionally a blood drinker would come through these lands, but they were taken by surprise, not expecting the wolves. Sometimes a wolf would die, but never were they decimated again like that first time. They'd learned how to fight the cold ones, and they passed the knowledge on, wolf mind to wolf mind, spirit to spirit, father to son.

"Time passed, and the descendants of Taha Aki no longer became wolves when they reached manhood. Only in a great while, if a cold one was near, would the wolves return. The cold ones always came in ones and twos, and the pack stayed small.

"A bigger coven came, and your own great-grandfathers prepared to fight them off. But the leader spoke to Ephraim Black as if he were a man, and promised not to harm the Quileutes. His strange yellow eyes gave some proof to his claim that they were not the same as other blood drinkers. The wolves were outnumbered; there was no need for the cold ones to offer a treaty when they could have won the fight. Ephraim accepted. They've stayed true to their side, though their presence does tend to draw in others.

"And their numbers have forced a larger pack than the tribe has ever seen," Old Quil said, and for one moment his black eyes, all but buried in the wrinkles of skin folded around them, seemed to rest on me. "Except, of course, in Taha Aki's time," he said, and then he sighed. "And so the sons of our tribe again carry the burden and share the sacrifice their fathers endured before them."

All was silent for a long moment. The living descendants of magic and legend stared at one another across the fire with sadness in their eyes. All but one.

"Burden," he scoffed in a low voice. "I think it's cool." Quil's full lower lip pouted out a little bit.

Across the dying fire, Seth Clearwater — his eyes wide with adulation for the fraternity of tribal protectors — nodded his agreement.

Billy chuckled, low and long, and the magic seemed to fade into the glowing embers. Suddenly, it was just a circle of friends again. Jared flicked a small stone at Quil, and everyone laughed when it made him jump. Low conversations murmured around us, teasing and casual.

Leah Clearwater's eyes did not open. I thought I saw something sparkling on her cheek like a tear, but when I looked back a moment later it was gone.

Neither Jacob nor I spoke. He was so still beside me, his breath so deep and even, that I thought he might be close to sleep.

My mind was a thousand years away. I was not thinking of Yaha Uta or the other wolves, or the beautiful Cold Woman — I could picture *her* only too easily. No, I was thinking of someone outside the magic altogether. I was trying to imagine the face of the unnamed woman who had saved the entire tribe, the third wife.

Just a human woman, with no special gifts or powers. Physically weaker and slower than any of the monsters in the story. But she had been the key, the solution. She'd saved her husband, her young sons, her tribe.

I wish they'd remembered her name. . . .

Something shook my arm.

"C'mon, Bells," Jacob said in my ear. "We're here."

I blinked, confused because the fire seemed to have disappeared. I glared into the unexpected darkness, trying to make sense of my surroundings. It took me a minute to realize that I was no longer on the cliff. Jacob and I were alone. I was still under his arm, but I wasn't on the ground anymore.

How did I get in Jacob's car?

"Oh, crap!" I gasped as I realized that I had fallen asleep. "How late is it? Dang it, where's that stupid phone?" I patted my pockets, frantic and coming up empty.

"Easy. It's not even midnight yet. And I already called him for you. Look — he's waiting there."

"Midnight?" I repeated stupidly, still disoriented. I stared into the darkness, and my heartbeat picked up when my eyes made out the shape of the Volvo, thirty yards away. I reached for the door handle.

"Here," Jacob said, and he put a small shape into my other hand. The phone.

"You called Edward for me?"

My eyes were adjusted enough to see the bright gleam of Jacob's smile. "I figured if I played nice, I'd get more time with you."

"Thanks, Jake," I said, touched. "Really, thank you. And thanks for inviting me tonight. That was . . ." Words failed me. "Wow. That was something else."

"And you didn't even stay up to watch me swallow a cow." He laughed. "No, I'm glad you liked it. It was . . . nice for me. Having you there."

There was a movement in the dark distance — something pale ghosting against the black trees. Pacing?

"Yeah, he's not so patient, is he?" Jacob said, noticing my distraction. "Go ahead. But come back soon, okay?"

"Sure, Jake," I promised, cracking the car door open. Cold air washed across my legs and made me shiver.

"Sleep tight, Bells. Don't worry about anything — I'll be watching out for you tonight."

I paused, one foot on the ground. "No, Jake. Get some rest, I'll be fine."

"Sure, sure," he said, but he sounded more patronizing than agreeing.

"'Night, Jake. Thanks."

"'Night, Bella," he whispered as I hurried into the darkness.

Edward caught me at the boundary line.

"Bella," he said, relief strong in his voice; his arms wound tightly around me.

"Hi. Sorry I'm so late. I fell asleep and —"

"I know. Jacob explained." He started toward the car, and I staggered woodenly at his side. "Are you tired? I could carry you."

"I'm fine."

"Let's get you home and in bed. Did you have a nice time?"

"Yeah — it was amazing, Edward. I wish you could have come. I can't even explain it. Jake's dad told us the old legends and it was like . . . like magic."

"You'll have to tell me about it. After you've slept."

"I won't get it right," I said, and then I yawned hugely.

Edward chuckled. He opened my door for me, lifted me in, and buckled my seat belt around me.

Bright lights flashed on and swept across us. I waved

toward Jacob's headlights, but I didn't know if he saw the gesture.

That night — after I'd gotten past Charlie, who didn't give me as much trouble as I'd expected because Jacob had called him, too — instead of collapsing in bed right away, I leaned out the open window while I waited for Edward to come back. The night was surprisingly cold, almost wintry. I hadn't noticed it at all on the windy cliffs; I imagined that had less to do with the fire than it did with sitting next to Jacob.

Icy droplets spattered against my face as the rain began to fall.

It was too dark to see much besides the black triangles of the spruces leaning and shaking with the wind. But I strained my eyes anyway, searching for other shapes in the storm. A pale silhouette, moving like a ghost through the black . . . or maybe the shadowy outline of an enormous wolf. . . . My eyes were too weak.

Then there was a movement in the night, right beside me. Edward slid through my open window, his hands colder than the rain.

"Is Jacob out there?" I asked, shivering as Edward pulled me into the circle of his arm.

"Yes . . . somewhere. And Esme's on her way home."

I sighed. "It's so cold and wet. This is silly." I shivered again.

He chuckled. "It's only cold to *you,* Bella."

It was cold in my dream that night, too, maybe because

I slept in Edward's arms. But I dreamt I was outside in the storm, the wind whipping my hair in my face and blinding my eyes. I stood on the rocky crescent of First Beach, trying to understand the quickly moving shapes I could only dimly see in the darkness at the shore's edge. At first, there was nothing but a flash of white and black, darting toward each other and dancing away. And then, as if the moon had suddenly broken from the clouds, I could see everything.

Rosalie, her hair swinging wet and golden down to the back of her knees, was lunging at an enormous wolf — its muzzle shot through with silver — that I instinctively recognized as Billy Black.

I broke into a run, but found myself moving in the frustrating slow motion of dreamers. I tried to scream to them, to tell them to stop, but my voice was stolen by the wind, and I could make no sound. I waved my arms, hoping to catch their attention. Something flashed in my hand, and I noticed for the first time that my right hand wasn't empty.

I held a long, sharp blade, ancient and silver, crusted in dried, blackened blood.

I cringed away from the knife, and my eyes snapped open to the quiet darkness of my bedroom. The first thing I realized was that I was not alone, and I turned to bury my face in Edward's chest, knowing the sweet scent of his skin would chase the nightmare away more effectively than anything else.

"Did I wake you?" he whispered. There was the sound of paper, the ruffling of pages, and a faint *thump* as something light fell to the wooden floor.

"No," I mumbled, sighing in contentment as his arms tightened around me. "I had a bad dream."

"Do you want to tell me about it?"

I shook my head. "Too tired. Maybe in the morning, if I remember."

I felt a silent laugh shake through him.

"In the morning," he agreed.

"What were you reading?" I muttered, not really awake at all.

"Wuthering Heights," he said.

I frowned sleepily. "I thought you didn't like that book."

"You left it out," he murmured, his soft voice lulling me toward unconsciousness. "Besides . . . the more time I spend with you, the more human emotions seem comprehensible to me. I'm discovering that I can sympathize with Heathcliff in ways I didn't think possible before."

"Mmm," I sighed.

He said something else, something low, but I was already asleep.

The next morning dawned pearl gray and still. Edward asked me about my dream, but I couldn't get a handle on it. I only remembered that I was cold, and that I was glad he was there when I woke up. He kissed me, long enough to get my pulse racing, and then headed home to change and get his car.

I dressed quickly, low on options. Whoever had ransacked my hamper had critically impaired my wardrobe. If it wasn't so frightening, it would be seriously annoying.

As I was about to head down for breakfast, I noticed my battered copy of *Wuthering Heights* lying open on the floor where Edward had dropped it in the night, holding his place the way the damaged binding always held mine.

I picked it up curiously, trying to remember what he'd said. Something about feeling sympathy for Heathcliff, of all people. That couldn't be right; I must have dreamed that part.

Three words on the open page caught my eye, and I bent my head to read the paragraph more closely. It was Heathcliff speaking, and I knew the passage well.

And there you see the distinction between our feelings: had he been in my place and I in his, though I hated him with a hatred that turned my life to gall, I never would have raised a hand against him. You may look incredulous, if you please! I never would have banished him from her society as long as she desired his. The moment her regard ceased, I would have torn his heart out, and drank his blood! But, till then — if you don't believe me, you don't know me — till then, I would have died by inches before I touched a single hair of his head!

The three words that had caught my eye were "drank his blood."

I shuddered.

Yes, surely I must have dreamt that Edward said anything positive about Heathcliff. And this page was probably not the page he'd been reading. The book could have fallen open to any page.

12. TIME

"I HAVE FORESEEN . . . ," ALICE BEGAN IN AN OMINOUS
tone.

Edward threw an elbow toward her ribs, which she
neatly dodged.

"Fine," she grumbled. "Edward is making me do this.
But I *did* foresee that you would be more difficult if I surprised you."

We were walking to the car after school, and I was
completely clueless as to what she was talking about.

"In English?" I requested.

"Don't be a baby about this. No tantrums."

"Now I'm scared."

"So you're — I mean *we're* — having a graduation

party. It's no big thing. Nothing to freak out over. But I saw that you *would* freak out if I tried to make it a surprise party" — she danced out of the way as Edward reached over to muss her hair — "and Edward said I had to tell you. But it's nothing. Promise."

I sighed heavily. "Is there any point in arguing?"

"None at all."

"Okay, Alice. I'll be there. And I'll hate every minute of it. Promise."

"That's the spirit! By the way, I love my gift. You shouldn't have."

"Alice, I didn't!"

"Oh, I know that. But you will."

I racked my brains in panic, trying to remember what I'd ever decided to get her for graduation that she might have seen.

"Amazing," Edward muttered. "How can someone so tiny be so annoying?"

Alice laughed. "It's a talent."

"Couldn't you have waited a few weeks to tell me about this?" I asked petulantly. "Now I'll just be stressed that much longer."

Alice frowned at me.

"Bella," she said slowly. "Do you know what day it is?"

"Monday?"

She rolled her eyes. "Yes. It is Monday . . . the fourth." She grabbed my elbow, spun me halfway around, and pointed toward a big yellow poster taped to the gym door. There, in sharp black letters, was the date of graduation. Exactly one week from today.

"It's the fourth? *Of June?* Are you sure?"

Neither one answered. Alice just shook her head sadly, feigning disappointment, and Edward's eyebrows lifted.

"It can't be! How did that happen?" I tried to count backwards in my head, but I couldn't figure out where the days had gone.

I felt like someone had kicked my legs out from under me. The weeks of stress, of worry . . . somehow in the middle of all my obsessing over the time, my time had disappeared. My space for sorting through it all, for making plans, had vanished. I was out of time.

And I wasn't ready.

I didn't know how to do this. How to say goodbye to Charlie and Renée . . . to Jacob . . . to being human.

I knew exactly what I wanted, but I was suddenly terrified of getting it.

In theory, I was anxious, even eager to trade mortality for immortality. After all, it was the key to staying with Edward forever. And then there was the fact that I was being hunted by known and unknown parties. I'd rather not sit around, helpless and delicious, waiting for one of them to catch up with me.

In theory, that all made sense.

In practice . . . being human was all I knew. The future beyond that was a big, dark abyss that I couldn't know until I leaped into it.

This simple knowledge, today's date — which was so obvious that I must have been subconsciously repressing it — made the deadline I'd been impatiently counting down toward feel like a date with the firing squad.

In a vague way, I was aware of Edward holding the car door for me, of Alice chattering from the backseat, of the rain hammering against the windshield. Edward seemed to realize I was only there in body; he didn't try to pull me out of my abstraction. Or maybe he did, and I was past noticing.

We ended up at my house, where Edward led me to the sofa and pulled me down next to him. I stared out the window, into the liquid gray haze, and tried to find where my resolve had gone. Why was I panicking now? I'd known the deadline was coming. Why should it frighten me that it was here?

I don't know how long he let me stare out the window in silence. But the rain was disappearing into darkness when it was finally too much for him.

He put his cold hands on either side of my face and fixed his golden eyes on mine.

"Would you please tell me what you are thinking? *Before* I go mad?"

What could I say to him? That I was a coward? I searched for words.

"Your lips are white. Talk, Bella."

I exhaled in a big gust. How long had I been holding my breath?

"The date took me off guard," I whispered. "That's all."

He waited, his face full of worry and skepticism.

I tried to explain. "I'm not sure what to do . . . what to tell Charlie . . . what to say . . . how to . . ." My voice trailed off.

"This isn't about the party?"

I frowned. "No. But thanks for reminding me."

The rain was louder as he read my face.

"You're not ready," he whispered.

"I am," I lied immediately, a reflex reaction. I could tell he saw through it, so I took a deep breath, and told the truth. "I have to be."

"You don't have to be anything."

I could feel the panic surfacing in my eyes as I mouthed the reasons. "Victoria, Jane, Caius, whoever was in my room . . . !"

"All the more reason to wait."

"That doesn't make any sense, Edward!"

He pressed his hands more tightly to my face and spoke with slow deliberation.

"Bella. Not one of us had a choice. You've seen what it's done . . . to Rosalie especially. We've all struggled, trying to reconcile ourselves with something we had no control over. I won't let it be that way for you. You *will* have a choice."

"I've already made my choice."

"You aren't going through with this because a sword is hanging over your head. We will take care of the problems, and I will take care of you," he vowed. "When we're through it, and there is nothing forcing your hand, then you can decide to join me, if you still want to. But not because you're afraid. You won't be forced into this."

"Carlisle promised," I mumbled, contrary out of habit. "After graduation."

"Not until you're ready," he said in a sure voice. "And definitely not while you feel threatened."

I didn't answer. I didn't have it in me to argue; I couldn't seem to find my commitment at the moment.

"There." He kissed my forehead. "Nothing to worry about."

I laughed a shaky laugh. "Nothing but impending doom."

"Trust me."

"I do."

He was still watching my face, waiting for me to relax.

"Can I ask you something?" I said.

"Anything."

I hesitated, biting my lip, and then asked a different question than the one I was worried about.

"What am I getting Alice for graduation?"

He snickered. "It looked like you were getting us both concert tickets —"

"That's right!" I was so relieved, I almost smiled. "The concert in Tacoma. I saw an ad in the paper last week, and I thought it would be something you'd like, since you said it was a good CD."

"It's a great idea. Thank you."

"I hope it's not sold out."

"It's the thought that counts. I ought to know."

I sighed.

"There's something else you meant to ask," he said.

I frowned. "You're good."

"I have lots of practice reading your face. Ask me."

I closed my eyes and leaned into him, hiding my face against his chest. "You don't want me to be a vampire."

"No, I don't," he said softly, and then he waited for

more. "That's not a question," he prompted after a moment.

"Well . . . I was worrying about . . . *why* you feel that way."

"Worrying?" He picked out the word with surprise.

"Would you tell me why? The whole truth, not sparing my feelings?"

He hesitated for a minute. "If I answer your question, will you then *explain* your question?"

I nodded, my face still hidden.

He took a deep breath before he answered. "You could do so much better, Bella. I know that *you* believe I have a soul, but I'm not entirely convinced on that point, and to risk yours . . ." He shook his head slowly. "For me to allow this — to let you become what I am just so that I'll never have to lose you — is the most selfish act I can imagine. I want it more than anything, for *myself*. But for you, I want so much more. Giving in — it feels criminal. It's the most selfish thing I'll ever do, even if I live forever.

"If there were any way for me to become human for you — no matter what the price was, I would pay it."

I sat very still, absorbing this.

Edward thought he was *being selfish*.

I felt the smile slowly spread across my face.

"So . . . it's not that you're afraid you won't . . . like me as much when I'm different — when I'm not soft and warm and I don't smell the same? You really do want to keep me, no matter how I turn out?"

He exhaled sharply. "You were worried I wouldn't *like* you?" he demanded. Then, before I could answer, he was laughing. "Bella, for a fairly intuitive person, you can be so obtuse!"

I knew he would think it silly, but I was relieved. If he really wanted me, I could get through the rest . . . somehow. *Selfish* suddenly seemed like a beautiful word.

"I don't think you realize how much easier it will be for me, Bella," he said, the echo of his humor still there in his voice, "when I don't have to concentrate all the time on not killing you. Certainly, there are things I'll miss. This for one . . ."

He stared into my eyes as he stroked my cheek, and I felt the blood rush up to color my skin. He laughed gently.

"And the sound of your heart," he continued, more serious but still smiling a little. "It's the most significant sound in my world. I'm so attuned to it now, I swear I could pick it out from miles away. But neither of these things matter. *This*," he said, taking my face in his hands. "*You*. That's what I'm keeping. You'll always be my Bella, you'll just be a little more durable."

I sighed and let my eyes close in contentment, resting there in his hands.

"Now will you answer a question for me? The whole truth, not sparing my feelings?" he asked.

"Of course," I answered at once, my eyes opening wide with surprise. What would he want to know?

He spoke the words slowly. "You don't want to be my wife."

My heart stopped, and then broke into a sprint. A cold

sweat dewed on the back of my neck and my hands turned to ice.

He waited, watching and listening to my reaction.

"That's not a question," I finally whispered.

He looked down, his lashes casting long shadows across his cheekbones, and dropped his hands from my face to pick up my frozen left hand. He played with my fingers while he spoke.

"I was worrying about why you felt that way."

I tried to swallow. "That's not a question, either," I whispered.

"Please, Bella?"

"The truth?" I asked, only mouthing the words.

"Of course. I can take it, whatever it is."

I took a deep breath. "You're going to laugh at me."

His eyes flashed up to mine, shocked. "Laugh? I cannot imagine that."

"You'll see," I muttered, and then I sighed. My face went from white to scarlet in a sudden blaze of chagrin. "Okay, fine! I'm sure this will sound like some big joke to you, but really! It's just so . . . so . . . so *embarrassing*!" I confessed, and I hid my face against his chest again.

There was a brief pause.

"I'm not following you."

I tilted my head back and glared at him, embarrassment making me lash out, belligerent.

"I'm not *that girl*, Edward. The one who gets married right out of high school like some small-town hick who got knocked up by her boyfriend! Do you know what people would think? Do you realize what century this is? People don't just get married at eighteen! Not smart people, not responsible, mature people! I wasn't going to be that girl! That's not who I am. . . ." I trailed off, losing steam.

Edward's face was impossible to read as he thought through my answer.

"That's all?" he finally asked.

I blinked. "Isn't that enough?"

"It's not that you were . . . more eager for immortality itself than for just me?"

And then, though I'd predicted that *he* would laugh, I was suddenly the one having hysterics.

"Edward!" I gasped out between the paroxysms of giggles. "And here . . . I always . . . thought that . . . you were . . . so much . . . *smarter* than me!"

He took me in his arms, and I could feel that he was laughing with me.

"Edward," I said, managing to speak more clearly with a little effort, "there's no point to forever without you. I wouldn't want one day without you."

"Well, that's a relief," he said.

"Still . . . it doesn't change anything."

"It's nice to understand, though. And I do understand your perspective, Bella, truly I do. But I'd like it very much if you'd try to consider mine."

I'd sobered up by then, so I nodded and struggled to keep the frown off my face.

His liquid gold eyes turned hypnotic as they held mine.

"You see, Bella, I was always *that boy*. In my world, I

was already a man. I wasn't looking for love — no, I was far too eager to be a soldier for that; I thought of nothing but the idealized glory of the war that they were selling prospective draftees then — but if I had found . . ." He paused, cocking his head to the side. "I was going to say if I had found *someone,* but that won't do. If I had found *you,* there isn't a doubt in my mind how I would have proceeded. I was *that boy,* who would have — as soon as I discovered that you were what I was looking for — gotten down on one knee and endeavored to secure your hand. I would have wanted you for eternity, even when the word didn't have quite the same connotations."

He smiled his crooked smile at me.

I stared at him with my eyes frozen wide.

"Breathe, Bella," he reminded me, smiling.

I breathed.

"Can you see my side, Bella, even a little bit?"

And for one second, I could. I saw myself in a long skirt and a high-necked lace blouse with my hair piled up on my head. I saw Edward looking dashing in a light suit with a bouquet of wildflowers in his hand, sitting beside me on a porch swing.

I shook my head and swallowed. I was just having *Anne of Green Gables* flashbacks.

"The thing is, Edward," I said in a shaky voice, avoiding the question, "in my mind, *marriage* and *eternity* are not mutually exclusive or mutually inclusive concepts. And since we're living in my world for the moment, maybe we should go with the times, if you know what I mean."

"But on the other hand," he countered, "you will soon

be leaving time behind you altogether. So why should the transitory customs of one local culture affect the decision so much?"

I pursed my lips. "When in Rome?"

He laughed at me. "You don't have to say yes or no today, Bella. It's good to understand both sides, though, don't you think?"

"So your condition . . . ?"

"Is still in effect. I do see your point, Bella, but if you want me to change you myself. . . ."

"Dum, dum, dah-dum," I hummed under my breath. I was going for the wedding march, but it sort of sounded like a dirge.

Time continued to move too fast.

That night flew by dreamlessly, and then it was morning and graduation was staring me in the face. I had a pile of studying to do for my finals that I knew I wouldn't get halfway through in the few days I had left.

When I came down for breakfast, Charlie was already gone. He'd left the paper on the table, and that reminded me that I had some shopping to do. I hoped the ad for the concert was still running; I needed the phone number to get the stupid tickets. It didn't seem like much of a gift now that all the surprise was gone. Of course, trying to surprise Alice wasn't the brightest plan to begin with.

I meant to flip right back to the entertainment section, but the thick black headline caught my attention. I felt a thrill of fear as I leaned closer to read the front-page story.

SEATTLE TERRORIZED BY SLAYINGS

It's been less than a decade since the city of Seattle was the hunting ground for the most prolific serial killer in U.S. history. Gary Ridgway, the Green River Killer, was convicted of the murders of 48 women.

And now a beleaguered Seattle must face the possibility that it could be harboring an even more horrifying monster at this very moment.

The police are not calling the recent rash of homicides and disappearances the work of a serial killer. Not yet, at least. They are reluctant to believe so much carnage could be the work of one individual. This killer — if, in fact, it is one person — would then be responsible for 39 linked homicides and disappearances within the last three months alone. In comparison, Ridgway's 48-count murder spree was scattered over a 21-year period. If these deaths can be linked to one man, then this is the most violent rampage of serial murder in American history.

The police are leaning instead toward the theory that gang activity is involved. This theory is supported by the sheer number of victims, and by the fact that there seems to be no pattern in the choice of victims.

From Jack the Ripper to Ted Bundy, the targets of serial killings are usually connected by similarities in age, gender, race, or a combination of the three. The victims of this crime wave range in age from 15-year-old honor student Amanda Reed, to 67-year-old retired postman Omar Jenks. The linked deaths include a nearly even 18 women and 21 men. The victims are racially diverse: Caucasians, African Americans, Hispanics and Asians.

The selection appears random. The motive seems to be killing for no other reason than to kill.

So why even consider the idea of a serial killer?

There are enough similarities in the modus operandi to rule out unrelated crimes. Every victim discovered has been burned to the extent that dental records were necessary for identification. The use of some kind of accelerant, like gasoline or alcohol, seems to be indicated in the conflagrations; however, no traces of any accelerant have yet been found. All of the bodies have been carelessly dumped with no attempt at concealment.

More gruesome yet, most of the remains show evidence of brutal violence — bones crushed and snapped by some kind of tremendous pressure — which medical examiners believe occurred before the time of death, though these conclusions are difficult to be sure of, considering the state of the evidence.

Another similarity that points to the possibility of a serial: every crime is perfectly clean of evidence, aside from the remains themselves. Not a fingerprint, not a tire tread mark nor a foreign hair is left behind. There have been no sightings of any suspect in the disappearances.

Then there are the disappearances themselves — hardly low profile by any means. None of the victims are what could be viewed as easy targets. None are runaways or the homeless, who vanish so easily and are seldom reported missing. Victims have vanished from their homes, from a fourth-story apartment, from a health club, from a wedding reception. Perhaps the most astounding: 30-

year-old amateur boxer Robert Walsh entered a movie theater with a date; a few minutes into the movie, the woman realized that he was not in his seat. His body was found only three hours later when fire fighters were called to the scene of a burning trash Dumpster, twenty miles away.

Another pattern is present in the slayings: all of the victims disappeared at night.

And the most alarming pattern? Acceleration. Six of the homicides were committed in the first month, 11 in the second. Twenty-two have occurred in the last 10 days alone. And the police are no closer to finding the responsible party than they were after the first charred body was discovered.

The evidence is conflicting, the pieces horrifying. A vicious new gang or a wildly active serial killer? Or something else the police haven't yet conceived of?

Only one conclusion is indisputable: something hideous is stalking Seattle.

It took me three tries to read the last sentence, and I realized the problem was my shaking hands.

"Bella?"

Focused as I was, Edward's voice, though quiet and not totally unexpected, made me gasp and whirl.

He was leaning in the doorway, his eyebrows pulled together. Then he was suddenly at my side, taking my hand.

"Did I startle you? I'm sorry. I did knock. . . ."

"No, no," I said quickly. "Have you seen this?" I pointed to the paper.

A frown creased his forehead.

"I hadn't seen today's news yet. But I knew it was getting worse. We're going to have to do something . . . quickly."

I didn't like that. I hated any of them taking chances, and whatever or whoever was in Seattle was truly beginning to frighten me. But the idea of the Volturi coming was just as scary.

"What does Alice say?"

"That's the problem." His frown hardened. "She can't see anything . . . though we've made up our minds half a dozen times to check it out. She's starting to lose confidence. She feels like she's missing too much these days, that something's wrong. That maybe her vision is slipping away."

My eyes were wide. "Can that happen?"

"Who knows? No one's ever done a study . . . but I really doubt it. These things tend to intensify over time. Look at Aro and Jane."

"Then what's wrong?"

"Self-fulfilling prophecy, I think. We keep waiting for Alice to see something so we can go . . . and she doesn't see anything because we won't really go until she does. So she can't see us there. Maybe we'll have to do it blind."

I shuddered. "No."

"Did you have a strong desire to attend class today? We're only a couple of days from finals; they won't be giving us anything new."

"I think I can live without school for a day. What are we doing?"

"I want to talk to Jasper."

Jasper, again. It was strange. In the Cullen family,

Jasper was always a little on the fringe, part of things but never the center of them. It was my unspoken assumption that he was only there for Alice. I had the sense that he would follow Alice anywhere, but that this lifestyle was not his first choice. The fact that he was less committed to it than the others was probably why he had more difficulty keeping it up.

At any rate, I'd never seen Edward feel dependent on Jasper. I wondered again what he'd meant about Jasper's expertise. I really didn't know much about Jasper's history, just that he had come from somewhere in the south before Alice found him. For some reason, Edward had always shied away from any questions about his newest brother. And I'd always been too intimidated by the tall, blond vampire who looked like a brooding movie star to ask him outright.

When we got to the house, we found Carlisle, Esme, and Jasper watching the news intently, though the sound was so low that it was unintelligible to me. Alice was perched on the bottom step of the grand staircase, her face in her hands and her expression discouraged. As we walked in, Emmett ambled through the kitchen door, seeming perfectly at ease. Nothing ever bothered Emmett.

"Hey, Edward. Ditching, Bella?" He grinned at me.

"We both are," Edward reminded him.

Emmett laughed. "Yes, but it's *her* first time through high school. She might miss something."

Edward rolled his eyes, but otherwise ignored his favorite brother. He tossed the paper to Carlisle.

"Did you see that they're considering a serial killer now?" he asked.

Carlisle sighed. "They've had two specialists debating that possibility on CNN all morning."

"We can't let this go on."

"Let's go now," Emmett said with sudden enthusiasm. "I'm dead bored."

A hiss echoed down the stairway from upstairs.

"She's such a pessimist," Emmett muttered to himself.

Edward agreed with Emmett. "We'll have to go sometime."

Rosalie appeared at the top of the stairs and descended slowly. Her face was smooth, expressionless.

Carlisle was shaking his head. "I'm concerned. We've never involved ourselves in this kind of thing before. It's not our business. We aren't the Volturi."

"I don't want the Volturi to have to come here," Edward said. "It gives us so much less reaction time."

"And all those innocent humans in Seattle," Esme murmured. "It's not right to let them die this way."

"I know," Carlisle sighed.

"Oh," Edward said sharply, turning his head slightly to look at Jasper. "I didn't think of that. I see. You're right, that has to be it. Well, that changes everything."

I wasn't the only one who stared at him in confusion, but I might have been the only one who didn't look slightly annoyed.

"I think you'd better explain to the others," Edward said to Jasper. "What could be the purpose of this?" Edward started to pace, staring at the floor, lost in thought.

I hadn't seen her get up, but Alice was there beside me.

"What is he rambling about?" she asked Jasper. "What are you thinking?"

Jasper didn't seem to enjoy the spotlight. He hesitated, reading every face in the circle — for everyone had moved in to hear what he would say — and then his eyes paused on my face.

"You're confused," he said to me, his deep voice very quiet.

There was no question in his assumption. Jasper knew what I was feeling, what everyone was feeling.

"We're all confused," Emmett grumbled.

"You can afford the time to be patient," Jasper told him. "Bella should understand this, too. She's one of us now."

His words took me by surprise. As little as I'd had to do with Jasper, especially since my last birthday when he'd tried to kill me, I hadn't realize that he thought of me that way.

"How much do you know about me, Bella?" Jasper asked.

Emmett sighed theatrically, and plopped down on the couch to wait with exaggerated impatience.

"Not much," I admitted.

Jasper stared at Edward, who looked up to meet his gaze.

"No," Edward answered his thought. "I'm sure you can understand why I haven't told her that story. But I suppose she needs to hear it now."

Jasper nodded thoughtfully, and then started to roll up the arm of his ivory sweater.

I watched, curious and confused, trying to figure out what he was doing. He held his wrist under the edge of the lampshade beside him, close to the light of the naked bulb, and traced his finger across a raised crescent mark on the pale skin.

It took me a minute to understand why the shape looked strangely familiar.

"Oh," I breathed as realization hit. "Jasper, you have a scar exactly like mine."

I held out my hand, the silvery crescent more prominent against my cream skin than against his alabaster.

Jasper smiled faintly. "I have a lot of scars like yours, Bella."

Jasper's face was unreadable as he pushed the sleeve of his thin sweater higher up his arm. At first my eyes could not make sense of the texture that was layered thickly across the skin. Curved half-moons crisscrossed in a feathery pattern that was only visible, white on white as it was, because the bright glow of the lamp beside him threw the slightly raised design into relief, with shallow shadows outlining the shapes. And then I grasped that the pattern was made of individual crescents like the one on his wrist . . . the one on my hand.

I looked back at my own small, solitary scar — and remembered how I'd received it. I stared at the shape of James's teeth, embossed forever on my skin.

And then I gasped, staring up at him. "Jasper, what *happened* to you?"

13. NEWBORN

"THE SAME THING THAT HAPPENED TO YOUR HAND," Jasper answered in a quiet voice. "Repeated a thousand times." He laughed a little ruefully and brushed at his arm. "Our venom is the only thing that leaves a scar."

"*Why?*" I breathed in horror, feeling rude but unable to stop staring at his subtly ravaged skin.

"I didn't have quite the same . . . upbringing as my adopted siblings here. My beginning was something else entirely." His voice turned hard as he finished.

I gaped at him, appalled.

"Before I tell you my story," Jasper said, "you must understand that there are places in *our* world, Bella, where the life span of the never-aging is measured in weeks, and not centuries."

The others had heard this before. Carlisle and Emmett turned their attention to the TV again. Alice moved silently to sit at Esme's feet. But Edward was just as absorbed as I was; I could feel his eyes on my face, reading every flicker of emotion.

"To really understand why, you have to look at the world from a different perspective. You have to imagine the way it looks to the powerful, the greedy . . . the perpetually thirsty.

"You see, there are places in this world that are more desirable to us than others. Places where we can be less restrained, and still avoid detection.

"Picture, for instance, a map of the western hemisphere. Picture on it every human life as a small red dot. The thicker the red, the more easily we — well, those who exist this way — can feed without attracting notice."

I shuddered at the image in my head, at the word *feed*. But Jasper wasn't worried about frightening me, not overprotective like Edward always was. He went on without a pause.

"Not that the covens in the South care much for what the humans notice or do not. It's the Volturi that keep them in check. They are the only ones the southern covens fear. If not for the Volturi, the rest of us would be quickly exposed."

I frowned at the way he pronounced the name — with respect, almost gratitude. The idea of the Volturi as the good guys in any sense was hard to accept.

"The North is, by comparison, very civilized. Mostly we are nomads here who enjoy the day as well as the night, who allow humans to interact with us unsuspectingly — anonymity is important to us all.

"It's a different world in the South. The immortals there come out only at night. They spend the day plotting their next move, or anticipating their enemy's. Because it has been war in the South, constant war for centuries, with never one moment of truce. The covens there barely note the existence of humans, except as soldiers notice a herd of cows by the wayside — food for the taking. They only hide from the notice of the herd because of the Volturi."

"But what are they fighting for?" I asked.

Jasper smiled. "Remember the map with the red dots?"

He waited, so I nodded.

"They fight for control of the thickest red.

"You see, it occurred to someone once that, if he were the only vampire in, let's say Mexico City, well then, he could feed every night, twice, three times, and no one would ever notice. He plotted ways to get rid of the competition.

"Others had the same idea. Some came up with more effective tactics than others.

"But the *most* effective tactic was invented by a fairly young vampire named Benito. The first anyone ever heard of him, he came down from somewhere north of Dallas and massacred the two small covens that shared the area near Houston. Two nights later, he took on the much stronger clan of allies that claimed Monterrey in northern Mexico. Again, he won."

"How did he win?" I asked with wary curiosity.

"Benito had created an army of newborn vampires. He was the first one to think of it, and, in the beginning, he was unstoppable. Very young vampires are volatile, wild, and almost impossible to control. One newborn can be reasoned with, taught to restrain himself, but ten, fifteen together are a nightmare. They'll turn on each other as easily as on the enemy you point them at. Benito had to keep making more as they fought amongst themselves, and as the covens he decimated took more than half his force down before they lost.

"You see, though newborns are dangerous, they are still possible to defeat if you know what you're doing. They're incredibly powerful physically, for the first year or so, and if they're allowed to bring strength to bear they can crush an older vampire with ease. But they are slaves to their instincts, and thus predictable. Usually, they have no skill in fighting, only muscle and ferocity. And in this case, overwhelming numbers."

"The vampires in southern Mexico realized what was coming for them, and they did the only thing they could think of to counteract Benito. They made armies of their own. . . .

"All hell broke loose — and I mean that more literally than you can possibly imagine. We immortals have our histories, too, and this particular war will never be forgotten. Of course, it was not a good time to be human in Mexico, either."

I shuddered.

"When the body count reached epidemic proportions —

in fact, your histories blame a disease for the population slump — the Volturi finally stepped in. The entire guard came together and sought out every newborn in the bottom half of North America. Benito was entrenched in Puebla, building his army as quickly as he could in order to take on the prize — Mexico City. The Volturi started with him, and then moved on to the rest.

"Anyone who was found with the newborns was executed immediately, and, since everyone was trying to protect themselves from Benito, Mexico was emptied of vampires for a time.

"The Volturi were cleaning house for almost a year. This was another chapter of our history that will always be remembered, though there were very few witnesses left to speak of what it was like. I spoke to someone once who had, from a distance, watched what happened when they visited Culiacán."

Jasper shuddered. I realized that I had never before seen him either afraid or horrified. This was a first.

"It was enough that the fever for conquest did not spread from the South. The rest of the world stayed sane. We owe the Volturi for our present way of life.

"But when the Volturi went back to Italy, the survivors were quick to stake their claims in the South.

"It didn't take long before covens began to dispute again. There was a lot of bad blood, if you'll forgive the expression. Vendettas abounded. The idea of newborns was already there, and some were not able to resist. However, the Volturi had not been forgotten, and the southern covens were more careful this time. The newborns were selected from the human pool with more care, and given more training. They were used circumspectly, and the humans remained, for the most part, oblivious. Their creators gave the Volturi no reason to return.

"The wars resumed, but on a smaller scale. Every now and then, someone would go too far, speculation would begin in the human newspapers, and the Volturi would return and clean out the city. But they let the others, the careful ones, continue. . . ."

Jasper was staring off into space.

"That's how you were changed." My realization was a whisper.

"Yes," he agreed. "When I was human, I lived in Houston, Texas. I was almost seventeen years old when I joined the Confederate Army in 1861. I lied to the recruiters and told them I was twenty. I was tall enough to get away with it.

"My military career was short-lived, but very promising. People always . . . liked me, listened to what I had to say. My father said it was charisma. Of course, now I know it was probably something more. But, whatever the reason, I was promoted quickly through the ranks, over older, more experienced men. The Confederate Army was new and scrambling to organize itself, so that provided opportunities, as well. By the first battle of Galveston — well, it was more of a skirmish, really — I was the youngest major in Texas, not even acknowledging my real age.

"I was placed in charge of evacuating the women and children from the city when the Union's mortar boats reached the harbor. It took a day to prepare them, and then

I left with the first column of civilians to convey them to Houston.

"I remember that one night very clearly.

"We reached the city after dark. I stayed only long enough to make sure the entire party was safely situated. As soon as that was done, I got myself a fresh horse, and I headed back to Galveston. There wasn't time to rest.

"Just a mile outside the city, I found three women on foot. I assumed they were stragglers and dismounted at once to offer them my aid. But, when I could see their faces in the dim light of the moon, I was stunned into silence. They were, without question, the three most beautiful women I had ever seen.

"They had such pale skin, I remember marveling at it. Even the little black-haired girl, whose features were clearly Mexican, was porcelain in the moonlight. They seemed young, all of them, still young enough to be called girls. I knew they were not lost members of our party. I would have remembered seeing these three.

"'He's speechless,' the tallest girl said in a lovely, delicate voice — it was like wind chimes. She had fair hair, and her skin was snow white.

"The other was blonder still, her skin just as chalky. Her face was like an angel's. She leaned toward me with half-closed eyes and inhaled deeply.

"'Mmm,' she sighed. 'Lovely.'

"The small one, the tiny brunette, put her hand on the girl's arm and spoke quickly. Her voice was too soft and musical to be sharp, but that seemed to be the way she intended it.

"'Concentrate, Nettie,' she said.

"I'd always had a good sense of how people related to each other, and it was immediately clear that the brunette was somehow in charge of the others. If they'd been military, I would have said that she outranked them.

"'He looks right — young, strong, an officer. . . . ' The brunette paused, and I tried unsuccessfully to speak. 'And there's something more . . . do you sense it?' she asked the other two. 'He's . . . compelling.'

"'Oh, yes,' Nettie quickly agreed, leaning toward me again.

"'Patience,' the brunette cautioned her. 'I want to keep this one.'

"Nettie frowned; she seemed annoyed.

"'You'd better do it, Maria,' the taller blonde spoke again. 'If he's important to you. I kill them twice as often as I keep them.'

"'Yes, I'll do it,' Maria agreed. 'I really do like this one. Take Nettie away, will you? I don't want to have to protect my back while I'm trying to focus.'

"My hair was standing up on the back of my neck, though I didn't understand the meaning of anything the beautiful creatures were saying. My instincts told me that there was danger, that the angel had meant it when she spoke of killing, but my judgment overruled my instincts. I had not been taught to fear women, but to protect them.

"'Let's hunt,' Nettie agreed enthusiastically, reaching for the tall girl's hand. They wheeled — they were so graceful! — and sprinted toward the city. They seemed to almost take flight, they were so fast — their white dresses blew out behind them like wings. I blinked in amazement, and they were gone.

"I turned to stare at Maria, who was watching me curiously.

"I'd never been superstitious in my life. Until that second, I'd never believed in ghosts or any other such nonsense. Suddenly, I was unsure.

"'What is your name, soldier?' Maria asked me.

"'Major Jasper Whitlock, ma'am,' I stammered, unable to be impolite to a female, even if she was a ghost.

"'I truly hope you survive, Jasper,' she said in her gentle voice. 'I have a good feeling about you.'

"She took a step closer, and inclined her head as if she were going to kiss me. I stood frozen in place, though my instincts were screaming at me to run."

Jasper paused, his face thoughtful. "A few days later," he finally said, and I wasn't sure if he had edited his story for my sake or because he was responding to the tension that even I could feel exuding from Edward, "I was introduced to my new life.

"Their names were Maria, Nettie, and Lucy. They hadn't been together long — Maria had rounded up the other two — all three were survivors of recently lost battles. Theirs was a partnership of convenience. Maria wanted revenge, and she wanted her territories back. The others were eager to increase their . . . herd lands, I suppose you could say. They were putting together an army, and going about it more carefully than was usual. It was Maria's idea. She wanted a superior army, so she sought out specific humans who had potential. Then she gave us much more attention, more training than anyone else had bothered with. She taught us to fight, and she taught us to be invisible to the humans. When we did well, we were rewarded. . . ."

He paused, editing again.

"She was in a hurry, though. Maria knew that the massive strength of the newborn began to wane around the year mark, and she wanted to act while we were strong.

"There were six of us when I joined Maria's band. She added four more within a fortnight. We were all male — Maria wanted soldiers — and that made it slightly more difficult to keep from fighting amongst ourselves. I fought my first battles against my new comrades in arms. I was quicker than the others, better at combat. Maria was pleased with me, though put out that she had to keep replacing the ones I destroyed. I was rewarded often, and that made me stronger.

"Maria was a good judge of character. She decided to put me in charge of the others — as if I were being promoted. It suited my nature exactly. The casualties went down dramatically, and our numbers swelled to hover around twenty.

"This was considerable for the cautious times we lived in. My ability, as yet undefined, to control the emotional atmosphere around me was vitally effective. We soon began to work together in a way that newborn vampires had never cooperated before. Even Maria, Nettie, and Lucy were able to work together more easily.

"Maria grew quite fond of me — she began to depend upon me. And, in some ways, I worshipped the ground she walked on. I had no idea that any other life was possible. Maria told us this was the way things were, and we believed.

"She asked me to tell her when my brothers and I were ready to fight, and I was eager to prove myself. I pulled together an army of twenty-three in the end — twenty-three unbelievably strong new vampires, organized and skilled as no others before. Maria was ecstatic.

"We crept down toward Monterrey, her former home, and she unleashed us on her enemies. They had only nine newborns at the time, and a pair of older vampires controlling them. We took them down more easily than Maria could believe, losing only four in the process. It was an unheard-of margin of victory.

"And we were well trained. We did it without attracting notice. The city changed hands without any human being aware.

"Success made Maria greedy. It wasn't long before she began to eye other cities. That first year, she extended her control to cover most of Texas and northern Mexico. Then the others came from the South to dislodge her."

He brushed two fingers along the faint pattern of scars on his arm.

"The fighting was intense. Many began to worry that the Volturi would return. Of the original twenty-three, I was the only one to survive the first eighteen months. We both won and lost. Nettie and Lucy turned on Maria eventually — but that one we won.

"Maria and I were able to hold on to Monterrey. It quieted a little, though the wars continued. The idea of conquest was dying out; it was mostly vengeance and feuding now. So many had lost their partners, and that is something our kind does not forgive. . . .

"Maria and I always kept a dozen or so newborns ready. They meant little to us — they were pawns, they were disposable. When they outgrew their usefulness, we *did* dispose of them. My life continued in the same violent pattern and the years passed. I was sick of it all for a very long time before anything changed . . .

"Decades later, I developed a friendship with a newborn who'd remained useful and survived his first three years, against the odds. His name was Peter. I liked Peter; he was . . . civilized — I suppose that's the right word. He didn't enjoy the fight, though he was good at it.

"He was assigned to deal with the newborns — babysit them, you could say. It was a full-time job.

"And then it was time to purge again. The newborns were outgrowing their strength; they were due to be replaced. Peter was supposed to help me dispose of them. We took them aside individually, you see, one by one . . . It was always a very long night. This time, he tried to convince me that a few had potential, but Maria had instructed that we get rid of them all. I told him no.

"We were about halfway through, and I could feel that it was taking a great toll on Peter. I was trying to decide whether or not I should send him away and finish up myself as I called out the next victim. To my surprise, he was suddenly angry, furious. I braced for whatever his mood might foreshadow — he was a good fighter, but he was never a match for me.

"The newborn I'd summoned was a female, just past her year mark. Her name was Charlotte. His feelings changed when she came into view; they gave him away. He yelled for her to run, and he bolted after her. I could have pursued them, but I didn't. I felt . . . averse to destroying him.

"Maria was irritated with me for that . . .

"Five years later, Peter snuck back for me. He picked a good day to arrive.

"Maria was mystified by my ever-deteriorating frame of mind. She'd never felt a moment's depression, and I wondered why I was different. I began to notice a change in her emotions when she was near me — sometimes there was fear . . . and malice — the same feelings that had given me advance warning when Nettie and Lucy struck. I was preparing myself to destroy my only ally, the core of my existence, when Peter returned.

"Peter told me about his new life with Charlotte, told me about options I'd never dreamed I had. In five years, they'd never had a fight, though they'd met many others in the north. Others who could co-exist without the constant mayhem.

"In one conversation, he had me convinced. I was ready to go, and somewhat relieved I wouldn't have to kill Maria. I'd been her companion for as many years as Carlisle and Edward have been together, yet the bond between us was nowhere near as strong. When you live for the fight, for the blood, the relationships you form are tenuous and easily broken. I walked away without a backward glance.

"I traveled with Peter and Charlotte for a few years, getting the feel of this new, more peaceful world. But the depression didn't fade. I didn't understand what was wrong with me, until Peter noticed that it was always worse after I'd hunted.

"I contemplated that. In so many years of slaughter and carnage, I'd lost nearly all of my humanity. I was undeniably a nightmare, a monster of the grisliest kind. Yet each time I found another human victim, I would feel a faint prick of remembrance for that other life. Watching their eyes widen in wonder at my beauty, I could see Maria and the others in my head, what they had looked like to me the last night that I was Jasper Whitlock. It was stronger for me — this borrowed memory — than it was for anyone else, because I could *feel* everything my prey was feeling. And I lived their emotions as I killed them.

"You've experienced the way I can manipulate the emotions around myself, Bella, but I wonder if you realize how the feelings in a room affect *me*. I live every day in a climate of emotion. For the first century of my life, I lived in a world of bloodthirsty vengeance. Hate was my constant companion. It eased some when I left Maria, but I still had to feel the horror and fear of my prey.

"It began to be too much.

"The depression got worse, and I wandered away from Peter and Charlotte. Civilized as they were, they didn't feel the same aversion I was beginning to feel. They only wanted peace from the fight. I was so wearied by killing — killing anyone, even mere humans.

"Yet I had to keep killing. What choice did I have? I tried to kill less often, but I would get too thirsty and I would give in. After a century of instant gratification, I found self-discipline . . . challenging. I still haven't perfected that."

Jasper was lost in the story, as was I. It surprised me when his desolate expression smoothed into a peaceful smile.

"I was in Philadelphia. There was a storm, and I was out during the day — something I was not completely comfortable with yet. I knew standing in the rain would attract attention, so I ducked into a little half-empty diner. My eyes were dark enough that no one would notice them, though this meant I was thirsty, and that worried me a little.

"She was there — expecting me, naturally." He chuckled once. "She hopped down from the high stool at the counter as soon as I walked in and came directly toward me.

"It shocked me. I was not sure if she meant to attack. That's the only interpretation of her behavior my past had to offer. But she was smiling. And the emotions that were emanating from her were like nothing I'd ever felt before.

"'You've kept me waiting a long time,' she said."

I didn't realize Alice had come to stand behind me again.

"And you ducked your head, like a good Southern gentleman, and said, 'I'm sorry, ma'am.'" Alice laughed at the memory.

Jasper smiled down at her. "You held out your hand, and I took it without stopping to make sense of what I was doing. For the first time in almost a century, I felt hope."

Jasper took Alice's hand as he spoke.

Alice grinned. "I was just relieved. I thought you were never going to show up."

They smiled at each other for a long moment, and then Jasper looked back to me, the soft expression lingering.

"Alice told me what she'd seen of Carlisle and his family. I could hardly believe that such an existence was possible. But Alice made me optimistic. So we went to find them."

"Scared the hell out of them, too," Edward said, rolling his eyes at Jasper before turning to me to explain. "Emmett and I were away hunting. Jasper shows up, covered in battle scars, towing this little freak" — he nudged Alice playfully — "who greets them all by name, knows everything about them, and wants to know which room she can move into."

Alice and Jasper laughed in harmony, soprano and bass.

"When I got home, all my things were in the garage," Edward continued.

Alice shrugged. "Your room had the best view."

They all laughed together now.

"That's a nice story," I said.

Three pairs of eyes questioned my sanity.

"I mean the last part," I defended myself. "The happy ending with Alice."

"Alice has made all the difference," Jasper agreed. "This is a climate I enjoy."

But the momentary pause in the stress couldn't last.

"An army," Alice whispered. "Why didn't you tell me?"

The others were intent again, their eyes locked on Jasper's face.

"I thought I must be interpreting the signs incorrectly. Because where is the motive? Why would someone create an army in Seattle? There is no history there, no vendetta. It makes no sense from a conquest standpoint, either; no one claims it. Nomads pass through, but there's no one to *fight* for it. No one to defend it from.

"But I've seen this before, and there's no other explanation. There is an army of newborn vampires in Seattle. Fewer than twenty, I'd guess. The difficult part is that they are totally untrained. Whoever made them just set them loose. It will only get worse, and it won't be much longer till the Volturi step in. Actually, I'm surprised they've let this go on so long."

"What can we do?" Carlisle asked.

"If we want to avoid the Volturi's involvement, we will have to destroy the newborns, and we will have to do it very soon." Jasper's face was hard. Knowing his story now, I could guess how this evaluation must disturb him. "I can teach you how. It won't be easy in the city. The young ones aren't concerned about secrecy, but we will have to be. It will limit us in ways that they are not. Maybe we can lure them out."

"Maybe we won't have to." Edward's voice was bleak. "Does it occur to anyone else that the only possible threat in the area that would call for the creation of an army is . . . us?"

Jasper's eyes narrowed; Carlisle's widened, shocked.

"Tanya's family is also near," Esme said slowly, unwilling to accept Edward's words.

"The newborns aren't ravaging Anchorage, Esme. I think we have to consider the idea that *we* are the targets."

"They're not coming after us," Alice insisted, and then paused. "Or . . . they don't *know* that they are. Not yet."

"What is that?" Edward asked, curious and tense. "What are you remembering?"

"Flickers," Alice said. "I can't see a clear picture when I try to see what's going on, nothing concrete. But I've been getting these strange flashes. Not enough to make sense of. It's as if someone's changing their mind, moving from one course of action to another so quickly that I can't get a good view. . . ."

"Indecision?" Jasper asked in disbelief.

"I don't know. . . ."

"Not indecision," Edward growled. "*Knowledge*. Someone who knows you can't see anything until the decision is made. Someone who is hiding from us. Playing with the holes in your vision."

"Who would know that?" Alice whispered.

Edward's eyes were hard as ice. "Aro knows you as well as you know yourself."

"But I would see if they'd decided to come. . . ."

"Unless they didn't want to get their hands dirty."

"A favor," Rosalie suggested, speaking for the first time. "Someone in the South . . . someone who already had trouble with the rules. Someone who should have been destroyed is offered a second chance — if they take care of this one small problem. . . . That would explain the Volturi's sluggish response."

"Why?" Carlisle asked, still shocked. "There's no reason for the Volturi —"

"It was there," Edward disagreed quietly. "I'm surprised it's come to this so soon, because the other thoughts were stronger. In Aro's head he saw me at his one side and Alice at his other. The present and the future, virtual omniscience. The power of the idea intoxicated him. I would have thought it would take him much longer to give up on that plan — he wanted it too much. But there was also the thought of you, Carlisle, of our family, growing stronger and larger. The jealousy and the fear: you having . . . not *more* than he had, but still, things that he wanted. He tried not to think about it, but he couldn't hide it completely. The idea of rooting out the competition was there; besides their own, ours is the largest coven they've ever found. . . ."

I stared at his face in horror. He'd never told me this, but I guessed I knew why. I could see it in my head now, Aro's dream. Edward and Alice in black, flowing robes, drifting along at Aro's side with their eyes cold and blood-red. . . .

Carlisle interrupted my waking nightmare. "They're too committed to their mission. They would never break the rules themselves. It goes against everything they've worked for."

"They'll clean up afterward. A double betrayal," Edward said in a grim voice. "No harm done."

Jasper leaned forward, shaking his head. "No, Carlisle

is right. The Volturi do not break rules. Besides, it's much too sloppy. This . . . person, this threat — they have no idea what they're doing. A first-timer, I'd swear to it. I cannot believe the Volturi are involved. But they will be."

They all stared at each other, frozen with stress.

"Then let's *go,*" Emmett almost roared. "What are we waiting for?"

Carlisle and Edward exchanged a long glance. Edward nodded once.

"We'll need you to teach us, Jasper," Carlisle finally said. "How to destroy them." Carlisle's jaw was hard, but I could see the pain in his eyes as he said the words. No one hated violence more than Carlisle.

There was something bothering me, and I couldn't put my finger on it. I was numb, horrified, deathly afraid. And yet, under that, I could feel that I was missing something important. Something that would make some sense out of the chaos. That would explain it.

"We're going to need help," Jasper said. "Do you think Tanya's family would be willing . . . ? Another five mature vampires would make an enormous difference. And then Kate and Eleazar would be especially advantageous on our side. It would be almost easy, with their aid."

"We'll ask," Carlisle answered.

Jasper held out a cell phone. "We need to hurry."

I'd never seen Carlisle's innate calm so shaken. He took the phone, and paced toward the windows. He dialed a number, held the phone to his ear, and laid the other hand against the glass. He stared out into the foggy morning with a pained and ambivalent expression.

Edward took my hand and pulled me to the white love-seat. I sat beside him, staring at his face while he stared at Carlisle.

Carlisle's voice was low and quick, difficult to hear. I heard him greet Tanya, and then he raced through the situation too fast for me to understand much, though I could tell that the Alaskan vampires were not ignorant of what was going on in Seattle.

Then something changed in Carlisle's voice.

"Oh," he said, his voice sharper in surprise. "We didn't realize . . . that Irina felt that way."

Edward groaned at my side and closed his eyes. "Damn it. Damn Laurent to the deepest pit of hell where he belongs."

"Laurent?" I whispered, the blood emptying from my face, but Edward didn't respond, focused on Carlisle's thoughts.

My short encounter with Laurent early this spring was not something that had faded or dimmed in my mind. I still remembered every word he'd said before Jacob and his pack had interrupted.

I actually came here as a favor to her. . . .

Victoria. Laurent had been her first maneuver — she'd sent him to observe, to see how hard it might be to get to me. He hadn't survived the wolves to report back.

Though he'd kept up his old ties with Victoria after James's death, he'd also formed new ties and new relationships. He'd gone to live with Tanya's family in Alaska — Tanya the strawberry blonde — the closest friends the Cullens had in the vampire world, practically extended family. Laurent had been with them for almost a year previous to his death.

Carlisle was still talking, his voice not quite pleading. Persuasive, but with an edge. Then the edge abruptly won out over the persuasion.

"There's no question of that," Carlisle said in a stern voice. "We have a truce. They haven't broken it, and neither will we. I'm sorry to hear that. . . . Of course. We'll just have to do our best alone."

Carlisle shut the phone without waiting for an answer. He continued to stare out into the fog.

"What's the problem?" Emmett murmured to Edward.

"Irina was more involved with our friend Laurent than we knew. She's holding a grudge against the wolves for destroying him to save Bella. She wants —" He paused, looking down at me.

"Go on," I said as evenly as I could.

His eyes tightened. "She wants revenge. To take down the pack. They would trade their help for our permission."

"No!" I gasped.

"Don't worry," he told me in a flat voice. "Carlisle would never agree to it." He hesitated, then sighed. "Nor would I. Laurent had it coming" — this was almost a growl — "and I still owe the wolves for that."

"This isn't good," Jasper said. "It's too even a fight. We'd have the upper hand in skill, but not numbers. We'd win, but at what price?" His tense eyes flashed to Alice's face and away.

I wanted to scream out loud as I grasped what Jasper meant.

We would win, but we would lose. Some wouldn't survive.

I looked around the room at their faces — Jasper, Alice, Emmett, Rose, Esme, Carlisle . . . Edward — the faces of my family.

14. DECLARATION

"You can't be serious," I said Wednesday afternoon. "You've completely lost your mind!"

"Say whatever you like about me," Alice answered.
"The party is still on."

I stared at her, my eyes so wide with disbelief it felt like
they might fall out and land on my lunch tray.

"Oh, calm down, Bella! There's no reason not to go
through with it. Besides, the invitations are already sent."

"But . . . the . . . you . . . I . . . insane!" I spluttered.

"You've already bought my present," she reminded me.
"You don't have to do anything but show up."

I made an effort to calm myself. "With everything that
is going on right now, a party is hardly appropriate."

"Graduation is what's going on right now, and a party is so appropriate it's almost passé."

"Alice!"

She sighed, and tried to be serious. "There are a few things we need to get in order now, and that's going to take a little time. As long as we're sitting here waiting, we might as well commemorate the good stuff. You're only going to graduate from high school — for the first time — once. You don't get to be human again, Bella. This is a once-in-a-lifetime shot."

Edward, silent through our little argument, flashed her a warning look. She stuck out her tongue at him. She was right — her soft voice would never carry over the babble of the cafeteria. And no one would understand the meaning behind her words in any case.

"What few things do we need to get in order?" I asked, refusing to be sidetracked.

Edward answered in a low voice. "Jasper thinks we could use some help. Tanya's family isn't the only choice we have. Carlisle's trying to track down a few old friends, and Jasper is looking up Peter and Charlotte. He's considering talking to Maria . . . but no one really wants to involve the southerners."

Alice shuddered delicately.

"It shouldn't be too hard to convince them to help," he continued. "Nobody wants a visit from Italy."

"But these friends — they're not going to be . . . *vegetarians,* right?" I protested, using the Cullens' tongue-in-cheek nickname for themselves.

"No," Edward answered, suddenly expressionless.

"Here? In Forks?"

"They're friends," Alice reassured me. "Everything's going to be fine. Don't worry. And then, Jasper has to teach us a few courses on newborn elimination. . . ."

Edward's eyes brightened at that, and a brief smile flashed across his face. My stomach suddenly felt like it was full of sharp little splinters of ice.

"When are you going?" I asked in a hollow voice. I couldn't stand this — the idea that someone might not come back. What if it was Emmett, so brave and thoughtless that he was never the least bit cautious? Or Esme, so sweet and motherly that I couldn't even imagine her in a fight? Or Alice, so tiny, so fragile-looking? Or . . . but I couldn't even think the name, consider the possibility.

"A week," Edward said casually. "That ought to give us enough time."

The icy splinters twisted uncomfortably in my stomach. I was suddenly nauseated.

"You look kind of green, Bella," Alice commented.

Edward put his arm around me and pulled me tightly against his side. "It's going to be fine, Bella. Trust me."

Sure, I thought to myself. Trust him. He wasn't the one who was going to have to sit behind and wonder whether or not the core of his existence was going to come home.

And then it occurred to me. Maybe I didn't need to sit behind. A week was more than enough time.

"You're looking for help," I said slowly.

"Yes." Alice's head cocked to the side as she processed the change in my tone.

I looked only at her as I answered. My voice was just slightly louder than a whisper. "*I could help.*"

Edward's body was suddenly rigid, his arm too tight around me. He exhaled, and the sound was a hiss.

But it was Alice, still calm, who answered. "That really wouldn't be *helpful.*"

"Why not?" I argued; I could hear the desperation in my voice. "Eight is better than seven. There's more than enough time."

"There's not enough time to make you helpful, Bella," she disagreed coolly. "Do you remember how Jasper described the young ones? You'd be no good in a fight. You wouldn't be able to control your instincts, and that would make you an easy target. And then Edward would get hurt trying to protect you." She folded her arms across her chest, pleased with her unassailable logic.

And I knew she was right, when she put it like that. I slumped in my seat, my sudden hope defeated. Beside me, Edward relaxed.

He whispered the reminder in my ear. "Not because you're afraid."

"Oh," Alice said, and a blank look crossed her face. Then her expression became surly. "I hate last-minute cancellations. So that puts the party attendance list down to sixty-five. . . ."

"*Sixty-five!*" My eyes bulged again. I didn't have that many friends. Did I even know that many people?

"Who canceled?" Edward wondered, ignoring me.

"Renée."

"What?" I gasped.

"She was going to surprise you for your graduation, but something went wrong. You'll have a message when you get home."

For a moment, I just let myself enjoy the relief. Whatever it was that went wrong for my mother, I was eternally grateful to it. If she had come to Forks *now* . . . I didn't want to think about it. My head would explode.

The message light was flashing when I got home. My feeling of relief flared again as I listened to my mother describe Phil's accident on the ball field — while demonstrating a slide, he'd tangled up with the catcher and broken his thigh bone; he was entirely dependent on her, and there was no way she could leave him. My mom was still apologizing when the message cut off.

"Well, that's one," I sighed.

"One what?" Edward asked.

"One person I don't have to worry about getting killed this week."

He rolled his eyes.

"Why won't you and Alice take this seriously?" I demanded. "This is *serious*."

He smiled. "Confidence."

"Wonderful," I grumbled. I picked up the phone and dialed Renée's number. I knew it would be a long conversation, but I also knew that I wouldn't have to contribute much.

I just listened, and reassured her every time I could get a word in: I wasn't disappointed, I wasn't mad, I wasn't hurt. She should concentrate on helping Phil get better. I passed on my "get well soon" to Phil, and promised to call her with every single detail from Forks High's generic graduation. Finally, I had to use my desperate need to study for finals to get off the phone.

Edward's patience was endless. He waited politely through the whole conversation, just playing with my hair and smiling whenever I looked up. It was probably superficial to notice such things while I had so many more important things to think about, but his smile still knocked the breath out of me. He was so beautiful that it made it hard sometimes to think about anything else, hard to concentrate on Phil's troubles or Renée's apologies or hostile vampire armies. I was only human.

As soon as I hung up, I stretched onto my tiptoes to kiss him. He put his hands around my waist and lifted me onto the kitchen counter, so I wouldn't have to reach as far. That worked for me. I locked my arms around his neck and melted against his cold chest.

Too soon, as usual, he pulled away.

I felt my face slip into a pout. He laughed at my expression as he extricated himself from my arms and legs. He leaned against the counter next to me and put one arm lightly around my shoulders.

"I know you think that I have some kind of perfect, unyielding self-control, but that's not actually the case."

"I wish," I sighed.

And he sighed, too.

"After school tomorrow," he said, changing the subject, "I'm going hunting with Carlisle, Esme, and Rosalie.

Just for a few hours — we'll stay close. Alice, Jasper, and Emmett should be able to keep you safe."

"Ugh," I grumbled. Tomorrow was the first day of finals, and it was only a half-day. I had Calculus and History — the only two challenges in my line-up — so I'd have almost the whole day without him, and nothing to do but worry. "I hate being babysat."

"It's temporary," he promised.

"Jasper will be bored. Emmett will make fun of me."

"They'll be on their best behavior."

"Right," I grumbled.

And then it occurred to me that I did have one option besides babysitters. "You know . . . I haven't been to La Push since the bonfire."

I watched his face carefully for any change in expression. His eyes tightened the tiniest bit.

"I'd be safe enough there," I reminded him.

He thought about it for a few seconds. "You're probably right."

His face was calm, but just a little too smooth. I almost asked if he'd rather I stayed here, but then I thought of the ribbing Emmett would no doubt dish out, and I changed the subject. "Are you thirsty already?" I asked, reaching up to stroke the light shadow beneath his eye. His irises were still a deep gold.

"Not really." He seemed reluctant to answer, and that surprised me. I waited for an explanation.

"We want to be as strong as possible," he explained, still reluctant. "We'll probably hunt again on the way, looking for big game."

"That makes you stronger?"

He searched my face for something, but there was nothing to find but curiosity.

"Yes," he finally said. "Human blood makes us the strongest, though only fractionally. Jasper's been thinking about cheating — adverse as he is to the idea, he's nothing if not practical — but he won't suggest it. He knows what Carlisle will say."

"Would that help?" I asked quietly.

"It doesn't matter. We aren't going to change who we are."

I frowned. If something helped even the odds . . . and then I shuddered, realizing I was willing to have a stranger die to protect him. I was horrified at myself, but not entirely able to deny it, either.

He changed the subject again. "That's why they're so strong, of course. The newborns are full of human blood — their own blood, reacting to the change. It lingers in the tissues and strengthens them. Their bodies use it up slowly, like Jasper said, the strength starting to wane after about a year."

"How strong will *I* be?"

He grinned. "Stronger than I am."

"Stronger than Emmett?"

The grin got bigger. "Yes. Do me a favor and challenge him to an arm-wrestling match. It would be a good experience for him."

I laughed. It sounded so ridiculous.

Then I sighed and hopped down from the counter, because I really couldn't put it off any longer. I had to cram, and cram hard. Luckily I had Edward's help, and Edward was an excellent tutor — since he knew absolutely everything. I figured my biggest problem would be just focusing on the tests. If I didn't watch myself, I might end up writing my History essay on the vampire wars of the South.

I took a break to call Jacob, and Edward seemed just as comfortable as he had when I was on the phone with Renée. He played with my hair again.

Though it was the middle of the afternoon, my call woke Jacob up, and he was grouchy at first. He cheered right up when I asked if I could visit the next day. The Quileute school was already out for the summer, so he told me to come over as early as I could. I was pleased to have an option besides being babysat. There was a tiny bit more dignity in spending the day with Jacob.

Some of that dignity was lost when Edward insisted again on delivering me to the border line like a child being exchanged by custodial guardians.

"So how do you feel you did on your exams?" Edward asked on the way, making small talk.

"History was easy, but I don't know about the Calculus. It seemed like it was making sense, so that probably means I failed."

He laughed. "I'm sure you did fine. Or, if you're really worried, I could bribe Mr. Varner to give you an A."

"Er, thanks, but no thanks."

He laughed again, but suddenly stopped when we turned the last bend and saw the red car waiting. He frowned in concentration, and then, as he parked the car, he sighed.

"What's wrong?" I asked, my hand on the door.

He shook his head. "Nothing." His eyes were narrowed as he stared through the windshield toward the other car. I'd seen that look before.

"You're not *listening* to Jacob, are you?" I accused.

"It's not easy to ignore someone when he's shouting."

"Oh." I thought about that for a second. "What's he shouting?" I whispered.

"I'm absolutely certain he'll mention it himself," Edward said in a wry tone.

I would have pressed the issue, but then Jacob honked his horn — two quick impatient honks.

"That's impolite," Edward growled.

"That's Jacob," I sighed, and I hurried out before Jacob did something to really set Edward's teeth on edge.

I waved to Edward before I got into the Rabbit and, from that distance, it looked like he was truly upset about the honking thing . . . or whatever Jacob was thinking about. But my eyes were weak and made mistakes all the time.

I wanted Edward to come to me. I wanted to make both of them get out of their cars and shake hands and be friends — be Edward and Jacob rather than *vampire* and *werewolf*. It was as if I had those two stubborn magnets in my hands again, and I was holding them together, trying to force nature to reverse herself. . . .

I sighed, and climbed in Jacob's car.

"Hey, Bells." Jake's tone was cheerful, but his voice dragged. I examined his face as he started down the road, driving a little faster than I did, but slower than Edward, on his way back to La Push.

Jacob looked different, maybe even sick. His eyelids drooped and his face was drawn. His shaggy hair stuck out in random directions; it was almost to his chin in some places.

"Are you all right, Jake?"

"Just tired," he managed to get out before he was overcome by a massive yawn. When he finished, he asked, "What do you want to do today?"

I eyed him for a moment. "Let's just hang out at your place for now," I suggested. He didn't look like he was up for much more than that. "We can ride our bikes later."

"Sure, sure," he said, yawning again.

Jacob's house was vacant, and that felt strange. I realized I thought of Billy as a nearly permanent fixture there.

"Where's your dad?"

"Over at the Clearwaters'. He's been hanging out there a lot since Harry died. Sue gets lonely."

Jacob sat down on the old couch that was no bigger than a loveseat and squished himself to the side to make room for me.

"Oh. That's nice. Poor Sue."

"Yeah . . . she's having some trouble. . . ." He hesitated. "With her kids."

"Sure, it's got to be hard on Seth and Leah, losing their dad. . . ."

"Uh-huh," he agreed, lost in thought. He picked up

the remote and flipped on the TV without seeming to think about it. He yawned.

"What's with you, Jake? You're like a zombie."

"I got about two hours of sleep last night, and four the night before," he told me. He stretched his long arms slowly, and I could hear the joints crack as he flexed. He settled his left arm along the back of the sofa behind me, and slumped back to rest his head against the wall. "I'm exhausted."

"Why aren't you sleeping?" I asked.

He made a face. "Sam's being difficult. He doesn't trust your bloodsuckers. I've been running double shifts for two weeks and nobody's touched me yet, but he still doesn't buy it. So I'm on my own for now."

"Double shifts? Is this because you're trying to watch out for *me?* Jake, that's wrong! You need to sleep. I'll be fine."

"It's no big deal." His eyes were abruptly more alert. "Hey, did you ever find out who was in your room? Is there anything new?"

I ignored the second question. "No, we didn't find anything out about my, um, visitor."

"Then I'll be around," he said as his eyes slid closed.

"Jake . . . ," I started to whine.

"Hey, it's the least I can do — I offered eternal servitude, remember. I'm your slave for life."

"I don't want a slave!"

His eyes didn't open. "What *do* you want, Bella?"

"I want my friend Jacob — and I don't want him half-dead, hurting himself in some misguided attempt —"

He cut me off. "Look at it this way — I'm hoping I can track down a vampire I'm allowed to kill, okay?"

I didn't answer. He looked at me then, peeking at my reaction.

"Kidding, Bella."

I stared at the TV.

"So, any special plans next week? You're graduating. Wow. That's big." His voice turned flat, and his face, already drawn, looked downright haggard as his eyes closed again — not in exhaustion this time, but in denial. I realized that graduation still had a horrible significance for him, though my intentions were now disrupted.

"No *special* plans," I said carefully, hoping he would hear the reassurance in my words without a more detailed explanation. I didn't want to get into it now. For one thing, he didn't look up for any difficult conversations. For another, I knew he would read too much into my qualms. "Well, I do have to go to a graduation party. Mine." I made a disgusted sound. "Alice *loves* parties, and she's invited the whole town to her place the night of. It's going to be horrible."

His eyes opened as I spoke, and a relieved smile made his face look less worn. "I didn't get an invitation. I'm hurt," he teased.

"Consider yourself invited. It's supposedly *my* party, so I should be able to ask who I want."

"Thanks," he said sarcastically, his eyes slipping closed once more.

"I wish you would come," I said without any hope. "It would be more fun. For me, I mean."

"Sure, sure," he mumbled. "That would be very . . . wise . . ." His voice trailed off.

A few seconds later, he was snoring.

Poor Jacob. I studied his dreaming face, and liked what I saw. While he slept, every trace of defensiveness and bitterness disappeared and suddenly he was the boy who had been my very best friend before all the werewolf nonsense had gotten in the way. He looked so much younger. He looked like my Jacob.

I nestled into the couch to wait out his nap, hoping he would sleep for a while and make up some of what he'd lost. I flipped through channels, but there wasn't much on. I settled for a cooking show, knowing, as I watched, that I'd never put that much effort into Charlie's dinner. Jacob continued to snore, getting louder. I turned up the TV.

I was strangely relaxed, almost sleepy, too. This house felt safer than my own, probably because no one had ever come looking for me here. I curled up on the sofa and thought about taking a nap myself. Maybe I would have, but Jacob's snoring was impossible to tune out. So, instead of sleeping, I let my mind wander.

Finals were done, and most of them had been a cakewalk. Calculus, the one exception, was behind me, pass or fail. My high school education was over. And I didn't really know how I felt about that. I couldn't look at it objectively, tied up as it was with my human life being over.

I wondered how long Edward planned to use this "not because you're scared" excuse. I was going to have to put my foot down sometime.

If I were thinking practically, I knew it made more

sense to ask Carlisle to change me the second I made it through the graduation line. Forks was becoming nearly as dangerous as a war zone. No, Forks *was* a war zone. Not to mention . . . it would be a good excuse to miss the graduation party. I smiled to myself as I thought of that most trivial of reasons for changing. Silly . . . yet still compelling.

But Edward was right — I wasn't quite ready yet.

And I didn't want to be practical. I wanted Edward to be the one. It wasn't a rational desire. I was sure that — about two seconds after someone actually bit me and the venom started burning through my veins — I really wouldn't care anymore who had done it. So it shouldn't make a difference.

It was hard to define, even to myself, why it mattered. There was just something about him being the one to make the choice — to want to keep me enough that he wouldn't just allow me to be changed, he would act to keep me. It was childish, but I liked the idea that *his* lips would be the last good thing I would feel. Even more embarrassingly, something I would never say aloud, I wanted *his* venom to poison my system. It would make me belong to him in a tangible, quantifiable way.

But I knew he was going to stick to his marriage scheme like glue — because a delay was what he was clearly after and it was working so far. I tried to imagine telling my parents that I was getting married this summer. Telling Angela and Ben and Mike. I couldn't. I couldn't think of the words to say. It would be easier to tell them I was becoming a vampire. And I was sure that at least my mother — were I to tell her every detail of the truth — would be more strenuously opposed to me getting married than to me becoming a vampire. I grimaced to myself as I imagined her horrified expression.

Then, for just a second, I saw that same odd vision of Edward and me on a porch swing, wearing clothes from another kind of world. A world where it would surprise no one if I wore his ring on my finger. A simpler place, where love was defined in simpler ways. One plus one equals two. . . .

Jacob snorted and rolled to his side. His arm swung off the back of the couch and pinned me against his body.

Holy crow, but he was heavy! And *hot.* It was sweltering after just a few seconds.

I tried to slide out from under his arm without waking him, but I had to shove a little bit, and when his arm fell off me, his eyes snapped open. He jumped to his feet, looking around anxiously.

"What? What?" he asked, disoriented.

"It's just me, Jake. Sorry I woke you."

He turned to look at me, blinking and confused. "Bella?"

"Hey, sleepy."

"Oh, man! Did I fall asleep? I'm sorry! How long was I out?"

"A few Emerils. I lost count."

He flopped back on the couch next to me. "Wow. Sorry about that, really."

I patted his hair, trying to smooth the wild disarray. "Don't feel bad. I'm glad you got some sleep."

He yawned and stretched. "I'm useless these days. No wonder Billy's always gone. I'm so boring."

"You're fine," I assured him.

"Ugh, let's go outside. I need to walk around or I'll pass out again."

"Jake, go back to sleep. I'm good. I'll call Edward to come pick me up." I patted my pockets as I spoke, and realized they were empty. "Shoot, I'll have to borrow your phone. I think I must have left his in the car." I started to unfold myself.

"No!" Jacob insisted, grabbing my hand. "No, stay. You hardly ever make it down. I can't believe I wasted all this time."

He pulled me off the couch as he spoke, and then led the way outside, ducking his head as he passed under the doorframe. It had gotten much cooler while Jacob slept; the air was unseasonably cold — there must be a storm on the way. It felt like February, not May.

The wintry air seemed to make Jacob more alert. He paced back and forth in front of the house for a minute, dragging me along with him.

"I'm an idiot," he muttered to himself.

"What's the matter, Jake? So you fell asleep." I shrugged.

"I wanted to talk to you. I can't believe this."

"Talk to me now," I said.

Jacob met my eyes for a second, and then looked away quickly toward the trees. It almost looked like he was blushing, but it was hard to tell with his dark skin.

I suddenly remembered what Edward had said when he

dropped me off — that Jacob would tell me whatever he was shouting in his head. I started gnawing on my lip.

"Look," Jacob said. "I was planning to do this a little bit differently." He laughed, and it sounded like he was laughing at himself. "Smoother," he added. "I was going to work up to it, but" — and he looked at the clouds, dimmer as the afternoon progressed — "I'm out of time to work."

He laughed again, nervous. We were still pacing slowly.

"What are you talking about?" I demanded.

He took a deep breath. "I want to tell you something. And you already know it . . . but I think I should say it out loud anyway. Just so there's never any confusion on the subject."

I planted my feet, and he came to a stop. I took my hand away and folded my arms across my chest. I was suddenly sure that I didn't want to know what he was building up to.

Jacob's eyebrows pulled down, throwing his deep-set eyes into shadow. They were pitch black as they bored into mine.

"I'm in love with you, Bella," Jacob said in a strong, sure voice. "Bella, I love you. And I want you to pick me instead of him. I know you don't feel that way, but I need the truth out there so that you know your options. I wouldn't want a miscommunication to stand in our way."

15. WAGER

I STARED AT HIM FOR A LONG MINUTE, SPEECHLESS. I could not think of one thing to say to him.

As he watched my dumbfounded expression, the seriousness left his face.

"Okay," he said, grinning. "That's all."

"Jake —" It felt like there was something big sticking in my throat. I tried to clear the obstruction. "I can't — I mean I don't . . . I have to go."

I turned, but he grabbed my shoulders and spun me around.

"No, wait. I *know* that, Bella. But, look, answer me this, all right? Do you want me to go away and never see you again? Be honest."

It was hard to concentrate on his question, so it took a minute to answer. "No, I don't want that," I finally admitted.

Jacob grinned again. "See."

"But I don't want you around for the same reason that you want me around," I objected.

"Tell me exactly why you want me around, then."

I thought carefully. "I miss you when you're not there. When you're happy," I qualified carefully, "it makes me happy. But I could say the same thing about Charlie, Jacob. You're family. I love you, but I'm not *in* love with you."

He nodded, unruffled. "But you do want me around."

"Yes." I sighed. He was impossible to discourage.

"Then I'll stick around."

"You're a glutton for punishment," I grumbled.

"Yep." He stroked the tips of his fingers across my right cheek. I slapped his hand away.

"Do you think you could behave yourself a little better, at least?" I asked, irritated.

"No, I don't. You decide, Bella. You can have me the way I am — bad behavior included — or not at all."

I stared at him, frustrated. "That's mean."

"So are you."

That pulled me up short, and I took an involuntary step back. He was right. If I wasn't mean — and greedy, too — I would tell him I didn't want to be friends and walk away. It was wrong to try to keep my friend when that would hurt him. I didn't know what I was doing here, but I was suddenly sure that it wasn't good.

"You're right," I whispered.

He laughed. "I forgive you. Just try not to get *too* mad at me. Because I recently decided that I'm not giving up. There really is something irresistible about a lost cause."

"Jacob." I stared into his dark eyes, trying to make him take me seriously. "I love *him,* Jacob. He's my whole life."

"You love me, too," he reminded me. He held up his hand when I started to protest. "Not the same way, I know. But he's not your whole life, either. Not anymore. Maybe he was once, but he left. And now he's just going to have to deal with the consequence of that choice — *me.*"

I shook my head. "You're impossible."

Suddenly, he was serious. He took my chin in his hand, holding it firmly so that I couldn't look away from his intent gaze.

"Until your heart stops beating, Bella," he said. "I'll be here — fighting. Don't forget that you have options."

"I don't want options," I disagreed, trying to yank my chin free unsuccessfully. "And my heartbeats are numbered, Jacob. The time is almost gone."

His eyes narrowed. "All the more reason to fight — fight harder now, while I can," he whispered.

He still had my chin — his fingers holding too tight, till it hurt — and I saw the resolve form abruptly in his eyes.

"N —" I started to object, but it was too late.

His lips crushed mine, stopping my protest. He kissed me angrily, roughly, his other hand gripping tight around the back of my neck, making escape impossible. I shoved against his chest with all my strength, but he didn't even seem to notice. His mouth was soft, despite the anger, his lips molding to mine in a warm, unfamiliar way.

I grabbed at his face, trying to push it away, failing again. He seemed to notice this time, though, and it aggravated him. His lips forced mine open, and I could feel his hot breath in my mouth.

Acting on instinct, I let my hands drop to my side, and shut down. I opened my eyes and didn't fight, didn't feel . . . just waited for him to stop.

It worked. The anger seemed to evaporate, and he pulled back to look at me. He pressed his lips softly to mine again, once, twice . . . a third time. I pretended I was a statue and waited.

Finally, he let go of my face and leaned away.

"Are you done now?" I asked in an expressionless voice.

"Yes," he sighed. He started to smile, closing his eyes.

I pulled my arm back and then let it snap forward, punching him in the mouth with as much power as I could force out of my body.

There was a crunching sound.

"Ow! *OW!*" I screamed, frantically hopping up and down in agony while I clutched my hand to my chest. It was broken, I could feel it.

Jacob stared at me in shock. "Are you all right?"

"No, dammit! *You broke my hand!*"

"Bella, *you* broke your hand. Now stop dancing around and let me look at it."

"Don't touch me! I'm going home right now!"

"I'll get my car," he said calmly. He wasn't even rubbing his jaw like they did in the movies. How pathetic.

"No, thanks," I hissed. "I'd rather walk." I turned toward the road. It was only a few miles to the border. As

soon as I got away from him, Alice would see me. She'd
send somebody to pick me up.

"Just let me drive you home," Jacob insisted. Unbelievably, he had the nerve to wrap his arm around my waist.

I jerked away from him.

"Fine!" I growled. "*Do!* I can't wait to see what Edward
does to you! I hope he snaps your neck, you pushy, obnoxious, moronic DOG!"

Jacob rolled his eyes. He walked me to the passenger
side of his car and helped me in. When he got in the
driver's side, he was whistling.

"Didn't I hurt you at all?" I asked, furious and annoyed.

"Are you kidding? If you hadn't started screaming, I
might not have figured out that you were trying to punch
me. I may not be made out of stone, but I'm not *that* soft."

"I hate you, Jacob Black."

"That's good. Hate is a passionate emotion."

"I'll give you passionate," I muttered under my breath.
"Murder, the ultimate crime of passion."

"Oh, c'mon," he said, all cheery and looking like he
was about to start whistling again. "That had to be better
than kissing a rock."

"Not even remotely close," I told him coldly.

He pursed his lips. "You could just be saying that."

"But I'm not."

That seemed to bother him for a second, but then he
perked up. "You're just mad. I don't have any experience
with this kind of thing, but I thought it was pretty incredible myself."

"Ugh," I groaned.

"You're going to think about it tonight. When he thinks you're asleep, you'll be thinking about your options."

"If I think about you tonight, it will be because I'm having a *nightmare.*"

He slowed the car to a crawl, turning to stare at me with his dark eyes wide and earnest. "Just think about how it could be, Bella," he urged in a soft, eager voice. "You wouldn't have to change anything for me. You know Charlie would be happy if you picked me. I could protect you just as well as your vampire can — maybe better. And I would make you happy, Bella. There's so much I could give you that he can't. I'll bet he couldn't even kiss you like that — because he would hurt you. I would never, never hurt you, Bella."

I held up my injured hand.

He sighed. "That wasn't my fault. You should have known better."

"Jacob, I can't *be* happy without him."

"You've never tried," he disagreed. "When he left, you spent all your energy holding on to him. You could be happy if you let go. You could be happy with me."

"I don't want to be happy with anyone but him," I insisted.

"You'll never be able to be as sure of him as you are of me. He left you once, he could do it again."

"No, he will not," I said through my teeth. The pain of the memory bit into me like the lash of a whip. It made me want to hurt him back. "You left me once," I reminded him in a cold voice, thinking of the weeks he'd hidden from me, the words he'd said to me in the woods beside his home. . . .

"I never did," he argued hotly. "They told me I couldn't tell you — that it wasn't safe *for you* if we were together. But I never left, never! I used to run around your house at night — like I do now. Just making sure you were okay."

I wasn't about to let him make me feel bad for him now.

"Take me home. My hand hurts."

He sighed, and started driving at a normal speed, watching the road.

"Just think about it, Bella."

"No," I said stubbornly.

"You will. Tonight. And I'll be thinking about you while you're thinking about me."

"Like I said, a nightmare."

He grinned over at me. "You kissed me back."

I gasped, unthinkingly balling my hands up into fists again, hissing when my broken hand reacted.

"Are you okay?" he asked.

"I did *not*."

"I think I can tell the difference."

"Obviously you can't — that was not kissing back, that was trying to get you the hell off of me, you *idiot*."

He laughed a low, throaty laugh. "Touchy. Almost *overly* defensive, I would say."

I took a deep breath. There was no point in arguing with him; he would twist anything I said. I concentrated on my hand, trying to stretch out my fingers, to ascertain where the broken parts were. Sharp pains stabbed along my knuckles. I groaned.

"I'm really sorry about your hand," Jacob said, sounding almost sincere. "Next time you want to hit me, use a baseball bat or a crowbar, okay?"

"Don't think I'll forget that," I muttered.

I didn't realize where we were going until we were on my road.

"Why are you taking me here?" I demanded.

He looked at me blankly. "I thought you said you were going home?"

"Ugh. I guess you can't take me to Edward's house, can you?" I ground my teeth in frustration.

Pain twisted across his face, and I could see that this affected him more than anything else I'd said.

"This is your home, Bella," he said quietly.

"Yes, but do any doctors live here?" I asked, holding up my hand again.

"Oh." He thought about that for a minute. "I'll take you to the hospital. Or Charlie can."

"I don't want to go to the hospital. It's embarrassing and unnecessary."

He let the Rabbit idle in front of the house, deliberating with an unsure expression. Charlie's cruiser was in the driveway.

I sighed. "Go home, Jacob."

I climbed out of the car awkwardly, heading for the house. The engine cut off behind me, and I was less surprised than annoyed to find Jacob beside me again.

"What are you going to do?" he asked.

"I am going to get some ice on my hand, and then I am going to call Edward and tell him to come and get me and take me to Carlisle so that he can fix my hand. Then, if you're still here, I am going to go hunt up a crowbar."

He didn't answer. He opened the front door and held it for me.

We walked silently past the front room where Charlie was lying on the sofa.

"Hey, kids," he said, sitting forward. "Nice to see *you* here, Jake."

"Hey, Charlie," Jacob answered casually, pausing. I stalked on to the kitchen.

"What's wrong with her?" Charlie wondered.

"She thinks she broke her hand," I heard Jacob tell him. I went to the freezer and pulled out a tray of ice cubes.

"How did she do that?" As my father, I thought Charlie ought to sound a bit less amused and a bit more concerned.

Jacob laughed. "She hit me."

Charlie laughed, too, and I scowled while I beat the tray against the edge of the sink. The ice scattered inside the basin, and I grabbed a handful with my good hand and wrapped the cubes in the dishcloth on the counter.

"Why did she hit you?"

"Because I kissed her," Jacob said, unashamed.

"Good for you, kid," Charlie congratulated him.

I ground my teeth and went for the phone. I dialed Edward's cell.

"Bella?" he answered on the first ring. He sounded more than relieved — he was delighted. I could hear the

Volvo's engine in the background; he was already in the car — that was good. "You left the phone . . . I'm sorry, did Jacob drive you home?"

"Yes," I grumbled. "Will you come and get me, please?"

"I'm on my way," he said at once. "What's wrong?"

"I want Carlisle to look at my hand. I think it's broken."

It had gone quiet in the front room, and I wondered when Jacob would bolt. I smiled a grim smile, imagining his discomfort.

"What happened?" Edward demanded, his voice going flat.

"I punched Jacob," I admitted.

"Good," Edward said bleakly. "Though I'm sorry you're hurt."

I laughed once, because he sounded as pleased as Charlie had.

"I wish I'd hurt *him*." I sighed in frustration. "I didn't do any damage at all."

"I can fix that," he offered.

"I was hoping you would say that."

There was a slight pause. "That doesn't sound like you," he said, wary now. "What did he *do*?"

"He kissed me," I growled.

All I heard on the other end of the line was the sound of an engine accelerating.

In the other room, Charlie spoke again. "Maybe you ought to take off, Jake," he suggested.

"I think I'll hang out here, if you don't mind."

"Your funeral," Charlie muttered.

"Is the dog still there?" Edward finally spoke again.

"Yes."

"I'm around the corner," he said darkly, and the line disconnected.

As I hung up the phone, smiling, I heard the sound of his car racing down the street. The brakes protested loudly as he slammed to a stop out front. I went to get the door.

"How's your hand?" Charlie asked as I walked by. Charlie looked uncomfortable. Jacob lolled next to him on the sofa, perfectly at ease.

I lifted the ice pack to show it off. "It's swelling."

"Maybe you should pick on people your own size," Charlie suggested.

"Maybe," I agreed. I walked on to open the door. Edward was waiting.

"Let me see," he murmured.

He examined my hand gently, so carefully that it caused me no pain at all. His hands were almost as cold as the ice, and they felt good against my skin.

"I think you're right about the break," he said. "I'm proud of you. You must have put some force behind this."

"As much as I have." I sighed. "Not enough, apparently."

He kissed my hand softly. "I'll take care of it," he promised. And then he called, "Jacob," his voice still quiet and even.

"Now, now," Charlie cautioned.

I heard Charlie heave himself off of the sofa. Jacob got to the hall first, and much more quietly, but Charlie was not far behind him. Jacob's expression was alert and eager.

"I don't want any fighting, do you understand?" Charlie looked only at Edward when he spoke. "I can go put my badge on if that makes my request more official."

"That won't be necessary," Edward said in a restrained tone.

"Why don't you arrest me, Dad?" I suggested. "I'm the one throwing punches."

Charlie raised an eyebrow. "Do you want to press charges, Jake?"

"No." Jacob grinned, incorrigible. "I'll take the trade any day."

Edward grimaced.

"Dad, don't you have a baseball bat somewhere in your room? I want to borrow it for a minute."

Charlie looked at me evenly. "Enough, Bella."

"Let's go have Carlisle look at your hand before you wind up in a jail cell," Edward said. He put his arm around me and pulled me toward the door.

"Fine," I said, leaning against him. I wasn't so angry anymore, now that Edward was with me. I felt comforted, and my hand didn't bother me as much.

We were walking down the sidewalk when I heard Charlie whispering anxiously behind me.

"What are you doing? Are you crazy?"

"Give me a minute, Charlie," Jacob answered. "Don't worry, I'll be right back."

I looked back and Jacob was following us, stopping to close the door in Charlie's surprised and uneasy face.

Edward ignored him at first, leading me to the car. He helped me inside, shut the door, and then turned to face Jacob on the sidewalk.

I leaned anxiously through the open window. Charlie was visible in the house, peeking through the drapes in the front room.

Jacob's stance was casual, his arms folded across his chest, but the muscles in his jaw were tight.

Edward spoke in a voice so peaceful and gentle that it made the words strangely more threatening. "I'm not going to kill you now, because it would upset Bella."

"Hmph," I grumbled.

Edward turned slightly to throw me a quick smile. His face was still calm. "It would bother you in the morning," he said, brushing his fingers across my cheek.

Then he turned back to Jacob. "But if you ever bring her back damaged again — and I don't care whose fault it is; I don't care if she merely trips, or if a meteor falls out of the sky and hits her in the head — if you return her to me in less than the perfect condition that I left her in, you will be running with three legs. Do you understand that, mongrel?"

Jacob rolled his eyes.

"Who's going back?" I muttered.

Edward continued as if he hadn't heard me. "And if you ever kiss her again, I *will* break your jaw for her," he promised, his voice still gentle and velvet and deadly.

"What if she wants me to?" Jacob drawled, arrogant.

"Hah!" I snorted.

"If that's what she wants, then I won't object." Edward shrugged, untroubled. "You might want to wait for her to *say* it, rather than trust your interpretation of body language — but it's your face."

Jacob grinned.

"You wish," I grumbled.

"Yes, he does," Edward murmured.

"Well, if you're done rummaging through my head," Jacob said with a thick edge of annoyance, "why don't you go take care of her hand?"

"One more thing," Edward said slowly. "I'll be fighting for her, too. You should know that. I'm not taking anything for granted, and I'll be fighting twice as hard as you will."

"Good," Jacob growled. "It's no fun beating someone who forfeits."

"She *is* mine." Edward's low voice was suddenly dark, not as composed as before. "I didn't say I would fight fair."

"Neither did I."

"Best of luck."

Jacob nodded. "Yes, may the best *man* win."

"That sounds about right . . . pup."

Jacob grimaced briefly, then he composed his face and leaned around Edward to smile at me. I glowered back.

"I hope your hand feels better soon. I'm really sorry you're hurt."

Childishly, I turned my face away from him.

I didn't look up again as Edward walked around the car and climbed into the driver's side, so I didn't know if Jacob went back into the house or continued to stand there, watching me.

"How do you feel?" Edward asked as we drove away.

"Irritated."

He chuckled. "I meant your hand."

I shrugged. "I've had worse."

"True," he agreed, and frowned.

Edward drove around the house to the garage. Emmett and Rosalie were there, Rosalie's perfect legs, recognizable even sheathed in jeans, were sticking out from under the bottom of Emmett's huge Jeep. Emmett was sitting beside her, one hand reached under the Jeep toward her. It took me a moment to realize that he was acting as the jack.

Emmett watched curiously as Edward helped me carefully out of the car. His eyes zeroed in on the hand I cradled against my chest.

Emmett grinned. "Fall down again, Bella?"

I glared at him fiercely. "No, Emmett. I punched a werewolf in the face."

Emmett blinked, and then burst into a roar of laughter.

As Edward led me past them, Rosalie spoke from under the car.

"Jasper's going to win the bet," she said smugly.

Emmett's laughter stopped at once, and he studied me with appraising eyes.

"What bet?" I demanded, pausing.

"Let's get you to Carlisle," Edward urged. He was staring at Emmett. His head shook infinitesimally.

"What bet?" I insisted as I turned on him.

"Thanks, Rosalie," he muttered as he tightened his arm around my waist and pulled me toward the house.

"Edward . . . ," I grumbled.

"It's infantile," he shrugged. "Emmett and Jasper like to gamble."

"Emmett will tell me." I tried to turn, but his arm was like iron around me.

He sighed. "They're betting on how many times you . . . slip up in the first year."

"Oh." I grimaced, trying to hide my sudden horror as I realized what he meant. "They have a bet about how many people I'll kill?"

"Yes," he admitted unwillingly. "Rosalie thinks your temper will turn the odds in Jasper's favor."

I felt a little high. "Jasper's betting high."

"It will make him feel better if you have a hard time adjusting. He's tired of being the weakest link."

"Sure. Of course it will. I guess I could throw in a few extra homicides, if it makes Jasper happy. Why not?" I was babbling, my voice a blank monotone. In my head, I was seeing newspaper headlines, lists of names. . . .

He squeezed me. "You don't need to worry about it now. In fact, you don't have to worry about it ever, if you don't want to."

I groaned, and Edward, thinking it was the pain in my hand that bothered me, pulled me faster toward the house.

My hand *was* broken, but there wasn't any serious damage, just a tiny fissure in one knuckle. I didn't want a cast, and Carlisle said I'd be fine in a brace if I promised to keep it on. I promised.

Edward could tell I was out of it as Carlisle worked to fit a brace carefully to my hand. He worried aloud a few times that I was in pain, but I assured him that that wasn't it.

As if I needed — or even had room for — one more thing to worry about.

All of Jasper's stories about newly created vampires had been percolating in my head since he'd explained his past. Now those stories jumped into sharp focus with the news of his and Emmett's wager. I wondered randomly what they were betting. What was a motivating prize when you had everything?

I'd always known that I would be different. I hoped that I would be as strong as Edward said I would be. Strong and fast and, most of all, beautiful. Someone who could stand next to Edward and feel like she belonged there.

I'd been trying not to think too much about the other things that I would be. Wild. Bloodthirsty. Maybe I would not be able to stop myself from killing people. Strangers, people who had never harmed me. People like the growing number of victims in Seattle, who'd had families and friends and futures. People who'd had *lives.* And I could be the monster who took that away from them.

But, in truth, I could handle that part — because I trusted Edward, trusted him absolutely, to keep me from doing anything I would regret. I knew he'd take me to Antarctica and hunt penguins if I asked him to. And I would do whatever it took to be a good person. A good vampire. That thought would have made me giggle, if not for this new worry.

Because, if I really were somehow like that — like the nightmarish images of newborns that Jasper had painted in my head — could I possibly be *me*? And if all I wanted was to kill people, what would happen to the things I wanted *now*?

Edward was so obsessed with me not missing anything while I was human. Usually, it seemed kind of silly. There weren't many human experiences that I worried about missing. As long as I got to be with Edward, what else could I ask for?

I stared at his face while he watched Carlisle fix my hand. There was nothing in this world that I wanted more than him. Would that, *could* that, change?

Was there a human experience that I was *not* willing to give up?

16. EPOCH

"I HAVE NOTHING TO WEAR!" I MOANED TO MYSELF.

Every item of clothing I owned was strewn across my bed; my drawers and closets were bare. I stared into the empty recesses, willing something suitable to appear.

My khaki skirt lay over the back of the rocking chair, waiting for me to discover something that went with it just exactly right. Something that would make me look beautiful and grown up. Something that said *special occasion.* I was coming up empty.

It was almost time to go, and I was still wearing my favorite old sweats. Unless I could find something better here — and the odds weren't looking good at this point — I was going to graduate in them.

I scowled at the pile of clothes on my bed.

The kicker was that I knew exactly what I would have worn if it were still available — my kidnapped red blouse. I punched the wall with my good hand.

"Stupid, thieving, annoying vampire!" I growled.

"What did I do?" Alice demanded.

She was leaning casually beside the open window as if she'd been there the whole time.

"Knock, knock," she added with a grin.

"Is it really so hard to wait for me to get the door?"

She threw a flat, white box onto my bed. "I'm just passing through. I thought you might need something to wear."

I looked at the big package lying on top of my unsatis-fying wardrobe and grimaced.

"Admit it," Alice said. "I'm a lifesaver."

"You're a lifesaver," I muttered. "Thanks."

"Well, it's nice to get something right for a change. You don't know how irritating it is — missing things the way I have been. I feel so useless. So . . . normal." She cringed in horror of the word.

"I can't imagine how awful that must feel. Being nor-mal? Ugh."

She laughed. "Well, at least this makes up for missing your annoying thief — now I just have to figure out what I'm not seeing in Seattle."

When she said the words that way — putting the two situations together in one sentence — right then it clicked. The elusive something that had been bothering me for days, the important connection that I couldn't quite put together, suddenly became clear. I stared at her, my face frozen with whatever expression was already in place.

"Aren't you going to open it?" she asked. She sighed when I didn't move immediately, and tugged the top of the box off herself. She pulled something out and held it up, but I couldn't concentrate on what it was. "Pretty, don't you think? I picked blue, because I know it's Edward's favorite on you."

I wasn't listening.

"It's the same," I whispered.

"What is?" she demanded. "You don't have anything like this. For crying out loud, you only own one skirt!"

"No, Alice! Forget the clothes, listen!"

"You don't like it?" Alice's face clouded with disappointment.

"Listen, Alice, don't you see? It's the *same*! The one who broke in and stole my things, and the new vampires in Seattle. They're together!"

The clothes slipped from her fingers and fell back into the box.

Alice focused now, her voice suddenly sharp. "Why do you think that?"

"Remember what Edward said? About someone using the holes in your vision to keep you from seeing the newborns? And then what you said before, about the timing being too perfect — how careful my thief was to make no contact, as if he knew you would see that. I think you were right, Alice, I think he did know. I think he was using those holes, too. And what are the odds that *two* different people not only know enough about you to do that, but also decided to do it at exactly the same time? No way. It's one person. The same one. The one who is making the army is the one who stole my scent."

Alice wasn't accustomed to being taken by surprise. She froze, and was still for so long that I started counting in my head as I waited. She didn't move for two minutes straight. Then her eyes refocused on me.

"You're right," she said in a hollow tone. "Of course you're right. And when you put it that way. . . ."

"Edward had it wrong," I whispered. "It was a test . . . to see if it would work. If he could get in and out safely as long as he didn't do anything you would be watching out for. Like trying to kill me. . . . And he didn't take my things to prove he'd found me. He stole my scent . . . so that *others* could find me."

Her eyes were wide with shock. I was right, and I could see that she knew it, too.

"Oh, no," she mouthed.

I was through expecting my emotions to make sense anymore. As I processed the fact that someone had created an army of vampires — the army that had gruesomely murdered dozens of people in Seattle — for the express purpose of destroying *me,* I felt a spasm of relief.

Part of it was finally solving that irritating feeling that I was missing something vital.

But the larger part was something else entirely.

"Well," I whispered, "everyone can relax. Nobody's trying to exterminate the Cullens after all."

"If you think that one thing has changed, you're

absolutely wrong," Alice said through her teeth. "If someone wants one of us, they're going to have to go through the rest of us to get to her."

"Thanks, Alice. But at least we know what they're really after. That has to help."

"Maybe," she muttered. She started pacing back and forth across my room.

Thud, thud — a fist hammered against my door.

I jumped. Alice didn't seem to notice.

"Aren't you ready yet? We're gonna be late!" Charlie complained, sounding edgy. Charlie hated occasions about as much as I did. In his case, a lot of the problem was having to dress up.

"Almost. Give me a minute," I said hoarsely.

He was quiet for half a second. "Are you crying?"

"No. I'm nervous. Go away."

I heard him clump down the stairs.

"I have to go," Alice whispered.

"Why?"

"Edward is coming. If he hears this . . ."

"Go, go!" I urged immediately. Edward would go berserk when he knew. I couldn't keep it from him for long, but maybe the graduation ceremony wasn't the best time for his reaction.

"Put it on," Alice commanded as she flitted out the window.

I did what she said, dressing in a daze.

I'd been planning to do something more sophisticated with my hair, but time was up, so it hung straight and boring as on any other day. It didn't matter. I didn't bother to look in the mirror, so I had no idea how Alice's sweater and skirt ensemble worked. That didn't matter, either. I threw the ugly yellow polyester graduation robe over my arm and hurried down the stairs.

"You look nice," Charlie said, already gruff with suppressed emotion. "Is that new?"

"Yeah," I mumbled, trying to concentrate. "Alice gave it to me. Thanks."

Edward arrived just a few minutes after his sister left. It wasn't enough time for me to pull together a calm façade. But, since we were riding in the cruiser with Charlie, he never had a chance to ask me what was wrong.

Charlie had gotten stubborn last week when he'd learned that I was intending to ride with Edward to the graduation ceremony. And I could see his point — parents should have some rights come graduation day. I'd conceded with good grace, and Edward had cheerfully suggested that we all go together. Since Carlisle and Esme had no problem with this, Charlie couldn't come up with a compelling objection; he'd agreed with poor grace. And now Edward rode in the backseat of my father's police car, behind the fiberglass divider, with an amused expression — probably due to my father's amused expression, and the grin that widened every time Charlie stole a glance at Edward in his rearview mirror. Which almost certainly meant that Charlie was imagining things that would get him in trouble with me if he said them out loud.

"Are you all right?" Edward whispered when he helped me from the front seat in the school parking lot.

"Nervous," I answered, and it wasn't even a lie.

"You are so beautiful," he said.

He looked like he wanted to say more, but Charlie, in an obvious maneuver that he meant to be subtle, shrugged in between us and put his arm around my shoulders.

"Are you excited?" he asked me.

"Not really," I admitted.

"Bella, this is a big deal. You're graduating from high school. It's the real world for you now. College. Living on your own. . . . You're not my little girl anymore." Charlie choked up a bit at the end.

"Dad," I moaned. "Please don't get all weepy on me."

"Who's weepy?" he growled. "Now, why aren't you excited?"

"I don't know, Dad. I guess it hasn't hit yet or something."

"It's good that Alice is throwing this party. You need something to perk you up."

"Sure. A party's exactly what I need."

Charlie laughed at my tone and squeezed my shoulders. Edward looked at the clouds, his face thoughtful.

My father had to leave us at the back door of the gym and go around to the main entrance with the rest of the parents.

It was pandemonium as Ms. Cope from the front office and Mr. Varner the math teacher tried to line everyone up alphabetically.

"Up front, Mr. Cullen," Mr. Varner barked at Edward.

"Hey, Bella!"

I looked up to see Jessica Stanley waving at me from the back of the line with a smile on her face.

Edward kissed me quickly, sighed, and went to go stand with the C's. Alice wasn't there. What was she going to do? Skip graduation? What poor timing on my part. I should have waited to figure things out until after this was over with.

"Down here, Bella!" Jessica called again.

I walked down the line to take my place behind Jessica, mildly curious as to why she was suddenly so friendly. As I got closer, I saw Angela five people back, watching Jessica with the same curiosity.

Jess was babbling before I was in earshot.

". . . so amazing. I mean, it seems like we just met, and now we're graduating together," she gushed. "Can you believe it's over? I feel like screaming!"

"So do I," I muttered.

"This is all just so incredible. Do you remember your first day here? We were friends, like, right away. From the first time we saw each other. Amazing. And now I'm off to California and you'll be in Alaska and I'm going to miss you so much! You have to promise that we'll get together sometimes! I'm so glad you're having a party. That's perfect. Because we really haven't spent much time together in a while and now we're all leaving. . . ."

She droned on and on, and I was sure the sudden return of our friendship was due to graduation nostalgia and gratitude for the party invite, not that I'd had anything to do with that. I paid attention as well as I could while I shrugged into my robe. And I found that I was glad that things could end on a good note with Jessica.

Because it was an ending, no matter what Eric, the

valedictorian, had to say about commencement meaning "beginning" and all the rest of the trite nonsense. Maybe more for me than for the rest, but we were all leaving something behind us today.

It went so quickly. I felt like I'd hit the fast forward button. Were we supposed to march quite that fast? And then Eric was speed talking in his nervousness, the words and phrases running together so they didn't make sense anymore. Principal Greene started calling names, one after the other without a long enough pause between; the front row in the gymnasium was rushing to catch up. Poor Ms. Cope was all thumbs as she tried to give the principal the right diploma to hand to the right student.

I watched as Alice, suddenly appearing, danced across the stage to take hers, a look of deep concentration on her face. Edward followed behind, his expression confused, but not upset. Only the two of them could carry off the hideous yellow and still look the way they did. They stood out from the rest of the crowd, their beauty and grace otherworldly. I wondered how I'd ever fallen for their human farce. A couple of angels, standing there with wings intact, would be less conspicuous.

I heard Mr. Greene call my name and I rose from my chair, waiting for the line in front of me to move. I was conscious of cheering in the back of the gym, and I looked around to see Jacob pulling Charlie to his feet, both of them hooting in encouragement. I could just make out the top of Billy's head beside Jake's elbow. I managed to throw them an approximation of a smile.

Mr. Greene finished with the list of names, and then

continued to hand out diplomas with a sheepish grin as we filed past.

"Congratulations, Miss Stanley," he mumbled as Jess took hers.

"Congratulations, Miss Swan," he mumbled to me, pressing the diploma into my good hand.

"Thanks," I murmured.

And that was it.

I went to stand next to Jessica with the assembled graduates. Jess was all red around the eyes, and she kept blotting her face with the sleeve of her robe. It took me a second to understand that she was crying.

Mr. Greene said something I didn't hear, and everyone around me shouted and screamed. Yellow hats rained down. I pulled mine off, too late, and just let it fall to the ground.

"Oh, Bella!" Jess blubbered over the sudden roar of conversation. "I can't believe we're done."

"I can't believe it's all over," I mumbled.

She threw her arms around my neck. "You have to promise we won't lose touch."

I hugged her back, feeling a little awkward as I dodged her request. "I'm so glad I know you, Jessica. It was a good two years."

"It was," she sighed, and sniffed. Then she dropped her arms. "Lauren!" she squealed, waving over her head and pushing through the massed yellow gowns. Families were beginning to converge, pressing us tighter together.

I caught sight of Angela and Ben, but they were surrounded by their families. I would congratulate them later.

I craned my head, looking for Alice.

"Congratulations," Edward whispered in my ear, his arms winding around my waist. His voice was subdued; he'd been in no hurry for me to reach this particular milestone.

"Um, thanks."

"You don't look like you're over the nerves yet," he noted.

"Not quite yet."

"What's left to worry about? The party? It won't be that horrible."

"You're probably right."

"Who are you looking for?"

My searching wasn't quite as subtle as I'd thought. "Alice — where is she?"

"She ran out as soon as she had her diploma."

His voice took on a new tone. I looked up to see his confused expression as he stared toward the back door of the gym, and I made an impulse decision — the kind I really should think twice about, but rarely did.

"Worrying about Alice?" I asked.

"Er . . ." He didn't want to answer that.

"What was she thinking about, anyway? To keep you out, I mean."

His eyes flashed down to my face, and narrowed in suspicion. "She was translating the Battle Hymn of the Republic into Arabic, actually. When she finished that, she moved on to Korean sign language."

I laughed nervously. "I suppose that *would* keep her head busy enough."

"You know what she's hiding from me," he accused.

"Sure." I smiled a weak smile. "I'm the one who came up with it."

He waited, confused.

I looked around. Charlie would be on his way through the crowd now.

"Knowing Alice," I whispered in a rush, "she'll probably try to keep this from you until after the party. But since I'm all for the party being canceled — well, don't go berserk, regardless, okay? It's always better to know as much as possible. It has to help somehow."

"What are you talking about?"

I saw Charlie's head bob up over the other heads as he searched for me. He spotted me and waved.

"Just stay calm, okay?"

He nodded once, his mouth a grim line.

In hurried whispers I explained my reasoning to him. "I think you're wrong about things coming at us from all sides. I think it's mostly coming at us from one side . . . and I think it's coming at me, really. It's all connected, it has to be. It's just one person who's messing with Alice's visions. The stranger in my room was a test, to see if someone could get around her. It's got to be the same one who keeps changing his mind, and the newborns, and stealing my clothes — all of it goes together. My scent is for them."

His face had turned so white that I had a hard time finishing.

"But no one's coming for you, don't you see? This is good — Esme and Alice and Carlisle, no one wants to hurt them!"

His eyes were huge, wide with panic, dazed and horrified. He could see that I was right, just as Alice had.

I put my hand on his cheek. "Calm," I pleaded.

"Bella!" Charlie crowed, pushing his way past the close-packed families around us.

"Congratulations, baby!" He was still yelling, even though he was right at my ear now. He wrapped his arms around me, ever so slyly shuffling Edward off to the side as he did so.

"Thanks," I muttered, preoccupied by the expression on Edward's face. He still hadn't gained control. His hands were halfway extended toward me, like he was about to grab me and make a run for it. Only slightly more in control of myself than he was, running didn't seem like such a terrible idea to me.

"Jacob and Billy had to take off — did you see that they were here?" Charlie asked, taking a step back, but keeping his hands on my shoulders. He had his back to Edward — probably an effort to exclude him, but that was fine at the moment. Edward's mouth was hanging open, his eyes still wide with dread.

"Yeah," I assured my father, trying to pay enough attention. "Heard them, too."

"It was nice of them to show up," Charlie said.

"Mm-hmm."

Okay, so telling Edward had been a really bad idea. Alice was right to keep her thoughts clouded. I should have waited till we were alone somewhere, maybe with the rest of his family. And nothing breakable close by — like windows . . . cars . . . school buildings. His face brought back all my fear and then some. Though his expression was past the fear now — it was pure fury that was suddenly plain on his features.

"So where do you want to go out for dinner?" Charlie asked. "The sky's the limit."

"I can cook."

"Don't be silly. Do you want to go to the Lodge?" he asked with an eager smile.

I did not particularly enjoy Charlie's favorite restaurant, but, at this point, what was the difference? I wasn't going to be able to eat anyway.

"Sure, the Lodge, cool," I said.

Charlie smiled wider, and then sighed. He turned his head halfway toward Edward, without really looking at him.

"You coming, too, Edward?"

I stared at him, my eyes beseeching. Edward pulled his expression together just before Charlie turned to see why he hadn't gotten an answer.

"No, thank you," Edward said stiffly, his face hard and cold.

"Do you have plans with your parents?" Charlie asked, a frown in his voice. Edward was always more polite than Charlie deserved; the sudden hostility surprised him.

"Yes. If you'll excuse me. . . ." Edward turned abruptly and stalked away through the dwindling crowd. He moved just a little bit too fast, too upset to keep up his usually perfect charade.

"What did I say?" Charlie asked with a guilty expression.

"Don't worry about it, Dad," I reassured him. "I don't think it's you."

"Are you two fighting again?"

"Nobody's fighting. Mind your own business."

"You *are* my business."

I rolled my eyes. "Let's go eat."

The Lodge was crowded. The place was, in my opinion, overpriced and tacky, but it was the only thing close to a formal restaurant in town, so it was always popular for events. I stared morosely at a depressed-looking stuffed elk head while Charlie ate prime rib and talked over the back of the seat to Tyler Crowley's parents. It was noisy — everyone there had just come from graduation, and most were chatting across the aisles and over the booth-tops like Charlie.

I had my back to the front windows, and I resisted the urge to turn around and search for the eyes I could feel on me now. I knew I wouldn't be able to see anything. Just as I knew there was no chance that he would leave me unguarded, even for a second. Not after this.

Dinner dragged. Charlie, busy socializing, ate too slowly. I picked at my burger, stuffing pieces of it into my napkin when I was sure his attention was somewhere else. It all seemed to take a very long time, but when I looked at the clock — which I did more often than necessary — the hands hadn't moved much.

Finally Charlie got his change back and put a tip on the table. I stood up.

"In a hurry?" he asked me.

"I want to help Alice set things up," I claimed.

"Okay." He turned away from me to say goodnight to everyone. I went out to wait by the cruiser.

I leaned against the passenger door, waiting for Charlie

to drag himself away from the impromptu party. It was almost dark in the parking lot, the clouds so thick that there was no telling if the sun had set or not. The air felt heavy, like it was about to rain.

Something moved in the shadows.

My gasp turned into a sigh of relief as Edward appeared out of the gloom.

Without a word, he pulled me tightly against his chest. One cool hand found my chin, and pulled my face up so that he could press his hard lips to mine. I could feel the tension in his jaw.

"How are you?" I asked as soon as he let me breathe.

"Not so great," he murmured. "But I've got a handle on myself. I'm sorry that I lost it back there."

"My fault. I should have waited to tell you."

"No," he disagreed. "This is something I needed to know. I can't believe I didn't see it!"

"You've got a lot on your mind."

"And you don't?"

He suddenly kissed me again, not letting me answer. He pulled away after just a second. "Charlie's on his way."

"I'll have him drop me at your house."

"I'll follow you there."

"That's not really necessary," I tried to say, but he was already gone.

"Bella?" Charlie called from the doorway of the restaurant, squinting into the darkness.

"I'm out here."

Charlie sauntered out to the car, muttering about impatience.

"So, how do you feel?" he asked me as we drove north along the highway. "It's been a big day."

"I feel fine," I lied.

He laughed, seeing through me easily. "Worried about the party?" he guessed.

"Yeah," I lied again.

This time he didn't notice. "You were never one for the parties."

"Wonder where I got that from," I murmured.

Charlie chuckled. "Well, you look really nice. I wish I'd thought to get you something. Sorry."

"Don't be silly, Dad."

"It's not silly. I feel like I don't always do everything for you that I should."

"That's ridiculous. You do a fantastic job. World's best dad. And . . ." It wasn't easy to talk about feelings with Charlie, but I persevered after clearing my throat. "And I'm really glad I came to live with you, Dad. It was the best idea I ever had. So don't worry — you're just experiencing post-graduation pessimism."

He snorted. "Maybe. But I'm sure I slipped up in a few places. I mean, look at your hand!"

I stared down blankly at my hands. My left hand rested lightly on the dark brace I rarely thought about. My broken knuckle didn't hurt much anymore.

"I never thought I needed to teach you how to throw a punch. Guess I was wrong about that."

"I thought you were on Jacob's side?"

"No matter what side I'm on, if someone kisses you without your permission, you should be able to make your feelings clear without hurting yourself. You didn't keep your thumb inside your fist, did you?"

"No, Dad. That's kind of sweet in a weird way, but I don't think lessons would have helped. Jacob's head is *really* hard."

Charlie laughed. "Hit him in the gut next time."

"Next time?" I asked incredulously.

"Aw, don't be too hard on the kid. He's young."

"He's obnoxious."

"He's still your friend."

"I know." I sighed. "I don't really know what the right thing to do here is, Dad."

Charlie nodded slowly. "Yeah. The right thing isn't always real obvious. Sometimes the right thing for one person is the wrong thing for someone else. So . . . good luck figuring that out."

"Thanks," I muttered dryly.

Charlie laughed again, and then frowned. "If this party gets too wild . . . ," he began.

"Don't worry about it, Dad. Carlisle and Esme are going to be there. I'm sure you can come, too, if you want."

Charlie grimaced as he squinted through the windshield into the night. Charlie enjoyed a good party just about as much as I did.

"Where's the turnoff, again?" he asked. "They ought to clear out their drive — it's impossible to find in the dark."

"Just around the next bend, I think." I pursed my lips. "You know, you're right — it is impossible to find. Alice said she put a map in the invitation, but even so, maybe everyone will get lost." I cheered up slightly at the idea.

"Maybe," Charlie said as the road curved to the east. "Or maybe not."

The black velvet darkness was interrupted ahead, just where the Cullens' drive should be. Someone had wrapped the trees on either side in thousands of twinkle lights, impossible to miss.

"Alice," I said sourly.

"Wow," Charlie said as we turned onto the drive. The two trees at the entry weren't the only ones lit. Every twenty feet or so, another shining beacon guided us toward the big white house. All the way — all three miles of the way.

"She doesn't do things halfway, does she?" Charlie mumbled in awe.

"Sure you don't want to come in?"

"Extremely sure. Have fun, kid."

"Thanks so much, Dad."

He was laughing to himself as I got out and shut the door. I watched him drive away, still grinning. With a sigh, I marched up the stairs to endure my party.

17. ALLIANCE

"BELLA?"

Edward's soft voice came from behind me. I turned to see him spring lightly up the porch steps, his hair windblown from running. He pulled me into his arms at once, just like he had in the parking lot, and kissed me again.

This kiss frightened me. There was too much tension, too strong an edge to the way his lips crushed mine — like he was afraid we only had so much time left to us.

I couldn't let myself think about that. Not if I was going to have to act human for the next several hours. I pulled away from him.

"Let's get this stupid party over with," I mumbled, not meeting his eyes.

He put his hands on either side of my face, waiting until I looked up.

"I won't let anything happen to you."

I touched his lips with the fingers of my good hand. "I'm not worried about myself so much."

"Why am I not surprised by that?" he muttered to himself. He took a deep breath, and then he smiled slightly. "Ready to celebrate?" he asked.

I groaned.

He held the door for me, keeping his arm securely around my waist. I stood frozen there for a minute, then I slowly shook my head.

"Unbelievable."

Edward shrugged. "Alice will be Alice."

The interior of the Cullens' home had been transformed into a nightclub — the kind that didn't often exist in real life, only on TV.

"Edward!" Alice called from beside a gigantic speaker. "I need your advice." She gestured toward a towering stack of CDs. "Should we give them familiar and comforting? Or" — she gestured to a different pile — "educate their taste in music?"

"Keep it comforting," Edward recommended. "You can only lead the horse to water."

Alice nodded seriously, and started throwing the educational CDs into a box. I noticed that she had changed into a sequined tank top and red leather pants. Her bare skin reacted oddly to the pulsing red and purple lights.

"I think I'm underdressed."

"You're perfect," Edward disagreed.

"You'll do," Alice amended.

"Thanks." I sighed. "Do you really think people will come?" Anyone could hear the hope in my voice. Alice made a face at me.

"Everyone will come," Edward answered. "They're all dying to see the inside of the reclusive Cullens' mystery house."

"Fabulous," I moaned.

There wasn't anything I could do to help. I doubted that — even after I didn't need sleep and moved at a much faster speed — I would ever be able to get things done the way Alice did.

Edward refused to let me go for a second, dragging me along with him as he hunted up Jasper and then Carlisle to tell them of my epiphany. I listened with quiet horror as they discussed their attack on the army in Seattle. I could tell that Jasper was not pleased with the way the numbers stood, but they'd been unable to contact anyone besides Tanya's unwilling family. Jasper didn't try to hide his desperation the way Edward would have. It was easy to see that he didn't like gambling with stakes this high.

I couldn't stay behind, waiting and hoping for them to come home. I wouldn't. I would go mad.

The doorbell rang.

All at once, everything was surreally normal. A perfect smile, genuine and warm, replaced the stress on Carlisle's face. Alice turned the volume of the music up, and then danced to get the door.

It was a Suburban-load of my friends, either too nervous or too intimidated to arrive on their own. Jessica was the first one in the door, with Mike right behind her. Tyler, Conner, Austin, Lee, Samantha . . . even Lauren trailing in last, her critical eyes alight with curiosity. They all were curious, and then overwhelmed as they took in the huge room decked out like a chic rave. The room wasn't empty; all the Cullens had taken their places, ready to put on their usual perfect human charade. Tonight I felt like I was acting every bit as much as they were.

I went to greet Jess and Mike, hoping the edge in my voice sounded like the right kind of excitement. Before I could get to anyone else, the bell rang again. I let Angela and Ben in, leaving the door wide, because Eric and Katie were just reaching the steps.

I didn't get another chance to panic. I had to talk to everyone, concentrate on being upbeat, a hostess. Though the party had been billed as a joint event for Alice, Edward, and me, there was no denying that I was the most popular target for congratulations and thanks. Maybe because the Cullens looked just slightly wrong under Alice's party lights. Maybe because those lights left the room dim and mysterious. Not an atmosphere to make your average human feel relaxed when standing next to someone like Emmett. I saw Emmett grin at Mike over the food table, the red lights gleaming off his teeth, and watched Mike take an automatic step back.

Probably Alice had done this on purpose, to force me into the center of attention — a place she thought I should enjoy more. She was forever trying to make me be human the way she thought humans should be.

The party was a clear success, despite the instinctive edginess caused by the Cullens' presence — or maybe that simply added a thrill to the atmosphere. The music was infectious, the lights almost hypnotic. From the way the food disappeared, that must have been good, too. The room was soon crowded, though never claustrophobic. The entire senior class seemed to be there, along with most of the juniors. Bodies swayed to the beat that rumbled under the soles of their feet, the party constantly on the edge of breaking into a dance.

It wasn't as hard as I'd thought it would be. I followed Alice's lead, mingling and chatting for a minute with everyone. They seemed easy enough to please. I was sure this party was far cooler than anything the town of Forks had experienced before. Alice was almost purring — no one here would forget this night.

I'd circled the room once, and was back to Jessica. She babbled excitedly, and it was not necessary to pay strict attention, because the odds were she wouldn't need a response from me anytime soon. Edward was at my side — still refusing to let go of me. He kept one hand securely at my waist, pulling me closer now and then in response to thoughts I probably didn't want to hear.

So I was immediately suspicious when he dropped his arm and edged away from me.

"Stay here," he murmured in my ear. "I'll be right back."

He passed gracefully through the crowd without seeming to touch any of the close-packed bodies, gone too quickly for me to ask why he was leaving. I stared after him with narrowed eyes while Jessica shouted over the music eagerly, hanging on to my elbow, oblivious to my distraction.

I watched him as he reached the dark shadow beside the kitchen doorway, where the lights only shone inter-mittently. He was leaning over someone, but I couldn't see past all the heads between us.

I stretched up on my toes, craning my neck. Right then, a red light flashed across his back and glinted off the red sequins of Alice's shirt. The light only touched her face for half a second, but it was enough.

"Excuse me for a minute, Jess," I mumbled, pulling my arm away. I didn't pause for her reaction, even to see if I'd hurt her feelings with my abruptness.

I ducked my way through the bodies, getting shoved around a bit. A few people were dancing now. I hurried to the kitchen door.

Edward was gone, but Alice was still there in the dark, her face blank — the kind of expressionless look you see on the face of someone who has just witnessed a horrible accident. One of her hands gripped the door frame, like she needed the support.

"What, Alice, what? What did you see?" My hands were clutched in front of me — begging.

She didn't look at me, she was staring away. I followed her gaze and watched as she caught Edward's eye across the room. His face was empty as a stone. He turned and disappeared into the shadows under the stair.

The doorbell rang just then, hours after the last time,

and Alice looked up with a puzzled expression that quickly turned into one of disgust.

"Who invited the werewolf?" she griped at me.

I scowled. "Guilty."

I'd thought I'd rescinded that invitation — not that I'd ever dreamed Jacob would come *here,* regardless.

"Well, you go take care of it, then. I have to talk to Carlisle."

"No, Alice, wait!" I tried to reach for her arm, but she was gone and my hand clutched the empty air.

"Damn it!" I grumbled.

I knew this was it. Alice had seen what she'd been waiting for, and I honestly didn't feel I could stand the suspense long enough to answer the door. The doorbell peeled again, too long, someone holding down the button. I turned my back toward the door resolutely, and scanned the darkened room for Alice.

I couldn't see anything. I started pushing for the stairs.

"Hey, Bella!"

Jacob's deep voice caught a lull in the music, and I looked up in spite of myself at the sound of my name.

I made a face.

It wasn't just one werewolf, it was three. Jacob had let himself in, flanked on either side by Quil and Embry. The two of them looked terribly tense, their eyes flickering around the room like they'd just walked into a haunted crypt. Embry's trembling hand still held the door, his body half-turned to run for it.

Jacob was waving at me, calmer than the others,

though his nose was wrinkled in disgust. I waved back —
waved goodbye — and turned to look for Alice. I squeezed
through a space between Conner's and Lauren's backs.

He came out of nowhere, his hand on my shoulder
pulling me back toward the shadow by the kitchen. I
ducked under his grip, but he grabbed my good wrist and
yanked me from the crowd.

"Friendly reception," he noted.

I pulled my hand free and scowled at him. "What are
you *doing* here?"

"You invited me, remember?"

"In case my right hook was too subtle for you, let me
translate: that was me *un*inviting you."

"Don't be a poor sport. I brought you a graduation
present and everything."

I folded my arms across my chest. I didn't want to fight
with Jacob right now. I wanted to know what Alice had
seen and what Edward and Carlisle were saying about it. I
craned my head around Jacob, searching for them.

"Take it back to the store, Jake. I've got to do something. . . ."

He stepped into my line of sight, demanding my attention.

"I can't take it back. I didn't get it from the store — I
made it myself. Took a really long time, too."

I leaned around him again, but I couldn't see any of the
Cullens. Where had they gone? My eyes scanned the darkened room.

"Oh, c'mon, Bell. Don't pretend like I'm not here!"

"I'm not." I couldn't see them anywhere. "Look, Jake, I've got a lot on my mind right now."

He put his hand under my chin and pulled my face up. "Could I please have just a few seconds of your undivided attention, Miss Swan?"

I jerked away from his touch. "Keep your hands to yourself, Jacob," I hissed.

"Sorry!" he said at once, holding his hands up in surrender. "I really am sorry. About the other day, I mean, too. I shouldn't have kissed you like that. It was wrong. I guess . . . well, I guess I deluded myself into thinking you wanted me to."

"Deluded — what a perfect description!"

"Be nice. You could accept my apology, you know."

"Fine. Apology accepted. Now, if you'll just excuse me for a moment . . ."

"Okay," he mumbled, and his voice was so different from before that I stopped searching for Alice and scrutinized his face. He was staring at the floor, hiding his eyes. His lower lip jutted out just a little bit.

"I guess you'd rather be with your *real* friends," he said in the same defeated tone. "I get it."

I groaned. "Aw, Jake, you know that's not fair."

"Do I?"

"You *should.*" I leaned forward, peering up, trying to look into his eyes. He looked up then, over my head, avoiding my gaze.

"Jake?"

He refused to look at me.

"Hey, you said you made me something, right?" I asked. "Was that just talk? Where's my present?" My attempt to fake enthusiasm was pretty sad, but it worked. He rolled his eyes and then grimaced at me.

I kept up the lame pretense, holding my hand open in front of me. "I'm waiting."

"Right," he grumbled sarcastically. But he also reached into the back pocket of his jeans and pulled out a small bag of a loose-woven, multi-colored fabric. It was tied shut with leather drawstrings. He set it on my palm.

"Hey, that's pretty, Jake. Thanks!"

He sighed. "The present is *inside,* Bella."

"Oh."

I had some trouble with the strings. He sighed again and took it from me, sliding the ties open with one easy tug of the right cord. I held my hand out for it, but he turned the bag upside down and shook something silver into my hand. Metal links clinked quietly against each other.

"I didn't make the bracelet," he admitted. "Just the charm."

Fastened to one of the links of the silver bracelet was a tiny wooden carving. I held it between my fingers to look at it closer. It was amazing the amount of detail involved in the little figurine — the miniature wolf was utterly realistic. It was even carved out of some red-brown wood that matched the color of his skin.

"It's beautiful," I whispered. "You *made* this? How?"

He shrugged. "It's something Billy taught me. He's better at it than I am."

"That's hard to believe," I murmured, turning the tiny wolf around and around in my fingers.

"Do you really like it?"

"Yes! It's unbelievable, Jake."

He smiled, happily at first, but then the expression soured. "Well, I figured that maybe it would make you remember me once in a while. You know how it is, out of sight, out of mind."

I ignored the attitude. "Here, help me put it on."

I held out my left wrist, since the right was stuck in the brace. He fastened the catch easily, though it looked too delicate for his big fingers to manage.

"You'll wear it?" he asked.

"Of course I will."

He grinned at me — it was the happy smile that I loved to see him wear.

I returned it for a moment, but then my eyes shot reflexively around the room again, anxiously scanning the crowd for some sign of Edward or Alice.

"Why're you so distracted?" Jacob wondered.

"It's nothing," I lied, trying to concentrate. "Thanks for the present, really. I love it."

"Bella?" His brows pulled together, throwing his eyes deep into their shadow. "Something's going on, isn't it?"

"Jake, I . . . no, there's nothing."

"Don't lie to me, you suck at lying. You should tell me what's going on. We want to know these things," he said, slipping into the plural at the end.

He was probably right; the wolves would certainly be

interested in what was happening. Only I wasn't sure what that *was* yet. I wouldn't know for sure until I found Alice.

"Jacob, I will tell you. Just let *me* figure out what's happening, okay? I need to talk to Alice."

Understanding lit his expression. "The psychic saw something."

"Yes, just when you showed up."

"Is this about the bloodsucker in your room?" he murmured, pitching his voice below the thrum of the music.

"It's related," I admitted.

He processed that for a minute, leaning his head to one side while he read my face. "You know something you're not telling me . . . something *big*."

What was the point in lying again? He knew me too well. "Yes."

Jacob stared at me for one short moment, and then turned to catch his pack brothers' eyes where they stood in the entry, awkward and uncomfortable. When they took in his expression, they started moving, weaving their way agilely through the partiers, almost like they were dancing, too. In half a minute, they stood on either side of Jacob, towering over me.

"Now. Explain," Jacob demanded.

Embry and Quil looked back and forth between our faces, confused and wary.

"Jacob, I don't know everything." I kept searching the room, now for a rescue. They had me backed into a corner in every sense.

"What you *do* know, then."

They all folded their arms across their chests at exactly

the same moment. It was a little bit funny, but mostly menacing.

And then I caught sight of Alice descending the stairs, her white skin glowing in the purple light.

"Alice!" I squeaked in relief.

She looked right at me as soon as I called her name, despite the thudding bass that should have drowned my voice. I waved eagerly, and watched her face as she took in the three werewolves leaning over me. Her eyes narrowed.

But, before that reaction, her face was full of stress and fear. I bit my lip as she skipped to my side.

Jacob, Quil, and Embry all leaned away from her with uneasy expressions. She put her arm around my waist.

"I need to talk to you," she murmured into my ear.

"Er, Jake, I'll see you later . . . ," I mumbled as we eased around them.

Jacob threw his long arm out to block our way, bracing his hand against the wall. "Hey, not so fast."

Alice stared up at him, eyes wide and incredulous. "Excuse me?"

"Tell us what's going on," he demanded in a growl.

Jasper appeared quite literally out of nowhere. One second it was just Alice and me against the wall, Jacob blocking our exit, and then Jasper was standing on the other side of Jake's arm, his expression terrifying.

Jacob slowly pulled his arm back. It seemed like the best move, going with the assumption that he wanted to keep that arm.

"We have a right to know," Jacob muttered, still glaring at Alice.

Jasper stepped in between them, and the three were-wolves braced themselves.

"Hey, hey," I said, adding a slightly hysterical chuckle. "This is a party, remember?"

Nobody paid any attention to me. Jacob glared at Alice while Jasper glowered at Jacob. Alice's face was suddenly thoughtful.

"It's okay, Jasper. He actually has a point."

Jasper did not relax his position.

I was sure the suspense was going to make my head explode in about one second. "What did you see, Alice?"

She stared at Jacob for one second, and then turned to me, evidently having chosen to let them hear.

"The decision's been made."

"You're going to Seattle?"

"No."

I felt the color drain out of my face. My stomach lurched. "They're coming here," I choked out.

The Quileute boys watched silently, reading every unconscious play of emotion on our faces. They were rooted in place, and yet not completely still. All three pairs of hands were trembling.

"Yes."

"To Forks," I whispered.

"Yes."

"For?"

She nodded, understanding my question. "One carried your red shirt."

I tried to swallow.

Jasper's expression was disapproving. I could tell he

didn't like discussing this in front of the werewolves, but he had something he needed to say. "We can't let them come that far. There aren't enough of us to protect the town."

"I know," Alice said, her face suddenly desolate. "But it doesn't matter where we stop them. There still won't be enough of us, and some of them will come here to search."

"No!" I whispered.

The noise of the party overwhelmed the sound of my denial. All around us, my friends and neighbors and petty enemies ate and laughed and swayed to the music, oblivious to the fact that they were about to face horror, danger, maybe death. Because of me.

"Alice," I mouthed her name. "I have to go, I have to get away from here."

"That won't help. It's not like we're dealing with a tracker. They'll still come looking here first."

"Then I have to go to meet them!" If my voice hadn't been so hoarse and strained, it might have been a shriek. "If they find what they're looking for, maybe they'll go away and not hurt anyone else!"

"Bella!" Alice protested.

"Hold it," Jacob ordered in a low, forceful voice. "*What* is coming?"

Alice turned her icy gaze on him. "Our kind. Lots of them."

"Why?"

"For Bella. That's all we know."

"There are too many for you?" he asked.

Jasper bridled. "We have a few advantages, dog. It will be an even fight."

"No," Jacob said, and a strange, fierce half-smile spread across his face. "It won't be *even*."

"Excellent!" Alice hissed.

I stared, still frozen in horror, at Alice's new expression. Her face was alive with exultation, all the despair wiped clean from her perfect features.

She grinned at Jacob, and he grinned back.

"Everything just disappeared, of course," she told him in a smug voice. "That's inconvenient, but, all things considered, I'll take it."

"We'll have to coordinate," Jacob said. "It won't be easy for us. Still, this is our job more than yours."

"I wouldn't go that far, but we need the help. We aren't going to be picky."

"Wait, wait, wait, wait," I interrupted them.

Alice was on her toes, Jacob leaning down toward her, both of their faces lit up with excitement, both of their noses wrinkled against the smell. They looked at me impatiently.

"Coordinate?" I repeated through my teeth.

"You didn't honestly think you were going to keep us out of this?" Jacob asked.

"You *are* staying out of this!"

"Your psychic doesn't think so."

"Alice — tell them no!" I insisted. "They'll get killed!"

Jacob, Quil, and Embry all laughed out loud.

"Bella," Alice said, her voice soothing, placating, "separately we all could get killed. Together —"

"It'll be no problem," Jacob finished her sentence. Quil laughed again.

"How many?" Quil asked eagerly.

"No!" I shouted.

Alice didn't even look at me. "It changes — twenty-one today, but the numbers are going down."

"Why?" Jacob asked, curious.

"Long story," Alice said, suddenly looking around the room. "And this isn't the place for it."

"Later tonight?" Jacob pushed.

"Yes," Jasper answered him. "We were already planning a . . . strategic meeting. If you're going to fight with us, you'll need some instruction."

The wolves all made a disgruntled face at the last part.

"No!" I moaned.

"This will be odd," Jasper said thoughtfully. "I never considered working together. This has to be a first."

"No doubt about that," Jacob agreed. He was in a hurry now. "We've got to get back to Sam. What time?"

"What's too late for you?"

All three rolled their eyes. "What time?" Jacob repeated.

"Three o'clock?"

"Where?"

"About ten miles due north of the Hoh Forest ranger station. Come at it from the west and you'll be able to follow our scent in."

"We'll be there."

They turned to leave.

"Wait, Jake!" I called after him. "*Please!* Don't do this!"

He paused, turning back to grin at me, while Quil and Embry headed impatiently for the door. "Don't be ridiculous, Bells. You're giving me a much better gift than the one I gave you."

"No!" I shouted again. The sound of an electric guitar drowned my cry.

He didn't respond; he hurried to catch up with his friends, who were already gone. I watched helplessly as Jacob disappeared.

18. INSTRUCTION

"THAT HAD TO BE THE LONGEST PARTY IN THE HISTORY of the world," I complained on the way home.

Edward didn't seem to disagree. "It's over now," he said, rubbing my arm soothingly.

Because I was the only one who needed soothing. Edward was fine now — all the Cullens were fine.

They'd all reassured me; Alice reaching up to pat my head as I left, eyeing Jasper meaningfully until a flood of peace swirled around me, Esme kissing my forehead and promising me everything was all right, Emmett laughing boisterously and asking why I was the only one who was allowed to fight with werewolves. . . . Jacob's solution had them all relaxed, almost euphoric after the long weeks of stress. Doubt had been replaced with confidence. The party had ended on a note of true celebration.

Not for me.

Bad enough — horrible — that the Cullens would fight for me. It was already too much that I would have to allow that. It already felt like more than I could bear.

Not Jacob, too. Not his foolish, eager brothers — most of them even younger than I was. They were just oversized, over-muscled children, and they looked forward to this like it was picnic on the beach. I could not have them in danger, too. My nerves felt frayed and exposed. I didn't know how much longer I could restrain the urge to scream out loud.

I whispered now, to keep my voice under control. "You're taking me with you tonight."

"Bella, you're worn out."

"You think I could sleep?"

He frowned. "This is an experiment. I'm not sure if it will be possible for us all to . . . cooperate. I don't want you in the middle of that."

As if that didn't make me all the more anxious to go. "If you won't take me, then I'll call Jacob."

His eyes tightened. That was a low blow, and I knew it. But there was no way I was being left behind.

He didn't answer; we were at Charlie's house now. The front light was on.

"See you upstairs," I muttered.

I tiptoed in the front door. Charlie was asleep in the living room, overflowing the too-small sofa, and snoring so loudly I could have ripped a chainsaw to life and it wouldn't have wakened him.

I shook his shoulder vigorously.

"Dad! Charlie!"

He grumbled, eyes still closed.

"I'm home now — you're going to hurt your back sleeping like that. C'mon, time to move."

It took a few more shakes, and his eyes never did open all the way, but I managed to get him off the couch. I helped him up to his bed, where he collapsed on top of the covers, fully dressed, and started snoring again.

He wasn't going to be looking for me anytime soon.

Edward waited in my room while I washed my face and changed into jeans and a flannel shirt. He watched me unhappily from the rocking chair as I hung the outfit Alice had given me in my closet.

"Come here," I said, taking his hand and pulling him to my bed.

I pushed him down on the bed and then curled up against his chest. Maybe he was right and I *was* tired enough to sleep. I wasn't going to let him sneak off without me.

He tucked my quilt in around me, and then held me close.

"Please relax."

"Sure."

"This is going to work, Bella. I can feel it."

My teeth locked together.

He was still radiating relief. Nobody but me cared if Jacob and his friends got hurt. Not even Jacob and his friends. Especially not them.

He could tell I was about to lose it. "Listen to me, Bella. This is going to be *easy*. The newborns will be completely taken by surprise. They'll have no more idea that were-wolves even exist than you did. I've seen how they act in a group, the way Jasper remembers. I truly believe that the wolves' hunting techniques will work flawlessly against them. And with them divided and confused, there won't be enough for the rest of us to do. Someone may have to sit out," he teased.

"Piece of cake," I mumbled tonelessly against his chest.

"Shhh," he stroked my cheek. "You'll see. Don't worry now."

He started humming my lullaby, but, for once, it didn't calm me.

People — well, vampires and werewolves really, but still — people I loved were going to get hurt. Hurt because of me. Again. I wished my bad luck would focus a little more carefully. I felt like yelling up at the empty sky: *It's me you want — over here! Just me!*

I tried to think of a way that I could do exactly that — force my bad luck to focus on me. It wouldn't be easy. I would have to wait, bide my time. . . .

I did not fall asleep. The minutes passed quickly, to my surprise, and I was still alert and tense when Edward pulled us both up into a sitting position.

"Are you sure you don't want to stay and sleep?"

I gave him a sour look.

He sighed, and scooped me up in his arms before he jumped from my window.

He raced through the black, quiet forest with me on his back, and even in his run I could feel the elation. He ran the way he did when it was just us, just for enjoyment, just for the feel of the wind in his hair. It was the kind of thing that, during less anxious times, would have made me happy.

When we got to the big open field, his family was there, talking casually, relaxed. Emmett's booming laugh echoed through the wide space now and then. Edward set me down and we walked hand in hand toward them.

It took me a minute, because it was so dark with the moon hidden behind the clouds, but I realized that we were in the baseball clearing. It was the same place where, more than a year ago, that first lighthearted evening with the Cullens had been interrupted by James and his coven. It felt strange to be here again — as if this gathering wouldn't be complete until James and Laurent and Victoria joined us. But James and Laurent were never coming back. That pattern wouldn't be repeated. Maybe all the patterns were broken.

Yes, someone had broken out of their pattern. Was it possible that the Volturi were the flexible ones in this equation?

I doubted it.

Victoria had always seemed like a force of nature to me — like a hurricane moving toward the coast in a straight line — unavoidable, implacable, but predictable. Maybe it was wrong to limit her that way. She had to be capable of adaptation.

"You know what I think?" I asked Edward.

He laughed. "No."

I almost smiled.

"What do you think?"

"I think it's *all* connected. Not just the two, but all three."

"You've lost me."

"Three bad things have happened since you came back." I ticked them off on my fingers. "The newborns in Seattle. The stranger in my room. And — first of all — Victoria came to look for me."

His eyes narrowed as he thought about it. "Why do you think so?"

"Because I agree with Jasper — the Volturi love their rules. They would probably do a better job anyway." And I'd be dead if they wanted me dead, I added mentally. "Remember when you were tracking Victoria last year?"

"Yes." He frowned. "I wasn't very good at it."

"Alice said you were in Texas. Did you follow her there?"

His eyebrows pulled together. "Yes. Hmm . . ."

"See — she could have gotten the idea there. But she doesn't know what she's doing, so the newborns are all out of control."

He started shaking his head. "Only Aro knows exactly how Alice's visions work."

"Aro would know *best,* but wouldn't Tanya and Irina and the rest of your friends in Denali know *enough*? Laurent lived with them for so long. And if he was still friendly enough with Victoria to be doing favors for her, why wouldn't he also tell her everything he knew?"

Edward frowned. "It wasn't Victoria in your room."

"She can't make new friends? Think about it, Edward.

If it *is* Victoria doing this in Seattle, she's *made* a lot of new friends. She's created them."

He considered it, his forehead creased in concentration.

"Hmm," he finally said. "It's possible. I still think the Volturi are most likely . . . But your theory — there's something there. Victoria's personality. Your theory suits her personality perfectly. She's shown a remarkable gift for self-preservation from the start — maybe it's a talent of hers. In any case, this plot would put her in no danger at all from us, if she sits safely behind and lets the newborns wreak their havoc here. And maybe little danger from the Volturi, either. Perhaps she's counting on us to win, in the end, though certainly not without heavy casualties of our own. But no survivors from her little army to bear witness against her. In fact," he continued, thinking it through, "if there were survivors, I'd bet she'd be planning to destroy them herself. . . . Hmm. Still, she'd have to have at least one friend who was a bit more mature. No fresh-made newborn left your father alive. . . ."

He frowned into space for a long moment, and then suddenly smiled at me, coming back from his reverie. "Definitely possible. Regardless, we've got to be prepared for anything until we know for sure. You're very perceptive today," he added. "It's impressive."

I sighed. "Maybe I'm just reacting to this place. It makes me feel like she's close by . . . like she sees me now."

His jaw muscles tensed at the idea. "She'll never touch you, Bella," he said.

In spite of his words, his eyes swept carefully across the

dark trees. While he searched their shadows, the strangest expression crossed his face. His lips pulled back over his teeth and his eyes shone with an odd light — a wild, fierce kind of hope.

"Yet, what I wouldn't give to have her that close," he murmured. "Victoria, and anyone else who's ever thought of hurting you. To have the chance to end this myself. To finish it with my own hands this time."

I shuddered at the ferocious longing in his voice, and clenched his fingers more tightly with mine, wishing I was strong enough to lock our hands together permanently.

We were almost to his family, and I noticed for the first time that Alice did not look as optimistic as the others. She stood a little aside, watching Jasper stretching his arms as if he were warming up to exercise, her lips pushed out in a pout.

"Is something wrong with Alice?" I whispered.

Edward chuckled, himself again. "The werewolves are on their way, so she can't see anything that will happen now. It makes her uncomfortable to be blind."

Alice, though the farthest from us, heard his low voice. She looked up and stuck her tongue out at him. He laughed again.

"Hey, Edward," Emmett greeted him. "Hey, Bella. Is he going to let you practice, too?"

Edward groaned at his brother. "Please, Emmett, don't give her any ideas."

"When will our guests arrive?" Carlisle asked Edward.

Edward concentrated for a moment, and then sighed.

"A minute and a half. But I'm going to have to translate. They don't trust us enough to use their human forms."

Carlisle nodded. "This is hard for them. I'm grateful they're coming at all."

I stared at Edward, my eyes stretched wide. "They're coming as wolves?"

He nodded, cautious of my reaction. I swallowed once, remembering the two times I'd seen Jacob in his wolf form — the first time in the meadow with Laurent, the second time on the forest lane where Paul had gotten angry at me. . . . They were both memories of terror.

A strange gleam came into Edward's eyes, as though something had just occurred to him, something that was not altogether unpleasant. He turned away quickly, before I could see any more, back to Carlisle and the others.

"Prepare yourselves — they've been holding out on us."

"What do you mean?" Alice demanded.

"Shh," he cautioned, and stared past her into the darkness.

The Cullens' informal circle suddenly widened out into a loose line with Jasper and Emmett at the spear point. From the way Edward leaned forward next to me, I could tell that he wished he was standing beside them. I tightened my hand around his.

I squinted toward the forest, seeing nothing.

"*Damn,*" Emmett muttered under his breath. "Did you ever see anything like it?"

Esme and Rosalie exchanged a wide-eyed glance.

"What is it?" I whispered as quietly as I could. "I can't see."

"The pack has grown," Edward murmured into my ear.

Hadn't I told him that Quil had joined the pack? I strained to see the six wolves in the gloom. Finally, something glittered in the blackness — their eyes, higher up than they should be. I'd forgotten how very tall the wolves were. Like horses, only thick with muscle and fur — and teeth like knives, impossible to overlook.

I could only see the eyes. And as I scanned, straining to see more, it occurred to me that there were more than six pairs facing us. *One, two, three* . . . I counted the pairs swiftly in my head. Twice.

There were ten of them.

"Fascinating," Edward murmured almost silently.

Carlisle took a slow, deliberate step forward. It was a careful movement, designed to reassure.

"Welcome," he greeted the invisible wolves.

"Thank you," Edward responded in a strange, flat tone, and I realized at once that the words came from Sam. I looked to the eyes shining in the center of the line, the highest up, the tallest of them all. It was impossible to separate the shape of the big black wolf from the darkness.

Edward spoke again in the same detached voice, speaking Sam's words. "We will watch and listen, but no more. That is the most we can ask of our self-control."

"That is more than enough," Carlisle answered. "My son Jasper" — he gestured to where Jasper stood, tensed and ready — "has experience in this area. He will teach us how they fight, how they are to be defeated. I'm sure you can apply this to your own hunting style."

"They are different from you?" Edward asked for Sam.

Carlisle nodded. "They are all very new — only months old to this life. Children, in a way. They will have no skill or strategy, only brute strength. Tonight their numbers stand at twenty. Ten for us, ten for you — it shouldn't be difficult. The numbers may go down. The new ones fight amongst themselves."

A rumble passed down the shadowy line of wolves, a low growling mutter that somehow managed to sound enthusiastic.

"We are willing to take more than our share, if necessary," Edward translated, his tone less indifferent now.

Carlisle smiled. "We'll see how it plays out."

"Do you know when and how they'll arrive?"

"They'll come across the mountains in four days, in the late morning. As they approach, Alice will help us intercept their path."

"Thank you for the information. We will watch."

With a sighing sound, the eyes sank closer to the ground one set at a time.

It was silent for two heartbeats, and then Jasper took a step into the empty space between the vampires and the wolves. It wasn't hard for me to see him — his skin was as bright against the darkness as the wolves' eyes. Jasper threw a wary glance toward Edward, who nodded, and then Jasper turned his back to the werewolves. He sighed, clearly uncomfortable.

"Carlisle's right." Jasper spoke only to us; he seemed to be trying to ignore the audience behind him. "They'll fight like children. The two most important things you'll need to remember are, first, don't let them get their arms around you and, second, don't go for the obvious kill. That's all they'll be prepared for. As long as you come at them from the side and keep moving, they'll be too confused to respond effectively. Emmett?"

Emmett stepped out of the line with a huge smile.

Jasper backed toward the north end of the opening between the allied enemies. He waved Emmett forward.

"Okay, Emmett first. He's the best example of a newborn attack."

Emmett's eyes narrowed. "I'll *try* not to break anything," he muttered.

Jasper grinned. "What I meant is that Emmett relies on his strength. He's very straightforward about the attack. The newborns won't be trying anything subtle, either. Just go for the easy kill, Emmett."

Jasper backed up a few more paces, his body tensing.

"Okay, Emmett — try to catch me."

And I couldn't see Jasper anymore — he was a blur as Emmett charged him like a bear, grinning while he snarled. Emmett was impossibly quick, too, but not like Jasper. It looked like Jasper had no more substance than a ghost — any time it seemed Emmett's big hands had him for sure, Emmett's fingers clenched around nothing but the air. Beside me, Edward leaned forward intently, his eyes locked on the brawl. Then Emmett froze.

Jasper had him from behind, his teeth an inch from his throat.

Emmett cussed.

There was a muttered rumble of appreciation from the watching wolves.

"Again," Emmett insisted, his smile gone.

"It's my turn," Edward protested. My fingers tensed around his.

"In a minute." Jasper grinned, stepping back. "I want to show Bella something first."

I watched with anxious eyes as he waved Alice forward.

"I know you worry about her," he explained to me as she danced blithely into the ring. "I want to show you why that's not necessary."

Though I knew that Jasper would never allow any harm to come to Alice, it was still hard to watch as he sank back into a crouch facing her. Alice stood motionlessly, looking tiny as a doll after Emmett, smiling to herself. Jasper shifted forward, then slinked to her left.

Alice closed her eyes.

My heart thumped unevenly as Jasper stalked toward where Alice stood.

Jasper sprang, disappearing. Suddenly he was on the other side of Alice. She didn't appear to have moved.

Jasper wheeled and launched himself at her again, only to land in a crouch behind her like the first time; all the while Alice stood smiling with her eyes closed.

I watched Alice more carefully now.

She *was* moving — I'd just been missing it, distracted by Jasper's attacks. She took a small step forward at the exact second that Jasper's body flew through the spot where she'd just been standing. She took another step, while Jasper's grasping hands whistled past where her waist had been.

Jasper closed in, and Alice began to move faster. She

was dancing — spiraling and twisting and curling in on herself. Jasper was her partner, lunging, reaching through her graceful patterns, never touching her, like every movement was choreographed. Finally, Alice laughed.

Out of nowhere she was perched on Jasper's back, her lips at his neck.

"Gotcha," she said, and kissed his throat.

Jasper chuckled, shaking his head. "You truly are one frightening little monster."

The wolves muttered again. This time the sound was wary.

"It's good for them to learn some respect," Edward murmured, amused. Then he spoke louder. "My turn."

He squeezed my hand before he let it go.

Alice came to take his place beside me. "Cool, huh?" she asked me smugly.

"Very," I agreed, not looking away from Edward as he glided noiselessly toward Jasper, his movements lithe and watchful as a jungle cat.

"I've got my eye on you, Bella," she whispered suddenly, her voice pitched so low that I could barely hear, though her lips were at my ear.

My gaze flickered to her face and then back to Edward. He was intent on Jasper, both of them feinting as he closed the distance.

Alice's expression was full of reproach.

"I'll warn him if your plans get any more defined," she threatened in the same low murmur. "It doesn't help anything for you to put yourself in danger. Do you think either of them would give up if you died? They'd still fight, we all would. You can't change anything, so just be good, okay?"

I grimaced, trying to ignore her.

"I'm watching," she repeated.

Edward had closed on Jasper now, and this fight was more even than either of the others. Jasper had the century of experience to guide him, and he tried to go on instinct alone as much as he could, but his thoughts always gave him away a fraction of a second before he acted. Edward was slightly faster, but the moves Jasper used were unfamiliar to him. They came at each other again and again, neither one able to gain the advantage, instinctive snarls erupting constantly. It was hard to watch, but harder to look away. They moved too fast for me to really understand what they were doing. Now and then the sharp eyes of the wolves would catch my attention. I had a feeling the wolves were getting more out of this than I was — maybe more than they should.

Eventually, Carlisle cleared his throat.

Jasper laughed, and took a step back. Edward straightened up and grinned at him.

"Back to work," Jasper consented. "We'll call it a draw."

Everyone took turns, Carlisle, then Rosalie, Esme, and Emmett again. I squinted through my lashes, cringing as Jasper attacked Esme. That one was the hardest to watch. Then he slowed down, still not quite enough for me to understand his motions, and gave more instruction.

"You see what I'm doing here?" he would ask. "Yes,

just like that," he encouraged. "Concentrate on the sides. Don't forget where their target will be. Keep moving."

Edward was always focused, watching and also listening to what others couldn't see.

It got more difficult to follow as my eyes got heavier. I hadn't been sleeping well lately, anyway, and it was approaching a solid twenty-four hours since the last time I'd slept. I leaned against Edward's side, and let my eyelids droop.

"We're about finished," he whispered.

Jasper confirmed that, turning toward the wolves for the first time, his expression uncomfortable again. "We'll be doing this tomorrow. Please feel welcome to observe again."

"Yes," Edward answered in Sam's cool voice. "We'll be here."

Then Edward sighed, patted my arm, and stepped away from me. He turned to his family.

"The pack thinks it would be helpful to be familiar with each of our scents — so they don't make mistakes later. If we could hold very still, it will make it easier for them."

"Certainly," Carlisle said to Sam. "Whatever you need."

There was a gloomy, throaty grumble from the wolf pack as they all rose to their feet.

My eyes were wide again, exhaustion forgotten.

The deep black of the night was just beginning to fade — the sun brightening the clouds, though it hadn't cleared the horizon yet, far away on the other side of the mountains. As they approached, it was suddenly possible to make out shapes . . . colors.

Sam was in the lead, of course. Unbelievably huge, black as midnight, a monster straight out of my nightmares — literally; after the first time I'd seen Sam and the others in the meadow, they'd starred in my bad dreams more than once.

Now that I could see them all, match the vastness with each pair of eyes, it looked like more than ten. The pack was overwhelming.

Out of the corner of my eye, I saw that Edward was watching me, carefully evaluating my reaction.

Sam approached Carlisle where he stood in the front, the huge pack right on his tail. Jasper stiffened, but Emmett, on the other side of Carlisle, was grinning and relaxed.

Sam sniffed at Carlisle, seeming to wince slightly as he did. Then he moved on to Jasper.

My eyes ran down the wary brace of wolves. I was sure I could pick out a few of the new additions. There was a light gray wolf that was much smaller than the others, the hackles on the back of his neck raised in distaste. There was another, the color of desert sand, who seemed gangly and uncoordinated beside the rest. A low whine broke through the sandy wolf's control when Sam's advance left him isolated between Carlisle and Jasper.

I stopped at the wolf just behind Sam. His fur was reddish-brown and longer than the others, shaggy in comparison. He was almost as tall as Sam, the second largest in the group. His stance was casual, somehow exuding nonchalance over what the rest obviously considered an ordeal.

The enormous russet-colored wolf seemed to feel my gaze, and he looked up at me with familiar black eyes.

I stared back at him, trying to believe what I already knew. I could feel the wonder and fascination on my face.

The wolf's muzzle fell open, pulling back over his teeth. It would have been a frightening expression, except that his tongue lolled out the side in a wolfy grin.

I giggled.

Jacob's grin widened over his sharp teeth. He left his place in line, ignoring the eyes of his pack as they followed him. He trotted past Edward and Alice to stand not two feet away from me. He stopped there, his gaze flickering briefly toward Edward.

Edward stood motionless, a statue, his eyes still assessing my reaction.

Jacob crouched down on his front legs and dropped his head so that his face was no higher than mine, staring at me, measuring my response just as much as Edward was.

"Jacob?" I breathed.

The answering rumble deep in his chest sounded like a chuckle.

I reached my hand out, my fingers trembling slightly, and touched the red-brown fur on the side of his face.

The black eyes closed, and Jacob leaned his huge head into my hand. A thrumming hum resonated in this throat.

The fur was both soft and rough, and warm against my skin. I ran my fingers through it curiously, learning the texture, stroking his neck where the color deepened. I hadn't realized how close I'd gotten; without warning, Jacob suddenly licked my face from chin to hairline.

"Ew! Gross, Jake!" I complained, jumping back and smacking at him, just as I would have if he were human. He dodged out of the way, and the coughing bark that came through his teeth was obviously laughter.

I wiped my face on the sleeve of my shirt, unable to keep from laughing with him.

It was at that point that I realized that everyone was watching us, the Cullens and the werewolves — the Cullens with perplexed and somewhat disgusted expressions. It was hard to read the wolves' faces. I thought Sam looked unhappy.

And then there was Edward, on edge and clearly disappointed. I realized he'd been hoping for a different reaction from me. Like screaming and running away in terror.

Jacob made the laughing sound again.

The other wolves were backing away now, not taking their eyes off the Cullens as they departed. Jacob stood by my side, watching them go. Soon, they disappeared into the murky forest. Only two hesitated by the trees, watching Jacob, their postures radiating anxiety.

Edward sighed, and — ignoring Jacob — came to stand on my other side, taking my hand.

"Ready to go?" he asked me.

Before I could answer, he was staring over me at Jacob.

"I've not quite figured out all the details yet," he said, answering a question in Jacob's thoughts.

The Jacob-wolf grumbled sullenly.

"It's more complicated than that," Edward said. "Don't concern yourself; I'll make sure it's safe."

"What are you talking about?" I demanded.

"Just discussing strategy," Edward said.

Jacob's head swiveled back and forth, looking at our faces. Then, suddenly, he bolted for the forest. As he darted away, I noticed for the first time a square of folded black fabric secured to his back leg.

"Wait," I called, one hand stretching out automatically to reach after him. But he disappeared into the trees in seconds, the other two wolves following.

"Why did he leave?" I asked, hurt.

"He's coming back," Edward said. He sighed. "He wants to be able to talk for himself."

I watched the edge of the forest where Jacob had vanished, leaning into Edward's side again. I was on the point of collapse, but I was fighting it.

Jacob loped back into view, on two legs this time. His broad chest was bare, his hair tangled and shaggy. He wore only a pair of black sweat pants, his feet bare to the cold ground. He was alone now, but I suspected that his friends lingered in the trees, invisible.

It didn't take him long to cross the field, though he gave a wide berth to the Cullens, who stood talking quietly in a loose circle.

"Okay, bloodsucker," Jacob said when he was a few feet from us, evidently continuing the conversation I'd missed. "What's so complicated about it?"

"I have to consider every possibility," Edward said, unruffled. "What if someone gets by you?"

Jacob snorted at that idea. "Okay, so leave her on the reservation. We're making Collin and Brady stay behind anyway. She'll be safe there."

I scowled. "Are you talking about me?"

"I just want to know what he plans to do with you during the fight," Jacob explained.

"*Do* with me?"

"You can't stay in Forks, Bella." Edward's voice was pacifying. "They know where to look for you there. What if someone slipped by us?"

My stomach dropped and the blood drained from my face. "Charlie?" I gasped.

"He'll be with Billy," Jacob assured me quickly. "If my dad has to commit a murder to get him there, he'll do it. Probably it won't take that much. It's this Saturday, right? There's a game."

"This Saturday?" I asked, my head spinning. I was too lightheaded to control my wildly random thoughts. I frowned at Edward. "Well, crap! There goes your graduation present."

Edward laughed. "It's the thought that counts," he reminded me. "You can give the tickets to someone else."

Inspiration came swiftly. "Angela and Ben," I decided at once. "At least that will get them out of town."

He touched my cheek. "You can't evacuate everyone," he said in a gentle voice. "Hiding you is just a precaution. I told you — we'll have no problem now. There won't be enough of them to keep us entertained."

"But what about keeping her in La Push?" Jacob interjected, impatient.

"She's been back and forth too much," Edward said. "She's left trails all over the place. Alice only sees very young vampires coming on the hunt, but obviously someone created them. There is someone more experienced behind this. Whoever he" — Edward paused to look at me — "or she is, this *could* all be a distraction. Alice will see if he decides to look himself, but we could be very busy at the time that decision is made. Maybe someone is counting on that. I can't leave her somewhere she's been frequently. She *has* to be hard to find, just in case. It's a very long shot, but I'm not taking chances."

I stared at Edward as he explained, my forehead creasing. He patted my arm.

"Just being overcautious," he promised.

Jacob gestured to the deep forest east of us, to the vast expanse of the Olympic Mountains.

"So hide her here," he suggested. "There's a million possibilities — places either one of us could be in just a few minutes if there's a need."

Edward shook his head. "Her scent is too strong and, combined with mine, especially distinct. Even if I carried her, it would leave a trail. *Our* trace is all over the range, but in conjunction with Bella's scent, it would catch their attention. We're not sure exactly which path they'll take, because *they* don't know yet. If they crossed her scent before they found us . . ."

Both of them grimaced at the same time, their eyebrows pulling together.

"You see the difficulties."

"There has to be a way to make it work," Jacob muttered. He glared toward the forest, pursing his lips.

I swayed on my feet. Edward put his arm around my waist, pulling me closer and supporting my weight.

"I need to get you home — you're exhausted. And Charlie will be waking up soon. . . ."

"Wait a sec," Jacob said, wheeling back to us, his eyes bright. "My scent disgusts you, right?"

"Hmm, not bad." Edward was two steps ahead. "It's possible." He turned toward his family. "Jasper?" he called.

Jasper looked up curiously. He walked over with Alice a half step behind. Her face was frustrated again.

"Okay, Jacob." Edward nodded at him.

Jacob turned toward me with a strange mixture of emotion on his face. He was clearly excited by whatever this new plan of his was, but he was also still uneasy so close to his enemy allies. And then it was my turn to be wary as he held his arms out toward me.

Edward took a deep breath.

"We're going to see if I can confuse the scent enough to hide your trail," Jacob explained.

I stared at his open arms suspiciously.

"You're going to have to let him carry you, Bella," Edward told me. His voice was calm, but I could hear the subdued distaste.

I frowned.

Jacob rolled his eyes, impatient, and reached down to yank me up into his arms.

"Don't be such a baby," he muttered.

But his eyes flickered to Edward, just like mine did. Edward's face was composed and smooth. He spoke to Jasper.

"Bella's scent is so much more potent to me — I thought it would be a fairer test if someone else tried."

Jacob turned away from them and paced swiftly into the woods. I didn't say anything as the dark closed around us. I was pouting, uncomfortable in Jacob's arms. It felt too intimate to me — surely he didn't need to hold me *quite* so tightly — and I couldn't help but wonder what it felt like to him. It reminded me of my last afternoon in La Push, and I didn't want to think about that. I folded my arms, annoyed when the brace on my hand intensified the memory.

We didn't go far; he made a wide arc and came back into the clearing from a different direction, maybe half a football field away from our original departure point. Edward was there alone and Jacob headed toward him.

"You can put me down now."

"I don't want to take a chance of messing up the experiment." His walk slowed and his arms tightened.

"You are *so* annoying," I muttered.

"Thanks."

Out of nowhere, Jasper and Alice stood beside Edward. Jacob took one more step, and then set me down a half dozen feet from Edward. Without looking back at Jacob, I walked to Edward's side and took his hand.

"Well?" I asked.

"As long as you don't touch anything, Bella, I can't *imagine* someone sticking their nose close enough to that trail to catch your scent," Jasper said, grimacing. "It was almost completely obscured."

"A definite success," Alice agreed, wrinkling her nose.

"And it gave me an idea."

"Which will work," Alice added confidently.

"Clever," Edward agreed.

"How do you *stand* that?" Jacob muttered to me.

Edward ignored Jacob and looked at me while he explained. "We're — well, *you're* — going to leave a false trail to the clearing, Bella. The newborns are hunting, your scent will excite them, and they'll come exactly the way we want them to without being careful about it. Alice can already see that this will work. When they catch *our* scent, they'll split up and try to come at us from two sides. Half will go through the forest, where her vision suddenly disappears. . . ."

"Yes!" Jacob hissed.

Edward smiled at him, a smile of true comradeship.

I felt sick. How could they be so eager for this? How could I stand having *both* of them in danger? I couldn't.

I wouldn't.

"Not a chance," Edward said suddenly, his voice disgusted. It made me jump, worrying that he'd somehow heard my resolve, but his eyes were on Jasper.

"I know, I know," Jasper said quickly. "I didn't even consider it, not really."

Alice stepped on his foot.

"If Bella was actually there in the clearing," Jasper explained to her, "it would drive them insane. They wouldn't be able to concentrate on anything but her. It would make picking them off truly easy. . . ."

Edward's glare had Jasper backtracking.

"Of course it's too dangerous for her. It was just an errant thought," he said quickly. But he looked at me from the corner of his eyes, and the look was wistful.

"No," Edward said. His voice rang with finality.

"You're right," Jasper said. He took Alice's hand and started back to the others. "Best two out of three?" I heard him ask her as they went to practice again.

Jacob stared after him in disgust.

"Jasper looks at things from a military perspective," Edward quietly defended his brother. "He looks at all the options — it's thoroughness, not callousness."

Jacob snorted.

He'd edged closer unconsciously, drawn by his absorption in the planning. He stood only three feet from Edward now, and, standing there between them, I could feel the physical tension in the air. It was like static, an uncomfortable charge.

Edward got back to business. "I'll bring her here Friday afternoon to lay the false trail. You can meet us afterward, and carry her to a place I know. Completely out of the way, and easily defensible, not that it will come to that. I'll take another route there."

"And then what? Leave her with a cell phone?" Jacob asked critically.

"You have a better idea?"

Jacob was suddenly smug. "Actually, I do."

"Oh. . . . Again, dog, not bad at all."

Jacob turned to me quickly, as if determined to play the good guy by keeping me in the conversation. "We tried to talk Seth into staying behind with the younger two. He's still too young, but he's stubborn and he's resisting. So I thought of a new assignment for him — cell phone."

I tried to look like I got it. No one was fooled.

"As long as Seth Clearwater is in his wolf form, he'll be connected to the pack," Edward said. "Distance isn't a problem?" he added, turning to Jacob.

"Nope."

"Three hundred miles?" Edward asked. "That's impressive."

Jacob was the good guy again. "That's the farthest we've ever gone to experiment," he told me. "Still clear as a bell."

I nodded absently; I was reeling from the idea that little Seth Clearwater was already a werewolf, too, and that made it difficult to concentrate. I could see his bright smile, so much like a younger Jacob, in my head; he couldn't be more than fifteen, if he was that. His enthusiasm at the council meeting bonfire suddenly took on new meaning. . . .

"It's a good idea." Edward seemed reluctant to admit this. "I'll feel better with Seth there, even without the instantaneous communication. I don't know if I'd be able to leave Bella there alone. To think it's come to this, though! Trusting werewolves!"

"Fighting *with* vampires instead of against them!" Jacob mirrored Edward's tone of disgust.

"Well, you still get to fight against some of them," Edward said.

Jacob smiled. "That's the reason we're here."

19. SELFISH

EDWARD CARRIED ME HOME IN HIS ARMS, EXPECTING that I wouldn't be able to hang on. I must have fallen asleep on the way.

When I woke up, I was in my bed and the dull light coming through my windows slanted in from a strange angle. Almost like it was afternoon.

I yawned and stretched, my fingers searching for him and coming up empty.

"Edward?" I mumbled.

My seeking fingers encountered something cool and smooth. His hand.

"Are you really awake this time?" he murmured.

"Mmm," I sighed in assent. "Have there been a lot of false alarms?"

"You've been very restless — talking all day."

"All *day*?" I blinked and looked at the windows again.

"You had a long night," he said reassuringly. "You'd earned a day in bed."

I sat up, and my head spun. The light *was* coming in my window from the west. "Wow."

"Hungry?" he guessed. "Do you want breakfast in bed?"

"I'll get it," I groaned, stretching again. "I need to get up and move around."

He held my hand on the way to the kitchen, eyeing me carefully, like I might fall over. Or maybe he thought I was sleepwalking.

I kept it simple, throwing a couple of Pop-Tarts in the toaster. I caught a glimpse of myself in the reflective chrome.

"Ugh, I'm a mess."

"It was a long night," he said again. "You should have stayed here and slept."

"Right! And missed *everything*. You know, you need to start accepting the fact that I'm part of the family now."

He smiled. "I could probably get used to that idea."

I sat down with my breakfast, and he sat next to me. When I lifted the Pop-Tart to take the first bite, I noticed him staring at my hand. I looked down, and saw that I was still wearing the gift that Jacob had given me at the party.

"May I?" he asked, reaching for the tiny wooden wolf.

I swallowed noisily. "Um, sure."

He moved his hand under the charm bracelet and balanced the little figurine in his snowy palm. For a fleeting moment, I was afraid. Just the slightest twist of his fingers could crush it into splinters.

But of course Edward wouldn't do that. I was embarrassed I'd even had the thought. He only weighed the wolf in his palm for a moment, and then let it fall. It swung lightly from my wrist.

I tried to read the expression in his eyes. All I could see was thoughtfulness; he kept everything else hidden, if there *was* anything else.

"Jacob Black can give you presents."

It wasn't a question, or an accusation. Just a statement of fact. But I knew he was referring to my last birthday and the fit I'd thrown over gifts; I hadn't wanted any. Especially not from Edward. It wasn't entirely logical, and, of course, everyone had ignored me anyway. . . .

"You've given me presents," I reminded him. "You know I like the homemade kind."

He pursed his lips for a second. "How about hand-me-downs? Are those acceptable?"

"What do you mean?"

"This bracelet." His finger traced a circle around my wrist. "You'll be wearing this a lot?"

I shrugged.

"Because you wouldn't want to hurt his feelings," he suggested shrewdly.

"Sure, I guess so."

"Don't you think it's fair, then," he asked, looking down at my hand as he spoke. He turned it palm up, and ran his finger along the veins in my wrist. "If I have a little representation?"

"Representation?"

"A charm — something to keep *me* on your mind."

"You're in every thought I have. I don't need reminders."

"If I gave you something, would you wear it?" he pressed.

"A hand-me-down?" I checked.

"Yes, something I've had for a while." He smiled his angel's smile.

If this was the only reaction to Jacob's gift, I would take it gladly. "Whatever makes you happy."

"Have you noticed the inequality?" he asked, and his voice turned accusing. "Because I certainly have."

"What inequality?"

His eyes narrowed. "Everyone else is able to get away with giving you things. Everyone but me. I would have loved to get you a graduation present, but I didn't. I knew it would have upset you more than if anyone else did. That's utterly unfair. How do you explain yourself?"

"Easy." I shrugged. "You're more important than everyone else. And you've given me *you*. That's already more than I deserve, and anything else you give me just throws us more out of balance."

He processed that for a moment, and then rolled his eyes. "The way you regard me is ludicrous."

I chewed my breakfast calmly. I knew he wouldn't listen if I told him that he had that backward.

Edward's phone buzzed.

He looked at the number before he opened it. "What is it, Alice?"

He listened, and I waited for his reaction, suddenly nervous. But whatever she said didn't surprise him. He sighed a few times.

"I sort of guessed as much," he told her, staring into my eyes, a disapproving arch to his brow. "She was talking in her sleep."

I flushed. What had I said now?

"I'll take care of it," he promised.

He glared at me as he shut his phone. "Is there something you'd like to talk to me about?"

I deliberated for a moment. Given Alice's warning last night, I could guess why she'd called. And then remembering the troubled dreams I'd had as I'd slept through the day — dreams where I chased after Jasper, trying to follow him and find the clearing in the maze-like woods, knowing I would find Edward there . . . Edward, and the monsters who wanted to kill me, but not caring about them because I'd already made my decision — I could also guess what Edward had overheard while I'd slept.

I pursed my lips for a moment, not quite able to meet his gaze. He waited.

"I like Jasper's idea," I finally said.

He groaned.

"I want to help. I have to do *something,*" I insisted.

"It wouldn't help to have you in danger."

"Jasper thinks it would. This is *his* area of expertise."

Edward glowered at me.

"You can't keep me away," I threatened. "I'm not going to hide out in the forest while you all take risks for me."

Suddenly, he was fighting a smile. "Alice doesn't see you *in* the clearing, Bella. She sees you stumbling around lost in the woods. You won't be able to find us; you'll just make it more time consuming for me to find you afterward."

I tried to keep as cool as he was. "That's because Alice didn't factor in Seth Clearwater," I said politely. "If she had, of course, she wouldn't have been able to see anything at all. But it sounds like Seth wants to be there as much as I do. It shouldn't be too hard to persuade him to show me the way."

Anger flickered across his face, and then he took a deep breath and composed himself. "That might have worked . . . if you hadn't told me. Now I'll just ask Sam to give Seth certain orders. Much as he might want to, Seth won't be able to ignore that kind of injunction."

I kept my smile pleasant. "But why would Sam give those orders? If I tell him how it would help for me to be there? I'll bet Sam would rather do me a favor than you."

He had to compose himself again. "Maybe you're right. But I'm sure Jacob would be only too eager to give those same orders."

I frowned. "Jacob?"

"Jacob is second in command. Did he never tell you that? His orders have to be followed, too."

He had me, and by his smile, he knew it. My forehead crumpled. Jacob would be on his side — in this one instance — I was sure. And Jacob never *had* told me that.

Edward took advantage of the fact that I was momentarily stumped, continuing in a suspiciously smooth and soothing voice.

"I got a fascinating look into the pack's mind last night. It was better than a soap opera. I had no idea how complex the dynamic is with such a large pack. The pull of the individual against the plural psyche . . . Absolutely fascinating."

He was obviously trying to distract me. I glared at him.

"Jacob's been keeping a lot of secrets," he said with a grin.

I didn't answer, I just kept glaring, holding on to my argument and waiting for an opening.

"For instance, did you note the smaller gray wolf there last night?"

I nodded one stiff nod.

He chuckled. "They take all of their legends so seriously. It turns out there are things that none of their stories prepared them for."

I sighed. "Okay, I'll bite. What are you talking about?"

"They always accepted without question that it was only the direct grandsons of the original wolf who had the power to transform."

"So someone changed who wasn't a direct descendant?"

"No. She's a direct descendant, all right."

I blinked, and my eyes widened. *"She?"*

He nodded. "She knows you. Her name is Leah Clearwater."

"Leah's a werewolf!" I shrieked. "What? For how long? Why didn't Jacob tell me?"

"There are things he wasn't allowed to share — their numbers, for instance. Like I said before, when Sam gives an order, the pack simply isn't able to ignore it. Jacob was very careful to think of other things when he was near me. Of course, after last night that's all out the window."

"I can't believe it. Leah Clearwater!" Suddenly, I remembered Jacob speaking of Leah and Sam, and the way he acted as if he'd said too much — after he'd said something about Sam having to look in Leah's eyes *every day* and know that he'd broken all his promises. . . . Leah on the cliff, a tear glistening on her cheek when Old Quil had spoken of the burden and sacrifice the Quileute *sons* shared. . . . And Billy, spending time with Sue because she was having trouble with her kids . . . and here the trouble actually was that both of them were werewolves now!

I hadn't given much thought to Leah Clearwater, just to grieve for her loss when Harry had passed away, and then to pity her again when Jacob had told her story, about how the strange imprinting between Sam and her cousin Emily had broken Leah's heart.

And now she was part of Sam's pack, hearing his thoughts . . . and unable to hide her own.

I really hate that part, Jacob had said. *Everything you're ashamed of, laid out for everyone to see.*

"Poor Leah," I whispered.

Edward snorted. "She's making life exceedingly unpleasant for the rest of them. I'm not sure she deserves your sympathy."

"What do you mean?"

"It's hard enough for them, having to share all their

thoughts. Most of them try to cooperate, make it easier. When even one member is deliberately malicious, it's painful for everyone."

"She has reason enough," I mumbled, still on her side.

"Oh, I know," he said. "The imprinting compulsion is one of the strangest things I've ever witnessed in my life, and I've seen some strange things." He shook his head wonderingly. "The way Sam is tied to his Emily is impossible to describe — or I should say *her Sam*. Sam really had no choice. It reminds me of *A Midsummer Night's Dream* with all the chaos caused by the fairies' love spells . . . like magic." He smiled. "It's very nearly as strong as the way I feel about you."

"Poor Leah," I said again. "But what do you mean, malicious?"

"She's constantly bringing up things they'd rather not think of," he explained. "For example, Embry."

"What's with Embry?" I asked, surprised.

"His mother moved down from the Makah reservation seventeen years ago, when she was pregnant with him. She's not Quileute. Everyone assumed she'd left his father behind with the Makahs. But then he joined the pack."

"So?"

"So the prime candidates for his father are Quil Ateara Sr., Joshua Uley, or Billy Black, all of them married at that point, of course."

"No!" I gasped. Edward was right — this was exactly like a soap opera.

"Now Sam, Jacob, and Quil all wonder which of them has a half-brother. They'd all like to think it's Sam, since his father was never much of a father. But the doubt is always there. Jacob's never been able to ask Billy about that."

"Wow. How did you get so much in one night?"

"The pack mind is mesmerizing. All thinking together and then separately at the same time. There's so much to read!"

He sounded faintly regretful, like someone who'd had to put down a good book just before the climax. I laughed.

"The pack is fascinating," I agreed. "Almost as fascinating as you are when you're trying to distract me."

His expression became polite again — a perfect poker face.

"I have to be in that clearing, Edward."

"No," he said in a very final tone.

A certain path occurred to me at that moment.

It wasn't so much that I had to be in the clearing. I just had to be where Edward was.

Cruel, I accused myself. *Selfish, selfish, selfish! Don't do it!*

I ignored my better instincts. I couldn't look at him while I spoke, though. The guilt had my eyes glued to the table.

"Okay, look, Edward," I whispered. "Here's the thing . . . I've already gone crazy once. I know what my limits are. *And I can't stand it if you leave me again.*"

I didn't look up to see his reaction, afraid to know how much pain I was inflicting. I did hear his sudden intake of breath and the silence that followed. I stared at the dark wooden tabletop, wishing I could take the words back. But knowing I probably wouldn't. Not if it worked.

Suddenly, his arms were around me, his hands stroking

my face, my arms. *He* was comforting *me*. The guilt went into spiral mode. But the survival instinct was stronger. There was no question that he was fundamental to my survival.

"You know it's not like that, Bella," he murmured. "I won't be far, and it will be over quickly."

"I can't stand it," I insisted, still staring down. "Not knowing whether or not you'll come back. How do I live through that, no matter how quickly it's over?"

He sighed. "It's going to be easy, Bella. There's no reason for your fears."

"None at all?"

"None."

"And everybody will be fine?"

"Everyone," he promised.

"So there's no way at all that I need to be in the clearing?"

"Of course not. Alice just told me that they're down to nineteen. We'll be able to handle it easily."

"That's right — you said it was so easy that someone could sit out," I repeated his words from last night. "Did you really mean that?"

"Yes."

It felt too simple — he had to see it coming.

"So easy that *you* could sit out?"

After a long moment of silence, I finally looked up at his expression.

The poker face was back.

I took a deep breath. "So it's one way or the other. Either there is more danger than you want me to know about, in which case it would be right for me to be there, to do what I can to help. Or . . . it's going to be so easy that they'll get by without you. Which way is it?"

He didn't speak.

I knew what he was thinking of — the same thing I was thinking of. Carlisle. Esme. Emmett. Rosalie. Jasper. And . . . I forced myself to think the last name. And Alice.

I wondered if I was a monster. Not the kind that he thought he was, but the real kind. The kind that hurt people. The kind that had no limits when it came to what they wanted.

What I wanted was to keep him safe, safe with me. Did I have a limit to what I would do, what I would sacrifice for that? I wasn't sure.

"You ask me to let them fight without my help?" he said in a quiet voice.

"Yes." I was surprised I could keep my voice even, I felt so wretched inside. "Or to let me be there. Either way, so long as we're together."

He took a deep breath, and then exhaled slowly. He moved his hands to place them on either side of my face, forcing me to meet his gaze. He looked into my eyes for a long time. I wondered what he was looking for, and what it was that he found. Was the guilt as thick on my face as it was in my stomach — sickening me?

His eyes tightened against some emotion I couldn't read, and he dropped one hand to pull out his phone again.

"Alice," he sighed. "Could you come babysit Bella for a bit?" He raised one eyebrow, daring me to object to the word. "I need to speak with Jasper."

She evidently agreed. He put the phone away and went back to staring at my face.

"What are you going to say to Jasper?" I whispered.

"I'm going to discuss . . . me sitting out."

It was easy to read in his face how difficult the words were for him.

"I'm sorry."

I *was* sorry. I hated to make him do this. Not enough that I could fake a smile and tell him to go on ahead without me. Definitely not that much.

"Don't apologize," he said, smiling just a little. "Never be afraid to tell me how you feel, Bella. If this is what you need . . ." He shrugged. "You are my first priority."

"I didn't mean it that way — like you have to choose me over your family."

"I know that. Besides, that's not what you asked. You gave me two alternatives that you could live with, and I chose the one that *I* could live with. That's how compromise is supposed to work."

I leaned forward and rested my forehead against his chest. "Thank you," I whispered.

"Anytime," he answered, kissing my hair. "Anything."

We didn't move for a long moment. I kept my face hidden, pressed against his shirt. Two voices struggled inside me. One that wanted to be good and brave, and one that told the good one to keep her mouth shut.

"Who's the third wife?" he asked me suddenly.

"Huh?" I said, stalling. I didn't remember having had that dream again.

"You were mumbling something about 'the third wife' last night. The rest made a little sense, but you lost me there."

"Oh. Um, yeah. That was just one of the stories that I heard at the bonfire the other night." I shrugged. "I guess it stuck with me."

Edward leaned away from me and cocked his head to the side, probably confused by the uncomfortable edge to my voice.

Before he could ask, Alice appeared in the kitchen doorway with a sour expression.

"You're going to miss all the fun," she grumbled.

"Hello, Alice," he greeted her. He put one finger under my chin and tilted my face up to kiss me goodbye.

"I'll be back later tonight," he promised me. "I'll go work this out with the others, rearrange things."

"Okay."

"There's not much to arrange," Alice said. "I already told them. Emmett is pleased."

Edward sighed. "Of course he is."

He walked out the door, leaving me to face Alice.

She glared at me.

"I'm sorry," I apologized again. "Do you think this will make it more dangerous for you?"

She snorted. "You worry too much, Bella. You're going to go prematurely gray."

"Why are you upset, then?"

"Edward is such a grouch when he doesn't get his way. I'm just anticipating living with him for the next few months." She made a face. "I suppose, if it keeps you sane, it's worth it. But I wish you could control the pessimism, Bella. It's so unnecessary."

"Would you let Jasper go without you?" I demanded.

Alice grimaced. "That's different."

"Sure it is."

"Go clean yourself up," she ordered me. "Charlie will be home in fifteen minutes, and if you look this ragged he's not going to want to let you out again."

Wow, I'd really lost the whole day. It felt like such a waste. I was glad I wouldn't always have to squander my time with sleeping.

I was entirely presentable when Charlie got home — fully dressed, hair decent, and in the kitchen putting his dinner on the table. Alice sat in Edward's usual place, and this seemed to make Charlie's day.

"Howdy, Alice! How are you, hon?"

"I'm fine, Charlie, thanks."

"I see you finally made it out of bed, sleepyhead," he said to me as I sat beside him, before turning back to Alice. "Everyone's talking about that party your parents threw last night. I'll bet you've got one heck of a clean-up job ahead of you."

Alice shrugged. Knowing her, it was already done.

"It was worth it," she said. "It was a great party."

"Where's Edward?" Charlie asked, a little grudgingly. "Is he helping clean up?"

Alice sighed and her face turned tragic. It was probably an act, but it was too perfect for me to be positive. "No. He's off planning the weekend with Emmett and Carlisle."

"Hiking again?"

Alice nodded, her face suddenly forlorn. "Yes. They're *all* going, except me. We always go backpacking at the end of the school year, sort of a celebration, but this year I decided I'd rather shop than hike, and not one of them will stay behind with me. I'm abandoned."

Her face puckered, the expression so devastated that Charlie leaned toward her automatically, one hand reaching out, looking for some way to help. I glared at her suspiciously. What was she doing?

"Alice, honey, why don't you come stay with us," Charlie offered. "I hate to think of you all alone in that big house."

She sighed. Something squashed my foot under the table.

"Ow!" I protested.

Charlie turned to me. "What?"

Alice shot me a frustrated look. I could tell she thought that I was very slow tonight.

"Stubbed my toe," I muttered.

"Oh." He looked back at Alice. "So, how 'bout it?"

She stepped on my foot again, not quite so hard this time.

"Er, Dad, you know, we don't really have the best accommodations here. I bet Alice doesn't want to sleep on my floor. . . ."

Charlie pursed his lips. Alice pulled out the devastated expression again.

"Maybe Bella should stay up there with you," he suggested. "Just until your folks get back."

"Oh, would you, Bella?" Alice smiled at me radiantly. "You don't mind shopping with me, right?"

"Sure," I agreed. "Shopping. Okay."

"When are they leaving?" Charlie asked.

Alice made another face. "Tomorrow."

"When do you want me?" I asked.

"After dinner, I guess," she said, and then put one finger to her chin, thoughtful. "You don't have anything going on Saturday, do you? I want to get out of town to shop, and it will be an all-day thing."

"Not Seattle," Charlie interjected, his eyebrows pulling together.

"Of course not," Alice agreed at once, though we both knew Seattle would be plenty safe on Saturday. "I was thinking Olympia, maybe. . . ."

"You'll like that, Bella." Charlie was cheerful with relief. "Go get your fill of the city."

"Yeah, Dad. It'll be great."

With one easy conversation, Alice had cleared my schedule for the battle.

Edward returned not much later. He accepted Charlie's wishes for a nice trip without surprise. He claimed they were leaving early in the morning, and said goodnight before the usual time. Alice left with him.

I excused myself soon after they left.

"You can't be tired," Charlie protested.

"A little," I lied.

"No wonder you like to skip the parties," he muttered. "It takes you so long to recover."

Upstairs, Edward was lying across my bed.

"What time are we meeting with the wolves?" I murmured as I went to join him.

"In an hour."

"That's good. Jake and his friends need to get some sleep."

"They don't need as much as you do," he pointed out.

I moved to another topic, assuming he was about to try to talk me into staying home. "Did Alice tell you that she's kidnapping me again?"

He grinned. "Actually, she's not."

I stared at him, confused, and he laughed quietly at my expression.

"I'm the only one who has permission to hold you hostage, remember?" he said. "Alice is going hunting with the rest of them." He sighed. "I guess I don't need to do that now."

"*You're* kidnapping me?"

He nodded.

I thought about that briefly. No Charlie listening downstairs, checking on me every so often. And no houseful of wide-awake vampires with their intrusively sensitive hearing. . . . Just him and me — really alone.

"Is that all right?" he asked, concerned by my silence.

"Well . . . sure, except for one thing."

"What thing?" His eyes were anxious. It was mind-boggling, but, somehow, he still seemed unsure of his hold on me. Maybe I needed to make myself more clear.

"Why didn't Alice tell Charlie you were leaving *tonight*?" I asked.

He laughed, relieved.

I enjoyed the trip to the clearing more than I had last night. I still felt guilty, still afraid, but I wasn't terrified anymore. I could function. I could see past what was coming, and almost believe that maybe it *would* be okay. Edward was apparently fine with the idea of missing the fight . . . and that made it very hard not to believe him when he said this would be easy. He wouldn't leave his family if he didn't believe it himself. Maybe Alice was right, and I did worry too much.

We got to the clearing last.

Jasper and Emmett were already wrestling — just warming up from the sounds of their laughter. Alice and Rosalie lounged on the hard ground, watching. Esme and Carlisle were talking a few yards away, heads close together, fingers linked, not paying attention.

It was much brighter tonight, the moon shining through the thin clouds, and I could easily see the three wolves that sat around the edge of the practice ring, spaced far apart to watch from different angles.

It was also easy to recognize Jacob; I would have known him at once, even if he hadn't looked up and stared at the sound of our approach.

"Where are the rest of the wolves?" I wondered.

"They don't all need to be here. One would do the job, but Sam didn't trust us enough to just send Jacob, though Jacob was willing. Quil and Embry are his usual . . . I guess you could call them his wingmen."

"Jacob trusts you."

Edward nodded. "He trusts us not to try to kill him. That's about it, though."

"Are you participating tonight?" I asked, hesitant. I knew this was going to be almost as hard for him as being left behind would have been for me. Maybe harder.

"I'll help Jasper when he needs it. He wants to try some unequal groupings, teach them how to deal with multiple attackers."

He shrugged.

And a fresh wave of panic shattered my brief sense of confidence.

They were still outnumbered. I was making that worse.

I stared at the field, trying to hide my reaction.

It was the wrong place to look, struggling as I was to lie to myself, to convince myself that everything would work out as I needed it to. Because when I forced my eyes away from the Cullens — away from the image of their play fighting that would be real and deadly in just a few days — Jacob caught my eyes and smiled.

It was the same wolfy grin as before, his eyes scrunching the way they did when he was human.

It was hard to believe that, not so long ago, I'd found the werewolves frightening — lost sleep to nightmares about them.

I knew, without asking, which of the others was Embry and which was Quil. Because Embry was clearly the thinner gray wolf with the dark spots on his back, who sat so patiently watching, while Quil — deep chocolate brown, lighter over his face — twitched constantly, looking like he was dying to join in the mock fight. They weren't monsters, even like this. They were friends.

Friends who didn't look nearly as indestructible as

Emmett and Jasper did, moving faster than cobra strikes while the moonlight glinted off their granite-hard skin. Friends who didn't seem to understand the danger involved here. Friends who were still somewhat mortal, friends who could bleed, friends who could die. . . .

Edward's confidence was reassuring, because it was plain that he wasn't truly worried about his family. But would it hurt him if something happened to the wolves? Was there any reason for him to be anxious, if that possibility didn't bother him? Edward's confidence only applied to one set of my fears.

I tried to smile back at Jacob, swallowing against the lump in my throat. I didn't seem to get it right.

Jacob sprang lightly to his feet, his agility at odds with his sheer mass, and trotted over to where Edward and I stood on the fringe of things.

"Jacob," Edward greeted him politely.

Jacob ignored him, his dark eyes on me. He put his head down to my level, as he had yesterday, cocking it to one side. A low whimper escaped his muzzle.

"I'm fine," I answered, not needing the translation that Edward was about to give. "Just worried, you know."

Jacob continued to stare at me.

"He wants to know why," Edward murmured.

Jacob growled — not a threatening sound, an annoyed sound — and Edward's lips twitched.

"What?" I asked.

"He thinks my translations leave something to be desired. What he actually thought was, 'That's really stupid.

What is there to be worried about?' I edited, because I thought it was rude."

I halfway smiled, too anxious to really feel amused. "There's plenty to be worried about," I told Jacob. "Like a bunch of really stupid wolves getting themselves hurt."

Jacob laughed his coughing bark.

Edward sighed. "Jasper wants help. You'll be okay without a translator?"

"I'll manage."

Edward looked at me wistfully for one minute, his expression hard to understand, then turned his back and strode over to where Jasper waited.

I sat down where I was. The ground was cold and uncomfortable.

Jacob took a step forward, then looked back at me, and a low whine rose in his throat. He took another half-step.

"Go on without me," I told him. "I don't want to watch."

Jacob leaned his head to the side again for a moment, and then folded himself on to the ground beside me with a rumbling sigh.

"Really, you can go ahead," I assured him. He didn't respond, he just put his head down on his paws.

I stared up at the bright silver clouds, not wanting to see the fight. My imagination had more than enough fuel. A breeze blew through the clearing, and I shivered.

Jacob scooted himself closer to me, pressing his warm fur against my left side.

"Er, thanks," I muttered.

After a few minutes, I leaned against his wide shoulder. It was much more comfortable that way.

The clouds moved slowly across the sky, dimming and brightening as thick patches crossed the moon and passed on.

Absently, I began pulling my fingers through the fur on his neck. That same strange humming sound that he'd made yesterday rumbled in his throat. It was a homey kind of sound. Rougher, wilder than a cat's purr, but conveying the same sense of contentment.

"You know, I never had a dog," I mused. "I always wanted one, but Renée's allergic."

Jacob laughed; his body shook under me.

"Aren't you worried about Saturday at all?" I asked.

He turned his enormous head toward me, so that I could see one of his eyes roll.

"I wish I could feel that positive."

He leaned his head against my leg and started humming again. And it did make me feel just a little bit better.

"So we've got some hiking to do tomorrow, I guess."

He rumbled; the sound was enthusiastic.

"It might be a *long* hike," I warned him. "Edward doesn't judge distances the way a normal person does."

Jacob barked another laugh.

I settled deeper into his warm fur, resting my head against his neck.

It was strange. Even though he was in this bizarre form, this felt more like the way Jake and I used to be — the easy, effortless friendship that was as natural as breathing in and out — than the last few times I'd been with

Jacob while he was human. Odd that I should find that again here, when I'd thought this wolf thing was the cause of its loss.

The killing games continued in the clearing, and I stared at the hazy moon.

20. COMPROMISE

Everything was ready.

I was packed for my two-day visit with "Alice," and my bag waited for me on the passenger seat of my truck. I'd given the concert tickets to Angela, Ben, and Mike. Mike was going to take Jessica, which was exactly as I'd hoped. Billy had borrowed Old Quil Ateara's boat and invited Charlie down for some open sea fishing before the afternoon game started. Collin and Brady, the two youngest werewolves, were staying behind to protect La Push — though they were just children, both of them only thirteen. Still, Charlie would be safer than anyone left in Forks.

I had done all that I could do. I tried to accept that, and

put the things that were outside of my control out of my head, for tonight at least. One way or another, this would all be over in forty-eight hours. The thought was almost comforting.

Edward had requested that I relax, and I was going to do my best.

"For this one night, could we try to forget everything besides just you and me?" he'd pleaded, unleashing the full force of his eyes on me. "It seems like I can never get enough time like that. I need to be with you. Just you."

That was not a hard request to agree to, though I knew that forgetting my fears would be much easier said than done. Other matters were on my mind now, knowing that we had this night to be alone, and that would help.

There were some things that had changed.

For instance, I was ready.

I was ready to join his family and his world. The fear and guilt and anguish I was feeling now had taught me that much. I'd had a chance to concentrate on this — as I'd gazed at the moon through the clouds and rested against a werewolf — and I knew I would not panic again. The next time something came at us, I would be ready. An asset, not a liability. He would never have to make the choice between me and his family again. We would be partners, like Alice and Jasper. Next time, I would do my part.

I would wait for the sword to be removed from over my head, so that Edward would be satisfied. But it wasn't necessary. I was ready.

There was only one missing piece.

One piece, because there were some things that had *not* changed, and that included the desperate way I loved him. I'd had plenty of time to think through the ramifications of Jasper and Emmett's bet — to figure out the things I was willing to lose with my humanity, and the part that I was not willing to give up. I knew which human experience I was going to insist on before I became inhuman.

So we had some things to work out tonight. After everything I'd seen in the past two years, I didn't believe in the word *impossible* anymore. It was going to take more than that to stop me now.

Okay, well, honestly, it was probably going to be much more complicated than that. But I was going to try.

As decided as I was, I wasn't surprised that I still felt nervous as I drove down the long path to his house — I didn't know how to do what I was trying to do, and that guaranteed me some serious jitters. He sat in the passenger seat, fighting a smile at my slow pace. I was surprised that he hadn't insisted on taking the wheel, but tonight he seemed content to go at my speed.

It was after dark when we reached the house. In spite of that, the meadow was bright in the light shining from every window.

As soon as I cut the engine he was at my door, opening it for me. He lifted me from the cab with one arm, slinging my bag out of the truck bed and over his shoulder with the other. His lips found mine as I heard him kick the truck's door shut behind me.

Without breaking the kiss, he swung me up so that I was cradled in his arms and carried me into the house.

Was the front door already open? I didn't know. We were inside, though, and I was dizzy. I had to remind myself to breathe.

This kissing did not frighten me. It wasn't like before when I could feel the fear and panic leaking through his control. His lips were not anxious, but enthusiastic now — he seemed as thrilled as I was that we had tonight to concentrate on being together. He continued to kiss me for several minutes, standing there in the entry; he seemed less guarded than usual, his mouth cold and urgent on mine.

I began to feel cautiously optimistic. Perhaps getting what I wanted would not be as difficult as I'd expected it to be.

No, of course it was going to be just exactly that difficult.

With a low chuckle, he pulled me away, holding me at arm's length.

"Welcome home," he said, his eyes liquid and warm.

"That sounds nice," I said, breathless.

He set me gently on my feet. I wrapped both my arms around him, refusing to allow any space between us.

"I have something for you," he said, his tone conversational.

"Oh?"

"Your hand-me-down, remember? You said that was allowable."

"Oh, that's right. I guess I did say that."

He chuckled at my reluctance.

"It's up in my room. Shall I go get it?"

His bedroom? "Sure," I agreed, feeling quite devious as I wound my fingers through his. "Let's go."

He must have been eager to give me my non-present, because human velocity was not fast enough for him. He scooped me up again and nearly flew up the stairs to his room. He set me down at the door, and darted into his closet.

He was back before I'd taken a step, but I ignored him and went to the huge gold bed, plopping down on the edge and then sliding to the center. I curled up in a ball, my arms wrapped around my knees.

"Okay," I grumbled. Now that I was where I wanted to be, I could afford a little reluctance. "Let me have it."

Edward laughed.

He climbed onto the bed to sit next to me, and my heart thumped unevenly. Hopefully he would write that off as some reaction to him giving me presents.

"A hand-me-down," he reminded me sternly. He pulled my left wrist away from my leg, and touched the silver bracelet for just a moment. Then he gave me my arm back.

I examined it cautiously. On the opposite side of the chain from the wolf, there now hung a brilliant heart-shaped crystal. It was cut in a million facets, so that even in the subdued light shining from the lamp, it sparkled. I inhaled in a low gasp.

"It was my mother's." He shrugged deprecatingly. "I inherited quite a few baubles like this. I've given some to Esme and Alice both. So, clearly, this is not a big deal in any way."

I smiled ruefully at his assurance.

"But I thought it was a good representation," he continued. "It's hard and cold." He laughed. "And it throws rainbows in the sunlight."

"You forgot the most important similarity," I murmured. "It's beautiful."

"My heart is just as silent," he mused. "And it, too, is yours."

I twisted my wrist so the heart would glimmer. "Thank you. For both."

"No, thank *you*. It's a relief to have you accept a gift so easily. Good practice for you, too." He grinned, flashing his teeth.

I leaned into him, ducking my head under his arm and cuddling into his side. It probably felt similar to snuggling with Michelangelo's *David,* except that this perfect marble creature wrapped his arms around me to pull me closer.

It seemed like a good place to start.

"Can we discuss something? I'd appreciate it if you could *begin* by being open-minded."

He hesitated for a moment. "I'll give it my best effort," he agreed, cautious now.

"I'm not breaking any rules here," I promised. "This is strictly about you and me." I cleared my throat. "So . . . I was impressed by how well we were able to compromise the other night. I was thinking I would like to apply the same principle to a different situation." I wondered why I was being so formal. Must be the nerves.

"What would you like to negotiate?" he asked, a smile in his voice.

I struggled, trying to find exactly the right words to open with.

"Listen to your heart fly," he murmured. "It's fluttering like a hummingbird's wings. Are you all right?"

"I'm great."

"Please go on then," he encouraged.

"Well, I guess, first, I wanted to talk to you about that whole ridiculous marriage condition thing."

"It's only ridiculous to you. What about it?"

"I was wondering . . . is *that* open to negotiation?"

Edward frowned, serious now. "I've already made the largest concession by far and away — I've agreed to take your life away against my better judgment. And that ought to entitle me to a few compromises on your part."

"No." I shook my head, focusing on keeping my face composed. "That part's a done deal. We're not discussing my . . . renovations right now. I want to hammer out some other details."

He looked at me suspiciously. "Which details do you mean exactly?"

I hesitated. "Let's clarify your prerequisites first."

"You know what I want."

"*Matrimony.*" I made it sound like a dirty word.

"Yes." He smiled a wide smile. "To start with."

The shock spoiled my carefully composed expression. "There's more?"

"Well," he said, and his face was calculating. "If you're my wife, then what's mine is yours . . . like tuition money. So there would be no problem with Dartmouth."

"Anything else? While you're already being absurd?"

"I wouldn't mind some *time*."

"No. No time. That's a deal breaker right there."

He sighed longingly. "Just a year or two?"

I shook my head, my lips set in a stubborn frown. "Move along to the next one."

"That's it. Unless you'd like to talk cars . . ."

He grinned widely when I grimaced, then took my hand and began playing with my fingers.

"I didn't realize there was anything else you wanted besides being transformed into a monster yourself. I'm extremely curious." His voice was low and soft. The slight edge would have been hard to detect if I hadn't known it so well.

I paused, staring at his hand on mine. I still didn't know how to begin. I felt his eyes watching me and I was afraid to look up. The blood began to burn in my face.

His cool fingers brushed my cheek. "You're blushing?" he asked in surprise. I kept my eyes down. "Please, Bella, the suspense is painful."

I bit my lip.

"Bella." His tone reproached me now, reminded me that it was hard for him when I kept my thoughts to myself.

"Well, I'm a little worried . . . about after," I admitted, finally looking at him.

I felt his body tense, but his voice was gentle and velvet. "What has you worried?"

"All of you just seem *so* convinced that the only thing I'm going to be interested in, afterward, is slaughtering everyone in town," I confessed, while he winced at my choice of words. "And I'm afraid I'll be so preoccupied with the mayhem that I won't be *me* anymore . . . and that I won't . . . I won't *want* you the same way I do now."

"Bella, that part doesn't last forever," he assured me.

He was missing the point.

"Edward," I said, nervous, staring at a freckle on my wrist. "There's something that I want to do before I'm not human anymore."

He waited for me to continue. I didn't. My face was all hot.

"Whatever you want," he encouraged, anxious and completely clueless.

"Do you promise?" I muttered, knowing my attempt to trap him with his words was not going to work, but unable to resist.

"Yes," he said. I looked up to see that his eyes were earnest and confused. "Tell me what you want, and you can have it."

I couldn't believe how awkward and idiotic I felt. I was too innocent — which was, of course, central to the discussion. I didn't have the faintest idea how to be seductive. I would just have to settle for flushed and self-conscious.

"You," I mumbled almost incoherently.

"I'm yours." He smiled, still oblivious, trying to hold my gaze as I looked away again.

I took a deep breath and shifted forward so that I was kneeling on the bed. Then I wrapped my arms around his neck and kissed him.

He kissed me back, bewildered but willing. His lips were gentle against mine, and I could tell his mind was elsewhere — trying to figure out what was on *my* mind. I decided he needed a hint.

My hands were slightly shaky as I unlocked my arms from around his neck. My fingers slid down his neck to the collar of his shirt. The trembling didn't help as I tried to hurry to undo the buttons before he stopped me.

His lips froze, and I could almost hear the click in his head as he put together my words and my actions.

He pushed me away at once, his face heavily disapproving.

"Be reasonable, Bella."

"You promised — whatever I wanted," I reminded him without hope.

"We're not having this discussion." He glared at me while he refastened the two buttons I'd managed to open.

My teeth clamped together.

"I say we are," I growled. I moved my hands to my blouse and yanked open the top button.

He grabbed my wrists and pinned them to my sides.

"I say we're not," he said flatly.

We glowered at each other.

"You wanted to know," I pointed out.

"I thought it would be something faintly realistic."

"So you can ask for any stupid, ridiculous thing *you* want — like getting *married* — but *I'm* not allowed to even *discuss* what I —"

While I was ranting, he pulled my hands together to restrain them in just one of his, and put his other hand over my mouth.

"No." His face was hard.

I took a deep breath to steady myself. And, as the anger began to fade, I felt something else.

It took me a minute to recognize why I was staring down again, the blush returning — why my stomach felt uneasy, why there was too much moisture in my eyes, why I suddenly wanted to run from the room.

Rejection washed through me, instinctive and strong.

I knew it was irrational. He'd been very clear on other occasions that my safety was the only factor. Yet I'd never made myself quite so vulnerable before. I scowled at the golden comforter that matched his eyes and tried to banish the reflex reaction that told me I was unwanted and unwantable.

Edward sighed. The hand over my mouth moved under my chin, and he pulled my face up until I had to look at him.

"What now?"

"Nothing," I mumbled.

He scrutinized my face for a long moment while I tried unsuccessfully to twist away from his gaze. His brow furrowed, and his expression became horrified.

"Did I hurt your feelings?" he asked, shocked.

"No," I lied.

So quickly that I wasn't even sure how it happened, I was in his arms, my face cradled between his shoulder and his hand, while his thumb stroked reassuringly against my cheek.

"You know why I have to say no," he murmured. "You know that I want you, too."

"Do you?" I whispered, my voice full of doubt.

"Of course I do, you silly, beautiful, oversensitive girl." He laughed once, and then his voice was bleak. "Doesn't everyone? I feel like there's a line behind me, jockeying for position, waiting for me to make a big enough mistake. . . . You're too desirable for your own good."

"Who's being silly now?" I doubted if awkward, self-conscious, and inept added up to *desirable* in anyone's book.

"Do I have to send a petition around to get you to believe? Shall I tell you whose names would be on the top of the list? You know a few of them, but some might surprise you."

I shook my head against his chest, grimacing. "You're just trying to distract me. Let's get back to the subject."

He sighed.

"Tell me if I have anything wrong." I tried to sound detached. "Your demands are marriage" — I couldn't say the word without making a face — "paying my tuition, more time, and you wouldn't mind if my vehicle went a little faster." I raised my eyebrows. "Did I get everything? That's a hefty list."

"Only the first is a demand." He seemed to be having a hard time keeping a straight face. "The others are merely requests."

"And my lone, solitary little demand is —"

"Demand?" he interrupted, suddenly serious again.

"Yes, demand."

His eyes narrowed.

"Getting married is a stretch for me. I'm not giving in unless I get something in return."

He leaned down to whisper in my ear. "No," he murmured silkily. "It's not possible now. Later, when you're less breakable. Be patient, Bella."

I tried to keep my voice firm and reasonable. "But that's the problem. It won't be the *same* when I'm less breakable. I won't be the same! I don't know *who* I'll be then."

"You'll still be Bella," he promised.

I frowned. "If I'm so far gone that I'd want to kill Charlie — that I'd drink Jacob's blood or Angela's if I got the chance — how can that be true?"

"It will pass. And I doubt you'll want to drink the dog's blood." He pretended to shudder at the thought. "Even as a newborn, you'll have better taste than that."

I ignored his attempt to sidetrack me. "But that will always be what I want most, won't it?" I challenged. "Blood, blood, and more blood!"

"The fact that you are still alive is proof that that is not true," he pointed out.

"Over eighty years later," I reminded him. "What I meant was *physically,* though. Intellectually, I know I'll be able to be myself . . . after a while. But just purely physically — I will always be thirsty, more than anything else."

He didn't answer.

"So I *will* be different," I concluded unopposed. "Because right now, physically, there's nothing I want more than you. More than food or water or oxygen. Intellectually, I have my priorities in a slightly more sensible order. But physically . . ."

I twisted my head to kiss the palm of his hand.

He took a deep breath. I was surprised that it sounded a little unsteady.

"Bella, I could kill you," he whispered.

"I don't think you could."

Edward's eyes tightened. He lifted his hand from my face and reached quickly behind himself for something I couldn't see. There was a muffled snapping sound, and the bed quivered beneath us.

Something dark was in his hand; he held it up for my curious examination. It was a metal flower, one of the roses that adorned the wrought iron posts and canopy of his bed frame. His hand closed for a brief second, his fingers contracting gently, and then it opened again.

Without a word, he offered me the crushed, uneven lump of black metal. It was a cast of the inside of his hand, like a piece of play dough squeezed in a child's fist. A half-second passed, and the shape crumbled into black sand in his palm.

I glared. "That's not what I meant. I already *know* how strong you are. You didn't have to break the furniture."

"What *did* you mean then?" he asked in a dark voice, tossing the handful of iron sand to the corner of the room; it hit the wall with a sound like rain.

His eyes were intent on my face as I struggled to explain.

"Obviously not that you aren't physically able to hurt me, if you wanted to . . . More that, you *don't* want to hurt me . . . so much so that I don't think that you ever could."

He started shaking his head before I was done.

"It might not work like that, Bella."

"*Might,*" I scoffed. "You have no more idea what you're talking about than I do."

"Exactly. Do you imagine I would ever take that kind of risk with you?"

I stared into his eyes for a long minute. There was no sign of compromise, no hint of indecision in them.

"Please," I finally whispered, hopeless. "It's all I want. Please." I closed my eyes in defeat, waiting for the quick and final no.

But he didn't answer immediately. I hesitated in disbelief, stunned to hear that his breathing was uneven again.

I opened my eyes, and his face was torn.

"Please?" I whispered again, my heartbeat picking up speed. My words tumbled out as I rushed to take advantage of the sudden uncertainty in his eyes. "You don't have to make me any guarantees. If it doesn't work out right, well, then that's that. Just let us *try* . . . only try. And I'll give you what you want," I promised rashly. "I'll marry you. I'll let you pay for Dartmouth, and I won't complain about the bribe to get me in. You can even buy me a fast car if that makes you happy! Just . . . *please.*"

His icy arms tightened around me, and his lips were at my ear; his cool breath made me shiver. "This is unbearable. So many things I've wanted to give you — and *this* is what you decide to demand. Do you have any idea how painful it is, trying to refuse you when you plead with me this way?"

"Then don't refuse," I suggested breathlessly.

He didn't respond.

"Please," I tried again.

"Bella . . ." He shook his head slowly, but it didn't feel like a denial as his face, his lips, moved back and forth across my throat. It felt more like surrender. My heart, racing already, spluttered frantically.

Again, I took what advantage I could. When his face turned toward mine with the slow movement of his indecision, I twisted quickly in his arms till my lips reached his. His hands seized my face, and I thought he was going to push me away again.

I was wrong.

His mouth was not gentle; there was a brand-new edge of conflict and desperation in the way his lips moved. I locked my arms around his neck, and, to my suddenly overheated skin, his body felt colder than ever. I trembled, but it was not from the chill.

He didn't stop kissing me. I was the one who had to break away, gasping for air. Even then his lips did not leave my skin, they just moved to my throat. The thrill of victory was a strange high; it made me feel powerful. Brave. My hands weren't unsteady now; I got through with the buttons on his shirt this time easily, and my fingers traced the perfect planes of his icy chest. He was too beautiful. What was the word he'd used just now? Unbearable — that was it. His beauty was too much to bear. . . .

I pulled his mouth back to mine, and he seemed just as eager as I was. One of his hands still cupped my face, his other arm was tight around my waist, straining me closer to him. It made it slightly more difficult as I tried to reach the front of my shirt, but not impossible.

Cold iron fetters locked around my wrists, and pulled my hands above my head, which was suddenly on a pillow.

His lips were at my ear again. "Bella," he murmured, his voice warm and velvet. "Would you *please* stop trying to take your clothes off?"

"Do you want to do that part?" I asked, confused.

"Not tonight," he answered softly. His lips were slower now against my cheek and jaw, all the urgency gone.

"Edward, don't —," I started to argue.

"I'm not saying no," he reassured me. "I'm just saying *not tonight.*"

I thought about that while my breathing slowed.

"Give me one good reason why tonight is not as good as any other night." I was still breathless; it made the frustration in my voice less impressive.

"I wasn't born yesterday." He chuckled in my ear. "Out of the two of us, which do you think is more unwilling to give the other what they want? You just promised to marry me before you do any changing, but if I give in tonight, what guarantee do I have that you won't go running off to Carlisle in the morning? I am — clearly — much less reluctant to give you what you want. Therefore . . . you first."

I exhaled with a loud huff. "I have to marry you first?" I asked in disbelief.

"That's the deal — take it or leave it. Compromise, remember?"

His arms wrapped around me, and he began kissing me in a way that should be illegal. Too persuasive — it was duress, coercion. I tried to keep a clear head . . . and failed quickly and absolutely.

"I think that's a really bad idea," I gasped when he let me breathe.

"I'm not surprised you feel that way." He smirked. "You have a one-track mind."

"How did this happen?" I grumbled. "I thought I was holding my own tonight — for once — and now, all of a sudden —"

"You're engaged," he finished.

"Ew! *Please* don't say that out loud."

"Are you going back on your word?" he demanded. He pulled away to read my face. His expression was entertained. He was having fun.

I glared at him, trying to ignore the way his smile made my heart react.

"Are you?" he pressed.

"Ugh!" I groaned. "No. I'm not. Are you happy now?"

His smile was blinding. "Exceptionally."

I groaned again.

"Aren't you happy at all?"

He kissed me again before I could answer. Another too-persuasive kiss.

"A little bit," I admitted when I could speak. "But not about getting married."

He kissed me another time. "Do you get the feeling that everything is backward?" he laughed in my ear. "Traditionally, shouldn't you be arguing my side, and I yours?"

"There isn't much that's traditional about you and me."

"True."

He kissed me again, and kept going until my heart was racing and my skin was flushed.

"Look, Edward," I murmured, my voice wheedling, when he paused to kiss the palm of my hand. "I said I would marry you, and I will. I promise. I swear. If you want, I'll sign a contract in my own blood."

"Not funny," he murmured against the inside of my wrist.

"What I'm saying is this — I'm not going to trick you or anything. You know me better than that. So there's really no reason to wait. We're completely alone — how often does that happen? — and you've provided this very large and comfortable bed. . . ."

"Not tonight," he said again.

"Don't you trust me?"

"Of course I do."

Using the hand that he was still kissing, I pulled his face back up to where I could see his expression.

"Then what's the problem? It's not like you didn't know you were going to win in the end." I frowned and muttered, "You always win."

"Just hedging my bets," he said calmly.

"There's something else," I guessed, my eyes narrowing. There was a defensiveness about his face, a faint hint of some secret motive he was trying to hide behind his casual manner. "Are *you* planning to go back on your word?"

"No," he promised solemnly. "I swear to you, we *will* try. After you marry me."

I shook my head, and laughed glumly. "You make me

feel like a villain in a melodrama — twirling my mustache while I try to steal some poor girl's virtue."

His eyes were wary as they flashed across my face, then he quickly ducked down to press his lips against my collarbone.

"That's it, isn't it?" The short laugh that escaped me was more shocked than amused. "You're trying to protect your virtue!" I covered my mouth with my hand to muffle the giggle that followed. The words were so . . . old-fashioned.

"No, silly girl," he muttered against my shoulder. "I'm trying to protect *yours*. And you're making it shockingly difficult."

"Of all the ridiculous —"

"Let me ask you something," he interrupted quickly. "We've had this discussion before, but humor me. How many people in this room have a soul? A shot at heaven, or whatever there is after this life?"

"Two," I answered immediately, my voice fierce.

"All right. Maybe that's true. Now, there's a world full of dissension about this, but the vast majority seem to think that there are some rules that have to be followed."

"Vampire rules aren't enough for you? You want to worry about the human ones too?"

"It couldn't hurt." He shrugged. "Just in case."

I glared at him through narrowed eyes.

"Now, of course, it might be too late for me, even if you are right about my soul."

"No, it isn't," I argued angrily.

"'Thou shalt not kill' *is* commonly accepted by most

major belief systems. And I've killed a lot of people, Bella."

"Only the bad ones."

He shrugged. "Maybe that counts, maybe it doesn't. But you haven't killed anyone —"

"That *you* know about," I muttered.

He smiled, but otherwise ignored the interruption. "And I'm going to do my best to keep you out of temptation's way."

"Okay. But we weren't fighting over committing murder," I reminded him.

"The same principle applies — the only difference is that this is the one area in which I'm just as spotless as you are. Can't I leave one rule unbroken?"

"One?"

"You know that I've stolen, I've lied, I've coveted . . . my virtue is all I have left." He grinned crookedly.

"I lie all the time."

"Yes, but you're such a bad liar that it doesn't really count. Nobody believes you."

"I really hope you're wrong about that — because otherwise Charlie is about to burst through the door with a loaded gun."

"Charlie is happier when he pretends to swallow your stories. He'd rather lie to himself than look too closely." He grinned at me.

"But what did you ever covet?" I asked doubtfully. "You have everything."

"I coveted you." His smile darkened. "I had no right to want you — but I reached out and took you anyway. And now look what's become of you! Trying to seduce a vampire." He shook his head in mock horror.

"You can covet what's already yours," I informed him. "Besides, I thought it was *my* virtue you were worried about."

"It is. If it's too late for me . . . Well, I'll be damned — no pun intended — if I'll let them keep you out, too."

"You can't make me go somewhere you won't be," I vowed. "That's my definition of hell. Anyway, I have an easy solution to all this: let's never die, all right?"

"Sounds simple enough. Why didn't I think of that?"

He smiled at me until I gave up with an angry *humph*. "So that's it. You won't sleep with me until we're *married*."

"Technically, I can't ever *sleep* with you."

I rolled my eyes. "Very mature, Edward."

"But, other than that detail, yes, you've got it right."

"I think you have an ulterior motive."

His eyes widened innocently. "Another one?"

"You know this will speed things up," I accused.

He tried not to smile. "There is only one thing I want to speed up, and the rest can wait forever . . . but for that, it's true, your impatient human hormones are my most powerful ally at this point."

"I can't believe I'm going along with this. When I think of Charlie . . . and Renée! Can you imagine what Angela will think? Or Jessica? Ugh. I can hear the gossip now."

He raised one eyebrow at me, and I knew why. What did it matter what they said about me when I was leaving soon and not coming back? Was I really so oversensitive that I couldn't bear a few weeks of sidelong glances and leading questions?

Maybe it wouldn't bug me so much if I didn't know that I would probably be gossiping just as condescendingly as the rest of them if it was someone else getting married this summer.

Gah. Married this summer! I shuddered.

And then, maybe it wouldn't bug me so much if I hadn't been raised to shudder at the thought of marriage.

Edward interrupted my fretting. "It doesn't have to be a big production. I don't need any fanfare. You won't have to tell anyone or make any changes. We'll go to Vegas — you can wear old jeans and we'll go to the chapel with the drive-through window. I just want it to be official — that you belong to me and *no one else*."

"It couldn't be any more official than it already is," I grumbled. But his description didn't sound that bad. Only Alice would be disappointed.

"We'll see about that." He smiled complacently. "I suppose you don't want your ring now?"

I had to swallow before I could speak. "You suppose correctly."

He laughed at my expression. "That's fine. I'll get it on your finger soon enough."

I glared at him. "You talk like you already have one."

"I do," he said, unashamed. "Ready to force upon you at the first sign of weakness."

"You're unbelievable."

"Do you want to see it?" he asked. His liquid topaz eyes were suddenly shining with excitement.

"No!" I almost shouted, a reflex reaction. I regretted it at once. His face fell ever so slightly. "Unless you really want to show it to me," I amended. I gritted my teeth together to keep my illogical terror from showing.

"That's all right," he shrugged. "It can wait."

I sighed. "Show me the damn ring, Edward."

He shook his head. "No."

I studied his expression for a long minute.

"Please?" I asked quietly, experimenting with my newly discovered weapon. I touched his face lightly with the tips of my fingers. "Please can I see it?"

His eyes narrowed. "You are the most dangerous creature I've ever met," he muttered. But he got up and moved with unconscious grace to kneel next to the small bedside table. He was back on the bed with me in an instant, sitting beside me with one arm around my shoulder. In his other hand was a little black box. He balanced it on my left knee.

"Go ahead and look, then," he said brusquely.

It was harder than it should have been to pick up the inoffensive little box, but I didn't want to hurt him again, so I tried to keep my hand from shaking. The surface was smooth with black satin. I brushed my fingers over it, hesitating.

"You didn't spend a *lot* of money, did you? Lie to me, if you did."

"I didn't spend anything," he assured me. "It's just another hand-me-down. This is the ring my father gave to my mother."

"Oh." Surprise colored my voice. I pinched the lid between my thumb and forefinger, but didn't open it.

"I suppose it's a little outdated." His tone was playfully apologetic. "Old-fashioned, just like me. I can get you something more modern. Something from Tiffany's?"

"I like old-fashioned things," I mumbled as I hesitantly lifted the lid.

Nestled into the black satin, Elizabeth Masen's ring sparkled in the dim light. The face was a long oval, set with slanting rows of glittering round stones. The band was gold — delicate and narrow. The gold made a fragile web around the diamonds. I'd never seen anything like it.

Unthinkingly, I stroked the shimmering gems.

"It's so *pretty*," I murmured to myself, surprised.

"Do you like it?"

"It's beautiful." I shrugged, feigning a lack of interest. "What's not to like?"

He chuckled. "See if it fits."

My left hand clenched into a fist.

"Bella," he sighed. "I'm not going to solder it to your finger. Just try it on so I can see if it needs to be sized. Then you can take it right off."

"Fine," I grumbled.

I reached for the ring, but his long fingers beat me there. He took my left hand in his, and slid the ring into place on my third finger. He held my hand out, and we both examined the oval sparkling against my skin. It wasn't quite as awful as I'd feared, having it there.

"A perfect fit," he said indifferently. "That's nice — saves me a trip to the jeweler's."

I could hear some strong emotion burning under the casual tone of his voice, and I stared up at his face. It was there in his eyes, too, visible despite the careful nonchalance of his expression.

"You like that, don't you?" I asked suspiciously, fluttering my fingers and thinking that it was really too bad that I had not broken my *left* hand.

He shrugged his shoulders. "Sure," he said, still casual. "It looks very nice on you."

I stared into his eyes, trying to decipher the emotion that smoldered just under the surface. He gazed back, and the casual pretense suddenly slipped away. He was glowing — his angel's face brilliant with joy and victory. He was so glorious that it knocked me breathless.

Before I could catch that breath, he was kissing me, his lips exultant. I was lightheaded when he moved his mouth to whisper in my ear — but his breathing was just as ragged as mine.

"Yes, I like it. You have *no* idea."

I laughed, gasping a little. "I believe you."

"Do you mind if I do something?" he murmured, his arms tightening around me.

"Anything you want."

But he let me go and slid away.

"Anything but that," I complained.

He ignored me, taking my hand and pulling me off the bed, too. He stood in front of me, hands on my shoulders, face serious.

"Now, I want to do this right. Please, *please*, keep in mind that you've already agreed to this, and don't ruin it for me."

"Oh, no," I gasped as he slid down onto one knee.

"Be nice," he muttered.

I took a deep breath.

"Isabella Swan?" He looked up at me through his impossibly long lashes, his golden eyes soft but, somehow, still scorching. "I promise to love you forever — every single day of forever. Will you marry me?"

There were many things I wanted to say, some of them not nice at all, and others more disgustingly gooey and romantic than he probably dreamed I was capable of. Rather than embarrass myself with either, I whispered, "Yes."

"Thank you," he said simply. He took my left hand and kissed each of my fingertips before he kissed the ring that was now mine.

21. TRAILS

I HATED TO WASTE ANY PART OF THE NIGHT IN SLEEP, but that was inevitable. The sun was bright outside the window-wall when I woke, with small clouds scuttling too quickly across the sky. The wind rocked the treetops till the whole forest looked as if it was going to shake apart.

He left me alone to get dressed, and I appreciated the chance to think. Somehow, my plan for last night had gone horribly awry, and I needed to come to grips with the consequences. Though I'd given back the hand-me-down ring as soon as I could do it without hurting his feelings, my left hand felt heavier, like it was still in place, just invisible.

This shouldn't bother me, I reasoned. It was no big thing — a road trip to Vegas. I would go one better than old jeans — I would wear old sweats. The ceremony certainly couldn't take very long; no more than fifteen minutes at the most, right? So I could handle that.

And then, when it was over, he'd have to fulfill his side of the bargain. I would concentrate on that, and forget the rest.

He said I didn't have to tell anyone, and I was planning to hold him to that. Of course, it was very stupid of me not to think of Alice.

The Cullens got home around noon. There was a new, businesslike feel to the atmosphere around them, and it pulled me back into the enormity of what was coming.

Alice seemed to be in an unusually bad mood. I chalked it up to her frustration with feeling normal, because her first words to Edward were a complaint about working with the wolves.

"I *think*" — she made a face as she used the uncertain word — "that you're going to want to pack for cold weather, Edward. I can't see where you are exactly, because you're taking off with that *dog* this afternoon. But the storm that's coming seems particularly bad in that general area."

Edward nodded.

"It's going to snow on the mountains," she warned him.

"Ew, snow," I muttered to myself. It was June, for crying out loud.

"Wear a jacket," Alice told me. Her voice was unfriendly, and that surprised me. I tried to read her face, but she turned away.

I looked at Edward, and he was smiling; whatever was bugging Alice amused him.

Edward had more than enough camping gear to choose from — props in the human charade; the Cullens were good customers at the Newton's store. He grabbed a down sleeping bag, a small tent, and several packets of dehydrated food — grinning when I made a face at them — and stuffed them all in a backpack.

Alice wandered into the garage while we were there, watching Edward's preparations without a word. He ignored her.

When he was done packing, Edward handed me his phone. "Why don't you call Jacob and tell him we'll be ready for him in an hour or so. He knows where to meet us."

Jacob wasn't home, but Billy promised to call around until he could find an available werewolf to pass the news to.

"Don't you worry about Charlie, Bella," Billy said. "I've got my part of this under control."

"Yeah, I know Charlie'll be fine." I didn't feel so confident about his son's safety, but I didn't add that.

"I wish I could be with the rest of them tomorrow." Billy chuckled regretfully. "Being an old man is a hardship, Bella."

The urge to fight must be a defining characteristic of the Y chromosome. They were all the same.

"Have fun with Charlie."

"Good luck, Bella," he answered. "And . . . pass that along to the, er, Cullens for me."

"I will," I promised, surprised by the gesture.

As I gave the phone back to Edward, I saw that he and Alice were having some kind of silent discussion. She was staring at him, pleading in her eyes. He was frowning back, unhappy with whatever she wanted.

"Billy said to tell you 'good luck.'"

"That was generous of him," Edward said, breaking away from her.

"Bella, could I please speak to you alone?" Alice asked swiftly.

"You're about to make my life harder than it needs to be, Alice," Edward warned her through his teeth. "I'd really rather you didn't."

"This isn't about you, Edward," she shot back.

He laughed. Something about her response was funny to him.

"It's not," Alice insisted. "This is a female thing."

He frowned.

"Let her talk to me," I told him. I was curious.

"You asked for it," he muttered. He laughed again — half angry, half amused — and strode out of the garage.

I turned to Alice, worried now, but she didn't look at me. Her bad mood hadn't passed yet.

She went to sit on the hood of her Porsche, her face dejected. I followed, and leaned against the bumper beside her.

"Bella?" Alice asked in a sad voice, shifting over and curling up against my side. Her voice sounded so miserable that I wrapped my arms around her shoulders in comfort.

"What's wrong, Alice?"

"Don't you love me?" she asked in that same sad tone.

"Of course I do. You know that."

"Then why do I see you sneaking off to Vegas to get married without inviting me?"

"Oh," I muttered, my cheeks turning pink. I could see that I had seriously hurt her feelings, and I hurried to defend myself. "You know how I hate to make a big deal out of things. It was Edward's idea, anyway."

"I don't care whose idea it was. How could *you* do this to me? I expect that kind of thing from *Edward,* but not from you. I love you like you were my own sister."

"To me, Alice, you *are* my sister."

"Words!" she growled.

"Fine, you can come. There won't be much to see."

She was still grimacing.

"What?" I demanded.

"How *much* do you love me, Bella?"

"Why?"

She stared at me with pleading eyes, her long black eyebrows slanting up in the middle and pulling together, her lips trembling at the corners. It was a heart-breaking expression.

"Please, please, please," she whispered. "Please, Bella, please — if you really love me . . . Please let me do your wedding."

"Aw, Alice!" I groaned, pulling away and standing up. "No! Don't do this to me."

"If you really, truly love me, Bella."

I folded my arms across my chest. "That is *so* unfair. And Edward kind of already used that one on me."

"I'll bet Edward would like it better if you did this traditionally, though he'd never tell you that. And Esme — think what it would mean to her!"

I groaned. "I'd rather face the newborns alone."

"I'll owe you for a decade."

"You'd owe me for a century!"

Her eyes glowed. "Is that a yes?"

"No! I don't want to *do* this!"

"You won't have to do anything but walk a few yards and then repeat after the minister."

"Ugh! Ugh, ugh!"

"Please?" She started bouncing in place. "Please, please, please, please, please?"

"I'll never, never ever forgive you for this, Alice."

"Yay!" she squealed, clapping her hands together.

"That's *not* a yes!"

"But it will be," she sang.

"Edward!" I yelled, stalking out of the garage. "I know you're listening. Get over here." Alice was right behind me, still clapping.

"Thanks so much, Alice," Edward said acidly, coming from behind me. I turned to let him have it, but his expression was so worried and upset that I couldn't speak my complaints. I threw my arms around him instead, hiding my face, just in case the angry moisture in my eyes made it look like I was crying.

"Vegas," Edward promised in my ear.

"Not a chance," Alice gloated. "Bella would never do that to me. You know, Edward, as a brother, you are sometimes a disappointment."

"Don't be mean," I grumbled at her. "He's trying to make me happy, unlike you."

"I'm trying to make you happy, too, Bella. It's just that I know better what will make you happy . . . in the long run. You'll thank me for this. Maybe not for fifty years, but definitely someday."

"I never thought I'd see the day where I'd be willing to take a bet against you, Alice, but it has arrived."

She laughed her silvery laugh. "So, are you going to show me the ring?"

I grimaced in horror as she grabbed my left hand and then dropped it just as quickly.

"Huh. I saw him put it on you. . . . Did I miss something?" she asked. She concentrated for half a second, furrowing her brow, before she answered her own questions. "No. Wedding's still on."

"Bella has issues with jewelry," Edward explained.

"What's one more diamond? Well, I guess the ring has lots of diamonds, but my point is that he's already got one on —"

"Enough, Alice!" Edward cut her off suddenly. The way he glared at her . . . he looked like a vampire again. "We're in a hurry."

"I don't understand. What's that about diamonds?" I asked.

"We'll talk about it later," Alice said. "Edward is right — you'd better get going. You've got to set a trap and make camp before the storm comes." She frowned, and her expression was anxious, almost nervous. "Don't forget your coat, Bella. It seems . . . unseasonably cold."

"I've already got it," Edward assured her.

"Have a nice night," she told us in farewell.

It was twice as far to the clearing as usual; Edward took a long detour, making sure my scent would be nowhere near the trail Jacob would hide later. He carried me in his arms, the bulky backpack in my usual spot.

He stopped at the farthest end of the clearing and set me on my feet.

"All right. Just walk north for a ways, touching as much as you can. Alice gave me a clear picture of their path, and it won't take long for us to intersect it."

"North?"

He smiled and pointed out the right direction.

I wandered into the woods, leaving the clear yellow light of the strangely sunny day in the clearing behind me. Maybe Alice's blurred sight would be wrong about the snow. I hoped so. The sky was mostly clear, though the wind whipped furiously through the open spaces. In the trees it was calmer, but much too cold for June — even in a long-sleeved shirt with a thick sweater over the top, there were goose bumps on my arms. I walked slowly, trailing my fingers over anything close enough: the rough tree bark, the wet ferns, the moss-covered rocks.

Edward stayed with me, walking a parallel line about twenty yards away.

"Am I doing this right?" I called.

"Perfectly."

I had an idea. "Will this help?" I asked as I ran my fingers through my hair and caught a few loose strands. I draped them over the ferns.

"Yes, that does make the trail stronger. But you don't need to pull your hair out, Bella. It will be fine."

"I've got a few extras I can spare."

It was gloomy under the trees, and I wished I could walk closer to Edward and hold his hand.

I wedged another hair into a broken branch that cut through my path.

"You don't need to let Alice have her way, you know," Edward said.

"Don't worry about it, Edward. I'm not going to leave you at the altar, regardless." I had a sinking feeling that Alice was going to get her way, mostly because she was totally unscrupulous when there was something she wanted, and also because I was a sucker for guilt trips.

"That's not what I'm worried about. I want this to be what you want it to be."

I repressed a sigh. It would hurt his feelings if I told the truth — that it didn't really matter, because it was all just varying degrees of awful anyway.

"Well, even if she does get her way, we can keep it small. Just us. Emmett can get a clerical license off the Internet."

I giggled. "That does sound better." It wouldn't feel very official if *Emmett* read the vows, which was a plus. But I'd have a hard time keeping a straight face.

"See," he said with a smile. "There's always a compromise."

It took a while for me to reach the spot where the new-born army would be certain to cross my trail, but Edward never got impatient with my pace.

He had to lead a bit more on the way back, to keep me on the same path. It all looked alike to me.

We were almost to the clearing when I fell. I could see the wide opening ahead, and that's probably why I got too eager and forgot to watch my feet. I caught myself before my head bashed into the nearest tree, but a small branch snapped off under my left hand and gouged into my palm.

"Ouch! Oh, fabulous," I muttered.

"Are you all right?"

"I'm fine. Stay where you are. I'm bleeding. It will stop in a minute."

He ignored me. He was right there before I could finish.

"I've got a first aid kit," he said, pulling off the back-pack. "I had a feeling I might need it."

"It's not bad. I can take care of it — you don't have to make yourself uncomfortable."

"I'm not uncomfortable," he said calmly. "Here — let me clean it."

"Wait a second, I just got another idea."

Without looking at the blood and breathing through my mouth, just in case my stomach might react, I pressed my hand against a rock within my reach.

"What are you doing?"

"Jasper will *love* this," I muttered to myself. I started for the clearing again, pressing my palm against every-thing in my path. "I'll bet this really gets them going."

Edward sighed.

"Hold your breath," I told him.

"I'm fine. I just think you're going overboard."

"This is all I get to do. I want to do a good job."

We broke through the last of the trees as I spoke. I let my injured hand graze across the ferns.

"Well, you have," Edward assured me. "The newborns will be frantic, and Jasper will be very impressed with your dedication. Now let me treat your hand — you've gotten the cut dirty."

"Let me do it, please."

He took my hand and smiled as he examined it. "This doesn't bother me anymore."

I watched him carefully as he cleaned the gash, looking for some sign of distress. He continued to breathe evenly in and out, the same small smile on his lips.

"Why not?" I finally asked as he smoothed a bandage across my palm.

He shrugged. "I got over it."

"You . . . *got over it*? When? How?" I tried to remember the last time he'd held his breath around me. All I could think of was my wretched birthday party last September.

Edward pursed his lips, seeming to search for the words. "I lived through an entire twenty-four hours thinking that you were dead, Bella. That changed the way I look at a lot of things."

"Did it change the way I smell to you?"

"Not at all. But . . . having experienced the way it feels to think I've lost you . . . my reactions have changed. My entire being shies away from any course that could inspire that kind of pain again."

I didn't know what to say to that.

He smiled at my expression. "I guess that you could call it a very educational experience."

The wind tore through the clearing then, lashing my hair around my face and making me shiver.

"All right," he said, reaching into his pack again. "You've done your part." He pulled out my heavy winter jacket and held it out for me to slide my arms in. "Now it's out of our hands. Let's go camping!"

I laughed at the mock enthusiasm in his voice.

He took my bandaged hand — the other was in worse shape, still in the brace — and started toward the other side of the clearing.

"Where are we meeting Jacob?" I asked.

"Right here." He gestured to the trees in front of us just as Jacob stepped warily from their shadows.

It shouldn't have surprised me to see him human. I wasn't sure why I'd been looking for the big red-brown wolf.

Jacob seemed bigger again — no doubt a product of my expectations; I must have unconsciously been hoping to see the smaller Jacob from my memory, the easygoing friend who hadn't made everything so difficult. He had his arms folded across his bare chest, a jacket clutched in one fist. His face was expressionless as he watched us.

Edward's lips pulled down at the corners. "There had to have been a better way to do this."

"Too late now," I muttered glumly.

He sighed.

"Hey, Jake," I greeted him when we got closer.

"Hi, Bella."

"Hello, Jacob," Edward said.

Jacob ignored the pleasantry, all business. "Where do I take her?"

Edward pulled a map from a side pocket on the pack and offered it to him. Jacob unfolded it.

"We're here now," Edward said, reaching over to touch the right spot. Jacob recoiled from his hand automatically, and then steadied himself. Edward pretended not to notice.

"And you're taking her up here," Edward continued, tracing a serpentine pattern around the elevation lines on the paper. "Roughly nine miles."

Jacob nodded once.

"When you're about a mile away, you should cross my path. That will lead you in. Do you need the map?"

"No, thanks. I know this area pretty well. I think I know where I'm going."

Jacob seemed to have to work harder than Edward to keep the tone polite.

"I'll take a longer route," Edward said. "And I'll see you in a few hours."

Edward stared at me unhappily. He didn't like this part of the plan.

"See you," I murmured.

Edward faded into the trees, heading in the opposite direction.

As soon as he was gone, Jacob turned cheerful.

"What's up, Bella?" he asked with a big grin.

I rolled my eyes. "Same old, same old."

"Yeah," he agreed. "Bunch of vampires trying to kill you. The usual."

"The usual."

"Well," he said as he shrugged into his jacket to free his arms. "Let's get going."

Making a face, I took a small step closer to him.

He bent down and swept his arm behind my knees, knocking them out from under me. His other arm caught me before my head hit the ground.

"Jerk," I muttered.

Jacob chuckled, already running through the trees. He kept a steady pace, a brisk jog that a fit human could keep up with . . . across a level plane . . . if they weren't burdened with a hundred-plus pounds as he was.

"You don't have to run. You'll get tired."

"Running doesn't make me tired," he said. His breathing was even — like the fixed tempo of a marathoner. "Besides, it will be colder soon. I hope he gets the camp set up before we get there."

I tapped my finger against the thick padding of his parka. "I thought you didn't get cold now."

"I don't. I brought this for you, just in case you weren't prepared." He looked at my jacket, almost as if he were disappointed that I was. "I don't like the way the weather feels. It's making me edgy. Notice how we haven't seen any animals?"

"Um, not really."

"I guess you wouldn't. Your senses are too dull."

I let that pass. "Alice was worried about the storm, too."

"It takes a lot to silence the forest this way. You picked a hell of a night for a camping trip."

"It wasn't entirely my idea."

The pathless way he took began to climb more and more steeply, but it didn't slow him down. He leapt easily from rock to rock, not seeming to need his hands at all. His perfect balance reminded me of a mountain goat.

"What's with the addition to your bracelet?" he asked.

I looked down, and realized that the crystal heart was facing up on my wrist.

I shrugged guiltily. "Another graduation present."

He snorted. "A rock. Figures."

A rock? I was suddenly reminded of Alice's unfinished sentence outside the garage. I stared at the bright white crystal and tried to remember what Alice had been saying before . . . about diamonds. Could she have been trying to say *he's already got one on you*? As in, I was already wearing one diamond from Edward? No, that was impossible. The heart would have to be five carats or something crazy like that! Edward wouldn't —

"So it's been a while since you came down to La Push," Jacob said, interrupting my disturbing conjectures.

"I've been busy," I told him. "And . . . I probably wouldn't have visited, anyway."

He grimaced. "I thought you were supposed to be the forgiving one, and I was the grudge-holder."

I shrugged.

"Been thinking about that last time a lot, have you?"

"Nope."

He laughed. "Either you're lying, or you are the stubbornest person alive."

"I don't know about the second part, but I'm not lying."

I didn't like having this conversation under the present conditions — with his too-warm arms wrapped tightly around me and nothing at all I could do about it. His face was closer than I wanted it to be. I wished I could take a step back.

"A smart person looks at all sides of a decision."

"I have," I retorted.

"If you haven't thought at all about our . . . er, conversation the last time you came over, then that's not true."

"That *conversation* isn't relevant to my decision."

"Some people will go to any lengths to delude themselves."

"I've noticed that werewolves in particular are prone to that mistake — do you think it's a genetic thing?"

"Does that mean that he's a better kisser than I am?" Jacob asked, suddenly glum.

"I really couldn't say, Jake. Edward is the only person I've ever kissed."

"Besides me."

"But I don't count that as a kiss, Jacob. I think of it more as an assault."

"Ouch! That's cold."

I shrugged. I wasn't going to take it back.

"I did apologize about that," he reminded me.

"And I forgave you . . . mostly. It doesn't change the way I remember it."

He muttered something unintelligible.

It was quiet then for a while; there was just the sound of his measured breathing and the wind roaring high above us in the treetops. A cliff face rose sheer beside us, bare, rough gray stone. We followed the base as it curved upward out of the forest.

"I still think it's pretty irresponsible," Jacob suddenly said.

"Whatever you're talking about, you're wrong."

"Think about it, Bella. According to you, you've kissed just one person — who isn't even really a person — in your whole life, and you're calling it quits? How do you know that's what you want? Shouldn't you play the field a little?"

I kept my voice cool. "I know exactly what I want."

"Then it couldn't hurt to double check. Maybe you should try kissing someone else — just for comparison's sake . . . since what happened the other day doesn't count. You could kiss *me*, for example. I don't mind if you want to use me to experiment."

He pulled me tighter against his chest, so that my face was closer to his. He was smiling at his joke, but I wasn't taking any chances.

"Don't mess with me, Jake. I swear I won't stop him if he wants to break your jaw."

The panicky edge to my voice made him smile wider. "If you *ask* me to kiss you, he won't have any reason to get upset. He said that was fine."

"Don't hold your breath, Jake — no, wait, I changed my mind. Go right ahead. Just hold your breath until I ask you to kiss me."

"You're in a bad mood today."

"I wonder why?"

"Sometimes I think you like me better as a wolf."

"Sometimes I do. It probably has something to do with the way you *can't talk.*"

He pursed his broad lips thoughtfully. "No, I don't think that's it. I think it's easier for you to be near me when I'm not human, because you don't have to pretend that you're not attracted to me."

My mouth fell open with a little popping sound. I snapped it shut at once, grinding my teeth together.

He heard that. His lips pulled tightly across his face in a triumphant smile.

I took a slow breath before I spoke. "No. I'm pretty sure it's because you can't talk."

He sighed. "Do you ever get tired of lying to yourself? You have to know how aware you are of me. Physically, I mean."

"How could anyone *not* be aware of you physically, Jacob?" I demanded. "You're an enormous monster who refuses to respect anyone else's personal space."

"I make you nervous. But only when I'm human. When I'm a wolf, you're more comfortable around me."

"Nervousness and irritation are not the same thing."

He stared at me for a minute, slowing to a walk, the amusement draining from his face. His eyes narrowed, turned black in the shadow of his brows. His breathing, so regular as he ran, started to accelerate. Slowly, he leaned his face closer to mine.

I stared him down, knowing exactly what he was trying to do.

"It's your face," I reminded him.

He laughed loudly and started jogging again. "I don't really want to fight with your vampire tonight — I mean, any other night, sure. But we both have a job to do tomorrow, and I wouldn't want to leave the Cullens one short."

The sudden, unexpected swell of shame distorted my expression.

"I know, I know," he responded, not understanding. "You think he could take me."

I couldn't speak. I was leaving them one short. What if someone got hurt because I was so weak? But what if I was brave and Edward . . . I couldn't even think it.

"What's the matter with you, Bella?" The joking bravado vanished from his face, revealing my Jacob underneath, like pulling a mask away. "If something I said upset you, you know I was only kidding. I didn't mean anything — hey, are you okay? Don't cry, Bella," he pled.

I tried to pull myself together. "I'm not going to cry."

"What did I say?"

"It's nothing you said. It's just, well, it's me. I did something . . . bad."

He stared at me, his eyes wide with confusion.

"Edward isn't going to fight tomorrow," I whispered the explanation. "I'm making him stay with me. I am a huge coward."

He frowned. "You think this isn't going to work? That they'll find you here? Do you know something I don't know?"

"No, no. I'm not afraid of that. I just . . . I *can't* let him go. If he didn't come back . . ." I shuddered, closing my eyes to escape the thought.

Jacob was quiet.

I kept whispering, my eyes shut. "If anyone gets hurt, it will always be my fault. And even if no one does . . . I was horrible. I had to be, to convince him to stay with me. *He* won't hold it against me, but I'll always know what I'm capable of." I felt just a tiny bit better, getting this off my chest. Even if I could only confess it to Jacob.

He snorted. My eyes opened slowly, and I was sad to see that the hard mask was back.

"I can't believe he let you talk him out of going. I wouldn't miss this for anything."

I sighed. "I know."

"That doesn't mean anything, though." He was suddenly backtracking. "That doesn't mean that he loves you more than I do."

"But *you* wouldn't stay with me, even if I begged."

He pursed his lips for a moment, and I wondered if he would try to deny it. We both knew the truth. "That's only because I know you better," he said at last. "Everything's going to go without a hitch. Even if you'd asked and I'd said no, you wouldn't be mad at me afterwards."

"If everything does go without a hitch, you're probably right. I wouldn't be mad. But the whole time you're gone, I'll be sick with worry, Jake. Crazy with it."

"Why?" he asked gruffly. "Why does it matter to you if something happens to me?"

"Don't say that. You know how much you mean to me.

I'm sorry it's not in the way you want, but that's just how it is. You're my best friend. At least, you used to be. And still sometimes are . . . when you let your guard down."

He smiled the old smile that I loved. "I'm always that," he promised. "Even when I don't . . . behave as well as I should. Underneath, I'm always in here."

"I know. Why else would I put up with all of your crap?"

He laughed with me, and then his eyes were sad. "*When* are you finally going to figure out that you're in love with me, too?"

"Leave it to you to ruin the moment."

"I'm not saying you don't love him. I'm not stupid. But it's possible to love more than one person at a time, Bella. I've seen it in action."

"I'm not some freaky werewolf, Jacob."

He wrinkled his nose, and I was about to apologize for that last jab, but he changed the subject.

"We're not far now, I can smell him."

I sighed in relief.

He misinterpreted my meaning. "I'd happily slow down, Bella, but you're going to want to be under shelter before *that* hits."

We both looked up at the sky.

A solid wall of purple-black cloud was racing in from the west, blackening the forest beneath it as it came.

"Wow," I muttered. "You'd better hurry, Jake. You'll want to get home before it gets here."

"I'm not going home."

I glared at him, exasperated. "You're not camping with us."

"Not technically — as in, sharing your tent or anything. I prefer the storm to the smell. But I'm sure your bloodsucker will want to keep in touch with the pack for coordination purposes, and so I will graciously provide that service."

"I thought that was Seth's job."

"He'll take over tomorrow, during the fight."

The reminder silenced me for a second. I stared at him, worry springing up again with sudden fierceness.

"I don't suppose there's any way you'd just stay since you're already here?" I suggested. "If I *did* beg? Or trade back the lifetime of servitude or something?"

"Tempting, but no. Then again, the begging might be interesting to see. You can give it a go if you like."

"There's really nothing, *nothing* at all I can say?"

"Nope. Not unless you can promise me a better fight. Anyway, Sam's calling the shots, not me."

That reminded me.

"Edward told me something the other day . . . about you."

He bristled. "It's probably a lie."

"Oh, really? You aren't second in command of the pack, then?"

He blinked, his face going blank with surprise. "Oh. That."

"How come you never told me that?"

"Why would I? It's no big thing."

"I don't know. Why not? It's interesting. So, how does that work? How did Sam end up as the Alpha, and you as the . . . the Beta?"

Jacob chuckled at my invented term. "Sam was the first, the oldest. It made sense for him to take charge."

I frowned. "But shouldn't Jared or Paul be second, then? They were the next to change."

"Well . . . it's hard to explain," Jacob said evasively.

"Try."

He sighed. "It's more about the lineage, you know? Sort of old-fashioned. Why should it matter who your grandpa was, right?"

I remembered something Jacob had told me a long time ago, before either of us had known anything about werewolves.

"Didn't you say that Ephraim Black was the last chief the Quileutes had?"

"Yeah, that's right. Because he was the Alpha. Did you know that, technically, Sam's the chief of the whole tribe now?" He laughed. "Crazy traditions."

I thought about that for a second, trying to make all the pieces fit. "But you also said that people listened to your dad more than anyone else on the council, because he was Ephraim's grandson?"

"What about it?"

"Well, if it's about the lineage . . . shouldn't you be the chief, then?"

Jacob didn't answer me. He stared into the darkening forest, as if he suddenly needed to concentrate on where he was going.

"Jake?"

"No. That's Sam's job." He kept his eyes on our path-less course.

"Why? His great-granddad was Levi Uley, right? Was Levi an Alpha, too?"

"There's only one Alpha," he answered automatically.

"So what was Levi?"

"Sort of a Beta, I guess." He snorted at my term. "Like me."

"That doesn't make sense."

"It doesn't matter."

"I just want to understand."

Jacob finally met my confused gaze, and then sighed. "Yeah. I was supposed to be the Alpha."

My eyebrows pulled together. "Sam didn't want to step down?"

"Hardly. I didn't want to step up."

"Why not?"

He frowned, uncomfortable with my questions. Well, it was his turn to feel uncomfortable.

"I didn't want any of it, Bella. I didn't want anything to change. I didn't want to be some legendary chief. I didn't want to be part of a pack of werewolves, let alone their leader. I wouldn't take it when Sam offered."

I thought about this for a long moment. Jacob didn't interrupt. He stared into the forest again.

"But I thought you were happier. That you were okay with this," I finally whispered.

Jacob smiled down at me reassuringly. "Yeah. It's really not so bad. Exciting sometimes, like with this thing to-morrow. But at first it sort of felt like being drafted into a war you didn't know existed. There was no choice, you know? And it was so final." He shrugged. "Anyway, I guess

I'm glad now. It has to be done, and could I trust someone else to get it right? It's better to make sure myself."

I stared at him, feeling an unexpected kind of awe for my friend. He was more of a grown-up than I'd ever given him credit for. Like with Billy the other night at the bonfire, there was a majesty here that I'd never suspected.

"Chief Jacob," I whispered, smiling at the way the words sounded together.

He rolled his eyes.

Just then, the wind shook more fiercely through the trees around us, and it felt like it was blowing straight off a glacier. The sharp sound of wood cracking echoed off the mountain. Though the light was vanishing as the grisly cloud covered the sky, I could still see the little white specks that fluttered past us.

Jacob stepped up the pace, keeping his eyes on the ground now as he flat out sprinted. I curled more willingly against his chest, recoiling from the unwelcome snow.

It was only minutes later that he dashed around to the lee side of the stony peak and we could see the little tent nestled up against the sheltering face. More flurries were falling around us, but the wind was too fierce to let them settle anywhere.

"Bella!" Edward called out in acute relief. We'd caught him in the middle of pacing back and forth across the little open space.

He flashed to my side, sort of blurring as he moved so swiftly. Jacob cringed, and then set me on my feet. Edward ignored his reaction and caught me in a tight hug.

"Thank you," Edward said over my head. His tone was

unmistakably sincere. "That was quicker than I expected, and I truly appreciate it."

I twisted to see Jacob's response.

Jacob merely shrugged, all the friendliness wiped clean from his face. "Get her inside. This is going to be bad — my hair's standing up on my scalp. Is that tent secure?"

"I all but welded it to the rock."

"Good."

Jacob looked up at the sky — now black with the storm, sprinkled with the swirling bits of snow. His nostrils flared.

"I'm going to change," he said. "I want to know what's going on back home."

He hung his jacket on a low, stubby branch, and walked into the murky forest without a backward glance.

22. FIRE AND ICE

THE WIND SHOOK THE TENT AGAIN, AND I SHOOK WITH IT.

The temperature was dropping. I could feel it through the down bag, through my jacket. I was fully dressed, my hiking boots still laced into place. It didn't make any difference. How could it be so cold? How could it *keep* getting colder? It had to bottom out sometime, didn't it?

"W-w-w-w-w-what t-t-t-t-time is it?" I forced the words through my rattling teeth.

"Two," Edward answered.

Edward sat as far from me as possible in the cramped space, afraid to even breathe on me when I was already so cold. It was too dark to see his face, but his voice was wild with worry, indecision, and frustration.

"Maybe . . ."

"No, I'm f-f-f-f-f-fine, r-r-r-really. I don't w-w-w-want to g-go outside."

He'd tried to talk me into making a run for it a dozen times already, but I was terrified of leaving my shelter. If it was this cold in here, protected from the raging wind, I could imagine how bad it would be if we were running through it.

And it would waste all our efforts this afternoon. Would we have enough time to reset ourselves when the storm was over? What if it didn't end? It made no sense to move now. I could shiver my way through one night.

I was worried that the trail I had laid would be lost, but he promised that it would still be plain to the coming monsters.

"What can I do?" he almost begged.

I just shook my head.

Out in the snow, Jacob whined unhappily.

"G-g-g-get out of h-h-h-ere," I ordered, again.

"He's just worried about you," Edward translated. "He's fine. *His* body is equipped to deal with this."

"H-h-h-h-h-h." I wanted to say that he should still leave, but I couldn't get it past my teeth. I nearly bit my tongue off trying. At least Jacob *did* seem to be well equipped for the snow, better even than the others in his pack with his thicker, longer, shaggy russet fur. I wondered why that was.

Jacob whimpered, a high-pitched, grating sound of complaint.

"What do you want me to do?" Edward growled, too

anxious to bother with politeness anymore. "Carry her through *that*? I don't see you making yourself useful. Why don't you go fetch a space heater or something?"

"I'm ok-k-k-k-k-*kay*," I protested. Judging from Edward's groan and the muted growl outside the tent, I hadn't convinced anyone. The wind rocked the tent roughly, and I shuddered in harmony with it.

A sudden howl ripped through the roar of the wind, and I covered my ears against the noise. Edward scowled.

"That was hardly necessary," he muttered. "And that's the worst idea I've ever heard," he called more loudly.

"Better than anything you've come up with," Jacob answered, his human voice startling me. *"Go fetch a space heater,"* he grumbled. "I'm not a St. Bernard."

I heard the sound of the zipper around the tent door pulling swiftly down.

Jacob slid through the smallest opening he could manage, while the arctic air flowed in around him, a few flecks of snow falling to the floor of the tent. I shivered so hard it was a convulsion.

"I don't like this," Edward hissed as Jake zipped the tent door shut. "Just give her the coat and get out."

My eyes were adjusted enough to see shapes — Jacob was carrying the parka that had been hanging on a tree next to the tent.

I tried to ask what they were talking about, but all that came out of my mouth was, "W-w-w-w-w-w," as the shivering made me stutter uncontrollably.

"The parka's for tomorrow — she's too cold to warm it up by herself. It's frozen." He dropped it by the door. "You said she needed a space heater, and here I am." Jacob held his arms as wide as the tent allowed. As usual, when he'd been running around as a wolf, he'd only thrown on the bare essentials — just a pair of sweats, no shirt, no shoes.

"J-J-J-J-Jake, you'll f-f-f-freez-z-z-ze," I tried to complain.

"Not me," he said cheerfully. "I run at a toasty one-oh-eight point nine these days. I'll have you sweating in no time."

Edward snarled, but Jacob didn't even look at him. Instead, he crawled to my side and started unzipping my sleeping bag.

Edward's hand was suddenly hard on his shoulder, restraining, snow white against the dark skin. Jacob's jaw clenched, his nostrils flaring, his body recoiling from the cold touch. The long muscles in his arms flexed automatically.

"Get your hand off of me," he growled through his teeth.

"Keep your hands off of her," Edward answered blackly.

"D-d-d-don't f-f-f-f-fight," I pleaded. Another tremor rocked through me. It felt like my teeth were going to shatter, they were slamming together so hard.

"I'm sure she'll thank you for this when her toes turn black and drop off," Jacob snapped.

Edward hesitated, then his hand fell away and he slid back to his position in the corner.

His voice was flat and frightening. "Watch yourself."

Jacob chuckled.

"Scoot over, Bella," he said, zipping the sleeping bag open farther.

I stared at him in outrage. No wonder Edward was reacting this way.

"N-n-n-n-n," I tried to protest.

"Don't be stupid," he said, exasperated. "Don't you *like* having ten toes?"

He crammed his body into the nonexistent space, forcing the zipper up behind himself.

And then I couldn't object — I didn't want to anymore. He was so warm. His arms constricted around me, holding me snugly against his bare chest. The heat was irresistible, like air after being underwater for too long. He cringed when I pressed my icy fingers eagerly against his skin.

"Jeez, you're freezing, Bella," he complained.

"S-s-s-s-sorry," I stuttered.

"Try to relax," he suggested as another shiver rippled through me violently. "You'll be warm in a minute. Of course, you'd warm up faster if you took your clothes off."

Edward growled sharply.

"That's just a simple fact," Jacob defended himself. "Survival one-oh-one."

"C-c-cut it out, Jake," I said angrily, though my body refused to even try to pull away from him. "N-n-n-nobody really n-n-n-n-needs all ten t-t-t-toes."

"Don't worry about the bloodsucker," Jacob suggested, and his tone was smug. "He's just jealous."

"Of course I am." Edward's voice was velvet again, under

control, a musical murmur in the darkness. "You don't have the faintest idea how much I wish I could do what you're doing for her, mongrel."

"Those are the breaks," Jacob said lightly, but then his tone soured. "At least you know she wishes it was you."

"True," Edward agreed.

The shuddering slowed, became bearable while they wrangled.

"There," Jacob said, pleased. "Feeling better?"

I was finally able to speak clearly. "Yes."

"Your lips are still blue," he mused. "Want me to warm those up for you, too? You only have to ask."

Edward sighed heavily.

"Behave yourself," I muttered, pressing my face against his shoulder. He flinched again when my cold skin touched his, and I smiled with slightly vindictive satisfaction.

It was already warm and snug inside the sleeping bag. Jacob's body heat seemed to radiate from every side — maybe because there was so *much* of him. I kicked my boots off, and pushed my toes against his legs. He jumped slightly, and then leaned his head down to press his hot cheek against my numb ear.

I noticed that Jacob's skin had a woodsy, musky scent — it fit the setting, here in the middle of the forest. It was nice. I wondered if the Cullens and the Quileutes weren't just playing up that whole odor issue because of their prejudices. Everyone smelled fine to me.

The storm howled like an animal attacking the tent, but it didn't worry me now. Jacob was out of the cold, and so was I. Plus, I was simply too exhausted to worry about anything — tired from just staying awake so late, and aching from the muscle spasms. My body relaxed slowly as I thawed, piece by frozen piece, and then turned limp.

"Jake?" I mumbled sleepily. "Can I ask you something? I'm not trying to be a jerk or anything, I'm honestly curious." They were the same words he'd used in my kitchen . . . how long ago was it now?

"Sure," he chuckled, remembering.

"Why are you so much furrier than your friends? You don't have to answer if I'm being rude." I didn't know the rules for etiquette as they applied to werewolf culture.

"Because my hair is longer," he said, amused — my question hadn't offended him, at least. He shook his head so that his unkempt hair — grown out to his chin now — tickled my cheek.

"Oh." I was surprised, but it made sense. So that was why they'd all cropped their hair in the beginning, when they joined the pack. "Then why don't you cut it? Do you like to be shaggy?"

He didn't answer right away this time, and Edward laughed under his breath.

"Sorry," I said, pausing to yawn. "I didn't mean to pry. You don't have to tell me."

Jacob made an annoyed sound. "Oh, he'll tell you anyway, so I might as well. . . . I was growing my hair out because . . . it seemed like you liked it better long."

"Oh." I felt awkward. "I, er, like it both ways, Jake. You don't need to be . . . inconvenienced."

He shrugged. "Turns out it was very convenient tonight, so don't worry about it."

I didn't have anything else to say. As the silence lengthened, my eyelids drooped and shut, and my breathing grew slower, more even.

"That's right, honey, go to sleep," Jacob whispered.

I sighed, content, already half-unconscious.

"Seth is here," Edward muttered to Jacob, and I suddenly understood the point of the howling.

"Perfect. Now you can keep an eye on everything else, while I take care of your girlfriend for you."

Edward didn't answer, but I groaned groggily. "Stop it," I muttered.

It was quiet then, inside at least. Outside, the wind shrieked insanely through the trees. The shimmying of the tent made it hard to sleep. The poles would suddenly jerk and quiver, pulling me back from the edge of unconsciousness each time I was close to slipping under. I felt so bad for the wolf, the boy that was stuck outside in the snow.

My mind wandered as I waited for sleep to find me. This warm little space made me think of the early days with Jacob, and I remembered how it used to be when he was my replacement sun, the warmth that made my empty life livable. It had been a while since I'd thought of Jake that way, but here he was, warming me again.

"*Please!*" Edward hissed. "Do you *mind*!"

"What?" Jacob whispered back, his tone surprised.

"Do you think you could *attempt* to control your thoughts?" Edward's low whisper was furious.

"No one said you had to listen," Jacob muttered, defiant, yet still embarrassed. "Get out of my head."

"I wish I *could.* You have no idea how loud your little fantasies are. It's like you're shouting them at me."

"I'll try to keep it down," Jacob whispered sarcastically. There was a brief moment of silence.

"Yes," Edward answered an unspoken thought in a murmur so low I barely made it out. "I'm jealous of that, too."

"I figured it was like that," Jacob whispered smugly. "Sort of evens the playing field up a little, doesn't it?"

Edward chuckled. "In your dreams."

"You know, she could still change her mind," Jacob taunted him. "Considering *all* the things I could do with her that you can't. At least, not without killing her, that is."

"Go to sleep, Jacob," Edward murmured. "You're starting to get on my nerves."

"I think I will. I'm really very comfortable."

Edward didn't answer.

I was too far gone to ask them to stop talking about me like I wasn't there. The conversation had taken on a dreamlike quality to me, and I wasn't sure I was really awake.

"Maybe I would," Edward said after a moment, answering a question I hadn't heard.

"But would you be honest?"

"You can always ask and see." Edward's tone made me wonder if I was missing out on a joke.

"Well, you see inside my head — let me see inside yours tonight, it's only fair," Jacob said.

"Your head is full of questions. Which one do you want me to answer?"

"The jealousy . . . it *has* to be eating at you. You can't

be as sure of yourself as you seem. Unless you have no emotions at all."

"Of course it is," Edward agreed, no longer amused. "Right now it's so bad that I can barely control my voice. Of course, it's even worse when she's away from me, with you, and I can't see her."

"Do you think about it all the time?" Jacob whispered. "Does it make it hard to concentrate when she's not with you?"

"Yes and no," Edward said; he seemed determined to answer honestly. "My mind doesn't work quite the same as yours. I can think of many more things at one time. Of course, that means that I'm *always* able to think of you, always able to wonder if that's where her mind is, when she's quiet and thoughtful."

They were both still for a minute.

"Yes, I would guess that she thinks about you often," Edward murmured in response to Jacob's thoughts. "More often than I like. She worries that you're unhappy. Not that you don't know that. Not that you don't *use* that."

"I have to use whatever I can," Jacob muttered. "I'm not working with your advantages — advantages like her knowing she's in love with you."

"That helps," Edward agreed in a mild tone.

Jacob was defiant. "She's in love with me, too, you know."

Edward didn't answer.

Jacob sighed. "But she *doesn't* know it."

"I can't tell you if you're right."

"Does that bother you? Do you wish you could see what she's thinking, too?"

"Yes . . . and no, again. She likes it better this way, and, though it sometimes drives me insane, I'd rather she was happy."

The wind ripped around the tent, shaking it like an earthquake. Jacob's arms tightened around me protectively.

"Thank you," Edward whispered. "Odd as this might sound, I suppose I'm glad you're here, Jacob."

"You mean, 'as much as I'd love to kill you, I'm glad she's warm,' right?"

"It's an uncomfortable truce, isn't it?"

Jacob's whisper was suddenly smug. "I knew you were just as crazy jealous as I am."

"I'm not such a fool as to wear it on my sleeve like you do. It doesn't help your case, you know."

"You have more patience than I do."

"I should. I've had a hundred years to gain it. A hundred years of waiting for *her.*"

"So . . . at what point did you decide to play the very patient good guy?"

"When I saw how much it was hurting her to make her choose. It's not usually this difficult to control. I can smother the . . . less civilized feelings I may have for you fairly easily most of the time. Sometimes I think she sees through me, but I can't be sure."

"I think you were just worried that if you really forced her to choose, she might not choose you."

Edward didn't answer right away. "That was a part of it,"

he finally admitted. "But only a small part. We all have our moments of doubt. Mostly I was worried that she'd hurt herself trying to sneak away to see you. After I'd accepted that she was more or less safe with you — as safe as Bella ever is — it seemed best to stop driving her to extremes."

Jacob sighed. "I'd tell her all of this, but she'd never believe me."

"I know." It sounded like Edward was smiling.

"You think you know everything," Jacob muttered.

"I don't know the future," Edward said, his voice suddenly unsure.

There was a long pause.

"What would you do if she changed her mind?" Jacob asked.

"I don't know that either."

Jacob chuckled quietly. "Would you try to kill me?" Sarcastic again, as if doubting Edward's ability to do it.

"No."

"Why not?" Jacob's tone was still jeering.

"Do you really think I would hurt her that way?"

Jacob hesitated for a second, and then sighed. "Yeah, you're right. I know that's right. But sometimes . . ."

"Sometimes it's an intriguing idea."

Jacob pressed his face into the sleeping bag to muffle his laughter. "Exactly," he eventually agreed.

What a strange dream this was. I wondered if it was the relentless wind that made me imagine all the whispering. Only the wind was screaming rather than whispering . . .

"What is it like? Losing her?" Jacob asked after a quiet

moment, and there was no hint of humor in his suddenly hoarse voice. "When you thought that you'd lost her forever? How did you . . . cope?"

"That's very difficult for me to talk about."

Jacob waited.

"There were two different times that I thought that." Edward spoke each word just a little slower than normal. "The first time, when I thought I could leave her . . . that was . . . almost bearable. Because I thought she would forget me and it would be like I hadn't touched her life. For over six months I was able to stay away, to keep my promise that I wouldn't interfere again. It was getting close — I was fighting but I knew I wasn't going to win; I would have come back . . . just to check on her. That's what I would have told myself, anyway. And if I'd found her reasonably happy . . . I like to think that I could have gone away again.

"But she wasn't happy. And I would have stayed. That's how she convinced me to stay with her tomorrow, of course. You were wondering about that before, what could possibly motivate me . . . what she was feeling so needlessly guilty about. She reminded me of what it did to her when I left — what it still does to her when I leave. She feels horrible about bringing that up, but she's right. I'll never be able to make up for that, but I'll never stop trying anyway."

Jacob didn't respond for a moment, listening to the storm or digesting what he'd heard, I didn't know which.

"And the other time — when you thought she was dead?" Jacob whispered roughly.

"Yes." Edward answered a different question. "It will probably feel like that to you, won't it? The way you perceive us, you might not be able to see her as *Bella* anymore. But that's who she'll be."

"That's not what I asked."

Edward's voice came back fast and hard. "I can't tell you how it felt. There aren't words."

Jacob's arms flexed around me.

"But you left because you didn't want to make her a bloodsucker. You *want* her to be human."

Edward spoke slowly. "Jacob, from the second that I realized that I loved her, I knew there were only four possibilities. The first alternative, the best one for Bella, would be if she didn't feel as strongly for me — if she got over me and moved on. I would accept that, though it would never change the way I felt. You think of me as a . . . living stone — hard and cold. That's true. We are set the way we are, and it is very rare for us to experience a real change. When that happens, as when Bella entered my life, it is a permanent change. There's no going back. . . .

"The second alternative, the one I'd originally chosen, was to stay with her throughout her human life. It wasn't a good option for her, to waste her life with someone who couldn't be human with her, but it was the alternative I could most easily face. Knowing all along that, when she died, I would find a way to die, too. Sixty years, seventy years — it would seem like a very, very short time to me. . . . But then it proved much too dangerous for her to live in such close proximity with my world. It seemed like everything that could go wrong did. Or hung over us . . .

waiting to go wrong. I was terrified that I wouldn't get those sixty years if I stayed near her while she was human.

"So I chose option three. Which turned out to be the worst mistake of my very long life, as you know. I chose to take myself out of her world, hoping to force her into the first alternative. It didn't work, and it very nearly killed us both.

"What do I have left but the fourth option? It's what she wants — at least, she thinks she does. I've been trying to delay her, to give her time to find a reason to change her mind, but she's very . . . stubborn. You know *that*. I'll be lucky to stretch this out a few more months. She has a horror of getting older, and her birthday is in September. . . ."

"I like option one," Jacob muttered.

Edward didn't respond.

"You know *exactly* how much I hate to accept this," Jacob whispered slowly, "but I can see that you do love her . . . in your way. I can't argue with that anymore.

"Given that, I don't think you should give up on the first alternative, not yet. I think there's a very good chance that she would be okay. After time. You know, if she hadn't jumped off a cliff in March . . . and if you'd waited another six months to check on her. . . . Well, you might have found her reasonably happy. I had a game plan."

Edward chuckled. "Maybe it would have worked. It was a well thought-out plan."

"Yeah." Jake sighed. "But . . . ," suddenly he was whispering so fast the words got tangled, "give me a year, bl — Edward. I really think I could make her happy. She's stubborn, no one knows that better than I do, but she's capable of healing. She would have healed before. And she could be human, with Charlie and Renée, and she could grow up, and have kids and . . . be Bella.

"You love her enough that you have to see the advantages of that plan. She thinks you're very unselfish . . . are you really? Can you consider the idea that I might be better for her than you are?"

"I *have* considered it," Edward answered quietly. "In some ways, you would be better suited for her than another human. Bella takes some looking after, and you're strong enough that you could protect her from herself, and from everything that conspires against her. You *have* done that already, and I'll owe you for that for as long as I live — forever — whichever comes first. . . ."

"I even asked Alice if she could see that — see if Bella would be better off with you. She couldn't, of course. She can't see you, and then Bella's sure of her course, for now.

"But I'm not stupid enough to make the same mistake I made before, Jacob. I won't try to force her into that first option again. As long as she wants me, I'm here."

"And if she were to decide that she wanted me?" Jacob challenged. "Okay, it's a long shot, I'll give you that."

"I would let her go."

"Just like that?"

"In the sense that I'd never show her how hard it was for me, yes. But I would keep watch. You see, Jacob, *you* might leave *her* someday. Like Sam and Emily, you wouldn't have a choice. I would always be waiting in the wings, hoping for that to happen."

Jacob snorted quietly. "Well, you've been much more honest than I had any right to expect . . . Edward. Thanks for letting me in your head."

"As I said, I'm feeling oddly grateful for your presence in her life tonight. It was the least I could do. . . . You know, Jacob, if it weren't for the fact that we're natural enemies and that you're also trying to steal away the reason for my existence, I might actually like you."

"Maybe . . . if you weren't a disgusting vampire who was planning to suck out the life of the girl I love . . . well, no, not even then."

Edward chuckled.

"Can I ask you something?" Edward said after a moment.

"Why would you have to ask?"

"I can only hear if you think of it. It's just a story that Bella seemed reluctant to tell me about the other day. Something about a third wife . . . ?"

"What about it?"

Edward didn't answer, listening to the story in Jacob's head. I heard his low hiss in the darkness.

"What?" Jacob demanded again.

"Of course," Edward seethed. "Of course! I rather wish your elders had kept *that* story to themselves, Jacob."

"You don't like the leeches being painted as the bad guys?" Jacob mocked. "You know, they *are*. Then *and* now."

"I really couldn't care less about that part. Can't you guess which character Bella would identify with?"

It took Jacob a minute. "Oh. Ugh. The third wife. Okay, I see your point."

"She wants to be there in the clearing. To do what little

she can, as she puts it." He sighed. "That was the second-ary reason for my staying with her tomorrow. She's quite inventive when she wants something."

"You know, your military brother gave her the idea just as much as the story did."

"Neither side meant any harm," Edward whispered, peace-making now.

"And when does *this* little truce end?" Jacob asked. "First light? Or do we wait until after the fight?"

There was a pause as they both considered.

"First light," they whispered together, and then laughed quietly.

"Sleep well, Jacob," Edward murmured. "Enjoy the moment."

It was quiet again, and the tent held still for a few min-utes. The wind seemed to have decided that it wasn't go-ing to flatten us after all, and was giving up the fight.

Edward groaned softly. "I didn't mean that quite so lit-erally."

"Sorry," Jacob whispered. "You could leave, you know — give us a little privacy."

"Would you like me to *help* you sleep, Jacob?" Edward offered.

"You could try," Jacob said, unconcerned. "It would be interesting to see who walked away, wouldn't it?"

"Don't tempt me too far, wolf. My patience isn't *that* perfect."

Jacob whispered a laugh. "I'd rather not move just now, if you don't mind."

Edward started humming to himself, louder than usual — trying to drown out Jacob's thoughts, I assumed. But it was my lullaby he hummed, and, despite my growing discomfort with this whispered dream, I sank deeper into unconsciousness . . . into other dreams that made better sense. . . .

23. MONSTER

When I woke up in the morning, it was very bright — even inside the tent, the sunlight hurt my eyes. And I *was* sweating, as Jacob had predicted. Jacob was snoring lightly in my ear, his arms still wrapped around me.

I pulled my head away from his feverishly warm chest and felt the sting of the cold morning on my clammy cheek. Jacob sighed in his sleep; his arms tightened unconsciously.

I squirmed, unable to loosen his hold, struggling to lift my head enough to see. . . .

Edward met my gaze evenly. His expression was calm, but the pain in his eyes was unconcealed.

"Is it any warmer out there?" I whispered.

"Yes. I don't think the space heater will be necessary today."

I tried to get to the zipper, but I couldn't free my arms. I strained, fighting against Jacob's inert strength. Jacob muttered, still fast asleep, his arms constricting again.

"Some help?" I asked quietly.

Edward smiled. "Did you want me to take his arms all the way off?"

"No, thank you. Just get me free. I'm going to get heat stroke."

Edward unzipped the sleeping bag in a swift, abrupt movement. Jacob fell out, his bare back hitting the icy floor of the tent.

"Hey!" he complained, his eyes flying open. Instinctively, he flinched away from the cold, rolling onto me. I gasped as his weight knocked the breath out of me.

And then his weight was gone. I felt the impact as Jacob flew into one of the tent poles and the tent shuddered.

The growling erupted from all around. Edward was crouching in front of me, and I couldn't see his face, but the snarls were ripping angrily out of his chest. Jacob was half-crouched, too, his whole body quivering, while growls rumbled through his clenched teeth. Outside the tent, Seth Clearwater's vicious snarls echoed off the rocks.

"Stop it, stop it!" I yelled, scrambling awkwardly to put myself between them. The space was so small that I didn't have to stretch far to put one hand on each of their chests. Edward wrapped his hand around my waist, ready to yank me out of the way.

"Stop it, now," I warned him.

Under my touch, Jacob began to calm himself. The shaking slowed, but his teeth were still bared, his eyes furiously focused on Edward. Seth continued to growl, a long unbroken sound, a violent background to the sudden silence in the tent.

"Jacob?" I asked, waiting until he finally dropped his glare to look at me. "Are you hurt?"

"Of course not!" he hissed.

I turned to Edward. He was looking at me, his expression hard and angry. "That wasn't nice. You should say sorry."

His eyes widened in disgust. "You must be joking — he was crushing you!"

"Because you dumped him on the floor! He didn't do it on purpose, and he didn't hurt me."

Edward groaned, revolted. Slowly, he looked up to glare at Jacob with hostile eyes. "My apologies, dog."

"No harm done," Jacob said, a taunting edge to his voice.

It was still cold, though not as cold as it had been. I curled my arms around my chest.

"Here," Edward said, calm again. He took the parka off the floor and wrapped it over the top of my coat.

"That's Jacob's," I objected.

"Jacob has a fur coat," Edward hinted.

"I'll just use the sleeping bag again, if you don't mind." Jacob ignored him, climbing around us and sliding into the down bag. "I wasn't quite ready to wake up. That wasn't the best night's sleep I ever had."

"It was your idea," Edward said impassively.

Jacob was curled up, his eyes already closed. He yawned.

"I didn't say it wasn't the best night I've ever spent. Just that I didn't get a lot of sleep. I thought Bella was never going to shut up."

I winced, wondering what might have come out of my mouth in my sleep. The possibilities were horrifying.

"I'm glad you enjoyed yourself," Edward murmured.

Jacob's dark eyes fluttered open. "Didn't you have a nice night, then?" he asked, smug.

"It wasn't the worst night of my life."

"Did it make the top ten?" Jacob asked with perverse enjoyment.

"Possibly."

Jacob smiled and closed his eyes.

"But," Edward went on, "if I had been able to take your place last night, it would not have made the top ten of the *best* nights of my life. Dream about that."

Jacob's eyes opened into a glare. He sat up stiffly, his shoulders tense.

"You know what? I think it's too crowded in here."

"I couldn't agree more."

I elbowed Edward in the ribs — probably giving myself a bruise.

"Guess I'll catch up on my sleep later, then." Jacob made a face. "I need to talk to Sam anyway."

He rolled to his knees and grabbed the door's zipper.

Pain crackled down my spine and lodged in my stomach as I abruptly realized that this could be the last time I would see him. He was going back to Sam, back to fight the horde of bloodthirsty newborn vampires.

"Jake, wait —" I reached after him, my hand sliding down his arm.

He jerked his arm away before my fingers could find purchase.

"Please, Jake? Won't you stay?"

"No."

The word was hard and cold. I knew my face gave away my pain, because he exhaled and half a smile softened his expression.

"Don't worry about me, Bells. I'll be fine, just like I always am." He forced a laugh. "'Sides, you think I'm going to let Seth go in my place — have all the fun and steal all the glory? Right." He snorted.

"Be careful —"

He shoved out of the tent before I could finish.

"Give it a rest, Bella," I heard him mutter as he re-zipped the door.

I listened for the sound of his retreating footsteps, but it was perfectly still. No more wind. I could hear morning birdsong far away on the mountain, and nothing else. Jacob moved in silence now.

I huddled in my coats, and leaned against Edward's shoulder. We were quiet for a long time.

"How much longer?" I asked.

"Alice told Sam it should be an hour or so," Edward said, soft and bleak.

"We stay together. No matter what."

"No matter what," he agreed, his eyes tight.

"I know," I said. "I'm terrified for them, too."

"They know how to handle themselves," Edward assured me, purposely making his voice light. "I just hate missing the fun."

Again with the *fun*. My nostrils flared.

He put his arm around my shoulder. "Don't worry," he urged, and then he kissed my forehead.

As if there was any way to avoid that. "Sure, sure."

"Do you want me to distract you?" He breathed, running his cold fingers along my cheekbone.

I shivered involuntarily; the morning was still frosty.

"Maybe not right now," he answered himself, pulling his hand away.

"There are other ways to distract me."

"What would you like?"

"You could tell me about your ten best nights," I suggested. "I'm curious."

He laughed. "Try to guess."

I shook my head. "There're too many nights I don't know about. A century of them."

"I'll narrow it down for you. All of my best nights have happened since I met you."

"Really?"

"Yes, really — and by quite a wide margin, too."

I thought for a minute. "I can only think of mine," I admitted.

"They might be the same," he encouraged.

"Well, there was the first night. The night you stayed."

"Yes, that's one of mine, too. Of course, you were unconscious for my favorite part."

"That's right," I remembered. "I was talking that night, too."

"Yes," he agreed.

My face got hot as I wondered again what I might have said while sleeping in Jacob's arms. I couldn't remember what I'd dreamed about, or if I'd dreamed at all, so that was no help.

"What did I say last night?" I whispered more quietly than before.

He shrugged instead of answering, and I winced.

"That bad?"

"Nothing too horrible," he sighed.

"Please tell me."

"Mostly you said my name, the same as usual."

"That's not bad," I agreed cautiously.

"Near the end, though, you started mumbling some nonsense about 'Jacob, my Jacob.'" I could hear the pain, even in the whisper. "Your Jacob enjoyed *that* quite a lot."

I stretched my neck up, straining to reach my lips to the edge of his jaw. I couldn't see into his eyes. He was staring up at the ceiling of the tent.

"Sorry," I murmured. "That's just the way I differentiate."

"Differentiate?"

"Between Dr. Jekyll and Mr. Hyde. Between the Jacob I like and the one who annoys the hell out of me," I explained.

"That makes sense." He sounded slightly mollified. "Tell me another favorite night."

"Flying home from Italy."

He frowned.

"Is that not one of yours?" I wondered.

"No, it *is* one of mine, actually, but I'm surprised it's on your list. Weren't you under the ludicrous impression I was just acting from a guilty conscience, and I was going to bolt as soon as the plane doors opened?"

"Yes." I smiled. "But, still, you were there."

He kissed my hair. "You love me more than I deserve."

I laughed at the impossibility of that idea. "Next would be the night after Italy," I continued.

"Yes, that's on the list. You were so funny."

"Funny?" I objected.

"I had no idea your dreams were so vivid. It took me forever to convince you that you were awake."

"I'm still not sure," I muttered. "You've always seemed more like a dream than reality. Tell me one of yours, now. Did I guess your first place?"

"No — that would be two nights ago, when you finally agreed to marry me."

I made a face.

"That doesn't make your list?"

I thought about the way he'd kissed me, the concession I'd gained, and changed my mind. "Yes . . . it does. But with reservations. I don't understand why it's so important to you. You already had me forever."

"A hundred years from now, when you've gained enough perspective to really appreciate the answer, I will explain it to you."

"I'll remind you to explain — in a hundred years."

"Are you warm enough?" he asked suddenly.

"I'm fine," I assured him. "Why?"

Before he could answer, the silence outside the tent was ripped apart by an earsplitting howl of pain. The sound ricocheted off the bare rock face of the mountain and filled the air so that it seared from every direction.

The howl tore through my mind like a tornado, both strange and familiar. Strange because I'd never heard such a tortured cry before. Familiar because I knew the voice at once — I recognized the sound and understood the meaning as perfectly as if I'd uttered it myself. It made no difference that Jacob was not human when he cried out. I needed no translation.

Jacob was close. Jacob had heard every word we'd said. Jacob was in agony.

The howl choked off into a peculiar gurgled sob, and then it was quiet again.

I did not hear his silent escape, but I could feel it — I could feel the absence I had wrongly assumed before, the empty space he left behind.

"Because your space heater has reached his limit," Edward answered quietly. "Truce over," he added, so low I couldn't be sure that was really what he'd said.

"Jacob was listening," I whispered. It wasn't a question.

"Yes."

"You knew."

"Yes."

I stared at nothing, seeing nothing.

"I never promised to fight fair," he reminded me quietly. "And he deserves to know."

My head fell into my hands.

"Are you angry with me?" he asked.

"Not you," I whispered. "I'm horrified at *me.*"

"Don't torment yourself," he pleaded.

"Yes," I agreed bitterly. "I should save my energy to torment Jacob some more. I wouldn't want to leave any part of him unharmed."

"He knew what he was doing."

"Do you think that matters?" I was blinking back tears, and this was easy to hear in my voice. "Do you think I care whether it's fair or whether he was adequately warned? I'm *hurting* him. Every time I turn around, I'm hurting him again." My voice was getting louder, more hysterical. "I'm a hideous person."

He wrapped his arms tightly around me. "No, you're not."

"I am! What's wrong with me?" I struggled against his arms, and he let them drop. "I have to go find him."

"Bella, he's already miles away, and it's cold."

"I don't care. I can't just *sit* here." I shrugged off Jacob's parka, shoved my feet into my boots, and crawled stiffly to the door; my legs felt numb. "I have to — I have to . . ." I didn't know how to finish the sentence, didn't know what there was to do, but I unzipped the door anyway, and climbed out into the bright, icy morning.

There was less snow than I would have thought after the fury of last night's storm. Probably it had blown away rather than melted in the sun that now shone low in the southeast, glancing off the snow that lingered and stabbing at my unadjusted eyes. The air still had a bite to it, but it was dead calm and slowly becoming more seasonable as the sun rose higher.

Seth Clearwater was curled up on a patch of dry pine needles in the shadow of a thick spruce, his head on his paws. His sand-colored fur was almost invisible against the dead needles, but I could see the bright snow reflect off his open eyes. He was staring at me with what I imagined was an accusation.

I knew Edward was following me as I stumbled toward the trees. I couldn't hear him, but the sun reflected off his skin in glittering rainbows that danced ahead of me. He didn't reach out to stop me until I was several paces into the forest shadows.

His hand caught my left wrist. He ignored it when I tried to yank myself free.

"You can't go after him. Not today. It's almost time. And getting yourself lost wouldn't help anyone, regardless."

I twisted my wrist, pulling uselessly.

"I'm sorry, Bella," he whispered. "I'm sorry I did that."

"You didn't do anything. It's my fault. I did this. I did everything wrong. I could have . . . When he . . . I shouldn't have . . . I . . . I . . ." I was sobbing.

"Bella, Bella."

His arms folded around me, and my tears soaked into his shirt.

"I should have — told him — I should — have said —" What? What could have made this right? "He shouldn't have — found out like this."

"Do you want me to see if I can bring him back, so that

you can talk to him? There's still a little time," Edward murmured, hushed agony in his voice.

I nodded into his chest, afraid to see his face.

"Stay by the tent. I'll be back soon."

His arms disappeared. He left so quickly that, in the second it took me to look up, he was already gone. I was alone.

A new sob broke from my chest. I was hurting everyone today. Was there anything I touched that didn't get spoiled?

I didn't know why it was hitting me so hard now. It wasn't like I hadn't known this was coming all along. But Jacob had never reacted so strongly — lost his bold overconfidence and shown the intensity of his pain. The sound of his agony still cut at me, somewhere deep in my chest. Right beside it was the other pain. Pain for feeling pain over Jacob. Pain for hurting Edward, too. For not being able to watch Jacob go with composure, knowing that it was the right thing, the only way.

I was selfish, I was hurtful. I tortured the ones I loved.

I was like Cathy, like *Wuthering Heights,* only my options were so much better than hers, neither one evil, neither one weak. And here I sat, crying about it, not doing anything productive to make it right. Just like Cathy.

I couldn't allow what hurt *me* to influence my decisions anymore. It was too little, much too late, but I had to do what was right now. Maybe it was already done for me. Maybe Edward would not be able to bring him back. And then I would accept that and get on with my life. Edward would never see me shed another tear for Jacob Black.

There would be no more tears. I wiped the last of them away with cold fingers now.

But if Edward did return with Jacob, that was it. I had to tell him to go away and never come back.

Why was that so hard? So very much more difficult than saying goodbye to my other friends, to Angela, to Mike? Why did that *hurt*? It wasn't right. That shouldn't be able to hurt me. I had what I wanted. I couldn't have them both, because Jacob could not be just my friend. It was time to give up wishing for that. How ridiculously greedy could any one person be?

I had to get over this irrational feeling that Jacob belonged in my life. He couldn't belong with me, could not be *my* Jacob, when I belonged to someone else.

I walked slowly back to the little clearing, my feet dragging. When I broke into the open space, blinking against the sharp light, I threw one quick glance toward Seth — he hadn't moved from his bed of pine needles — and then looked away, avoiding his eyes.

I could feel that my hair was wild, twisted into clumps like Medusa's snakes. I yanked through it with my fingers, and then gave up quickly. Who cared what I looked like, anyway?

I grabbed the canteen hanging beside the tent door and shook it. It sloshed wetly, so I unscrewed the lid and took a swig to rinse my mouth with the ice water. There was food somewhere nearby, but I didn't feel hungry enough to look for it. I started pacing across the bright little space, feeling Seth's eyes on me the whole time. Because I wouldn't look at him, in my head he became the boy again, rather than the gigantic wolf. So much like a younger Jacob.

I wanted to ask Seth to bark or give some other sign if Jacob was coming back, but I stopped myself. It didn't matter if Jacob came back. It might be easier if he didn't. I wished I had some way to call Edward.

Seth whined at that moment, and got to his feet.

"What is it?" I asked him stupidly.

He ignored me, trotting to the edge of the trees, and pointing his nose toward the west. He began whimpering.

"Is it the others, Seth?" I demanded. "In the clearing?"

He looked at me and yelped softly once, and then turned his nose alertly back to the west. His ears laid back and he whined again.

Why was I such a fool? What was I thinking, sending Edward away? How was I supposed to know what was going on? I didn't speak wolf.

A cold trickle of fear began to ooze down my spine. What if the time had run out? What if Jacob and Edward got too close? What if Edward decided to join in the fight?

The icy fear pooled in my stomach. What if Seth's distress had nothing to do with the clearing, and his yelp had been a denial? What if Jacob and Edward were fighting with each other, far away somewhere in the forest? They wouldn't do that, would they?

With sudden, chilling certainty I realized that they would — if the wrong words were said. I thought of the tense standoff in the tent this morning, and I wondered if I'd underestimated how close it had come to a fight.

It would be no more than I deserved if I somehow lost them both.

The ice locked around my heart.

Before I could collapse with fear, Seth grumbled slightly, deep in his chest, and then turned away from his watch and sauntered back toward his resting place. It calmed me, but irritated me. Couldn't he scratch a message in the dirt or something?

The pacing was starting to make me sweat under all my layers. I threw my jacket into the tent, and then I went back to wearing a path across the center of the tiny break in the trees.

Seth jumped to his feet again suddenly, the hackles on the back of his neck standing up stiffly. I looked around, but saw nothing. If Seth didn't cut it out, I was going to throw a pinecone at him.

He growled, a low warning sound, slinking back toward the western rim, and I rethought my impatience.

"It's just us, Seth," Jacob called from a distance.

I tried to explain to myself why my heart kicked into fourth gear when I heard him. It was just fear of what I was going to have to do now, that was all. I could not allow myself to be relieved that he'd come back. That would be the opposite of helpful.

Edward walked into view first, his face blank and smooth. When he stepped out from the shadows, the sun shimmered on his skin like it did on the snow. Seth went to greet him, looking intently into his eyes. Edward nodded slowly, and worry creased his forehead.

"Yes, that's all we need," he muttered to himself before addressing the big wolf. "I suppose we shouldn't be surprised. But the timing is going to be very close. Please have Sam ask Alice to try to nail the schedule down better."

Seth dipped his head once, and I wished I was able to growl. Sure, he could nod *now.* I turned my head, annoyed, and realized that Jacob was there.

He had his back to me, facing the way he'd come. I waited warily for him to turn around.

"Bella," Edward murmured, suddenly right beside me. He stared down at me with nothing but concern showing in his eyes. There was no end to his generosity. I deserved him now less than I ever had.

"There's a bit of a complication," he told me, his voice carefully unworried. "I'm going to take Seth a little ways away and try to straighten it out. I won't go far, but I won't listen, either. I know you don't want an audience, no matter which way you decide to go."

Only at the very end did the pain break into his voice.

I had to never hurt him again. That would be my mission in life. Never again would I be the reason for this look to come into his eyes.

I was too upset to even ask him what the new problem was. I didn't need anything else right now.

"Hurry back," I whispered.

He kissed me lightly on the lips, and then disappeared into the forest with Seth at his side.

Jacob was still in the shadow of the trees; I couldn't see his expression clearly.

"I'm in a hurry, Bella," he said in a dull voice. "Why don't you get it over with?"

I swallowed, my throat suddenly so dry I wasn't sure if I could make sound come out.

"Just say the words, and be done with it."

I took a deep breath.

"I'm sorry I'm such a rotten person," I whispered. "I'm sorry I've been so selfish. I wish I'd never met you, so I couldn't hurt you the way I have. I won't do it anymore, I promise. I'll stay far away from you. I'll move out of the state. You won't have to look at me ever again."

"That's not much of an apology," he said bitterly.

I couldn't make my voice louder than a whisper. "Tell me how to do it right."

"What if I don't want you to go away? What if I'd rather you stayed, selfish or not? Don't I get any say, if you're trying to make things up to me?"

"That won't help anything, Jake. It was wrong to stay with you when we wanted such different things. It's not going to get better. I'll just keep hurting you. I don't want to hurt you anymore. I hate it." My voice broke.

He sighed. "Stop. You don't have to say anything else. I understand."

I wanted to tell him how much I would miss him, but I bit my tongue. That would not help anything, either.

He stood quietly for a moment, staring at the ground, and I fought against the urge to go and put my arms around him. To comfort him.

And then his head snapped up.

"Well, you're not the only one capable of self-sacrifice," he said, his voice stronger. "Two can play at that game."

"What?"

"I've behaved pretty badly myself. I've made this much harder for you than I needed to. I could have given up with good grace in the beginning. But I hurt you, too."

"This is my fault."

"I won't let you claim all the blame here, Bella. Or all the glory either. I know how to redeem myself."

"What are you talking about?" I demanded. The sudden, frenzied light in his eyes frightened me.

He glanced up at the sun and then smiled at me. "There's a pretty serious fight brewing down there. I don't think it will be that difficult to take myself out of the picture."

His words sank into my brain, slowly, one by one, and I couldn't breathe. Despite all my intentions to cut Jacob out of my life completely, I didn't realize until that precise second exactly how deep the knife would have to go to do it.

"Oh, no, Jake! No, no no no," I choked out in horror. "No, Jake, no. Please, no." My knees began to tremble.

"What's the difference, Bella? This will only make it more convenient for everyone. You won't even have to move."

"No!" My voice got louder. "No, Jacob! I won't let you!"

"How will you stop me?" he taunted lightly, smiling to take the sting out of his tone.

"Jacob, I'm begging you. Stay with me." I would have fallen to my knees, if I could have moved at all.

"For fifteen minutes while I miss a good brawl? So that you can run away from me as soon as you think I'm safe again? You've got to be kidding."

"I won't run away. I've changed my mind. We'll work something out, Jacob. There's always a compromise. Don't go!"

"You're lying."

"I'm not. You know what a terrible liar I am. Look in my eyes. I'll stay if you do."

His face hardened. "And I can be *your* best man at the wedding?"

It was a moment before I could speak, and still the only answer I could give him was, "Please."

"That's what I thought," he said, his face going calm again, but for the turbulent light in his eyes.

"I love you, Bella," he murmured.

"I love you, Jacob," I whispered brokenly.

He smiled. "I know that better than you do."

He turned to walk away.

"Anything," I called after him in a strangled voice. "Anything you want, Jacob. Just don't do this!"

He paused, turning slowly.

"I don't really think you mean that."

"Stay," I begged.

He shook his head. "No, I'm going." He paused, as if deciding something. "But I could leave it to fate."

"What do you mean?" I choked out.

"I don't have to do anything deliberate — I could just do my best for my pack and let what happens happen." He shrugged. "*If* you could convince me you really did want me to come back — more than you wanted to do the selfless thing."

"How?" I asked.

"You could ask me," he suggested.

"Come back," I whispered. How could he doubt that I meant it?

He shook his head, smiling again. "That's not what I'm talking about."

It took me a second to grasp what he was saying, and all the while he was looking at me with this superior expression — so sure of my reaction. As soon as the realization hit, though, I blurted out the words without stopping to count the cost.

"Will you kiss me, Jacob?"

His eyes widened in surprise, then narrowed suspiciously. "You're bluffing."

"Kiss me, Jacob. Kiss me, and then come back."

He hesitated in the shadow, warring with himself. He half-turned again to the west, his torso twisting away from me while his feet stayed planted where they were. Still looking away, he took one uncertain step in my direction, and then another. He swung his face around to look at me, his eyes doubtful.

I stared back. I had no idea what expression was on my face.

Jacob rocked back on his heels, and then lurched forward, closing the distance between us in three long strides.

I knew he would take advantage of the situation. I expected it. I held very still — my eyes closed, my fingers curled into fists at my sides — as his hands caught my face and his lips found mine with an eagerness that was not far from violence.

I could feel his anger as his mouth discovered my passive resistance. One hand moved to the nape of my neck, twisting into a fist around the roots of my hair. The other hand grabbed roughly at my shoulder, shaking me, then dragging me to him. His hand continued down my arm, finding my wrist and pulling my arm up around his neck. I left it there, my hand still tightly balled up, unsure how far I could go in my desperation to keep him alive. All the while his lips, disconcertingly soft and warm, tried to force a response out of mine.

As soon as he was sure I wouldn't drop my arm, he freed my wrist, his hand feeling its way down to my waist. His burning hand found the skin at the small of my back, and he yanked me forward, bowing my body against his.

His lips gave up on mine for a moment, but I knew he was nowhere close to finished. His mouth followed the line of my jaw, and then explored the length of my neck. He freed my hair, reaching for my other arm to draw it around his neck like the first.

Then both of his arms were constricted around my waist, and his lips found my ear.

"You can do better than this, Bella," he whispered huskily. "You're overthinking it."

I shivered as I felt his teeth graze my earlobe.

"That's right," he murmured. "For once, just let yourself feel what you feel."

I shook my head mechanically until one of his hands wound back into my hair and stopped me.

His voice turned acidic. "Are you sure you want me to come back? Or did you really want me to die?"

Anger rocked through me like the whiplash after a heavy punch. That was too much — he wasn't fighting fair.

My arms were already around his neck, so I grabbed two fistfuls of his hair — ignoring the stabbing pain in my right hand — and fought back, struggling to pull my face away from his.

And Jacob misunderstood.

He was too strong to recognize that my hands, trying to yank his hair out by the roots, meant to cause him pain. Instead of anger, he imagined passion. He thought I was finally responding to him.

With a wild gasp, he brought his mouth back to mine, his fingers clutching frantically against the skin at my waist.

The jolt of anger unbalanced my tenuous hold on self-control; his unexpected, ecstatic response overthrew it entirely. If there had been only triumph, I might have been able to resist him. But the utter defenselessness of his sudden joy cracked my determination, disabled it. My brain disconnected from my body, and I was kissing him back. Against all reason, my lips were moving with his in strange, confusing ways they'd never moved before — because I didn't have to be careful with Jacob, and he certainly wasn't being careful with me.

My fingers tightened in his hair, but I was pulling him closer now.

He was everywhere. The piercing sunlight turned my eyelids red, and the color fit, matched the heat. The heat was everywhere. I couldn't see or hear or feel anything that wasn't Jacob.

The tiny piece of my brain that retained sanity screamed questions at me.

Why wasn't I stopping this? Worse than that, why couldn't I find in myself even the desire to *want* to stop? What did it mean that I didn't want *him* to stop? That my hands clung to his shoulders, and liked that they were wide and strong? That his hands pulled me too tight against his body, and yet it was not tight enough for me?

The questions were stupid, because I knew the answer: I'd been lying to myself.

Jacob was right. He'd been right all along. He was more than just my friend. That's why it was so impossible to tell him goodbye — because I was in love with him. Too. I loved him, much more than I should, and yet, still nowhere near enough. I was in love with him, but it was not enough to change anything; it was only enough to hurt us both more. To hurt him worse than I ever had.

I didn't care about more than that — than his pain. I more than deserved whatever pain this caused me. I hoped it was bad. I hoped I would really suffer.

In this moment, it felt as though we were the same person. His pain had always been and would always be my pain — now his joy was my joy. I felt joy, too, and yet his happiness was somehow also pain. Almost tangible — it burned against my skin like acid, a slow torture.

For one brief, never-ending second, an entirely different path expanded behind the lids of my tear-wet eyes. As if I were looking through the filter of Jacob's thoughts, I could see exactly what I was going to give up, exactly what this new self-knowledge would not save me from losing. I could see Charlie and Renée mixed into a strange collage with Billy and Sam and La Push. I could see years passing, and meaning something as they passed, changing me. I could see the enormous red-brown wolf that I loved, always standing as protector if I needed him. For the tiniest fragment of that second, I saw the bobbing heads of two small, black-haired children, running away from me into the familiar forest. When they disappeared, they took the rest of the vision with them.

And then, quite distinctly, I felt the splintering along the fissure line in my heart as the smaller part wrenched itself away from the whole.

Jacob's lips were still before mine were. I opened my eyes and he was staring at me with wonder and elation.

"I have to leave," he whispered.

"No."

He smiled, pleased by my response. "I won't be long," he promised. "But one thing first . . ."

He bent to kiss me again, and there was no reason to resist. What would be the point?

This time was different. His hands were soft on my face

and his warm lips were gentle, unexpectedly hesitant. It was brief, and very, very sweet.

His arms curled around me, and he hugged me securely while he whispered in my ear.

"*That* should have been our first kiss. Better late than never."

Against his chest, where he couldn't see, the tears welled up and spilled over.

24. SNAP DECISION

I LAY FACEDOWN ACROSS THE SLEEPING BAG, WAITING for justice to find me. Maybe an avalanche would bury me here. I wished it would. I never wanted to have to see my face in the mirror again.

There was no sound to warn me. Out of nowhere, Edward's cold hand stroked against my knotted hair. I shuddered guiltily at his touch.

"Are you all right?" he murmured, his voice anxious.

"No. I want to die."

"That will never happen. I won't allow it."

I groaned and then whispered, "You might change your mind about that."

"Where's Jacob?"

"He went to fight," I mumbled into the floor.

Jacob had left the little camp joyfully — with a cheerful "I'll be right back" — running full tilt for the clearing, already quivering as he prepared to shift to his other self. By now the whole pack knew everything. Seth Clearwater, pacing outside the tent, was an intimate witness to my disgrace.

Edward was silent for a long moment. "Oh," he finally said.

The tone of his voice worried me that my avalanche wasn't coming fast enough. I peeked up at him and, sure enough, his eyes were unfocused as he listened to something I'd rather die than have him hear. I dropped my face back to the floor.

It stunned me when Edward chuckled reluctantly.

"And I thought *I* fought dirty," he said with grudging admiration. "He makes me look like the patron saint of ethics." His hand brushed against the part of my cheek that was exposed. "I'm not mad at you, love. Jacob's more cunning than I gave him credit for. I do wish you hadn't asked him, though."

"Edward," I whispered to the rough nylon. "I . . . I . . . I'm —"

"Shh," he hushed me, his fingers soothing against my cheek. "That's not what I meant. It's just that he would have kissed you anyway — even if you hadn't fallen for it — and now I don't have an excuse to break his face. I would have really enjoyed that, too."

"Fallen for it?" I mumbled almost incomprehensibly.

"Bella, did you really believe he was that noble? That

he would go out in a flame of glory just to clear the way for me?"

I raised my head slowly to meet his patient gaze. His expression was soft; his eyes were full of understanding rather than the revulsion I deserved to see.

"Yes, I did believe that," I muttered, and then looked away. But I didn't feel any anger at Jacob for tricking me. There wasn't enough room in my body to contain anything besides the hatred I felt toward myself.

Edward laughed softly again. "You're such a bad liar, you'll believe anyone who has the least bit of skill."

"Why aren't you angry with me?" I whispered. "Why don't you hate me? Or haven't you heard the whole story yet?"

"I think I got a fairly comprehensive look," he said in a light, easy voice. "Jacob makes vivid mental pictures. I feel almost as bad for his pack as I do for myself. Poor Seth was getting nauseated. But Sam is making Jacob focus now."

I closed my eyes and shook my head in agony. The sharp nylon fibers of the tent floor scraped against my skin.

"You're only human," he whispered, stroking my hair again.

"That's the most miserable defense I've ever heard."

"But you are human, Bella. And, as much as I might wish otherwise, so is he. . . . There are holes in your life that I can't fill. I understand that."

"But that's not *true*. That's what makes me so horrible. There are no holes."

"You love him," he murmured gently.

Every cell in my body ached to deny it.

"I love you more," I said. It was the best I could do.

"Yes, I know that, too. But . . . when I left you, Bella, I left you bleeding. Jacob was the one to stitch you back up again. That was bound to leave its mark — on both of you. I'm not sure those kinds of stitches dissolve on their own. I can't blame either of you for something I made necessary. I may gain forgiveness, but that doesn't let me escape the consequences."

"I should have known you'd find some way to blame yourself. Please stop. I can't stand it."

"What would you like me to say?"

"I want you to call me every bad name you can think of, in every language you know. I want you to tell me that you're disgusted with me and that you're going to leave so that I can beg and grovel on my knees for you to stay."

"I'm sorry." He sighed. "I can't do that."

"At least stop trying to make me feel better. Let me suffer. I deserve it."

"No," he murmured.

I nodded slowly. "You're right. Keep on being too understanding. That's probably worse."

He was silent for a moment, and I sensed a charge in the atmosphere, a new urgency.

"It's getting close," I stated.

"Yes, a few more minutes now. Just enough time to say one more thing. . . ."

I waited. When he finally spoke again, he was whispering. "*I* can be noble, Bella. I'm not going to make you choose between us. Just be happy, and you can have whatever part of me you want, or none at all, if that's better. Don't let any debt you feel you owe me influence your decision."

I pushed off the floor, shoving myself up onto my knees.

"Dammit, stop that!" I shouted at him.

His eyes widened in surprise. "No — you don't understand. I'm not just trying to make you feel better, Bella, I really mean it."

"I *know* you do," I groaned. "What happened to fighting back? Don't start with the noble self-sacrifice now! Fight!"

"How?" he asked, and his eyes were ancient with their sadness.

I scrambled into his lap, throwing my arms around him.

"I don't care that it's cold here. I don't care that I stink like a dog right now. Make me forget how awful I am. Make me forget him. Make me forget my own name. Fight back!"

I didn't wait for him to decide — or to have the chance to tell me he wasn't interested in a cruel, faithless monster like me. I pulled myself against him and crushed my mouth to his snow-cold lips.

"Careful, love," he murmured under my urgent kiss.

"No," I growled.

He gently pushed my face a few inches back. "You don't have to prove anything to me."

"I'm not trying to prove something. You said I could have any part of you I wanted. I want this part. I want *every* part." I wrapped my arms around his neck and strained to reach his lips. He bent his head to kiss me back, but his cool mouth was hesitant as my impatience grew more pronounced. My body was making my intentions clear, giving me away. Inevitably, his hands moved to restrain me.

"Perhaps this isn't the best moment for that," he suggested, too calm for my liking.

"Why not?" I grumbled. There was no point in fighting if he was going to be rational; I dropped my arms.

"Firstly, because it *is* cold." He reached out to pull the sleeping bag off the floor; he wrapped it around me like a blanket.

"Wrong," I said. "First, because you are bizarrely moral for a vampire."

He chuckled. "All right, I'll give you that. The cold is second. And thirdly . . . well, you do actually stink, love."

He wrinkled his nose.

I sighed.

"Fourthly," he murmured, dropping his face so that he was whispering in my ear. "We *will* try, Bella. I'll make good on my promise. But I'd much rather it wasn't in reaction to Jacob Black."

I cringed, and buried my face against his shoulder.

"And fifthly . . ."

"This is a very long list," I muttered.

He laughed. "Yes, but did you want to listen to the fight or not?"

As he spoke, Seth howled stridently outside the tent.

My body stiffened to the sound. I didn't realize my left hand was clenched into a fist, nails biting into my bandaged palm, until Edward took it and gently smoothed my fingers out.

"It's going to be fine, Bella," he promised. "We've got skill, training, and surprise on our side. It will be over very soon. If I didn't truly believe that, I would be down there now — and you'd be here, chained to a tree or something along those lines."

"Alice is so small," I moaned.

He chuckled. "That might be a problem . . . if it were possible for someone to catch her."

Seth started to whimper.

"What's wrong?" I demanded.

"He's just angry that he's stuck here with us. He knows the pack kept him out of the action to protect him. He's salivating to join them."

I scowled in Seth's general direction.

"The newborns have reached the end of the trail — it worked like a charm, Jasper's a genius — and they've caught the scent of the ones in the meadow, so they're splitting into two groups now, as Alice said," Edward murmured, his eyes focused on something far away. "Sam's taking us around to head off the ambush party." He was so intent on what he was hearing that he used the pack plural.

Suddenly he looked down at me. "Breathe, Bella."

I struggled to do what he asked. I could hear Seth's heavy panting just outside the tent wall, and I tried to keep my lungs on the same even pace, so that I wouldn't hyperventilate.

"The first group is in the clearing. We can hear the fighting."

My teeth locked together.

He laughed once. "We can hear Emmett — he's enjoying himself."

I made myself take another breath with Seth.

"The second group is getting ready — they aren't paying attention, they haven't heard us yet."

Edward growled.

"What?" I gasped.

"They're talking about you." His teeth clenched together. "They're supposed to make sure you don't escape. . . . Nice move, Leah! Mmm, she's quite fast," he murmured in approval. "One of the newborns caught our scent, and Leah took him down before he could even turn. Sam's helping her finish him off. Paul and Jacob got another one, but the others are on the defensive now. They have no idea what to make of us. Both sides are feinting. . . . No, let Sam lead. Stay out of the way," he muttered. "Separate them — don't let them protect each other's backs."

Seth whined.

"That's better, drive them toward the clearing," Edward approved. His body was shifting unconsciously as he watched, tensing for moves he would have made. His hands still held mine; I twisted my fingers through his. At least he wasn't down there.

The sudden absence of sound was the only warning.

The deep rush of Seth's breathing cut off, and — as I'd paced my breaths with his — I noticed.

I stopped breathing, too — too frightened to even

make my lungs work as I realized that Edward had frozen into a block of ice beside me.

Oh, no. No. No.

Who had been lost? Theirs or ours? Mine, all mine. What was *my* loss?

So quickly that I wasn't exactly sure how it happened, I was on my feet and the tent was collapsing in ragged shreds around me. Had Edward ripped our way out? Why?

I blinked, shocked, into the brilliant light. Seth was all I could see, right beside us, his face only six inches from Edward's. They stared at each other with absolute concentration for one infinite second. The sun shattered off Edward's skin and sent sparkles dancing across Seth's fur.

And then Edward whispered urgently, "Go, Seth!"

The huge wolf wheeled and disappeared into the forest shadows.

Had two entire seconds passed? It felt like hours. I was terrified to the point of nausea by the knowledge that something horrible had gone awry in the clearing. I opened my mouth to demand that Edward take me there, and do it now. They needed him, and they needed *me*. If I had to bleed to save them, I would do it. I would die to do it, like the third wife. I had no silver dagger in my hand, but I would find a way —

Before I could get the first syllable out, I felt as if I was being flung through the air. But Edward's hands never let go of me — I was only being moved, so quickly that the sensation was like falling sideways.

I found myself with my back pressed against the sheer

cliff face. Edward stood in front of me, holding a posture that I knew at once.

Relief washed through my mind at the same time that my stomach dropped through the soles of my feet.

I'd misunderstood.

Relief — nothing had gone wrong in the clearing.

Horror — the crisis was *here*.

Edward held a defensive position — half-crouched, his arms extended slightly — that I recognized with sickening certainty. The rock at my back could have been the ancient brick walls of the Italian alley where he had stood between me and the black-cloaked Volturi warriors.

Something was coming for us.

"Who?" I whispered.

The words came through his teeth in a snarl that was louder than I expected. Too loud. It meant that it was far too late to hide. We were trapped, and it didn't matter who heard his answer.

"Victoria," he said, spitting the word, making it a curse. "She's not alone. She crossed my scent, following the newborns in to watch — she never meant to fight with them. She made a spur-of-the-moment decision to find me, guessing that you would be wherever I was. She was right. You were right. It was always Victoria."

She was close enough that he could hear her thoughts.

Relief again. If it had been the Volturi, we were both dead. But with Victoria, it didn't have to be *both*. Edward could survive this. He was a good fighter, as good as Jasper. If she didn't bring too many others, he could fight his way out, back to his family. Edward was faster than anyone. He could make it.

I was so glad he'd sent Seth away. Of course, there was no one Seth could run to for help. Victoria had timed her decision perfectly. But at least Seth was safe; I couldn't see the huge sandy wolf in my head when I thought his name — just the gangly fifteen-year-old boy.

Edward's body shifted — only infinitesimally, but it told me where to look. I stared at the black shadows of the forest.

It was like having my nightmares walk forward to greet me.

Two vampires edged slowly into the small opening of our camp, eyes intent, missing nothing. They glistened like diamonds in the sun.

I could barely look at the blond boy — yes, he was just a boy, though he was muscular and tall, maybe my age when he was changed. His eyes — a more vivid red than I had ever seen before — could not hold mine. Though he was closest to Edward, the nearest danger, I could not watch him.

Because, a few feet to the side and a few feet back, Victoria was staring at me.

Her orange hair was brighter than I'd remembered, more like a flame. There was no wind here, but the fire around her face seemed to shimmer slightly, as if it were alive.

Her eyes were black with thirst. She did not smile, as she always had in my nightmares — her lips were pressed into a tight line. There was a striking feline quality to the way she held her coiled body, a lioness waiting for an opening to spring. Her restless, wild gaze flickered between Edward and me, but never rested on him for more than a half-second. She could not keep her eyes from my face any more than I could keep mine from hers.

Tension rolled off of her, nearly visible in the air. I could feel the desire, the all-consuming passion that held her in its grip. Almost as if I could hear her thoughts, too, I knew what she was thinking.

She was so close to what she wanted — the focus of her whole existence for more than a year now was just *so close*.

My death.

Her plan was as obvious as it was practical. The big blond boy would attack Edward. As soon as Edward was sufficiently distracted, Victoria would finish me.

It would be quick — she had no time for games here — but it would be thorough. Something that it would be impossible to recover from. Something that even vampire venom could not repair.

She'd have to stop my heart. Perhaps a hand shoved through my chest, crushing it. Something along those lines.

My heart beat furiously, loudly, as if to make her target more obvious.

An immense distance away, from far across the black forest, a wolf's howl echoed in the still air. With Seth gone, there was no way to interpret the sound.

The blond boy looked at Victoria from the corner of his eye, waiting on her command.

He was young in more ways than one. I guessed from

his brilliant crimson irises that he couldn't have been a vampire for very long. He would be strong, but inept. Edward would know how to fight him. Edward would survive.

Victoria jerked her chin toward Edward, wordlessly ordering the boy forward.

"Riley," Edward said in a soft, pleading voice.

The blond boy froze, his red eyes widening.

"She's lying to you, Riley," Edward told him. "Listen to me. She's lying to you just like she lied to the others who are dying now in the clearing. You know that she's lied to them, that she had *you* lie to them, that neither of you were ever going to help them. Is it so hard to believe that she's lied to you, too?"

Confusion swept across Riley's face.

Edward shifted a few inches to the side, and Riley automatically compensated with an adjustment of his own.

"She doesn't love you, Riley." Edward's soft voice was compelling, almost hypnotic. "She never has. She loved someone named James, and you're no more than a tool to her."

When he said James's name, Victoria's lips pulled back in a teeth-baring grimace. Her eyes stayed locked on me.

Riley cast a frantic glance in her direction.

"Riley?" Edward said.

Riley automatically refocused on Edward.

"She knows that I will kill you, Riley. She *wants* you to die so that she doesn't have to keep up the pretense anymore. Yes — you've seen that, haven't you? You've read the reluctance in her eyes, suspected a false note in her promises. You were right. She's never wanted you. Every kiss, every touch was a lie."

Edward moved again, moved a few inches toward the boy, a few inches away from me.

Victoria's gaze zeroed in on the gap between us. It would take her less than a second to kill me — she only needed the tiniest margin of opportunity.

Slower this time, Riley repositioned himself.

"You don't have to die," Edward promised, his eyes holding the boy's. "There are other ways to live than the way she's shown you. It's not all lies and blood, Riley. You can walk away right now. You don't have to die for her lies."

Edward slid his feet forward and to the side. There was a foot of space between us now. Riley circled too far, over-compensating this time. Victoria leaned forward onto the balls of her feet.

"Last chance, Riley," Edward whispered.

Riley's face was desperate as he looked to Victoria for answers.

"He's the liar, Riley," Victoria said, and my mouth fell open in shock at the sound of her voice. "I told you about their mind tricks. You know I love only you."

Her voice was not the strong, wild, catlike growl I would have put with her face and stance. It was soft, it was high — a babyish, soprano tinkling. The kind of voice that went with blond curls and pink bubble gum. It made no sense coming through her bared, glistening teeth.

Riley's jaw tightened, and he squared his shoulders. His eyes emptied — there was no more confusion, no more suspicion. There was no thought at all. He tensed himself to attack.

Victoria's body seemed to be trembling, she was so tightly wound. Her fingers were ready claws, waiting for Edward to move just one more inch away from me.

The snarl came from none of them.

A mammoth tan shape flew through the center of the opening, throwing Riley to the ground.

"No!" Victoria cried, her baby voice shrill with disbelief.

A yard and a half in front of me, the huge wolf ripped and tore at the blond vampire beneath him. Something white and hard smacked into the rocks by my feet. I cringed away from it.

Victoria did not spare one glance for the boy she'd just pledged her love to. Her eyes were still on me, filled with a disappointment so ferocious that she looked deranged.

"No," she said again, through her teeth, as Edward started to move toward her, blocking her path to me.

Riley was on his feet again, looking misshapen and haggard, but he was able to fling a vicious kick into Seth's shoulder. I heard the bone crunch. Seth backed off and started to circle, limping. Riley had his arms out, ready, though he seemed to be missing part of one hand. . . .

Only a few yards away from that fight, Edward and Victoria were dancing.

Not quite circling, because Edward was not allowing her to position herself closer to me. She sashayed back, moving from side to side, trying to find a hole in his defense. He shadowed her footwork lithely, stalking her with perfect concentration. He began to move just a fraction of a second *before* she moved, reading her intentions in her thoughts.

Seth lunged at Riley from the side, and something tore with a hideous, grating screech. Another heavy white chunk flew into the forest with a thud. Riley roared in fury, and Seth skipped back — amazingly light on his feet for his size — as Riley took a swipe at him with one mangled hand.

Victoria was weaving through the tree trunks at the far end of the little opening now. She was torn, her feet pulling her toward safety while her eyes yearned toward me as if I were a magnet, reeling her in. I could see the burning desire to kill warring with her survival instinct.

Edward could see that, too.

"Don't go, Victoria," he murmured in that same hypnotic tone as before. "You'll never get another chance like this."

She showed her teeth and hissed at him, but she seemed unable to move farther away from me.

"You can always run later," Edward purred. "Plenty of time for that. It's what you do, isn't it? It's why James kept you around. Useful, if you like to play deadly games. A partner with an uncanny instinct for escaping. He shouldn't have left you — he could have used your skills when we caught up to him in Phoenix."

A snarl ripped from between her lips.

"That's all you ever were to him, though. Silly to waste so much energy avenging someone who had less affection for you than a hunter for his mount. You were never more than a convenience to him. I would know."

Edward's lips pulled up on one side as he tapped his temple.

With a strangled screech, Victoria darted out of the trees again, feinting to the side. Edward responded, and the dance began again.

Just then, Riley's fist caught Seth's flank, and a low yelp coughed out of Seth's throat. Seth backed away, his shoulders twitching as if he were trying to shake off the pain.

Please, I wanted to plead with Riley, but I couldn't find the muscles to make my mouth open, to pull the air up from my lungs. *Please, he's just a child!*

Why hadn't Seth run away? Why didn't he run now?

Riley was closing the distance between them again, driving Seth toward the cliff face beside me. Victoria was suddenly interested in her partner's fate. I could see her, from the corner of her eyes, judge the distance between Riley and me. Seth snapped at Riley, forcing him back again, and Victoria hissed.

Seth wasn't limping anymore. His circling took him within inches of Edward; his tail brushed Edward's back, and Victoria's eyes bulged.

"No, he won't turn on me," Edward said, answering the question in Victoria's head. He used her distraction to slide closer. "You provided us with a common enemy. You allied us."

She clenched her teeth, trying to keep her focus on Edward alone.

"Look more closely, Victoria," he murmured, pulling at the threads of her concentration. "Is he really so much like the monster James tracked across Siberia?"

Her eyes popped wide open, and then began flickering wildly from Edward to Seth to me, around and around. "Not the same?" she snarled in her little girl's soprano. "Impossible!"

"Nothing is impossible," Edward murmured, voice velvet soft as he moved another inch closer to her. "Except what you want. You'll never touch her."

She shook her head, fast and jerky, fighting his diversions, and tried to duck around him, but he was in place to block her as soon as she'd thought of the plan. Her face contorted in frustration, and then she shifted lower into her crouch, a lioness again, and stalked deliberately forward.

Victoria was no inexperienced, instinct-driven newborn. She was lethal. Even I could tell the difference between her and Riley, and I knew that Seth wouldn't have lasted so long if he'd been fighting *this* vampire.

Edward shifted, too, as they closed on each other, and it was lion versus lioness.

The dance increased in tempo.

It was like Alice and Jasper in the meadow, a blurred spiraling of movement, only this dance was not as perfectly choreographed. Sharp crunches and crackings reverberated off the cliff face whenever someone slipped in their formation. But they were moving too fast for me to see who was making the mistakes. . . .

Riley was distracted by the violent ballet, his eyes anxious for his partner. Seth struck, crunching off another small piece of the vampire. Riley bellowed and launched a massive backhanded blow that caught Seth full in his broad chest. Seth's huge body soared ten feet and crashed into the rocky wall over my head with a force that seemed to shake the whole peak. I heard the breath whoosh from his lungs, and I ducked out of the way as he rebounded off the stone and collapsed on the ground a few feet in front of me.

A low whimper escaped through Seth's teeth.

Sharp fragments of gray stone showered down on my head, scratching my exposed skin. A jagged spike of rock rolled down my right arm and I caught it reflexively. My fingers clenched around the long shard as my own survival instincts kicked in; since there was no chance of flight, my body — not caring how ineffectual the gesture was — prepared for a fight.

Adrenaline jolted through my veins. I knew the brace was cutting into my palm. I knew the crack in my knuckle was protesting. I knew it, but I could not feel the pain.

Behind Riley, all I could see was the twisting flame of Victoria's hair and a blur of white. The increasingly frequent metallic snaps and tears, the gasps and shocked hissings, made it clear that the dance was turning deadly for someone.

But *which* someone?

Riley lurched toward me, his red eyes brilliant with fury. He glared at the limp mountain of sand-colored fur between us, and his hands — mangled, broken hands — curled into talons. His mouth opened, widened, his teeth glistening, as he prepared to rip out Seth's throat.

A second kick of adrenaline hit like an electric shock, and everything was suddenly very clear.

Both fights were too close. Seth was about to lose his, and I had no idea if Edward was winning or losing. They needed help. A distraction. Something to give them an edge.

My hand gripped the stone spike so tightly that a support in the brace snapped.

Was I strong enough? Was I brave enough? How hard could I shove the rough stone into my body? Would this buy Seth enough time to get back on his feet? Would he heal fast enough for my sacrifice to do him any good?

I raked the point of the shard up my arm, yanking my thick sweater back to expose the skin, and then pressed the sharp tip to the crease at my elbow. I already had a long scar there from my last birthday. That night, my flowing blood had been enough to catch every vampire's attention, to freeze them all in place for an instant. I prayed it would work that way again. I steeled myself and sucked in one deep breath.

Victoria was distracted by the sound of my gasp. Her eyes, holding still for one tiny portion of a second, met mine. Fury and curiosity mingled strangely in her expression.

I wasn't sure how I heard the low sound with all the other noises echoing off the stone wall and hammering inside my head. My own heartbeat should have been enough to drown it out. But, in the split second that I stared into Victoria's eyes, I thought I heard a familiar, exasperated sigh.

In that same short second, the dance broke violently apart. It happened so quickly that it was over before I could follow the sequence of events. I tried to catch up in my head.

Victoria had flown out of the blurred formation and smashed into a tall spruce about halfway up the tree. She dropped back to the earth already crouched to spring.

Simultaneously, Edward — all but invisible with speed — had twisted backward and caught the unsuspecting Riley by the arm. It had looked like Edward planted his foot against Riley's back, and heaved —

The little campsite was filled with Riley's piercing shriek of agony.

At the same time, Seth leaped to his feet, cutting off most of my view.

But I could still see Victoria. And, though she looked oddly deformed — as if she were unable to straighten up completely — I could see the smile I'd been dreaming of flash across her wild face.

She coiled and sprang.

Something small and white whistled through the air and collided with her mid-flight. The impact sounded like an explosion, and it threw her against another tree — this one snapped in half. She landed on her feet again, crouched and ready, but Edward was already in place. Relief swelled in my heart when I saw that he stood straight and perfect.

Victoria kicked something aside with a flick of her bare foot — the missile that had crippled her attack. It rolled toward me, and I realized what it was.

My stomach lurched.

The fingers were still twitching; grasping at blades of grass, Riley's arm began to drag itself mindlessly across the ground.

Seth was circling Riley again, and now Riley was retreating. He backed away from the advancing werewolf, his face rigid with pain. He raised his one arm defensively.

Seth rushed Riley, and the vampire was clearly off-balance. I saw Seth sink his teeth into Riley's shoulder and tear, jumping back again.

With an earsplitting metallic screech, Riley lost his other arm.

Seth shook his head, flinging the arm into the woods. The broken hissing noise that came through Seth's teeth sounded like snickering.

Riley screamed out a tortured plea. "Victoria!"

Victoria did not even flinch to the sound of her name. Her eyes did not flicker once toward her partner.

Seth launched himself forward with the force of a wrecking ball. The thrust carried both Seth and Riley into the trees, where the metallic screeching was matched by Riley's screams. Screams that abruptly cut off, while the sounds of rock being ripped to shreds continued.

Though she spared Riley no farewell glance, Victoria seemed to realize that she was on her own. She began to back away from Edward, frenzied disappointment blazing in her eyes. She threw me one short, agonized stare of longing, and then she started to retreat faster.

"No," Edward crooned, his voice seductive. "Stay just a little longer."

She wheeled and flew toward the refuge of the forest like an arrow from a bow.

But Edward was faster — a bullet from a gun.

He caught her unprotected back at the edge of the trees and, with one last, simple step, the dance was over.

Edward's mouth brushed once across her neck, like a caress. The squealing clamor coming from Seth's efforts covered every other noise, so there was no discernible sound to make the image one of violence. He could have been kissing her.

And then the fiery tangle of hair was no longer connected to the rest of her body. The shivering orange waves fell to the ground, and bounced once before rolling toward the trees.

25. MIRROR

I FORCED MY EYES — FROZEN WIDE OPEN WITH SHOCK — to move, so that I could not examine too closely the oval object wrapped in tendrils of shivering, fiery hair.

Edward was in motion again. Swift and coolly businesslike, he dismembered the headless corpse.

I could not go to him — I could not make my feet respond; they were bolted to the stone beneath them. But I scrutinized his every action minutely, looking for any evidence that he had been harmed. My heart slowed to a healthier rhythm when I found nothing. He was lithe and graceful as ever. I couldn't even see a tear in his clothes.

He did not look at me — where I stood frozen to the cliff wall, horrified — while he piled the quivering, twitching limbs and then covered them with dry pine needles. He still did not meet my shocked gaze as he darted into the forest after Seth.

I didn't have time to recover before both he and Seth were back, Edward with his arms full of Riley. Seth was carrying a large chunk — the torso — in his mouth. They added their burden to the pile, and Edward pulled a silver rectangle from his pocket. He flipped open the butane lighter and held the flame to the dry tinder. It caught at once; long tongues of orange fire licked rapidly across the pyre.

"Get every piece," Edward said in a low aside to Seth.

Together, the vampire and the werewolf scoured the campsite, occasionally tossing small lumps of white stone into the blaze. Seth handled the pieces with his teeth. My brain wasn't working well enough for me to understand why he didn't change back to a form with hands.

Edward kept his eyes on his work.

And then they were done, and the raging fire was sending a pillar of choking purple toward the sky. The thick smoke curled up slowly, looking more solid than it should; it smelled like burning incense, and the scent was uncomfortable. It was heavy, too strong.

Seth made that snickering sound again, deep in his chest.

A smile flickered across Edward's tense face.

Edward stretched out his arm, his hand curled into a fist. Seth grinned, revealing the long row of dagger teeth, and bumped his nose against Edward's hand.

"Nice teamwork," Edward murmured.

Seth coughed a laugh.

Then Edward took a deep breath, and turned slowly to face me.

I did not understand his expression. His eyes were as wary as if I were another enemy — more than wary, they were afraid. Yet he'd shown no fear at all when he'd faced Victoria and Riley. . . . My mind was stuck, stunned and useless as my body. I stared at him, bewildered.

"Bella, love," he said in his softest tone, walking toward me with exaggerated slowness, his hands held up, palms forward. Dazed as I was, it reminded me oddly of a suspect approaching a policeman, showing that he wasn't armed. . . .

"Bella, can you drop the rock, please? Carefully. Don't hurt yourself."

I'd forgotten all about my crude weapon, though I realized now that I was grasping it so hard that my knuckle was screaming in protest. Was it rebroken? Carlisle would put me in a cast for sure this time.

Edward hesitated a few feet from me, his hands still in the air, his eyes still fearful.

It took me a few long seconds to remember how to move my fingers. Then the rock clattered to the ground, while my hand stayed frozen in the same position.

Edward relaxed slightly when my hands were empty, but came no closer.

"You don't have to be afraid, Bella," Edward murmured. "You're safe. I won't hurt you."

The mystifying promise only confused me further. I stared at him like an imbecile, trying to understand.

"It's going to be all right, Bella. I know you're frightened now, but it's over. No one is going to hurt you. I won't touch you. I won't hurt you," he said again.

My eyes blinked furiously, and I found my voice. "Why do you keep saying that?"

I took an unsteady step toward him, and he leaned away from my advance.

"What's wrong?" I whispered. "What do you mean?"

"Are you . . ." His golden eyes were suddenly as confused as I felt. "Aren't you afraid of me?"

"Afraid of you? *Why?*"

I staggered forward another step, and then tripped over something — my own feet probably. Edward caught me, and I buried my face in his chest and started to sob.

"Bella, Bella, I'm so sorry. It's over, it's over."

"I'm fine," I gasped. "I'm okay. I'm just. Freaking out. Give me. A minute."

His arms tightened around me. "I'm so sorry," he murmured again and again.

I clung to him until I could breathe, and then I was kissing him — his chest, his shoulder, his neck — every part of him that I could reach. Slowly, my brain started to work again.

"Are you okay?" I demanded between kisses. "Did she hurt you at all?"

"I am absolutely fine," he promised, burying his face in my hair.

"Seth?"

Edward chuckled. "More than fine. Very pleased with himself, in fact."

"The others? Alice, Esme? The wolves?"

"All fine. It's over there, too. It went just as smoothly as I promised. We got the worst of it here."

I let myself absorb that for a moment, let it sink in and settle in my head.

My family and my friends were safe. Victoria was never coming after me again. It was over.

We were all going to be fine.

But I couldn't completely take in the good news while I was still so confused.

"Tell me why," I insisted. "Why did you think I would be afraid of you?"

"I'm sorry," he said, apologizing yet again — for what? I had no idea. "So sorry. I didn't want you to see that. See *me* like that. I know I must have terrified you."

I had to think about that for another minute, about the hesitant way he'd approached me, his hands in the air. Like I was going to run if he moved too fast. . . .

"Seriously?" I finally asked. "You . . . what? Thought you'd scared me off?" I snorted. Snorting was good; a voice couldn't tremble or break during a snort. It sounded impressively offhand.

He put his hand under my chin and tilted my head back to read my face.

"Bella, I just" — he hesitated and then forced the words out — "I just beheaded and dismembered a sentient creature not twenty yards from you. That doesn't *bother* you?"

He frowned at me.

I shrugged. Shrugging was good, too. Very blasé. "Not really. I was only afraid that you and Seth were going to get hurt. I wanted to help, but there's only so much I can do. . . ."

His suddenly livid expression made my voice fade out.

"Yes," he said, his tone clipped. "Your little stunt with the rock. You know that you nearly gave me a heart attack? Not the easiest thing to do, that."

His furious glower made it hard to answer.

"I wanted to help . . . Seth was hurt. . . ."

"Seth was only feigning that he was hurt, Bella. It was a trick. And then you . . . !" He shook his head, unable to finish. "Seth couldn't see what you were doing, so I had to step in. Seth's a bit disgruntled that he can't claim a single-handed defeat now."

"Seth was . . . faking?"

Edward nodded sternly.

"Oh."

We both looked at Seth, who was studiously ignoring us, watching the flames. Smugness radiated from every hair in his fur.

"Well, I didn't know that," I said, on the offense now. "And it's not easy being the only helpless person around. Just you wait till I'm a vampire! I'm not going to be sitting on the sidelines next time."

A dozen emotions flitted across his face before he settled on being amused. "Next time? Did you anticipate another war soon?"

"With my luck? Who knows?"

He rolled his eyes, but I could see that he was flying — the relief was making us both lightheaded. It was over.

Or . . . was it?

"Hold on. Didn't you say something before — ?" I flinched, remembering what *exactly* it had been before — what was I going to say to Jacob? My splintered heart throbbed out a painful, aching beat. It was hard to believe, almost impossible, but the hardest part of this day was *not* behind me — and then I soldiered on. "About a complication? And Alice, needing to nail down the schedule for Sam. You said it was going to be close. What was going to be close?"

Edward's eyes flickered back to Seth, and they exchanged a loaded glance.

"Well?" I asked.

"It's nothing, really," Edward said quickly. "But we do need to be on our way. . . ."

He started to pull me into place on his back, but I stiffened and drew away.

"Define nothing."

Edward took my face between his palms. "We only have a minute, so don't panic, all right? I told you that you had no reason to be afraid. Trust me on that, please?"

I nodded, trying to hide the sudden terror — how much more could I handle before I collapsed? "No reason to be afraid. Got it."

He pursed his lips for a second, deciding what to say. And then he glanced abruptly at Seth, as if the wolf had called him.

"What's she doing?" Edward asked.

Seth whined; it was an anxious, uneasy sound. It made the hair on the back of my neck rise.

Everything was dead silent for one endless second.

And then Edward gasped, "No!" and one of his hands flew out as if to grab something that I couldn't see. "Don't —!"

A spasm rocked through Seth's body, and a howl, blistering with agony, ripped from his lungs.

Edward fell to his knees at the exact same moment, gripping the sides of his head with two hands, his face furrowed in pain.

I screamed once in bewildered terror, and dropped to my knees beside him. Stupidly, I tried to pull his hands from his face; my palms, clammy with sweat, slid off his marble skin.

"Edward! Edward!"

His eyes focused on me; with obvious effort, he pulled his clenched teeth apart.

"It's okay. We're going to be fine. It's —" He broke off, and winced again.

"What's happening?" I cried out while Seth howled in anguish.

"We're fine. We're going to be okay," Edward gasped. "Sam — help him —"

And I realized in that instant, when he said Sam's name, that he was not speaking of himself and Seth. No unseen force was attacking them. This time, the crisis was not here.

He was using the pack plural.

I'd burned through all my adrenaline. My body had nothing left. I sagged, and Edward caught me before I could hit the rocks. He sprang to his feet, me in his arms.

"Seth!" Edward shouted.

Seth was crouched, still tensed in agony, looking as if he meant to launch himself into the forest.

"No!" Edward ordered. "You go *straight home*. Now. As fast as you can!"

Seth whimpered, shaking his great head from side to side.

"Seth. Trust me."

The huge wolf stared into Edward's agonized eyes for one long second, and then he straightened up and flew into the trees, disappearing like a ghost.

Edward cradled me tightly against his chest, and then we were also hurtling through the shadowy forest, taking a different path than the wolf.

"Edward." I fought to force the words through my constricted throat. "What happened, Edward? What happened to Sam? Where are we going? What's happening?"

"We have to go back to the clearing," he told me in a low voice. "We knew there was a good probability of this happening. Earlier this morning, Alice saw it and passed it through Sam to Seth. The Volturi decided it was time to intercede."

The Volturi.

Too much. My mind refused to make sense of the words, pretended it couldn't understand.

The trees jolted past us. He was running downhill so fast that it felt as if we were plummeting, falling out of control.

"Don't panic. They aren't coming for us. It's just the normal contingent of the guard that usually cleans up this kind of mess. Nothing momentous, they're merely doing their job. Of course, they seem to have timed their arrival very carefully. Which leads me to believe that no one in Italy would mourn if these newborns *had* reduced the size of the Cullen family." The words came through his teeth, hard and bleak. "I'll know for sure what they were thinking when they get to the clearing."

"Is that why we're going back?" I whispered. Could I handle this? Images of flowing black robes crept into my unwilling mind, and I flinched away from them. I was close to a breaking point.

"It's part of the reason. Mostly, it will be safer for us to present a united front at this point. They have no reason to harass us, but . . . Jane's with them. If she thought we were alone somewhere away from the others, it might tempt her. Like Victoria, Jane will probably guess that I'm with you. Demetri, of course, is with her. He could find me, if Jane asked him to."

I didn't want to think that name. I didn't want to see that blindingly exquisite, childlike face in my head. A strange sound came out of my throat.

"Shh, Bella, shh. It's all going to be fine. Alice can see that."

Alice could see? But . . . then where were the wolves? Where was the pack?

"The pack?"

"They had to leave quickly. The Volturi do not honor truces with werewolves."

I could hear my breathing get faster, but I couldn't control it. I started to gasp.

"I swear they will be fine," Edward promised me. "The Volturi won't recognize the scent — they won't realize the wolves are here; this isn't a species they are familiar with. The pack will be fine."

I couldn't process his explanation. My concentration was ripped to shreds by my fears. *We're going to be fine,* he had said before . . . and Seth, howling in agony . . . Edward had avoided my first question, distracted me with the Volturi. . . .

I was very close to the edge — just clinging by my fingertips.

The trees were a racing blur that flowed around him like jade waters.

"What happened?" I whispered again. "Before. When Seth was howling? When you were hurt?"

Edward hesitated.

"Edward! Tell me!"

"It was all over," he whispered. I could barely hear him over the wind his speed created. "The wolves didn't count their half . . . they thought they had them all. Of course, Alice couldn't see. . . ."

"What happened?!"

"One of the newborns was hiding. . . . Leah found him — she was being stupid, cocky, trying to prove something. She engaged him alone. . . ."

"Leah," I repeated, and I was too weak to feel shame for the relief that flooded through me. "Is she going to be okay?"

"Leah wasn't hurt," Edward mumbled.

I stared at him for a long second.

Sam — help him — Edward had gasped. Him, not her.

"We're almost there," Edward said, and he stared at a fixed point in the sky.

Automatically, my eyes followed his. There was a dark purple cloud hanging low over the trees. A cloud? But it was so abnormally sunny. . . . No, not a cloud — I recognized the thick column of smoke, just like the one at our campsite.

"Edward," I said, my voice nearly inaudible. "Edward, someone got hurt."

I'd heard Seth's agony, seen the torture in Edward's face.

"Yes," he whispered.

"Who?" I asked, though, of course, I already knew the answer.

Of course I did. Of course.

The trees were slowing around us as we came to our destination.

It took him a long moment to answer me.

"Jacob," he said.

I was able to nod once.

"Of course," I whispered.

And then I slipped off the edge I was clinging to inside my head.

Everything went black.

*   *   *

I was first aware of the cool hands touching me. More than one pair of hands. Arms holding me, a palm curved to fit my cheek, fingers stroking my forehead, and more fingers pressed lightly into my wrist.

Then I was aware of the voices. They were just a humming at first, and then they grew in volume and clarity like someone was turning up a radio.

"Carlisle — it's been five minutes." Edward's voice, anxious.

"She'll come around when she's ready, Edward." Carlisle's voice, always calm and sure. "She's had too much to deal with today. Let her mind protect itself."

But my mind was not protected. It was trapped in the knowledge that had not left me, even in unconsciousness — the pain that was part of the blackness.

I felt totally disconnected from my body. Like I was caged in some small corner of my head, no longer at the controls. But I couldn't do anything about it. I couldn't think. The agony was too strong for that. There was no escape from it.

Jacob.

Jacob.

No, no, no, no, no . . .

"Alice, how long do we have?" Edward demanded, his voice still tense; Carlisle's soothing words had not helped.

From farther away, Alice's voice. It was brightly chipper. "Another five minutes. And Bella will open her eyes in thirty-seven seconds. I wouldn't doubt that she can hear us now."

"Bella, honey?" This was Esme's soft, comforting voice. "Can you hear me? You're safe now, dear."

Yes, *I* was safe. Did that really matter?

Then cool lips were at my ear, and Edward was speaking the words that allowed me to escape from the torture that had me caged inside my own head.

"He's going to live, Bella. Jacob Black is healing as I speak. He'll be fine."

As the pain and dread eased, I found my way back to my body. My eyelids fluttered.

"Oh, Bella," Edward sighed in relief, and his lips touched mine.

"Edward," I whispered.

"Yes, I'm here."

I got my lids to open, and I stared into warm gold.

"Jacob is okay?" I asked.

"Yes," he promised.

I watched his eyes carefully for some sign that he was placating me, but they were perfectly clear.

"I examined him myself," Carlisle said then; I turned my head to find his face, only a few feet away. Carlisle's expression was serious and reassuring at the same time. It was impossible to doubt him. "His life is not in any danger. He was healing at an incredible rate, though his injuries were extensive enough that it will still be a few days before he is back to normal, even if the rate of repair holds steady. As soon as we're done here, I will do what I can to help him. Sam is trying to get him to phase back to his human form. That will make treating him easier."

Carlisle smiled slightly. "I've never been to veterinarian school."

"What happened to him?" I whispered. "How bad are his injuries?"

Carlisle's face was serious again. "Another wolf was in trouble —"

"Leah," I breathed.

"Yes. He knocked her out of the way, but he didn't have time to defend himself. The newborn got his arms around him. Most of the bones on the right half of his body were shattered."

I flinched.

"Sam and Paul got there in time. He was already improving when they took him back to La Push."

"He'll be back to normal?" I asked.

"Yes, Bella. He won't have any permanent damage."

I took a deep breath.

"Three minutes," Alice said quietly.

I struggled, trying to get vertical. Edward realized what I was doing and helped me to my feet.

I stared at the scene in front of me.

The Cullens stood in a loose semicircle around the bonfire. There were hardly any flames visible, just the thick, purple-black smoke, hovering like a disease against the bright grass. Jasper stood closest to the solid-seeming haze, in its shadow so that his skin did not glitter brilliantly in the sun the way the others did. He had his back to me, his shoulders tense, his arms slightly extended. There was something there, in his shadow. Something he crouched over with wary intensity. . . .

I was too numb to feel more than a mild shock when I realized what it was.

There were eight vampires in the clearing.

The girl was curled into a small ball beside the flames, her arms wrapped around her legs. She was very young. Younger than me — she looked maybe fifteen, dark-haired and slight. Her eyes were focused on me, and the irises were a shocking, brilliant red. Much brighter than Riley's, almost glowing. They wheeled wildly, out of control.

Edward saw my bewildered expression.

"She surrendered," he told me quietly. "That's one I've never seen before. Only Carlisle would think of offering. Jasper doesn't approve."

I couldn't tear my gaze away from the scene beside the fire. Jasper was rubbing absently at his left forearm.

"Is Jasper all right?" I whispered.

"He's fine. The venom stings."

"He was bitten?" I asked, horrified.

"He was trying to be everywhere at once. Trying to make sure Alice had nothing to do, actually." Edward shook his head. "Alice doesn't need anyone's help."

Alice grimaced toward her true love. "Overprotective fool."

The young female suddenly threw her head back like an animal and wailed shrilly.

Jasper growled at her and she cringed back, but her fingers dug into the ground like claws and her head whipped back and forth in anguish. Jasper took a step toward her, slipping deeper into his crouch. Edward moved with overdone casualness, turning our bodies so that he was between the girl and me. I peeked around his arm to watch the thrashing girl and Jasper.

Carlisle was at Jasper's side in an instant. He put a restraining hand on his most recent son's arm.

"Have you changed your mind, young one?" Carlisle asked, calm as ever. "We don't want to destroy you, but we will if you can't control yourself."

"How can you stand it?" the girl groaned in a high, clear voice. "I *want* her." Her bright crimson irises focused on Edward, through him, beyond him to me, and her nails ripped through the hard soil again.

"You must stand it," Carlisle told her gravely. "You must exercise control. It is possible, and it is the only thing that will save you now."

The girl clutched her dirt-encrusted hands around her head, yowling quietly.

"Shouldn't we move away from her?" I whispered, tugging on Edward's arm. The girl's lips pulled back over her teeth when she heard my voice, her expression one of torment.

"We have to stay here," Edward murmured. "*They* are coming to the north end of the clearing now."

My heart burst into a sprint as I scanned the clearing, but I couldn't see anything past the thick pall of smoke.

After a second of fruitless searching, my gaze crept back to the young female vampire. She was still watching me, her eyes half-mad.

I met the girl's stare for a long moment. Chin-length dark hair framed her face, which was alabaster pale. It was hard to tell if her features were beautiful, twisted as they were by rage and thirst. The feral red eyes were dominant — hard to look away from. She glared at me viciously, shuddering and writhing every few seconds.

I stared at her, mesmerized, wondering if I were looking into a mirror of my future.

Then Carlisle and Jasper began to back toward the rest of us. Emmett, Rosalie, and Esme all converged hastily around where Edward stood with Alice and me. A united front, as Edward had said, with me at the heart, in the safest place.

I tore my attention away from the wild girl to search for the approaching monsters.

There was still nothing to see. I glanced at Edward, and his eyes were locked straight ahead. I tried to follow his gaze, but there was only the smoke — dense, oily smoke twisting low to the ground, rising lazily, undulating against the grass.

It billowed forward, darker in the middle.

"Hmm," a dead voice murmured from the mist. I recognized the apathy at once.

"Welcome, Jane." Edward's tone was coolly courteous.

The dark shapes came closer, separating themselves from the haze, solidifying. I knew it would be Jane in the front — the darkest cloak, almost black, and the smallest figure by more than two feet. I could just barely make out Jane's angelic features in the shade of the cowl.

The four gray-shrouded figures hulking behind her were also somewhat familiar. I was sure I recognized the biggest one, and while I stared, trying to confirm my suspicion, Felix looked up. He let his hood fall back slightly so that I could see him wink at me and smile. Edward was very still at my side, tightly in control.

Jane's gaze moved slowly across the luminous faces of the Cullens and then touched on the newborn girl beside the fire; the newborn had her head in her hands again.

"I don't understand." Jane's voice was toneless, but not quite as uninterested as before.

"She has surrendered," Edward explained, answering the confusion in her mind.

Jane's dark eyes flashed to his face. "Surrendered?"

Felix and another shadow exchanged a quick glance.

Edward shrugged. "Carlisle gave her the option."

"There are no options for those who break the rules," Jane said flatly.

Carlisle spoke then, his voice mild. "That's in your hands. As long as she was willing to halt her attack on us, I saw no need to destroy her. She was never taught."

"That is irrelevant," Jane insisted.

"As you wish."

Jane stared at Carlisle in consternation. She shook her head infinitesimally, and then composed her features.

"Aro hoped that we would get far enough west to see you, Carlisle. He sends his regards."

Carlisle nodded. "I would appreciate it if you would convey mine to him."

"Of course." Jane smiled. Her face was almost too lovely when it was animated. She looked back toward the smoke. "It appears that you've done our work for us today . . . for the most part." Her eyes flickered to the hostage. "Just out of professional curiosity, how many were there? They left quite a wake of destruction in Seattle."

"Eighteen, including this one," Carlisle answered.

Jane's eyes widened, and she looked at the fire again, seeming to reassess the size of it. Felix and the other shadow exchanged a longer glance.

"Eighteen?" she repeated, her voice sounding unsure for the first time.

"All brand-new," Carlisle said dismissively. "They were unskilled."

"All?" Her voice turned sharp. "Then who was their creator?"

"Her name was Victoria," Edward answered, no emotion in his voice.

"Was?" Jane asked.

Edward inclined his head toward the eastern forest. Jane's eyes snapped up and focused on something far in the distance. The other pillar of smoke? I didn't look away to check.

Jane stared to the east for a long moment, and then examined the closer bonfire again.

"This Victoria — she was in addition to the eighteen here?"

"Yes. She had only one other with her. He was not as young as this one here, but no older than a year."

"Twenty," Jane breathed. "Who dealt with the creator?"

"I did," Edward told her.

Jane's eyes narrowed, and she turned to the girl beside the fire.

"You there," she said, her dead voice harsher than before. "Your name."

The newborn shot a baleful glare at Jane, her lips pressed tightly together.

Jane smiled back angelically.

The newborn girl's answering scream was ear-piercing; her body arched stiffly into a distorted, unnatural position. I looked away, fighting the urge to cover my ears. I gritted my teeth, hoping to control my stomach. The screaming intensified. I tried to concentrate on Edward's face, smooth and unemotional, but that made me remember when it had been Edward under Jane's torturing gaze, and I felt sicker. I looked at Alice instead, and Esme next to her. Their faces were as empty as his.

Finally, it was quiet.

"Your name," Jane said again, her voice inflectionless.

"Bree," the girl gasped.

Jane smiled, and the girl shrieked again. I held my breath until the sound of her agony stopped.

"She'll tell you anything you want to know," Edward said through his teeth. "You don't have to do that."

Jane looked up, sudden humor in her usually dead eyes. "Oh, I know," she said to Edward, grinning at him before she turned back to the young vampire, Bree.

"Bree," Jane said, her voice cold again. "Is his story true? Were there twenty of you?"

The girl lay panting, the side of her face pressed against the earth. She spoke quickly. "Nineteen or twenty, maybe

more, I don't know!" She cringed, terrified that her igno-
rance might bring on another round of torture. "Sara and
the one whose name I don't know got in a fight on the
way. . . ."

"And this Victoria — did she create you?"

"I don't know," she said, flinching again. "Riley never
said her name. I didn't see that night . . . it was so dark,
and it hurt. . . ." Bree shuddered. "He didn't want us to be
able to think of her. He said that our thoughts weren't
safe. . . ."

Jane's eyes flickered to Edward, and then back to the
girl.

Victoria had planned this well. If she hadn't followed
Edward, there would have been no way to know for certain
that she was involved. . . .

"Tell me about Riley," Jane said. "Why did he bring
you here?"

"Riley told us that we had to destroy the strange
yellow-eyes here," Bree babbled quickly and willingly.
"He said it would be easy. He said that the city was theirs,
and they were coming to get us. He said once they were
gone, all the blood would be ours. He gave us her scent."
Bree lifted one hand and stabbed a finger in my direction.
"He said we would know that we had the right coven, because she would be with them. He said whoever got to her
first could have her."

I heard Edward's jaw flex beside me.

"It looks like Riley was wrong about the easy part,"
Jane noted.

Bree nodded, seeming relieved that the conversation

had taken this non-painful course. She sat up carefully. "I don't know what happened. We split up, but the others never came. And Riley left us, and he didn't come to help like he promised. And then it was so confusing, and everybody was in pieces." She shuddered again. "I was afraid. I wanted to run away. That one" — she looked at Carlisle — "said they wouldn't hurt me if I stopped fighting."

"Ah, but that wasn't his gift to offer, young one," Jane murmured, her voice oddly gentle now. "Broken rules demand a consequence."

Bree stared at her, not comprehending.

Jane looked at Carlisle. "Are you sure you got all of them? The other half that split off?"

Carlisle's face was very smooth as he nodded. "We split up, too."

Jane half-smiled. "I can't deny that I'm impressed." The big shadows behind her murmured in agreement. "I've never seen a coven escape this magnitude of offensive intact. Do you know what was behind it? It seems like extreme behavior, considering the way you live here. And why was the girl the key?" Her eyes rested unwilling on me for one short second.

I shivered.

"Victoria held a grudge against Bella," Edward told her, his voice impassive.

Jane laughed — the sound was golden, the bubbling laugh of a happy child. "This one seems to bring out bizarrely strong reactions in our kind," she observed, smiling directly at me, her face beatific.

Edward stiffened. I looked at him in time to see his face turning away, back to Jane.

"Would you please not do that?" he asked in a tight voice.

Jane laughed again lightly. "Just checking. No harm done, apparently."

I shivered, deeply grateful that the strange glitch in my system — which had protected me from Jane the last time we'd met — was still in effect. Edward's arm tightened around me.

"Well, it appears that there's not much left for us to do. Odd," Jane said, apathy creeping back into her voice. "We're not used to being rendered unnecessary. It's too bad we missed the fight. It sounds like it would have been entertaining to watch."

"Yes," Edward answered her quickly, his voice sharp. "And you were so close. It's a shame you didn't arrive just a half hour earlier. Perhaps then you could have fulfilled your purpose here."

Jane met Edward's glare with unwavering eyes. "Yes. Quite a pity how things turned out, isn't it?"

Edward nodded once to himself, his suspicions confirmed.

Jane turned to look at the newborn Bree again, her face completely bored. "Felix?" she drawled.

"Wait," Edward interjected.

Jane raised one eyebrow, but Edward was staring at Carlisle while he spoke in an urgent voice. "We could explain the rules to the young one. She doesn't seem unwilling to learn. She didn't know what she was doing."

"Of course," Carlisle answered. "We would certainly be prepared to take responsibility for Bree."

Jane's expression was torn between amusement and disbelief.

"We don't make exceptions," she said. "And we don't give second chances. It's bad for our reputation. Which reminds me . . ." Suddenly, her eyes were on me again, and her cherubic face dimpled. "Caius will be *so* interested to hear that you're still human, Bella. Perhaps he'll decide to visit."

"The date is set," Alice told Jane, speaking for the first time. "Perhaps we'll come to visit you in a few months."

Jane's smile faded, and she shrugged indifferently, never looking at Alice. She turned to face Carlisle. "It was nice to meet you, Carlisle — I'd thought Aro was exaggerating. Well, until we meet again . . ."

Carlisle nodded, his expression pained.

"Take care of that, Felix," Jane said, nodding toward Bree, her voice dripping boredom. "I want to go home."

"Don't watch," Edward whispered in my ear.

I was only too eager to follow his instruction. I'd seen more than enough for one day — more than enough for one lifetime. I squeezed my eyes tightly together and turned my face into Edward's chest.

But I could still hear.

There was a deep, rumbling growl, and then a high-pitched keen that was horribly familiar. That sound cut off quickly, and then the only sound was a sickening crunching and snapping.

Edward's hand rubbed anxiously against my shoulders.

"Come," Jane said, and I looked up in time to see the backs of the tall gray cloaks drifting away toward the curling smoke. The incense smell was strong again — fresh.

The gray cloaks disappeared into the thick mist.

26. ETHICS

THE COUNTER IN ALICE'S BATHROOM WAS COVERED WITH
a thousand different products, all claiming to beautify a
person's surface. Since everyone in this house was both
perfect and impermeable, I could only assume that she'd
bought most of these things with me in mind. I read the
labels numbly, struck by the waste.

I was careful never to look in the long mirror.

Alice combed through my hair with a slow, rhythmic
motion.

"That's enough, Alice," I said tonelessly. "I want to go
back to La Push."

How many hours had I waited for Charlie to *finally*

leave Billy's house so that I could see Jacob? Each minute, not knowing if Jacob was still breathing or not, had seemed like ten lifetimes. And then, when at last I'd been allowed to go, to see for myself that Jacob was alive, the time had gone so quickly. I felt like I'd barely caught my breath before Alice was calling Edward, insisting that I keep up this ridiculous sleepover façade. It seemed so insignificant. . . .

"Jacob's still unconscious," Alice answered. "Carlisle or Edward will call when he's awake. Anyway, you need to go see Charlie. He was there at Billy's house, he saw that Carlisle and Edward are back in from their trip, and he's bound to be suspicious when you get home."

I already had my story memorized and corroborated. "I don't care. I want to be there when Jacob wakes up."

"You need to think of Charlie now. You've had a long day — sorry, I know that doesn't begin to cover it — but that doesn't mean that you can shirk your responsibilities." Her voice was serious, almost chiding. "It's more important now than ever that Charlie stays safely in the dark. Play your role first, Bella, and then you can do what you want second. Part of being a Cullen is being meticulously responsible."

Of course she was right. And if not for this same reason — a reason that was more powerful than all my fear and pain and guilt — Carlisle would never have been able to talk me into leaving Jacob's side, unconscious or not.

"Go home," Alice ordered. "Talk to Charlie. Flesh out your alibi. Keep him safe."

I stood, and the blood flowed down to my feet, stinging like the pricks of a thousand needles. I'd been sitting still for a long time.

"That dress is adorable on you," Alice cooed.

"Huh? Oh. Er — thanks again for the clothes," I mumbled out of courtesy rather than real gratitude.

"You need the evidence," Alice said, her eyes innocent and wide. "What's a shopping trip without a new outfit? It's very flattering, if I do say so myself."

I blinked, unable to remember what she'd dressed me in. I couldn't keep my thoughts from skittering away every few seconds, insects running from the light. . . .

"Jacob is fine, Bella," Alice said, easily interpreting my preoccupation. "There's no hurry. If you realized how much extra morphine Carlisle had to give him — what with his temperature burning it off so quickly — you would know that he's going to be out for a while."

At least he wasn't in any pain. Not yet.

"Is there anything you want to talk about before you leave?" Alice asked sympathetically. "You must be more than a little traumatized."

I knew what she was curious about. But I had other questions.

"Will I be like that?" I asked her, my voice subdued. "Like that girl Bree in the meadow?"

There were many things I needed to think of, but I couldn't seem to get her out of my head, the newborn whose other life was now — abruptly — over. Her face, twisted with desire for my blood, lingered behind my eyelids.

Alice stroked my arm. "Everyone is different. But something like that, yes."

I was very still, trying to imagine.

"It passes," she promised.

"How soon?"

She shrugged. "A few years, maybe less. It might be different for you. I've never seen anyone go through this who's chosen it beforehand. It should be interesting to see how that affects you."

"Interesting," I repeated.

"We'll keep you out of trouble."

"I know that. I trust you." My voice was monotone, dead.

Alice's forehead puckered. "If you're worried about Carlisle and Edward, I'm sure they'll be fine. I believe Sam is beginning to trust us . . . well, to trust Carlisle, at least. It's a good thing, too. I imagine the atmosphere got a little tense when Carlisle had to rebreak the fractures —"

"Please, Alice."

"Sorry."

I took a deep breath to steady myself. Jacob had begun healing too quickly, and some of his bones had set wrong. He'd been out cold for the process, but it was still hard to think about.

"Alice, can I ask you a question? About the future?"

She was suddenly wary. "You know I don't see everything."

"It's not that, exactly. But you *do* see my future, sometimes. Why is that, do you think, when nothing else works on me? Not what Jane can do, or Edward or Aro . . ." My sentence trailed off with my interest level. My curiosity on this point was fleeting, heavily overshadowed by more pressing emotions.

Alice, however, found the question very interesting. "Jasper, too, Bella — his talent works on your body just as well as it does on anyone else's. That's the difference, do you see it? Jasper's abilities affect the body physically. He really does calm your system down, or excite it. It's not an illusion. And I see visions of outcomes, not the reasons and thoughts behind the decisions that create them. It's outside the mind, not an illusion, either; reality, or at least one version of it. But Jane and Edward and Aro and Demetri — they work *inside* the mind. Jane only creates an illusion of pain. She doesn't really hurt your body, you only think you feel it. You see, Bella? You are safe inside your mind. No one can reach you there. It's no wonder that Aro was so curious about your future abilities."

She watched my face to see if I was following her logic. In truth, her words had all started to run together, the syllables and sounds losing their meaning. I couldn't concentrate on them. Still, I nodded. Trying to look like I got it.

She wasn't fooled. She stroked my cheek and murmured, "He's going to be okay, Bella. I don't need a vision to know that. Are you ready to go?"

"One more thing. Can I ask you another question about the future? I don't want specifics, just an overview."

"I'll do my best," she said, doubtful again.

"Can you still see me becoming a vampire?"

"Oh, that's easy. Sure, I do."

I nodded slowly.

She examined my face, her eyes unfathomable. "Don't you know your own mind, Bella?"

"I do. I just wanted to be sure."

"I'm only as sure as you are, Bella. You know that. If you were to change your mind, what I see would change . . . or disappear, in your case."

I sighed. "That isn't going to happen, though."

She put her arms around me. "I'm sorry. I can't really *empathize*. My first memory is of seeing Jasper's face in my future; I always knew that he was where my life was headed. But I can *sympathize*. I'm so sorry you have to choose between two good things."

I shook off her arms. "Don't feel sorry for me." There were people who deserved sympathy. I wasn't one of them. And there wasn't any choice to make — there was just breaking a good heart to attend to now. "I'll go deal with Charlie."

I drove my truck home, where Charlie was waiting just as suspiciously as Alice had expected.

"Hey, Bella. How was your shopping trip?" he greeted me when I walked into the kitchen. He had his arms folded over his chest, his eyes on my face.

"Long," I said dully. "We just got back."

Charlie assessed my mood. "I guess you already heard about Jake, then?"

"Yes. The rest of the Cullens beat us home. Esme told us where Carlisle and Edward were."

"Are you okay?"

"Worried about Jake. As soon as I make dinner, I'm going down to La Push."

"I told you those motorcycles were dangerous. I hope this makes you realize that I wasn't kidding around."

I nodded as I started pulling things out of the fridge. Charlie settled himself in at the table. He seemed to be in a more talkative mood than usual.

"I don't think you need to worry about Jake too much. Anyone who can cuss with that kind of energy is going to recover."

"Jake was awake when you saw him?" I asked, spinning to look at him.

"Oh, yeah, he was awake. You should have heard him — actually, it's better you didn't. I don't think there was anyone in La Push who *couldn't* hear him. I don't know where he picked up that vocabulary, but I hope he hasn't been using that kind of language around you."

"He had a pretty good excuse today. How did he look?"

"Messed up. His friends carried him in. Good thing they're big boys, 'cause that kid's an armful. Carlisle said his right leg is broken, and his right arm. Pretty much the whole right side of his body got crushed when he wrecked that damn bike." Charlie shook his head. "If I ever hear of you riding again, Bella —"

"No problem there, Dad. You won't. Do you really think Jake's okay?"

"Sure, Bella, don't worry. He was himself enough to tease me."

"Tease you?" I echoed in shock.

"Yeah — in between insulting somebody's mother and taking the Lord's name in vain, he said, 'Bet you're glad she loves Cullen instead of me today, huh, Charlie?'"

I turned back to the fridge so that he couldn't see my face.

"And I couldn't argue. Edward's more mature than Jacob when it comes to your safety, I'll give him that much."

"Jacob's plenty mature," I muttered defensively. "I'm sure this wasn't his fault."

"Weird day today," Charlie mused after a minute. "You know, I don't put much stock in that superstitious crap, but it was odd. . . . It was like Billy knew something bad was going to happen to Jake. He was nervous as a turkey on Thanksgiving all morning. I don't think he heard anything I said to him.

"And then, weirder than that — remember back in February and March when we had all that trouble with the wolves?"

I bent down to get a frying pan out of the cupboard, and hid there an extra second or two.

"Yeah," I mumbled.

"I hope we're not going to have a problem with that again. This morning, we were out in the boat, and Billy wasn't paying any attention to me or the fish, when all of a sudden, you could hear wolves yowling in the woods. More than one, and, boy, was it loud. Sounded like they were right there in the village. Weirdest part was, Billy turned the boat around and headed straight back to the harbor like they were calling to him personally. Didn't even hear me ask what he was doing.

"The noise stopped before we got the boat docked. But all of a sudden Billy was in the biggest hurry not to miss the game, though we had hours still. He was mumbling some nonsense about an earlier showing . . . of a live game? I tell you, Bella, it was odd.

"Well, he found some game he said he wanted to watch, but then he just ignored it. He was on the phone the whole time, calling Sue, and Emily, and your friend Quil's grandpa. Couldn't quite make out what he was looking for — he just chatted real casual with them.

"Then the howling started again right outside the house. I've never heard anything like it — I had goose bumps on my arms. I asked Billy — had to shout over the noise — if he'd been setting traps in his yard. It sounded like the animal was in serious pain."

I winced, but Charlie was so caught up in his story that he didn't notice.

"'Course I forgot all about that till just this minute, 'cause that's when Jake made it home. One minute it was that wolf yowling, and then you couldn't hear it any- more — Jake's cussing drowned it right out. Got a set of lungs on him, that boy does."

Charlie paused for a minute, his face thoughtful. "Funny that some good should come out of this mess. I didn't think they were ever going to get over that fool prejudice they have against the Cullens down there. But somebody called Carlisle, and Billy was real grateful when he showed up. I thought we should get Jake up to the hos- pital, but Billy wanted to keep him home, and Carlisle agreed. I guess Carlisle knows what's best. Generous of him to sign up for such a long stretch of house calls."

"And . . ." he paused, as if unwilling to say something. He sighed, and then continued. "And Edward was really . . .

nice. He seemed as worried about Jacob as you are — like that was his brother lying there. The look in his eyes . . ." Charlie shook his head. "He's a decent guy, Bella. I'll try to remember that. No promises, though." He grinned at me.

"I won't hold you to it," I mumbled.

Charlie stretched his legs and groaned. "It's nice to be home. You wouldn't believe how crowded Billy's little place gets. Seven of Jake's friends all squished themselves into that little front room — I could hardly breathe. Have you ever noticed how big those Quileute kids all are?"

"Yeah, I have."

Charlie stared at me, his eyes abruptly more focused. "Really, Bella, Carlisle said Jake will be up and around in no time. Said it looked a lot worse than it was. He's going to be fine."

I just nodded.

Jacob had looked so . . . strangely fragile when I'd hurried down to see him as soon as Charlie had left. He'd had braces everywhere — Carlisle said there was no point in plaster, as fast as he was healing. His face had been pale and drawn, deeply unconscious though he was at the time. Breakable. Huge as he was, he'd looked very breakable. Maybe that had just been my imagination, coupled with the knowledge that I was going to have to break him.

If only I could be struck by lightning and be split in two. Preferably painfully. For the first time, giving up being human felt like a true sacrifice. Like it might be too much to lose.

I put Charlie's dinner on the table next to his elbow and headed for the door.

"Er, Bella? Could you wait just a second?"

"Did I forget something?" I asked, eyeing his plate.

"No, no. I just . . . want to ask a favor." Charlie frowned and looked at the floor. "Have a seat — this won't take long."

I sat across from him, a little confused. I tried to focus. "What do you need, Dad?"

"Here's the gist of it, Bella." Charlie flushed. "Maybe I'm just feeling . . . superstitious after hanging out with Billy while he was being so strange all day. But I have this . . . hunch. I feel like . . . I'm going to lose you soon."

"Don't be silly, Dad," I mumbled guiltily. "You want me to go to school, don't you?"

"Just promise me one thing."

I was hesitant, ready to rescind. "Okay . . ."

"Will you tell me before you do anything major? Before you run off with him or something?"

"Dad . . . ," I moaned.

"I'm serious. I won't kick up a fuss. Just give me some advance notice. Give me a chance to hug you goodbye."

Cringing mentally, I held up my hand. "This is silly. But, if it makes you happy, . . . I promise."

"Thanks, Bella," he said. "I love you, kid."

"I love you, too, Dad." I touched his shoulder, and then shoved away from the table. "If you need anything, I'll be at Billy's."

I didn't look back as I ran out. This was just perfect, just what I needed right now. I grumbled to myself all the way to La Push.

Carlisle's black Mercedes was not in front of Billy's

house. That was both good and bad. Obviously, I needed to talk to Jacob alone. Yet I still wished I could somehow hold Edward's hand, like I had before, when Jacob was unconscious. Impossible. But I missed Edward — it had seemed like a very long afternoon alone with Alice. I supposed that made my answer quite obvious. I already knew that I couldn't live without Edward. That fact wasn't going to make this any less painful.

I tapped quietly on the front door.

"Come in, Bella," Billy said. The roar of my truck was easy to recognize.

I let myself in.

"Hey, Billy. Is he awake?" I asked.

"He woke up about a half hour ago, just before the doctor left. Go on in. I think he's been waiting for you."

I flinched, and then took a deep breath. "Thanks."

I hesitated at the door to Jacob's room, not sure whether to knock. I decided to peek first, hoping — coward that I was — that maybe he'd gone back to sleep. I felt like I could use just a few more minutes.

I opened the door a crack and leaned hesitantly in.

Jacob was waiting for me, his face calm and smooth. The haggard, gaunt look was gone, but only a careful blankness took its place. There was no animation in his dark eyes.

It was hard to look at his face, knowing that I loved him. It made more of a difference than I would have thought. I wondered if it had always been this hard for him, all this time.

Thankfully, someone had covered him with a quilt. It was a relief not to have to see the extent of the damage.

I stepped in and shut the door quietly behind me.

"Hi, Jake," I murmured.

He didn't answer at first. He looked at my face for a long moment. Then, with some effort, he rearranged his expression into a slightly mocking smile.

"Yeah, I sort of thought it might be like that." He sighed. "Today has definitely taken a turn for the worse. First I pick the wrong place, miss the best fight, and Seth gets all the glory. Then Leah has to be an idiot trying to prove she's as tough as the rest of us and I have to be the idiot who saves her. And now this." He waved his left hand toward me where I hesitated by the door.

"How are you feeling?" I mumbled. What a stupid question.

"A little stoned. Dr. Fang isn't sure how much pain medication I need, so he's going with trial and error. Think he overdid it."

"But you're not in pain."

"No. At least, I can't feel my injuries," he said, smiling mockingly again.

I bit my lip. I was never going to get through this. Why didn't anyone ever try to kill me when I *wanted* to die?

The wry humor left his face, and his eyes warmed up. His forehead creased, like he was worried.

"How about you?" he asked, sounding really concerned. "Are you okay?"

"*Me?*" I stared at him. Maybe he *had* taken too many drugs. "*Why?*"

"Well, I mean, I was pretty sure that he wouldn't actually *hurt* you, but I wasn't sure how bad it was going to be. I've been going a little crazy with worrying about you ever since I woke up. I didn't know if you were going to be allowed to visit or anything. The suspense was terrible. How did it go? Was he mean to you? I'm sorry if it was bad. I didn't mean for you to have to go through that alone. I was thinking I'd be there. . . ."

It took me a minute to even understand. He babbled on, looking more and more awkward, until I got what he was saying. Then I hurried to reassure him.

"No, no, Jake! I'm fine. Too fine, really. Of course he wasn't mean. I wish!"

His eyes widened in what looked like horror. *"What?"*

"He wasn't even mad at me — he wasn't even mad at *you*! He's so unselfish it makes me feel even worse. I wish he would have yelled at me or something. It's not like I don't deserve . . . well, much worse than getting yelled at. But he doesn't care. He just wants me to be *happy.*"

"He wasn't mad?" Jacob asked, incredulous.

"No. He was . . . much too kind."

Jacob stared for another minute, and then he suddenly frowned. "Well, *damn!*" he growled.

"What's wrong, Jake? Does it hurt?" My hands fluttered uselessly as I looked around for his medication.

"No," he grumbled in a disgusted tone. "I can't believe this! He didn't give you an ultimatum or anything?"

"Not even close — what's wrong with you?"

He scowled and shook his head. "I was sort of counting on his reaction. Damn it all. He's better than I thought."

The way he said it, though angrier, reminded me of

Edward's tribute to Jacob's lack of ethics in the tent this morning. Which meant that Jake was still hoping, still fighting. I winced as that stabbed deep.

"He's not playing any game, Jake," I said quietly.

"You bet he is. He's playing every bit as hard as I am, only he knows what he's doing and I don't. Don't blame me because he's a better manipulator than I am — I haven't been around long enough to learn all his tricks."

"He isn't manipulating me!"

"Yes, he is! When are you going to wake up and realize that he's not as perfect as you think he is?"

"At least he didn't threaten to kill himself to make me kiss him," I snapped. As soon as the words were out, I flushed with chagrin. "Wait. Pretend that didn't slip out. I swore to myself that I wasn't going to say anything about that."

He took a deep breath. When he spoke, he was calmer. "Why not?"

"Because I didn't come here to blame you for anything."

"It's true, though," he said evenly. "I did do that."

"I don't care, Jake. I'm not mad."

He smiled. "I don't care, either. I knew you'd forgive me, and I'm glad I did it. I'd do it again. At least I have that much. At least I made you see that you *do* love me. That's worth something."

"Is it? Is it really better than if I was still in the dark?"

"Don't you think you ought to know how you feel — just so that it doesn't take you by surprise someday when it's too late and you're a married vampire?"

I shook my head. "No — I didn't mean better for me. I meant better for *you*. Does it make things better or worse for you, having me know that I'm in love with you? When it doesn't make a difference either way. Would it have been better, easier for you, if I never clued in?"

He took my question as seriously as I'd meant it, thinking carefully before he answered. "Yes, it's better to have you know," he finally decided. "If you hadn't figured it out . . . I'd have always wondered if your decision would have been different if you had. Now I know. I did everything I could." He dragged in an unsteady breath, and closed his eyes.

This time I did not — could not — resist the urge to comfort him. I crossed the small room and kneeled by his head, afraid to sit on the bed in case I jostled it and hurt him, and leaned in to touch my forehead to his cheek.

Jacob sighed, and put his hand on my hair, holding me there.

"I'm so sorry, Jake."

"I always knew this was a long shot. It's not your fault, Bella."

"Not you, too," I moaned. "Please."

He pulled away to look at me. "What?"

"It *is* my fault. And I'm so sick of being told it's not."

He grinned. It didn't touch his eyes. "You want me to haul you over the coals?"

"Actually . . . I think I do."

He pursed his lips as he measured how much I meant it. A smile flashed across his face briefly, and then he twisted his expression into a fierce scowl.

"Kissing me back like that was inexcusable." He spit the words at me. "If you knew you were just going to take it back, maybe you shouldn't have been quite so convincing about it."

I winced and nodded. "I'm so sorry."

"Sorry doesn't make anything better, Bella. What were you thinking?"

"I wasn't," I whispered.

"You should have told me to go die. That's what you want."

"No, Jacob," I whimpered, fighting against the budding tears. "No! Never."

"You're not crying?" he demanded, his voice suddenly back to its normal tone. He twitched impatiently on the bed.

"Yeah," I muttered, laughing weakly at myself through the tears that were suddenly sobs.

He shifted his weight, throwing his good leg off the bed as if he were going to try to stand.

"What are you doing?" I demanded through the tears. "Lie down, you idiot, you'll hurt yourself!" I jumped to my feet and pushed his good shoulder down with two hands.

He surrendered, leaning back with a gasp of pain, but he grabbed me around my waist and pulled me down on the bed, against his good side. I curled up there, trying to stifle the silly sobs against his hot skin.

"I can't believe you're crying," he mumbled. "You know I just said those things because you wanted me to. I didn't mean them." His hand rubbed against my shoulders.

"I know." I took a deep, ragged breath, trying to control myself. How did I end up being the one crying while he did the comforting? "It's all still true, though. Thanks for saying it out loud."

"Do I get points for making you cry?"

"Sure, Jake." I tried to smile. "As many as you want."

"Don't worry, Bella, honey. It's all going to work out."

"I don't see how," I muttered.

He patted the top of my head. "I'm going to give in and be good."

"More games?" I wondered, tilting my chin so that I could see his face.

"Maybe." He laughed with a bit of effort, and then winced. "But I'm going to try."

I frowned.

"Don't be so pessimistic," he complained. "Give me a little credit."

"What do you mean by 'be good'?"

"I'll be your friend, Bella," he said quietly. "I won't ask for more than that."

"I think it's too late for that, Jake. How can we be friends, when we love each other like this?"

He looked at the ceiling, his stare intent, as if he were reading something that was written there. "Maybe . . . it will have to be a long-distance friendship."

I clenched my teeth together, glad he wasn't looking at my face, fighting against the sobs that threatened to overtake me again. I needed to be strong, and I had no idea how. . . .

"You know that story in the Bible?" Jacob asked

suddenly, still reading the blank ceiling. "The one with the king and the two women fighting over the baby?"

"Sure. King Solomon."

"That's right. King Solomon," he repeated. "And he said, cut the kid in half . . . but it was only a test. Just to see who would give up their share to protect it."

"Yeah, I remember."

He looked back at my face. "I'm not going to cut you in half anymore, Bella."

I understood what he was saying. He was telling me that he loved me the most, that his surrender proved it. I wanted to defend Edward, to tell Jacob how Edward would do the same thing if I wanted, if I would *let* him. I was the one who wouldn't renounce my claim there. But there was no point in starting an argument that would only hurt him more.

I closed my eyes, willing myself to control the pain. I couldn't impose that on him.

We were quiet for a moment. He seemed to be waiting for me to say something; I was trying to think of something to say.

"Can I tell you what the worst part is?" he asked hesitantly when I said nothing. "Do you mind? I *am* going to be good."

"Will it help?" I whispered.

"It might. It couldn't hurt."

"What's the worst part, then?"

"The worse part is knowing what would have been."

"What *might* have been." I sighed.

"No." Jacob shook his head. "I'm exactly right for you, Bella. It would have been effortless for us — comfortable, easy as breathing. I was the natural path your life would have taken. . . ." He stared into space for a moment, and I waited. "If the world was the way it was supposed to be, if there were no monsters and no magic . . ."

I could see what he saw, and I knew that he was right. If the world was the sane place it was supposed to be, Jacob and I would have been together. And we would have been happy. He was my soul mate in that world — would have been my soul mate still if his claim had not been overshadowed by something stronger, something so strong that it could not exist in a rational world.

Was it out there for Jacob, too? Something that would trump a soul mate? I had to believe that it was.

Two futures, two soul mates . . . too much for any one person. And so unfair that I wouldn't be the only one to pay for it. Jacob's pain seemed too high a price. Cringing at the thought of that price, I wondered if I would have wavered, if I hadn't lost Edward once. If I didn't know what it was like to live without him. I wasn't sure. That knowledge was so deep a part of me, I couldn't imagine how I would feel without it.

"He's like a drug for you, Bella." His voice was still gentle, not at all critical. "I see that you can't live without him now. It's too late. But I would have been healthier for you. Not a drug; I would have been the air, the sun."

The corner of my mouth turned up in a wistful half-smile. "I used to think of you that way, you know. Like the sun. My personal sun. You balanced out the clouds nicely for me."

He sighed. "The clouds I can handle. But I can't fight with an eclipse."

I touched his face, laying my hand against his cheek. He exhaled at my touch and closed his eyes. It was very quiet. For a minute I could hear the beating of his heart, slow and even.

"Tell me the worst part for you," he whispered.

"I think that might be a bad idea."

"Please."

"I think it will hurt."

"Please."

How could I deny him anything at this point?

"The worst part . . ." I hesitated, and then let words spill out in a flood of truth. "The worst part is that I saw the whole thing — our whole life. And I want it bad, Jake, I want it all. I want to stay right here and never move. I want to love you and make you happy. And I can't, and it's killing me. It's like Sam and Emily, Jake — I never had a choice. I always knew nothing would change. Maybe that's why I was fighting against you so hard."

He seemed to be concentrating on breathing evenly.

"I knew I shouldn't have told you that."

He shook his head slowly. "No. I'm glad you did. Thank you." He kissed the top of my head, and then he sighed. "I'll be good now."

I looked up, and he was smiling.

"So you're going to get married, huh?"

"We don't have to talk about that."

"I'd like to know some of the details. I don't know when I'll talk to you again."

I had to wait for a minute before I could speak. When I was pretty sure that my voice wouldn't break, I answered his question.

"It's not really my idea . . . but, yes. It means a lot to him. I figure, why not?"

Jake nodded. "That's true. It's not such a big thing — in comparison."

His voice was very calm, very practical. I stared at him, curious about how he was managing, and that ruined it. He met my eyes for a second, and then twisted his head away. I waited to speak until his breathing was under control.

"Yes. In comparison," I agreed.

"How long do you have left?"

"That depends on how long it takes Alice to pull a wedding together." I suppressed a groan, imagining what Alice would do.

"Before or after?" he asked quietly.

I knew what he meant. "After."

He nodded. This was a relief to him. I wondered how many sleepless nights the thought of my graduation had given him.

"Are you scared?" he whispered.

"Yes," I whispered back.

"What are you afraid of?" I could barely hear his voice now. He stared down at my hands.

"Lots of things." I worked to make my voice lighter, but I stayed honest. "I've never been much of a masochist, so I'm not looking forward to the pain. And I wish there was some way to keep *him* away — I don't want him to suffer with me, but I don't think there's any way around it. There's dealing with Charlie, too, and Renée. . . . And then afterward, I hope I'll be able to control myself *soon*. Maybe I'll be such a menace that the pack will have to take me out."

He looked up with a disapproving expression. "I'd hamstring any one of my brothers who tried."

"Thanks."

He smiled halfheartedly. Then he frowned. "But isn't it more dangerous than that? In all of the stories, they say it's too hard . . . they lose control . . . people die. . . ." He gulped.

"No, I'm not afraid of that. Silly Jacob — don't you know better than to believe vampire stories?"

He obviously didn't appreciate my attempt at humor.

"Well, anyway, lots to worry about. But worth it, in the end."

He nodded unwillingly, and I knew that he in no way agreed with me.

I stretched my neck up to whisper in his ear, laying my cheek against his warm skin. "You know I love you."

"I know," he breathed, his arm tightening automatically around my waist. "You know how much I wish it was enough."

"Yes."

"I'll always be waiting in the wings, Bella," he promised, lightening his tone and loosening his arm. I pulled away with a dull, dragging sense of loss, feeling the tearing separation as I left a part of me behind, there on the bed next to him. "You'll always have that spare option if you want it."

I made an effort to smile. "Until my heart stops beating."

He grinned back. "You know, I think maybe I'd still take you — maybe. I guess that depends on how much you stink."

"Should I come back to see you? Or would you rather I didn't?"

"I'll think it through and get back to you," he said. "I might need the company to keep from going crazy. The vampire surgeon extraordinaire says I can't phase until he gives the okay — it might mess up the way the bones are set." Jacob made a face.

"Be good and do what Carlisle tells you to do. You'll get well faster."

"Sure, sure."

"I wonder when it will happen," I said. "When the right girl is going to catch your eye."

"Don't get your hopes up, Bella." Jacob's voice was abruptly sour. "Though I'm sure it would be a relief for you."

"Maybe, maybe not. I probably won't think she's good enough for you. I wonder how jealous I'll be."

"That part might be kind of fun," he admitted.

"Let me know if you want me to come back, and I'll be here," I promised.

With a sigh, he turned his cheek toward me.

I leaned in and kissed his face softly. "Love you, Jacob."

He laughed lightly. "Love you more."

He watched me walk out of his room with an unfathomable expression in his black eyes.

27. NEEDS

I DIDN'T GET VERY FAR BEFORE DRIVING BECAME IMPOS-
sible.

When I couldn't see anymore, I let my tires find the
rough shoulder and rolled slowly to a stop. I slumped over
on the seat and allowed the weakness I'd fought in Jacob's
room crush me. It was worse than I'd thought — the force
of it took me by surprise. Yes, I had been right to hide this
from Jacob. No one should ever see this.

But I wasn't alone for very long — just exactly long
enough for Alice to see me here, and then the few minutes
it took him to arrive. The door creaked open, and he
pulled me into his arms.

At first it was worse. Because there was that smaller part of me — smaller, but getting louder and angrier every minute, screaming at the rest of me — that craved a different set of arms. So then there was fresh guilt to season the pain.

He didn't say anything, he just let me sob until I began to blubber out Charlie's name.

"Are you really ready to go home?" he asked doubtfully.

I managed to convey, after several attempts, that it wasn't going to get any better anytime soon. I needed to get past Charlie before it got late enough for him to call Billy.

So he drove me home — for once not even getting close to my truck's internal speed limit — keeping one arm wrapped tightly around me. The whole way, I fought for control. It seemed to be a doomed effort at first, but I didn't give up. Just a few seconds, I told myself. Just time for a few excuses, or a few lies, and then I could break down again. I had to be able to do that much. I scrambled around in my head, searching desperately for a reserve of strength.

There was just enough for me to quiet the sobs — hold them back but not end them. The tears didn't slow. I couldn't seem to find any handle to even begin to work with those.

"Wait for me upstairs," I mumbled when we were in front of the house.

He hugged me closer for one minute, and then he was gone.

Once inside, I headed straight for the stairs.

"Bella?" Charlie called after me from his usual place on the sofa as I walked by.

I turned to look at him without speaking. His eyes bugged wide, and he lurched to his feet.

"What happened? Is Jacob . . . ?" he demanded.

I shook my head furiously, trying to find my voice. "He's fine, he's fine," I promised, my voice low and husky. And Jacob *was* fine, physically, which is all Charlie was worried about at the moment.

"But what happened?" He grabbed my shoulders, his eyes still anxious and wide. "What happened to you?"

I must look worse than I'd imagined.

"Nothing, Dad. I . . . just had to talk to Jacob about . . . some things that were hard. I'm fine."

The anxiety calmed, and was replaced by disapproval.

"Was this really the best time?" he asked.

"Probably not, Dad, but I didn't have any alternatives — it just got to the point where I had to choose. . . . Sometimes, there isn't any way to compromise."

He shook his head slowly. "How did he handle it?"

I didn't answer.

He looked at my face for a minute, and then nodded. That must have been answer enough.

"I hope you didn't mess up his recovery."

"He's a quick healer," I mumbled.

Charlie sighed.

I could feel the control slipping.

"I'll be in my room," I told him, shrugging out from underneath his hands.

"'Kay," Charlie agreed. He could probably see the waterworks starting to escalate. Nothing scared Charlie worse than tears.

I made my way to my room, blind and stumbling.

Once inside, I fought with the clasp on my bracelet, trying to undo it with shaking fingers.

"No, Bella," Edward whispered, capturing my hands. "It's part of who you are."

He pulled me into the cradle of his arms as the sobs broke free again.

This longest of days seemed to stretch on and on and on. I wondered if it would ever end.

But, though the night dragged relentlessly, it was not the worst night of my life. I took comfort from that. And I was not alone. There was a great deal of comfort in that, too.

Charlie's fear of emotional outbursts kept him from checking on me, though I was not quiet — he probably got no more sleep than I did.

My hindsight seemed unbearably clear tonight. I could see every mistake I'd made, every bit of harm I'd done, the small things and the big things. Each pain I'd caused Jacob, each wound I'd given Edward, stacked up into neat piles that I could not ignore or deny.

And I realized that I'd been wrong all along about the magnets. It had not been Edward and Jacob that I'd been trying to force together, it was the two parts of myself, Edward's Bella and Jacob's Bella. But they could not exist together, and I never should have tried.

I'd done so much damage.

At some point in the night, I remembered the promise I'd made to myself early this morning — that I would never make Edward see me shed another tear for Jacob Black. The thought brought on a round of hysteria which frightened Edward more than the weeping. But it passed, too, when it had run its course.

Edward said little; he just held me on the bed and let me ruin his shirt, staining it with salt water.

It took longer than I thought it would for that smaller, broken part of me to cry herself out. It happened, though, and I was eventually exhausted enough to sleep. Unconsciousness did not bring full relief from the pain, just a numbing, dulling ease, like medicine. Made it more bearable. But it was still there; I was aware of it, even asleep, and that helped me to make the adjustments I needed to make.

The morning brought with it, if not a brighter outlook, at least a measure of control, some acceptance. Instinctively, I knew that the new tear in my heart would always ache. That was just going to be a part of me now. Time would make it easier — that's what everyone always said. But I didn't care if time healed me or not, so long as Jacob could get better. Could be happy again.

When I woke up, there was no disorientation. I opened my eyes — finally dry — and met his anxious gaze.

"Hey," I said. My voice was hoarse. I cleared my throat. He didn't answer. He watched me, waiting for it to start.

"No, I'm fine," I promised. "That won't happen again."

His eyes tightened at my words.

"I'm sorry that you had to see that," I said. "That wasn't fair to you."

He put his hands on either side of my face.

"Bella . . . are you *sure*? Did you make the right choice? I've never seen you in so much pain —" His voice broke on the last word.

But I had known worse pain.

I touched his lips. "Yes."

"I don't know. . . ." His brow creased. "If it hurts you so much, how can it possibly be the right thing for you?"

"Edward, I know who I can't live without."

"But . . ."

I shook my head. "You don't understand. You may be brave enough or strong enough to live without me, if that's what's best. But I could never be that self-sacrificing. I have to be with you. It's the only way I can live."

He still looked dubious. I should never have let him stay with me last night. But I had needed him so much. . . .

"Hand me that book, will you?" I asked, pointing over his shoulder.

His eyebrows pulled together in confusion, but he gave it to me quickly.

"This again?" he asked.

"I just wanted to find this one part I remembered . . . to see how she said it. . . ." I flipped through the book, finding the page I wanted easily. The corner was dog-eared from the many times I'd stopped here. "Cathy's a monster, but there were a few things she got right," I muttered. I read the lines quietly, mostly to myself. "'If all else perished, and he remained, I should still continue to be; and if all else remained, and he were annihilated, the universe would turn to a mighty stranger.'" I nodded, again to myself. "I know exactly what she means. And I know who I can't live without."

Edward took the book from my hands and flipped it across the room — it landed with a light *thud* on my desk. He wrapped his arms around my waist.

A small smile lit his perfect face, though worry still lined his forehead. "Heathcliff had his moments, too," he said. He didn't need the book to get it word perfect. He pulled me closer and whispered in my ear, "'I *cannot* live without my life! I *cannot* live without my soul!'"

"Yes," I said quietly. "That's my point."

"Bella, I can't stand for you to be miserable. Maybe . . ."

"No, Edward. I've made a real mess of things, and I'm going to have to live with that. But I know what I want and what I need . . . and what I'm going to do now."

"What are *we* going to do now?"

I smiled just a bit at his correction, and then I sighed. "We are going to go see Alice."

Alice was on the bottom porch step, too hyper to wait for us inside. She looked about to break into a celebration dance, so excited was she about the news she knew I was there to deliver.

"Thank you, Bella!" she sang as we got out of the truck.

"Hold it, Alice," I warned her, lifting a hand up to halt her glee. "I've got a few limitations for you."

"I know, I know, I know. I only have until August thirteenth at the latest, you have veto power on the guest list, and if I go overboard on anything, you'll never speak to me again."

"Oh, okay. Well, yeah. You know the rules, then."

"Don't worry, Bella, it will be perfect. Do you want to see your dress?"

I had to take a few deep breaths. *Whatever makes her happy,* I said to myself.

"Sure."

Alice's smile was smug.

"Um, Alice," I said, keeping the casual, unruffled tone in my voice. "When did you get me a dress?"

It probably wasn't much of a show. Edward squeezed my hand.

Alice led the way inside, heading for the stairs. "These things take time, Bella," Alice explained. Her tone seemed . . . evasive. "I mean, I wasn't *sure* things were going to turn out this way, but there was a distinct possibility. . . ."

"When?" I asked again.

"Perrine Bruyere has a waiting list, you know," she said, defensive now. "Fabric masterpieces don't happen overnight. If I hadn't thought ahead, you'd be wearing something off the rack!"

It didn't look like I was going to get a straight answer. "Per — who?"

"He's not a major designer, Bella, so there's no need to throw a hissy fit. He's got promise, though, and he specializes in what I needed."

"I'm not throwing a fit."

"No, you're not." She eyed my calm face suspiciously. Then, as we walked into her room, she turned on Edward.

"You — out."

"Why?" I demanded.

"Bella," she groaned. "You know the rules. He's not supposed to see the dress till the day of."

I took another deep breath. "It doesn't matter to me. And you know he's already seen it in your head. But if that's how you want it. . . ."

She shoved Edward back out the door. He didn't even look at her — his eyes were on me, wary, afraid to leave me alone.

I nodded, hoping my expression was tranquil enough to reassure him.

Alice shut the door in his face.

"All right!" she muttered. "C'mon."

She grabbed my wrist and towed me to her closet — which was bigger than my bedroom — and then dragged me to the back corner, where a long white garment bag had a rack all to itself.

She unzipped the bag in one sweeping movement, and then slipped it carefully off the hanger. She took a step back, holding her hand out to the dress like she was a game show hostess.

"Well?" she asked breathlessly.

I appraised it for a long moment, playing with her a bit. Her expression turned worried.

"Ah," I said, and I smiled, letting her relax. "I see."

"What do you think?" she demanded.

It was my *Anne of Green Gables* vision all over again.

"It's perfect, of course. Exactly right. You're a genius." She grinned. "I know."

"Nineteen-eighteen?" I guessed.

"More or less," she said, nodding. "Some of it is *my* design, the train, the veil. . . ." She touched the white satin as she spoke. "The lace is vintage. Do you like it?"

"It's beautiful. It's just right for him."

"But is it just right for you?" she insisted.

"Yes, I think it is, Alice. I think it's just what I need. I know you'll do a great job with this . . . if you can keep yourself in check."

She beamed.

"Can I see your dress?" I asked.

She blinked, her face blank.

"Didn't you order your bridesmaid dress at the same time? I wouldn't want my maid of honor to wear something off the *rack*." I pretended to wince in horror.

She threw her arms around my waist. "Thank you, Bella!"

"How could you not see that one coming?" I teased, kissing her spiky hair. "Some psychic you are!"

Alice danced back, and her face was bright with fresh enthusiasm. "I've got so much to do! Go play with Edward. I have to get to work."

She dashed out of the room, yelling, "Esme!" as she disappeared.

I followed at my own pace. Edward was waiting for me in the hallway, leaning against the wood-paneled wall.

"That was very, very nice of you," he told me.

"She seems happy," I agreed.

He touched my face; his eyes — too dark, it had been so long since he'd left me — searched my expression minutely.

"Let's get out of here," he suddenly suggested. "Let's go to our meadow."

It sounded very appealing. "I guess I don't have to hide out anymore, do I?"

"No. The danger is behind us."

He was quiet, thoughtful, as he ran. The wind blew on my face, warmer now that the storm had really passed. The clouds covered the sky, the way they usually did.

The meadow was a peaceful, happy place today. Patches of summer daisies interrupted the grass with splashes of white and yellow. I lay back, ignoring the slight dampness of the ground, and looked for pictures in the clouds. They were too even, too smooth. No pictures, just a soft, gray blanket.

Edward lay next to me and held my hand.

"August thirteenth?" he asked casually after a few minutes of comfortable silence.

"That gives me a month till my birthday. I didn't want to cut it too close."

He sighed. "Esme is three years older than Carlisle — technically. Did you know that?"

I shook my head.

"It hasn't made any difference to them."

My voice was serene, a counterpoint to his anxiety. "My age is not really that important. Edward, I'm ready. I've chosen my life — now I want to start living it."

He stroked my hair. "The guest list veto?"

"I don't care really, but I . . ." I hesitated, not wanting to explain this one. Best to get it over with. "I'm not sure if Alice would feel the need to invite . . . a few were-wolves. I don't know if . . . Jake would feel like . . . like he *should* come. Like that's the right thing to do, or that I'd get my feelings hurt if he didn't. He shouldn't have to go through that."

Edward was quiet for a minute. I stared at the tips of the treetops, almost black against the light gray of the sky.

Suddenly, Edward grabbed me around the waist and pulled me onto his chest.

"Tell me why you're doing this, Bella. Why did you decide, now, to give Alice free rein?"

I repeated for him the conversation I had with Charlie last night before I'd gone to see Jacob.

"It wouldn't be fair to keep Charlie out of this," I concluded. "And that means Renée and Phil. I might as well let Alice have her fun, too. Maybe it will make the whole thing easier for Charlie if he gets his proper goodbye. Even if he thinks it's much too early, I wouldn't want to cheat him out of the chance to walk me down the aisle." I grimaced at the words, then took another deep breath. "At least my mom and dad and my friends will know the best part of my choice, the most I'm allowed to tell them. They'll know I chose you, and they'll know we're together.

They'll know I'm happy, wherever I am. I think that's the best I can do for them."

Edward held my face, searching it for a brief time.

"Deal's off," he said abruptly.

"*What?*" I gasped. "You're backing out? No!"

"I'm not backing out, Bella. I'll still keep my side of the bargain. But you're off the hook. Whatever you want, no strings attached."

"Why?"

"Bella, I see what you're doing. You're trying to make everyone else happy. And I don't care about anyone else's feelings. I only need *you* to be happy. Don't worry about breaking the news to Alice. I'll take care of it. I promise she won't make you feel guilty."

"But I —"

"No. We're doing this your way. Because my way doesn't work. I call you stubborn, but look at what *I've* done. I've clung with such idiotic obstinacy to my idea of what's best for you, though it's only hurt you. Hurt you so deeply, time and time again. I don't trust myself anymore. You can have happiness your way. My way is always wrong. So." He shifted under me, squaring his shoulders. "We're doing it *your way,* Bella. Tonight. Today. The sooner the better. I'll speak to Carlisle. I was thinking that maybe if we gave you enough morphine, it wouldn't be so bad. It's worth a try." He gritted his teeth.

"Edward, no —"

He put his finger to my lips. "Don't worry, Bella, love. I haven't forgotten the rest of your demands."

His hands were in my hair, his lips moving softly — but very seriously — against mine, before I realized what he was saying. What he was doing.

There wasn't much time to act. If I waited too long, I wouldn't be able to remember why I needed to stop him. Already, I couldn't breathe right. My hands were gripping his arms, pulling myself tighter to him, my mouth glued to his and answering every unspoken question his asked.

I tried to clear my head, to find a way to speak.

He rolled gently, pressing me into the cool grass.

Oh, never mind! my less noble side exulted. My head was full of the sweetness of his breath.

No, no, no, I argued with myself. I shook my head, and his mouth moved to my neck, giving me a chance to breathe.

"Stop, Edward. Wait." My voice was as weak as my will.

"Why?" he whispered into the hollow of my throat.

I labored to put some resolve into my tone. "I don't want to do this now."

"Don't you?" he asked, a smile in his voice. He moved his lips back to mine and made speaking impossible. Heat coursed through my veins, burning where my skin touched his.

I made myself focus. It took a great deal of effort just to force my hands to free themselves from his hair, to move them to his chest. But I did it. And then I shoved against him, trying to push him away. I could not succeed alone, but he responded as I knew he would.

He pulled back a few inches to look at me, and his eyes

did nothing to help my resolve. They were black fire. They smoldered.

"Why?" he asked again, his voice low and rough. "I love you. I want you. Right now."

The butterflies in my stomach flooded my throat. He took advantage of my speechlessness.

"Wait, wait," I tried to say around his lips.

"Not for me," he murmured in disagreement.

"*Please?*" I gasped.

He groaned, and pushed himself away from me, rolling onto his back again.

We both lay there for a minute, trying to slow our breathing.

"Tell me why not, Bella," he demanded. "This had better not be about me."

Everything in my world was about him. What a silly thing to expect.

"Edward, this is very important to me. I *am* going to do this right."

"Who's definition of right?"

"Mine."

He rolled onto his elbow and stared at me, his expression disapproving.

"*How* are you going to do this right?"

I took a deep breath. "Responsibly. Everything in the right order. I will not leave Charlie and Renée without the best resolution I can give them. I won't deny Alice her fun, if I'm having a wedding anyway. And I *will* tie myself to you in every human way, before I ask you to make me immortal. I'm following all the rules, Edward. Your soul is far, far too important to me to take chances with. You're not going to budge me on this."

"I'll bet I *could*," he murmured, his eyes burning again.

"But you wouldn't," I said, trying to keep my voice level. "Not knowing that this is what I really need."

"You don't fight fair," he accused.

I grinned at him. "Never said I did."

He smiled back, wistful. "If you change your mind . . ."

"You'll be the first to know," I promised.

The rain started to drip through the clouds just then, a few scattered drops that made faint *thuds* as they struck the grass.

I glowered at the sky.

"I'll get you home." He brushed the tiny beads of water from my cheeks.

"Rain's not the problem," I grumbled. "It just means that it's time to go do something that will be very unpleasant and possibly even highly dangerous."

His eyes widened in alarm.

"It's a good thing you're bulletproof." I sighed. "I'm going to need that ring. It's time to tell Charlie."

He laughed at the expression on my face. "Highly dangerous," he agreed. He laughed again and then reached into the pocket of his jeans. "But at least there's no need for a side trip."

He once again slid my ring into place on the third finger of my left hand.

Where it would stay — conceivably for the rest of eternity.

EPILOGUE — CHOICE

JACOB BLACK

"Jacob, do you think this is going to take too much longer?" Leah demanded. Impatient. Whiney.

My teeth clenched together.

Like anyone in the pack, Leah knew everything. She knew why I came here — to the very edge of the earth and sky and sea. To be alone. She knew that this was all I wanted. Just to be alone.

But Leah was going to force her company on me, anyway.

Besides being crazy annoyed, I did feel smug for a brief second. Because I didn't even have to think about controlling my temper. It was easy now, something I just did, natural. The red haze didn't wash over my eyes. The heat didn't shiver down my spine. My voice was calm when I answered.

"Jump off a cliff, Leah." I pointed to the one at my feet.

"Really, kid." She ignored me, throwing herself into a sprawl on the ground next to me. "You have no idea how hard this is for me."

"For *you*?" It took me a minute to believe she was serious. "You have to be the most self-absorbed person alive, Leah. I'd hate to shatter the dream world you live in — the one where the sun is orbiting the place where you stand — so I won't tell you how little I care what your problem is. *Go. Away.*"

"Just look at this from my perspective for a minute, okay?" she continued as if I hadn't said anything.

If she was trying to break my mood, it worked. I started laughing. The sound hurt in strange ways.

"Stop snorting and pay attention," she snapped.

"If I pretend to listen, will you leave?" I asked, glancing over at the permanent scowl on her face. I wasn't sure if she had any other expressions anymore.

I remembered back to when I used to think that Leah was pretty, maybe even beautiful. That was a long time ago. No one thought of her that way now. Except for Sam. He was never going to forgive himself. Like it was his fault that she'd turned into this bitter harpy.

Her scowl heated up, as if she could guess what I was thinking. Probably could.

"This is making me sick, Jacob. Can you imagine what

this feels like to *me*? I don't even *like* Bella Swan. And you've got me grieving over this leech-lover like I'm in love with her, too. Can you see where that might be a little confusing? I dreamed about kissing her last night! What the hell am I supposed to do with *that*?"

"Do I care?"

"I can't stand being in your head anymore! Get over her already! She's going to *marry* that thing. He's going to try to change her into one of them! Time to move on, boy."

"Shut *up*," I growled.

It would be wrong to strike back. I knew that. I was biting my tongue. But she'd be sorry if she didn't walk away. Now.

"He'll probably just kill her anyway," Leah said. Sneering. "All the stories say that happens more often than not. Maybe a funeral will be better closure than a wedding. Ha."

This time I had to work. I closed my eyes and fought the hot taste in my mouth. I pushed and shoved against the slide of fire down my back, wrestling to keep my shape together while my body tried to shake apart.

When I was in control again, I glowered at her. She was watching my hands as the tremors slowed. Smiling.

Some joke.

"If you're upset about gender confusion, Leah . . . ," I said. Slow, emphasizing each word. "How do you think the rest of us like looking at Sam through your eyes? It's bad enough that Emily has to deal with *your* fixation. She doesn't need us guys panting after him, too."

Pissed as I was, I still felt guilty when I watched the spasm of pain shoot across her face.

She scrambled to her feet — pausing only to spit in my direction — and ran for the trees, vibrating like a tuning fork.

I laughed darkly. "You missed."

Sam was going to give me hell for that, but it was worth it. Leah wouldn't bug me anymore. And I'd do it again if I had the chance.

Because her words were still there, scratching themselves into my brain, the pain of it so strong that I could hardly breathe.

It didn't matter so much that Bella'd chosen someone else over me. That agony was nothing at all. That agony I could live with for the rest of my stupid, too long, stretched-out life.

But it did matter that she was giving up everything — that she was letting her heart stop and her skin ice over and her mind twist into some crystallized predator's head. A monster. A stranger.

I would have thought there was nothing worse than that, nothing more painful in the whole world.

But, if he *killed* her . . .

Again, I had to fight the rage. Maybe, if not for Leah, it would be good to let the heat change me into a creature who could deal with it better. A creature with instincts so much stronger than human emotions. An animal who couldn't feel pain in the same way. A different pain. Some variety, at least. But Leah was running now, and I didn't want to share her thoughts. I cussed her under my breath for taking away that escape, too.

My hands were shaking in spite of me. What shook

them? Anger? Agony? I wasn't sure what I was fighting now.

I had to believe that Bella would survive. But that required trust — a trust I didn't want to feel, a trust in that bloodsucker's ability to keep her alive.

She would be different, and I wondered how that would affect me. Would it be the same as if she had died, to see her standing there like a stone? Like ice? When her scent burned in my nostrils and triggered the instinct to rip, to tear . . . How would that be? Could I want to kill *her*? Could I not want to kill one of *them*?

I watched the swells roll toward the beach. They disappeared from sight under the edge of the cliff, but I heard them beat against the sand. I watched them until it was late, long after dark.

Going home was probably a bad idea. But I was hungry, and I couldn't think of another plan.

I made a face as I pulled my arm through the retarded sling and grabbed my crutches. If only Charlie hadn't seen me that day and spread the word of my "motorcycle accident." Stupid props. I hated them.

Going hungry started to look better when I walked in the house and got a look at my dad's face. He had something on his mind. It was easy to tell — he always overdid it. Acted all casual.

He also talked too much. He was rambling about his day before I could get to the table. He never jabbered like this unless there was something that he didn't want to say. I ignored him as best I could, concentrating on the food. The faster I choked it down . . .

". . . and Sue stopped by today." My dad's voice was loud. Hard to ignore. As always. "Amazing woman. She's tougher than grizzlies, that one. I don't know how she deals with that daughter of hers, though. Now Sue, she would have made one hell of a wolf. Leah's more of a wolverine." He chuckled at his own joke.

He waited briefly for my response, but didn't seem to see my blank, bored-out-of-my-mind expression. Most days that bugged him. I wished he would shut up about Leah. I was trying not to think about her.

"Seth's a lot easier. Of course, you were easier than your sisters, too, until . . . well, you have more to deal with than they did."

I sighed, long and deep, and stared out the window.

Billy was quiet for a second too long. "We got a letter today."

I could tell that this was the subject he'd been avoiding.

"A letter?"

"A . . . wedding invitation."

Every muscle in my body locked into place. A feather of heat seemed to brush down my back. I held onto the table to keep my hands steady.

Billy went on like he hadn't noticed. "There's a note inside that's addressed to you. I didn't read it."

He pulled a thick ivory envelope from where it was wedged between his leg and the side of his wheelchair. He laid it on the table between us.

"You probably don't need to read it. Doesn't really matter what it says."

Stupid reverse psychology. I yanked the envelope off the table.

It was some heavy, stiff paper. Expensive. Too fancy for Forks. The card inside was the same, too done-up and formal. Bella'd had nothing to do with this. There was no sign of her personal taste in the layers of see-through, petal-printed pages. I'd bet she didn't like it at all. I didn't read the words, not even to see the date. I didn't care.

There was a piece of the thick ivory paper folded in half with my name handwritten in black ink on the back. I didn't recognize the handwriting, but it was as fancy as the rest of it. For half a second, I wondered if the bloodsucker was into gloating.

I flipped it open.

Jacob,

I'm breaking the rules by sending you this. She was afraid of hurting you, and she didn't want to make you feel obligated in any way. But I know that, if things had gone the other way, I would have wanted the choice.

I promise I will take care of her, Jacob. Thank you — for her — for everything.

Edward

"Jake, we only have the one table," Billy said. He was staring at my left hand.

My fingers were clamped down on the wood hard enough that it really was in danger. I loosened them one by one, concentrating on that action alone, and then clenched my hands together so I couldn't break anything.

"Yeah, doesn't matter anyway," Billy muttered.

I got up from the table, shrugging out of my t-shirt as I stood. Hopefully Leah had gone home by now.

"Not too late," Billy mumbled as I punched the front door out of my way.

I was running before I hit the trees, my clothes strewn out behind me like a trail of crumbs — as if I wanted to find my way back. It was almost too easy now to phase. I didn't have to think. My body already knew where I was going and, before I asked it to, it gave me what I wanted.

I had four legs now, and I was flying.

The trees blurred into a sea of black flowing around me. My muscles bunched and released in an effortless rhythm. I could run like this for days and I would not be tired. Maybe, this time, I wouldn't stop.

But I wasn't alone.

So sorry, Embry whispered in my head.

I could see through his eyes. He was far away, to the north, but he had wheeled around and was racing to join me. I growled and pushed myself faster.

Wait for us, Quil complained. He was closer, just starting out from the village.

Leave me alone, I snarled.

I could feel their worry in my head, try hard as I might to drown it in the sound of the wind and the forest. This was what I hated most — seeing myself through their eyes, worse now that their eyes were full of pity. They saw the hate, but they kept running after me.

A new voice sounded in my head.

Let him go. Sam's thought was soft, but still an order. Embry and Quil slowed to a walk.

If only I could stop hearing, stop seeing what they saw. My head was so crowded, but the only way to be alone again was to be human, and I couldn't stand the pain.

Phase back, Sam directed them. *I'll pick you up, Embry.*

First one, then another awareness faded into silence. Only Sam was left.

Thank you, I managed to think.

Come home when you can. The words were faint, trailing off into blank emptiness as he left, too. And I was alone.

So much better. Now I could hear the faint rustle of the matted leaves beneath my toenails, the whisper of an owl's wings above me, the ocean — far, far in the west — moaning against the beach. Hear this, and nothing more. Feel nothing but speed, nothing but the pull of muscle, sinew, and bone, working together in harmony as the miles disappeared behind me.

If the silence in my head lasted, I would never go back. I wouldn't be the first one to choose this form over the other. Maybe, if I ran far enough away, I would never have to hear again. . . .

I pushed my legs faster, letting Jacob Black disappear behind me.

Acknowledgments

I would be very remiss if I did not thank the many people
who helped me survive the birthing of another novel:

My parents have been my rock; I don't know how anyone does this
without a dad's good advice and a mom's shoulder to cry on.

My husband and sons have been incredibly long-suffering—
anyone else would have had me committed to an asylum long ago.
Thanks for keeping me around, guys.

My Elizabeth—Elizabeth Eulberg, publicist extraordinaire—
has made all the difference to my sanity both on and off the road.
Few people are lucky enough to work so closely with their BFF,
and I am eternally grateful for the wholesomeness of
cheese-loving Midwestern girls.

Jodi Reamer continues to guide my career with genius and finesse.
It is very comforting to know that I am in such good hands.

It is also wonderful to have my manuscripts in the right hands.
Thanks to Rebecca Davis for being so in tune with the story in my head
and helping me find the best ways to express it.
Thanks to Megan Tingley, first for your unwavering faith in my work,
and second for polishing that work until it shines.

Everyone at Little, Brown and Company Books for Young Readers has taken such
amazing care of my creations. I can tell it is a true labor of love for you all,
and I appreciate it more than you know. Thank you Chris Murphy, Shawn Foster,
Andrew Smith, Stephanie Voros, Gail Doobinin, Tina McIntyre, Ames O'Neill,
and the many others who have made the Twilight series a success.

I can't believe how lucky I was to discover Lori Joffs,
who somehow manages to be both the fastest and the most meticulous reader
at the same time. I am thrilled to have a friend and accomplice
who is so insightful, talented, and patient with my whining.

Lori Joffs again, along with Laura Cristiano, Michaela Child, and Ted Joffs,
for creating and maintaining the brightest star in the Twilight online universe,
the Twilight Lexicon. I truly appreciate all the hard work
you put into providing a happy place for my fans to hang out.
Thanks also to my international friends at Crepusculo-es.com
for a site so amazing it transcends the language barrier.
Kudos as well to Brittany Gardener's fabulous work
on the Twilight and New Moon by Stephenie Meyer MySpace Group,
a fan site so large that the idea of keeping track of it boggles my mind;
Brittany, you amaze me.
Katie and Audrey, Bella Penombra is a thing of beauty.
Heather, the Nexus rocks.
I can't mention all the amazing sites and their creators here,
but thank you very much to each of you.

Many thanks to my cold readers, Laura Cristiano, Michelle Vieira,
Bridget Creviston, and Kimberlee Peterson, for their invaluable input
and encouraging enthusiasm.

Every writer needs an independent bookstore for a friend;
I'm so grateful for my hometown supporters at Changing Hands Bookstore
in Tempe, Arizona, and especially to Faith Hochhalter,
who has brilliant taste in literature.

I am in your debt, rock gods of Muse, for yet another inspiring album.
Thank you for continuing to create my favorite writing music.
I am also grateful to all the other bands on my playlist
who help me through the writer's block, and to my new discoveries,
Ok Go, Gomez, Placebo, Blue October, and Jack's Mannequin.

Most of all, a gargantuan thank-you to all of my fans.
I firmly believe that my fans are the most attractive, intelligent,
exciting, and dedicated fans in the whole world.
I wish I could give you each a big hug and a Porsche 911 Turbo.